Granger's Threat

**A Murder Mystery Laced with a
Web of Lies and Familial Contempt**

D1706618

Granger's Threat

A Murder Mystery Laced with a Web of Lies and Familial Contempt

Teresa Pijoan

SUNSTONE
PRESS

SANTA FE

Sunstone books may be purchased for educational, business, or sales promotional use. For information please write: Special Markets Department, Sunstone Press, P.O. Box 2321, Santa Fe, New Mexico 87504-2321.

Book and Cover design › Vicki Ahl
Body typeface › Granjon LT Std
Printed on acid-free paper
∞
eBook 978-1-61139-253-1

Library of Congress Cataloging-in-Publication Data

Pijoan, Teresa, 1951-
 Granger's Threat : a murder mystery laced with a web of lies and familial contempt / by Teresa Pijoan.
   pages cm
 ISBN 978-0-86534-983-4 (softcover : alk. paper)
 1. Murder--Investigation--New Mexico--Fiction. 2. Family secrets--Fiction.
 3. Mystery fiction. I. Title.
 PS3572.A4365G73 2014
 813'.54--dc23
                        2014003979

WWW.SUNSTONEPRESS.COM
SUNSTONE PRESS / POST OFFICE BOX 2321 / SANTA FE, NM 87504-2321 /USA
(505) 988-4418 / ORDERS ONLY (800) 243-5644 / FAX (505) 988-1025

Dedicated
to
Sue Vliet
and
Carol C. Pijoan

"Oh what a tangled web we weave,
When first we practice to deceive!"
—Sir Walter Scott, *Marmion*, Canto vi. Stanza 17

1

Calavera, New Mexico
Early morning, Thursday, January, 1988

Margaret sat in the wooden Captain's chair beside the rented hospital bed, causing Margaret's bed to be pushed into the corner of the large bedroom. The one lamp on the bedside table gave an ominous glow to the white walls. She stared at her eighty year old husband.

He was a slip of his former self. His body was now a frail, weak skeleton covered in skin, opaque skin. The odor emanating from his body was wretched as was the way of the dead or dying. The man was curled in a fetal position. His claw like hands were wrapped one around the other. His feet were pointed downward as his knees were bent almost up to his hairless chest. The toenails were thick, dark orange, and cracked. Margaret pulled the white cotton sheet over his feet. She didn't want to look at them anymore.

Her son's deep voice permeated the silence. "You know this wouldn't have been so difficult if you would have just let him die from pneumonia last month?"

The sixty year old Margaret began rocking back and forth with her arms wrapped around her waist. She tugged at the sweater of lavender blue that hugged her thin frame. "Granger, I couldn't do it then. I just couldn't. The doctor had the visiting nurse come in and she was the one who called the ambulance. What was I to do?" She glared at her son through her long eyelashes, "There was no choice. What was I to do?"

Granger grimaced. This was her way to blame others for her own lack of action. She had always been this way. He sat back on the rolling medical stool on the opposite side of the hospital bed from his mother. He lifted his head to study the large painting on the wall over her bed. The dancing ballerinas were always dancing east, they never sat down and they never had a break. Granger sighed. He never got a break from her either.

When he was small boy, being raised on an isolated farm way out on the flat lands, his mother would wait up for her husband, his father, to come home from the hospital only to hand him a list of all the troubles their children had caused during the day. She made sure that the children were punished for their 'sins.'

If her husband did not beat the children to a pulp, then he was not allowed to get into her bed. He was hardly home as it was, right? He was always at the hospital. He was one of four doctors for about five hundred miles of flat dry farmland. He rarely came home. If he did come home, well, he needed to prove that he was worthy of being a father and do his fatherly duty of punishing the children. He was to keep them in line!

Granger remembered those nights when his mother leaned against the door frame of the bedroom to watch her husband as he would grab the kids who were sound asleep. Both Sophia and Granger were blissfully unaware of the hell that was soon descending upon their weak and fragile bodies. Granger's father was six-two and weighed around two hundred and forty pounds. He was strong and powerful in spirit with his striking Mediterranean good looks. Father would throw them, one by one onto the floor, kick them only to pick them up and pitch them back onto the bed with a loud remark to their mother, "There, are you happy now?" Then his father would hurry out the door, down the hall to fall into bed for desperate sleep.

Now his father was struggling to stay alive and Granger was the one with the power. His mother jerked when father started to wheeze and then cough. The phlegm in his father's throat had settled. Father would aspirate if he wasn't lifted to a sitting position. Usually either the visiting nurse or Granger's sister Sophia, would be here to lift father, but tonight they had sent his sister home to her husband and kids. Tonight was the night to do the deed.

The wind continued to howl in the cold January night. The dog and the cats had been locked out of the bedroom by his mother. She was terrified of witnesses yet she would not, could not ever do any deed by herself. Granger sucked in air. His father's face was contorting. His father had not been able to speak for almost two years and in the last three months only a grunt was given when the catheter had been put in or when his head was lifted for eye drops. The cough was becoming more labored, more difficult. Dark brown eyes shot open struggling to see anyone who would or could help him.

Granger's mother covered her mouth as tears fell from her round blue eyes. The tree branches outside rubbed against the side of the roof squeaking, scratching a morbid rhythm. A loud whistle broke through the silence. Some air worked through the phlegm and then the whistling stopped. Legs jerked out as father's head shot back and then fell forward. The chest heaved as fluids gushed from the lower extremities of his body. Granger froze. His large eyes stared at his father.

Margaret fell to her knees on the polished brick floor. "Our Father who art in Heaven, hallowed be Thy name, Thy kingdom come, Thy will be done, earth as it is in Heaven. Oh, God. No!" She reached over the dead body for Granger's hand.

Granger pulled his hand away quickly to wipe them on his corduroy pants. "That's right, Mom, Thy will be done in Heaven as done here." Dark hair fell forward onto Granger's forehead. Quickly he pushed it back.

Margaret screamed out, "No! Oh, no what have we done? We've sinned! We're going to burn in hell for all eternity!" She struggled to stand, pushing the chair back away from her. "Granger, get him back, bring him back! What have we done?"

"Mom, you killed him. You chose to kill him and now he is dead. This is all yours. All of this is yours. I wash my hands of this completely." Granger now stood. He reached down to pull the sheet over his father's face. "You wanted him dead and dead he is." Shadows played against the white wall as Granger hovered over the dead body.

"Not this way! Granger, not like this!" She hurried to him and grabbed his arms, "Do something! I can't burn in hell. I have lived in hell all my life and I refuse to live in hell in the hereafter! Do something, damn you!" Her eyes flowed with tears. Her face was white and wrinkled.

"Mom, you asked me here to do this." Granger used his calm voice, "Mom, you have already taken over his accounts, declared him incompetent, you are already spending his death insurance money. This was your personal choice, not mine." Granger pulled away from her to lift his hands in a stance of being noncommittal. "The deed is done. Now you are the one who has to call the police and your daughter. Mom, this was your choice. It is done."

Granger turned on his heel, rubbing his upper arms where she had held him. He opened the door, letting in the dark calico cat. The cat ran across the floor to jump on the high hospital bed.

"No, Granger, get the cat out of here. Get the cat!"

"Mom, this is your home, your house, your place of death. I leave all of this to you."

Not caring what the neighbors would think now, Granger moved down the hall turning on the lights. His leather soled boots echoed as they hit the polished brick floors. Swinging around the corner into the living room, he pulled his heavy jacket from the coat rack by the front door. "Bye, Mom. Good luck with this." He went out into the night, slamming the heavy wooden front door behind him. The glass in the front windows rattled.

Carefully, Granger drove down her driveway in his Mercedes with the lights off. It would not do for the neighbors to see him leaving his father's death bed at one in the morning. Probably was not a good idea to slam the front door, but he did have a point to make. "That woman has lived to make my life a living hell."

Margaret stood over her dead husband. "Are you really dead?" Her voice whispered out in the silence. The tree branches continued to scrape along the roof. "You must do something about those trees, dear. They are ruining the roof and we don't want to spend money on the roof now do we?"

Quietly, Margaret moved to the dial phone that sat on her bedside table overflowing with magazines. She sat on the edge of the bed smoothing her skirt of grey wool over her knees. "No, I should get into my nightgown and set the stage for a natural death. Yes, I will set the stage. I am innocent, Sir, innocent of any wrong doing."

Margaret moved to the walk-in closet, flipped on the light and disrobed. She pulled her nightgown of blue flannel over her head. Closing the door, she hurried around the hospital bed into the joining bathroom. There she brushed her shoulder length brown hair one hundred times. She brushed her teeth with the electric toothbrush and straightened all of her husband's medicines on the shelf. Turning off the bathroom light she stated, "There, now everything is neat and tidy."

She turned and stared at the hospital bed. "Oh, dear, you can't be dead yet!" She hurried to her husband and took the sheet off of his face to fold it under his chin. "There, you aren't really dead yet. We can pretend." She picked up the cat and threw her out into the hall, closing the door quietly.

The heavy quilt was folded back, then the wool blanket and finally her pink sheets. Margaret crawled under the sheets pulling each layer over her. The pillows were plumped as she sat erect staring at the painting of her husband that hung opposite her bed. "Well, there you are at forty- tall, dark, and handsome in your medical coat. Sharp eyes, drop dead smile, women fawning all over you, but I was the one who caught you, you bastard! How many women did you impregnate while married to me? There must have been at least three and Sophia knows of two others who would be her sisters if I had not paid them to go away. So, now the famous doctor with the gorgeous looks has dropped dead! Hah!" Margaret pulled one of the pillows from behind her and threw it at the painting. The pillow fell short hitting the bureau and then falling to the floor.

A scream rang through the room. Margaret jumped a foot in the air, "My God, what?" The phone echoed its ring. Margaret cautiously reached for the phone of black plastic. It was cold as she placed it to her ear. "Hello?"

"Mom, it's me Granger. Listen, Mom, Sophia will know what we did. She will figure this out and she will know. You have to wait until around six o'clock to call the police because if you call sooner than that, they will know what happened. Sophia will know, Mom, she will." Granger's voice was tight and tired.

Margaret took a calming breath, "Do you know that you almost gave me a heart attack?"

Granger smiled at the phone to mumble, "That will be the day."

"What do you mean Sophia will know? What will she know?"

"Mom, Sophia will know that we caused Dad to aspirate. She will know."

"She will not know, Granger, because no one will tell her! You are not to tell her and I certainly shan't. No, Sophia will only guess and she will be wrong." Margaret pulled the blanket up closer to her neck. "She will not know!"

There was a sigh on the other end of the phone, "All right, Mom, your concept of reality is different from mine. But don't call the cops until almost daylight. You can tell them you were asleep and were awakened by a strong smell and found dad dead."

Margaret sniffed the air, "Oh, you're so right. This room stinks. I should open a window, but it is cold outside and the wind is blowing." Margaret pulled the sheet over her head as she scrunched down under the covers. "Granger, it stinks in here. What should I do until then, that's about three hours away?"

"Just deal with it, Mom. Deal with it. I'm going to fix myself a stiff drink and go to bed. Call me when you have the cops in the house. Good night."

"Wait, Granger, we will have to deal with your sister."

"Mom, what do you mean by 'deal with her'?"

"Granger, she must not know. Sophia must not tell anyone. If she figures this out and she tells someone, she will put us in jeopardy. You know this?"

"Good night, it has been a long night. I can't think anymore tonight. Just go to bed."

Margaret held the phone as the dial tone hummed in her ear. "Good night," she whispered. The radiator creaked beside the bureau. The air was heavy with body odor. Margaret pulled the pillow over her head and tried to sleep. Quietly, she whispered, "Sophia cannot know for if she does this will be the end of her!"

The wind softened into a breeze as the pink fingers of dawn rose over the Puerco Mountains. The horse in the barn began to kick the metal water trough for it was sealed with ice. Last night had been a cold, cold night for certain.

The bright sunrise reflected red and orange off the high clouds. This morning was a welcoming sight to Margaret as she held her mug of steaming tea in her left hand and used the phone to dial Granger's phone number. It was ten minutes past eight and the sun had risen to a gloriously clear day with little wind. The phone rang twice. "Hello

"Granger, this is your mother. Your father died sometime last night. I felt it best to call and alert you to this development. I am in the process of calling your sister. Then I shall call the EMT's to come and see if they can revive him." Margaret lifted the steaming mug of tea to her lips to blow on the hot tea.

"Mom, I know dad is dead. I was there, remember? You should call the police, not the EMT's."

"No, Granger, I am calling the EMT's. I am an elderly woman who does not know how to handle these situations. I still have hope that your father can be resuscitated. Don't give me any grief. I know what you did." Margaret hung up the phone to take a sip of her tea. "So, there."

The Yellow Pages were opened on the counter beside the kitchen sink. "All right, if you need to call an EMT where-oh-where do you find them?" Margaret flipped through the pages in the front of the phonebook, nothing.

She then looked under hospitals. There was nothing there. Margaret closed the book with a sigh and punched in 911.

"I believe my husband is dead! Please can you send someone right away?" Margaret's voice was harried and confused. She even gulped a few times for effect.

"Ma'am, do you feel that you are in danger or anyone in your home is in danger?"

Margaret smiled. "No, we're not in danger anymore. I mean my husband has been very ill and now he has stopped breathing! What do I do? I can't lift him? I don't know what to do?" Margaret let forth a sob.

"Ma'am, please stay on the phone. I will call the sheriff's department for you. The sheriff must declare the emergency. He will notify the paramedics to investigate and photograph the room. What is the location of you home?"

Margaret explained that her mailing address was different from her house location. She then gave perfect directions to the farm house with the large silver Mercedes out front by the hand carved perfect oak gate that could be opened from the outside using the French made pulley.

"All right, Ma'am, you appear to have settled down. Would you please give me your phone number in case we get disconnected?"

"Get disconnected! Why should we be disconnected? Are you planning on hanging up on me while I am in this emotional confusion?"

"No, Ma'am, no, the sheriff should be arriving shortly. Do you hear the siren?"

The mug of tea was pressed to Margaret's lips. She blew into the steaming mug as the sound of sirens wound their way to her home. "Yes, I do hear sirens. Thank you, for your help."

A man leaned forward out of the sheriff's cruiser. He turned sideways to pick up his cowboy hat on the passenger seat. Placing it on his head, he sighed. Deaths were always messy. The clipboard, two way radio, and his felt tipped pen were inventoried to deal with the demise of a local citizen. His polished boots set off his pressed uniform. His belt held his baton and handcuffs. Grabbing the top of the car's door frame he lifted his six foot four body to stand.

At the oak gate, no more than eight feet from where he parked, stood a woman of about sixty, smiling. The sheriff shook his head. He held the clip board in his right hand against his hip and walked to her, slamming the driver's door as he did so. She was still smiling with her lips yet her eyes appeared to be squinting into the cold January morning light. She yelled out at him, "Are you the sheriff?"

He gently shook his head as he grunted under his breath, "Yes, Ma'am. I am the sheriff's deputy and I am here to assist you. What appears to be the problem?"

"Oh!" Flustered by his ignorance she flung open the oak gate smacking him directly in the shoulder. "Oh, I am sorry, sir! My husband appears to have passed away in the night." She held her eyes wide and her mouth in an 'O.'

Rubbing his shoulder, the deputy questioned, "Ma'am, can you direct me to your husband? Then I can call in the paramedics."

The woman held her body between him and the front door, which was partially open. "I don't know who you are, do I?" She put out her hand.

The Sheriff's deputy smiled as he reached into his back left pocket to remove his wallet. On his chest was pinned a deputy's metal with his name stamped in highlighted black. He flipped open his ID and handed it to her. "Ma'am, if you look at my shirt," his finger pointed to his name tag clearly visible on his jacket, "You see my name, my division, and my rank."

"Well, Deputy Sheriff Ignacio Cruz, it wasn't obvious to me. I don't usually have involvement with the police. I am a law abiding citizen. Thank you, for showing me your ID. At least it had your picture attached to help me understand who you are."

She held the door. The wind was buffeting her hair about and without a jacket or coat the sheriff deputy was sure she must be cold, "Ma'am, perhaps it would be best if we spoke inside. You must certainly be feeling the weather?"

"Yes, yes." She pushed the front door open. "Come in, please, come in."

She stood aside, allowing him to close the heavy door. "I am sorry. It's just you're here and everything appears more surreal. He's this way down the hall to your right. I will let you go by yourself." Margaret quietly retreated to the kitchen. She sat down heavily on the bar chair at the high counter. Sipping on her tea, she whispered. "Oh, dear, the drama begins."

"Ma'am, excuse me?" The sheriff's deputy stood in the hall calling out to her. "Ma'am, I have notified the paramedics and they are on their way. Once they establish the scene they will send for the OMI. I'll just wait out in the cruiser."

Margaret hurried into the front hall, "Wait, Sir, please wait. What is an OMI?"

Sheriff Cruz let his hand remain on the door knob, "The OMI is the Officer of Medical Investigation. We call him the medical examiner. He will work with the paramedics to determine the cause of death."

Margaret gasped, "Cause of death?"

"Yes, Ma'am, it's important to document the cause of death. Even if the deceased had been ill for a long period of time we need to know the cause of death. The Medical Examiner is the one who will decide exactly how and why the person died."

Margaret reached out to take his arm. Sheriff Deputy Ignacio Cruz stepped back from her, "Ma'am, is there something more?"

Margaret peered up at him through her eyelashes, "Sir, my husband died of natural causes. There is no need for an investigation."

Sheriff Cruz lifted his clipboard to bring a divide between them, 'The M.E. will remove everything with your husband's body, Ma'am. He will take the tubes, medicines, and all medical information he needs to determine if the death was natural. After he confirms the cause of death, he will sign off on the report."

"How do I get a copy of the death certificate?" Margaret stepped back against the bookcase in the hall. Sheriff Cruz pulled open the front door, "Ma'am, I believe your questions would be best answered by the Medical Examiner. His job is to verify the cause of death without a doubt. If he signs off on the case, the report returns to me and I will send it to New Mexico records. They will be the ones who will disperse the death certificate." He touched the tip of his hat, "Ma'am, I will be outside waiting for the paramedics."

He left her standing in the hall as he returned to his sheriff's cruiser. He sat staring across the fields of dried alfalfa watching the clouds drift lazily to the northeast. Ducks and sand hill cranes flew in their V pattern back and forth across the sky. Blasts of sand plummeted all sides of his cruiser.

Margaret bit her lip as she paced in the kitchen with the phone pressed against her ear, "Granger, you need to get over here! They are going to search for cause of death. This will be tricky. Granger, please come now. This isn't feeling good at all. Thank you, sweetheart." She replaced the phone to sip her tea.

A grey van bounced down the driveway to park behind the sheriff's cruiser. The taller fellow, who was driving, blew cigarette smoke out the window. The sheriff's deputy rolled down his window. "Hey, guys, the deceased is inside with the wife watching over the body. Where is the M.E.?"

The paramedic on the passenger's side shook his head, "We had to pull him from Rio Grodno. There was a motorcycle fatality up there about two hours ago. Not pretty at all, but then motorcycle accidents are nasty especially when no one was wearing a helmet or protective gear." The young man explained, "But doc should be here any minute. They have it all wrapped up and the cops are cleaning the street."

The radio squawked on the young paramedic's belt. He clicked it off. "The doc wants us to go ahead and do photos and draw up the scene. Do you want to come and observe or hide out here?"

The sheriff's deputy frowned, "No, you go on in, I'll wait for the M.E. Then I'll start interviewing the family."

The two paramedics were invited into the house by Margaret. They followed her down the hall. They noticed her tailored wool jumper with the expensive red cashmere sweater. Her hair, flecked with gray was neatly combed and had been curled under to a perfect page-boy. Her black shoes complimented her gray skirt and were polished to a sparkling sheen. The floor of red tiles had been recently swept and the smell of lemon polish wafted in the air.

Once the bedroom door was opened, the air was heavy with stale body odor. Both paramedics stepped back as if hit with a hurricane wind. "Whoa, there he is. You know no matter how many times we do this the foul smell is something I'll never get used to, the air freshener doesn't help." The younger paramedic with the wavy red hair wrinkled up his nose. The older paramedic in his sixties pulled two white paper masks from his handheld black kit. "Here, put this on, Doug."

Doug turned to glare at his partner. "Hey, the wife's right behind you, Fred."

Fred shook his head to mumble under his breath, "She knows, Doug, she already knows." The men walked into the bedroom, shutting the door firmly behind them. Margaret sniffed as the door closed in front of her face.

She returned to the kitchen. She sat on the counter stool and dialed Sophia's phone number.

The phone rang six times. "Sophia, it's your mother, dear." Margaret gritted her teeth.

"Mom, this isn't a good time!" Sophia pulled on her brown robe as if her perfect mother could see through the phone. "Geoffrey and I are late getting the girls ready for school. We're running around all over trying to find clean pink socks for Donna!" Sophia dropped the phone only to catch it in midair. "Oh, Mom, I will be there around ten to help with dad, don't worry. It's my day to wash him. Is everything all right?"

Margaret took a deep breath, "Sophia, your father is dead. He is cold stone dead. You need to get over here and stop running around." Abruptly, Margaret hung up the phone.

2

Rocoso, New Mexico
Thursday, January, 1988

Sophia hung up the phone. She fell back onto a kitchen chair. The kitchen table was covered with dripping cereal bowls, half eaten pieces of toast smeared with strawberry jam. "Geoffrey!"

Geoffrey came hurrying down the hall into the kitchen. "What? What's the matter?" His tall frame hurried past her to reach for his black coffee container by the sink. Breathlessly drinking in the coffee, he added, "You do know your six-year old daughter Donna absolutely doesn't want to go to school today because she doesn't have any pink socks like her friend Carrie? You know this right?" Glancing at Sophia, Geoffrey put the coffee container down. "What is it? Sophia, what's wrong?"

Sophia shook her head tears falling down her cheeks to the table. "Geoffrey, they did it. They did it, they killed him."

Geoffrey sat in the kitchen chair next to her. He leaned forward with his elbows on his knees, he studied her face. Her brown hair was curly in total disarray. Her high cheek bones and brown eyes were filled with distress.

"They, you mean Granger and your mother?" His big hands clasped the black coffee mug, "But, Sophia, he was getting better. The doc said the new Parkinson's meds were helping him. They found he was able to move his fingers. He was trying to move his lips to speak. Why would they kill him now?" Geoffrey reached over to push Sophia's short bangs away from her eyebrows. "Wouldn't it be obvious if they killed him now that he was getting better?"

Sophia sat back, wiping her nose with a dirty napkin. Her eyes pleaded with him to understand, "Geoffrey, they were already spending his money, you know that? Mom, wanted to buy Granger the house on the hill." Loud voices diverted their attention to the back bedrooms.

Geoffrey lifted his lanky body up from the kitchen chair. He rubbed his head as was his sign of distress. His blue eyes peered out through his glasses,

"Sophia, I will take the girls to school. We better get a move on it." He gingerly rubbed her back and arms, "Don't let your brother know you know what happened."

As an afterthought Geoffrey shook his head, "Sophia, how can you be sure? Your father was in bad shape for the last two years. He was almost a vegetable last month until the doc found the new medicine, wasn't he?"

Sophia leaned forward in the kitchen chair to start rocking back and forth, "Geoffrey, he wasn't ready to die. He was fighting for his life. He was fighting."

"Sophia, sooner or later you would've had to let go of him. He treated you terribly when you were a child. If it wouldn't have been for you and the nurse he wouldn't have had a chance in hell." Geoffrey pulled her up into his embrace. "Don't beat yourself up. What's done is done, but for the love of God, please," He lifted her face to his, "don't let them know you believe they killed him! Please!"

Sophia stared through his glass lenses into his eyes, " Geoffrey, they are my family. I can't lie to them. I hate lies. I hate all of this!" She pushed away from him, hugging her arms around her waist.

"Sophia, we're your family now. We are! The girls and I love you! You are our life, too! You can't go to the viper's den and tell the truth. It will come back to bite you!"

"Dad," their nine year old daughter Sybil stood in the hall, "Dad, what's going on?"

Geoffrey put his arms around Sophia, hugging her into his chest. He spoke to Sybil over Sophia's right shoulder, "Sybil, grandpa died last night and your mother's upset. I'm going to take you and Donna to school. Please see to your sister. She needs to have her backpack and her jacket. You need to help me with her this morning, all right?"

Sybil pouted, "Sure, Dad, whatever!" Sybil disappeared down the hallway. Sophia wiped her nose on a napkin. Strawberry jam stuck to her cheek. "Well, I have to clean this up and then myself. Thanks, Geoffrey, for the advice. I will just go and observe. It is important for me to be there and help Mom, I suppose. Although..."

"Just go, call me later. Here come my girls!" Geoffrey took Donna's pink princess backpack from Sybil's hand. Donna had obviously been crying. Her eyes were red and her cheeks were flushed. Sophia knelt down to zip up her pink jacket. "Donna, wow, you will be the only girl in First Grade with yellow socks. Stand tall and be proud!"

Donna stared at her ankles, "Mom, they aren't yellow! They're yellow-ish!" Geoffrey wrapped his arms around Donna's small waist to lift her up to his shoulder. "All right, the magic van is leaving! We shall all return here later for the Star Ship Enterprise lift off!"

Sophia took Sybil's hand, "You look lovely today, Sybil. How do you like your new green jacket?"

Sybil pulled the zipper to her chin, "I like it just fine, Mom." Sybil yanked her black backpack strap higher on her shoulder. "Mom, I am sorry about Grandpa, but he was a mean man. He never liked Donna or me much. To be honest, Mom, you are over there all the time and Daddy doesn't cook anything but macaroni and cheese. We're beginning to turn orange."

Sybil rubbed her nose, "Mommy, does this mean you will be home more?"

"Sybil, you are my number one girl and sometimes I have had to count on you to take care of things, but you know this right?"

"Yeah, well, sometimes I can't do everything!" Sybil laughed at repeating her father's favorite phrase. Sophia joined her as they went outside into the cold January morning. Geoffrey tooted the horn as he backed the old yellow Dodge van out of their dirt driveway.

Tall mesas surrounded their mountain home on the edge of a cliff. Rocoso was an area of wide open spaces, running canyons, soaring ravens, and strong stark mesas. Sophia stared at the vast expanse of land and sky. "Papa, wherever you are please be out of pain."

Sophia's and Geoffrey's home was at the top of a foothill, sloping off of the Puerco Mountains. It was an undulating landscape of endless open arid land, framed with mesas of sufficient height to interrupt the skyline.

Running into the house out of the cold weather, Sophia called out, "Oh, Spirits, let courage run through my veins!"

3

Calavera, New Mexico
Thursday, January, 1988

Sophia drove down the road of dirt to her mother's farm. The hard ridges jutting across the road gave it a corrugated texture. At either side of the road were detached properties of Southwestern stucco, many with trees for shade and small gardens consisting of native plants considerably older than the buildings. Barns of elaborate design accentuated the wealth of the neighborhood. Fences of white poles, white wood, or barbed wire separated the mink and manure acreage from one another. Her mother prided herself on living in a prestigious area of elite farmhouses with terraced irrigated fields, the last word in urban elegance.

Her mother's front drive was filled with cars parked everywhere. The wooden gate reflected traces of care from better days. It was propped open with a block of wood. Old steel hooks hung rusted and broken, swinging in the wind. Two miles west, sitting on a sandstone cliff, six smokestacks broke the open range with thick plumes of chemical smoke. The natural landscape conflicted with the smog and the sterile buildings filled with scientists stamping out computer chips for industries' latest technology.

Over the years citizens had submitted numerous petitions to close the computer plant regarding documented health issues. The government prefers jobs over health and the industrial center keeps chugging out cancerous fumes to fall on the small farming community.

Skirting around the paramedics' ambulance, Sophia noticed the Medical Examiner's van. A sheriff's cruiser was parked in front of Granger's metallic green Mercedes. A silver truck was parked at an odd angle beside Granger's Mercedes and Margaret's neighbor Charlotte's white pickup truck. Sophia parked outside of the property. A yellow Volkswagen Bug was backed into a space under her father's cottonwood tree. The VW had a drooling dog sitting in the passenger seat. Sophia laughed when she saw Daisy dog strapped into her seat belt. Daisy smiled with her brown eyes as Sophia knocked on the window.

Sophia's scarf was wrapped around her neck and folded into the front of her warm jacket. She wore her old jeans in case she had to muck out the horse's stall and her brown mittens warmed her hands. The red wool tam Geoffrey had given her for their first Christmas together kept her short hair tucked out of the wind.

Sophia slowly wound her way through the parked cars to her parents' home. She noticed the stucco high on the wall curling from water damage. The window frames shed skins of white paint revealing discolored wood underneath. She blinked at this dilapidated house. How had it become so run down without notice? The house was certainly in a state of disrepair. Sophia turned when she heard her name being called.

Dr. Milligan was hurrying to her, "Sophia, wait up! Wait for me, please!" He wore his long coat over his white scrubs. His stethoscope was banging against his chest. The wind blew his heavy coat open allowing it to float around him. His reading glasses were on top of his head, keeping his short white hair from lifting.

He grabbed her right forearm, "Sophia, there is no reason for your father to be dead. I suspect foul play. Honestly! Your father was to be elevated forty degrees in his bed. His saliva should have run out of his mouth. There was no reason for him to stop breathing, unless..." Dr. Milligan wiped his white up turned mustache with his gloved hand, "unless, someone put his bed flat."

Sophia moved away from him. "Doctor, are you accusing my family of murder?"

Dr. Milligan stepped back. He hit the side mirror on the ambulance with his back. "What? Ouch! Sophia, are you siding with them?" He shook his head, "Sophia, we have been a team here. We have been trying to get your father's life back, weren't we?"

Sophia turned away from him to enter the stucco cracked home. She heard his footsteps behind her. "Sophia, please allow me to explain. This may have been an accident. Your mother may have not realized how important it was to have him elevated. Do you think she lowered his bed, by accident?"

She needed to see what was being done, what had happened, and who was inside the house. She followed the sounds of voices as she entered. The house smelled heavily of furniture polish. The tile floor had been cleaned recently. A floor to ceiling bookcase on her left revealed stacked books covered in thick dust. They were in stark contrast to the fresh lemon smell, which hovered in the air.

Leaves had blown into the front entry room gathering into a pile under a shelf of knick-knacks. Margaret's authoritative voice could be heard emanating from the kitchen. Granger's velvet voice was radiating from the back bedroom down the hall. Sophia chose to go into the bedroom where perhaps she could view her father one last time. Dr. Milligan followed her.

Granger's formidable presence blocked the painted wooden door to the bedroom. He had on a dark jacket with pinstriped trousers and polished shoes. He was clearly a man with a serious attitude about his position. He invited Sophia and Dr. Milligan into the room with a wave of his well manicured hand. "There wasn't much chance of him getting better." Granger's voice was subtle in tone as he continued, "Ah, here are my sister and his doctor. They took care of him most of the time. I really haven't seen him lately. My wife and daughter are in California visiting my wife's family. I have been busy with my medical practice. I haven't had time to do much for my father."

Granger reached out to take Dr. Milligan's gloved hand, "Dr. Milligan, good of you to come. This is a surprise, way above your duty. I would suppose." Granger gave a respectful nod to the doctor. Completely ignoring Sophia he left the room. His leather shoes echoed on the brick floor of the hall.

Sophia stared. There in the hospital bed was her Papa. There was no warmth. His brown eyes were frozen staring straight ahead. The Medical Examiner and a paramedic were trying to straighten his body unto his back. There was a long black plastic bag being pushed under his body by a younger paramedic. The smell in the room was a mixture of stale air and pine scent air freshener. Dr. Milligan quickly caught Sophia as she fell back, her knees giving way. "Whoa, girl, hold on there. Death is not something you can approach head on. Would someone get her a chair?"

The young paramedic closest to them grabbed a wooden chair and shoved it to Dr. Milligan. "Here you go."

Sophia gently dropped into the chair as Dr. Milligan moved to stand next to the Medical Examiner. "So, what's the verdict, Ralph?"

"Hey, Brian, well, won't know for certain until I get him on the table. It appears he aspirated, choked. He had fluid in his trachea or in layman's terms he died from respiratory failure." The Medical Examiner pointed to Sophia, "She the caretaker?"

Sophia whispered out. "Papa, what happened to you?"

Dr. Milligan turned his back to Sophia as he spoke, "She's his daughter and helped with Nurse Carol Grover. They both were his constant companions, until last night."

"What happened last night?"

"Evidently, the deceased's wife felt that Sophia, the daughter over there, and the nurse needed a night off to be with their families. So, the wife decided to take care of her husband by herself."

The Medical Examiner lifted his eyebrows, "Well, I guess she did then, didn't she? There is some petechial hemorrhaging, but not enough to suggest purposeful suffocation. If he was as weak and as his frail as his body appears then he probably aspirated. The bed was flat when we arrived. The wife may have put it down once she saw he was dead. Again, I will know more once I have examined the body thoroughly on the table at the lab."

The Medical Examiner gently cleared his throat, "Ah, Brian, if the son is in medicine why didn't he care for his father?"

Dr. Milligan slowly let a smile work its way across his face, "Oh, he told you he was in medicine, didn't he?" Shaking his head, he smothered a laugh, "Mr. Granger Pino is not a medical man. He has a license to practice pain management with massage and chiropractic skills. The two of us have had problems many a time for he seriously knows nothing about Western medical procedures or Western medicine. Give him rubbing oil and a towel and he goes to work. A stethoscope would be beyond him."

The Medical Examiner turned to the older paramedic, "Where is Ignacio? He needs to start the interviews with the family."

The older paramedic shook his head, "He told me he preferred to interview them down at the station."

"Call him. He needs to be here for this. I know he is shy and cautious, but he needs to follow procedures. I covered for him last time and told him never again. Get him on the radio, get him in here now!"

Dr. Milligan turned back to Sophia, "Let me get her out of here so you guys can get on with your work. I'll call you later this afternoon." He turned to Sophia, "Come, we should go and let these men do their jobs."

She shook her head, "No, I want to see this."

"Brian, she shouldn't be here for this." The Medical Examiner shook his head.

Dr. Milligan knelt down and hugged her by the shoulders, "Come on, Sophia, this isn't something you need to see. This is a messy job. Please remember your father the way he was ten years ago. Come on, let's go into the kitchen and get you some hot tea."

Sophia allowed him to lead her out of the room and down the hall. She quickly came face to face with Carol Grover. "Sophia, come with me. You're just the person I need to speak with, Sophia, come outside, we need to talk now!"

Carol was of a solid frame. She was five feet tall and five feet wide. She was excellent at lifting patients with her firm muscles. She pushed Sophia ahead of her down the hall. Carol's frosted dark hair bounced as she walked. Her ready smile was now a stern frown. She followed Sophia out the front door, sideways onto the wooden bench against the front porch wall. Sophia sat down with a groan. "Carol, he's dead, did you see him? He's really dead!"

"Sophia, get a grip! You and I both know he was doing better! We both know this! If his bed was kept upright he would still be getting better. Someone put the bed flat or at least low enough for him to not be able to swallow." Carol's bright blue eyes flashed with anger as she gulped for air, "I want you to file charges against your brother Granger."

Carol placed her plump hands on her hips and began to pace, "God, Sophia, I am sorry, but I absolutely cannot stand your brother with his smooth velvet demeanor. He's repulsive to me, absolutely repulsive. How can you two be so completely different? In all of my fifty-three years on this planet I have never met anyone who is as phony as your brother! How can he stand there as if he is sorry when he is the cause? Sophia, answer me!" Carol stood over Sophia, glaring.

"What do you want me to say, Carol? You want me to admit that he killed my father, his father? I can't do that, I can't!" Sophia stared at the dirt ground in front of her. "Besides I heard Granger tell the Sheriff in there he was at home last night. He never came over here to help Mom."

Carol threw her arms up into the air to scream, "What? You believe that slimy slug? Sophia, how can you believe a word that comes out of his mouth? Are you going to let them get away with this?" Carol gently pushed Sophia so she could sit beside her. Carol's nose was inches away from Sophia's. "You know he lives within minutes of here, just over the ditch road? You know this? He's already using your father's money to buy the fancy Mercedes he drives! Sophia, what part of this don't you get?"

Sophia pulled her red cap forward to protect her forehead from the wind, "What do you want me to do? This is my family, Carol!" Sophia stood. "This is my family, as confused and bizarre as it maybe—this is my family. I am not sure what happened, my mind is reeling. My father is dead. Right now what can we do? There is nothing more to do. Carol, there is nothing more anyone can do."

Carol firmly grit her teeth, "Oh, so, then the deed is done? Is that it? Let's just bury the man and forget all about this? Sophia, this is a crime! What the two of them did was murder!"

Sophia swung around, "Carol, no! Now you listen to me! My brother, my mother, whoever it was who put my father's bed down killed him. You know it. I know it and apparently most of the medical staff knows it. How does that make my father any less dead? Huh? How does this help anyone? We are all in mourning and you want to argue and press charges. How is that going to bring my father back?" Sophia wiped the tears from her cheek.

Carol shook her head, "Fine, then! But listen to me, Sophia. I may walk away from here, but by golly I will not forgive. No! I liked your dad, I liked him a lot. Sure he wasn't the easiest person in the world, but he was getting better! Sophia, you're just as bad as they are!"

Carol kicked dirt in Sophia's direction as she walked between the cars to her yellow Volkswagen. Sophia screamed out to her, "I am NOT like them. I am not like them at all!" She flung her red scarf over her shoulder and ran to the barn.

Her mother's horse stood expectantly waiting for his breakfast. The sixteen hand Quarter horse bay leaned his broad chest on the paint peeling wooden fence. He nodded his head up and down. Sophia rubbed his nose and then hurried through the wooden barn gate into the large metal barn. "All right, Geordie, it's way past breakfast time." Sophia scooped some alfalfa and timothy grass onto her cupped forearms. Using her mittened fingers, she lifted the metal latch of the stall gate and dropped the food into Geordie's empty trough.

"You could probably do with a good brushing. You don't want to get involved with what's going on in the house." Geordie got a good neck rub and a pat on his withers. "It's hard to believe everyone forgot about you. You perfect animal you!" Sophia removed her right mitten to stroke Geordie on his forelegs. "Your arthritis has gotten worse, huh, old boy?"

Geordie snorted in the alfalfa and timothy grass causing dust to float through the air.

"What's this on your chest?" Sophia felt a large lump the size of a grapefruit on his shoulder muscle. "Let's get you rubbed down and your blanket buckled. The weather is turning for the worse and it is cold in here." After Sophia brushed Geordie, she gathered up his green horse blanket from the neighboring stall. Gingerly placing it on his back so as not to startle him, she buckled the leather belt across his chest.

"Geordie, you haven't eaten anything. What are you doing with your breakfast? You're just pushing your food around, making a mess. Are you trying for more attention?" Sophia rubbed his cheek.

The leather buckle that went under his abdomen was buckled and in a fluid movement Sophia reached under his tail to buckle the final belt. This would keep the blanket from moving forward. Her arm came away with a smear of dried blood. "Oh, Geordie, you have blood coming out of your rear end, buddy boy! What's going on with you?" Sophia buckled the leather belt to study the dried blood from his rectum. "Geordie, everyone was so preoccupied with Papa we didn't take time for you. We need to get a vet out here to check you. Everyone needs care around here these days."

Sophia hugged Geordie's neck as he continued to shuffle the alfalfa around with his nose in the bin. She opened the stall gate to re-enter the main barn. The grey light from the stall doors allowed the dirt particles to dance. Sophia took the plastic cup hanging from a hook on the wall to scoop out a cup and a half of molasses senior feed with bran. "Don't know about the bran for you seem to have no problem dropping your horse apples, old boy." Sophia laughed as she poured the mixture into Geordie's grain bucket, which hung into his stall from a rope on her side in the barn.

"Well, now you're hungry!" Sophia smiled as Geordie's eyes sparkled. He licked up the mixture, banging the bucket against the stall wall for more. "Geordie, I wish life was simpler. I would feed you peppermints and ride you across fields of clover." She rubbed his forehead.

"Hey, thought I would find you here with the ancient horse!" Granger laughed as he came behind Sophia. His fingers tightly latched onto her shoulder. Sophia felt a chill and shuddered at his touch. She ducked down and pulled away from him.

He released her, "Sophia, this has been hard for you. We all know how difficult this is for you and Carol, but you have to let go of what happened to Papa. I am the Papa of the family now."

Granger moved to stand behind her and started rubbing Sophia's back. His velvet voice purred out of his white smile, "This is hard to understand, sure, but this wasn't anyone's fault. Papa was suffering, lying there. He was dying day by day, night by night, not able to speak. Dad was dead anyway, he just needed to let go." Granger's voice became softer, trying to sound soothing, "It's all right if you want to blame someone. You can blame me if this makes you feel better? I don't mind. I'm your older brother and it is my duty to take care of you and Mom."

His gloved hand dragged across the top of the stable door. "Yuck, this place is filthy."

Sophia smirked, "Granger, it's a barn not an operating room. Why don't you leave since you aren't welcome and I don't like or want your company?"

He grabbed her upper left arm in a death grip, "Sophia, I'm not the enemy. Understand I care for you and want the best for you and for Mom. But if you need to blame me, like Carol did then go ahead. I will never turn away from you."

Sophia tugged her arm free from him. Her arm throbbed. Granger stroked his moustache as he spoke to her over his shoulder, "You know, Sophia, we have a history together which gives us an affinity. You and I have a certain awareness of what goes on in this family. Papa may be dead, but you and I still have a true bond." Sophia rubbed her bruised arm through her heavy jacket. She heard him greet someone as he stepped out of the barn door.

"Granger, been in to check on the animals, have you?"

Sophia could hear Granger chuckle, "Yeah, you said it not me. I better get back to the house now, back to the grieving widow."

Dr. Milligan called out into the dark cavernous barn, "Sophia, are you in here? I'm going and wanted to share something with you." He reached to the right and flipped on the light switch. Sophia counted as she had done since she was a young girl. Slowly one by one the florescent barn lights flickered to illuminate. Her father once had told her of a little man who ran from the light switch on the wall, up the wire then to each florescent fixture, lighting them as he ran. When the last ceiling light lit up, Sophia turned to Dr. Milligan. "Hi, thank you for coming, Dr. Milligan. If no one else appreciated your presence I did. This must appear strange to you what with the family, the police or sheriffs, and the whole emotional upheaval. But I'm not ready to point blame at my family for my father's death."

"I've done this for many years, Sophia, it is important to assist in the grieving process. I am a geriatric doctor after all." Dr. Milligan leaned against Geordie's stall gate to watch him lick his grain bucket. "This fellow here doesn't look so hot. Has he been updated by a vet?"

Sophia frowned, "No, and he has dried blood on his rectum. He doesn't appear to want to eat his alfalfa and it's the good stuff like chocolate."

"I'm not a vet, but his eyes are glazed as well. Perhaps you should mention this to your mother." Dr. Milligan moved to sit on a bale of alfalfa. "There is one thing that I feel you should be aware of, Sophia. This is for your own safety and is probably none of my business. I bring this up more for my peace of mind than possibly for yours. I want you to be careful now that your father has passed."

He pulled off his leather gloves and folded them on his lap. Smiling, he studied Sophia, "Carol and I both took an immediate liking to you. Your care of your father appeared to be genuine. At least I believed this to be true?" He lowered his chin to stare at her.

Sophia pulled a stem of alfalfa from her mitten, "Yes, I truly loved my father. We may not have always been friends, but I loved him very much. My care for him was genuine."

Dr. Milligan nodded, "I believe you. There is something you may know about since you are an ethnology professor. Are you aware of the internecine family? Do you know what this term means?"

"Yes, of course." Sophia proudly smiled, "Internecine occurs frequently in history. This happened more in royal families than in any other for they had the means and the motive to interact in such a manner. Internecine refers to a disjointed family fighting for power of land, wealth or the throne. This causes slaughter among one another for each person of the family is equally deadly and powerful."

Dr. Milligan laughed as he clapped his hands, "Yes, you've got it, by golly she's got it! Remember the Henrys of Olde England and how they betrayed and backstabbed each other for the sole purpose of taking control. Remember internecine, Sophia, with this group of people you call family." He jabbed his thumb toward the house. Shaking his head as he chortled, he backed out of the barn bowing to her. "Madam, I leave you to the piranha of life."

4

Calavera, New Mexico
Thursday, January, 1988

Sophia pushed through the groups of neighbors on her mother's back porch. Now and then someone put their hand on her arm or her shoulder to say, "Sorry, Sophia, we are so sorry." Sophia smiled and bent her head determined to get into the house and warm her hands. Sophia noticed her mother sitting in the living room. Beside her on the wooden stool was a sheriff with a clipboard.

Margaret enjoyed her poise as a self righteous woman with a fragile build. The sitting room was neat and cleanly kept. All perfect in dignity for a householder of Margaret's age and means. Margaret's late father's large, dark landscape oil paintings were carefully placed on the widest area of walls. The predominant color in each of her father's paintings was a pale blue. This had brought many a comment from viewers who knew Margaret's father to be a dam builder during the WPA.

A twelve foot by twelve foot Peruvian tapestry similar in style to a Matisse painting hung over the expensive leather couch. The horizontal striped bright colors of the hanging tapestry brought life to the otherwise sedate furniture. Like the rest of the house, the clean walls were white, which in many places had chipped or worn off to reveal a fawn colored brick underneath. The room smelled heavily of lemon furniture polish. Margaret perched on a worn leather armchair in the corner of the room. She leaned forward, listening to the sheriff who was beside her.

When Margaret noticed Sophia entering the sitting room she excused herself. Hurrying to Sophia, she whispered, "This man is interrogating each one of us! I don't like this at all. He took Granger into your father's den to speak with him. I couldn't hear anything they said. What if I say the wrong thing?" Margaret kept glancing back at the sheriff as she spoke.

Sophia took her mother's hand, "Mom, if you tell the truth you don't have to worry. It's when people lie they get into trouble. Tell the man the truth about last night."

"Sophia, your hands are freezing. Did you feed Geordie?" Margaret lifted to her toes to peer over Sophia's shoulder.

"Yes, I did. He needs the vet to come give him a check up. Something's off with his eating and his health appears to have deteriorated." As Sophia spoke her mother began to cry. "Mom, what is it? What's wrong?"

Margaret pulled a cotton handkerchief from the sleeve of her sweater, "Oh, Sophia, I miss your father. I wish he hadn't gotten ill and left us alone to fight for our own. I don't want to talk to the sheriff right now. Do you think I could speak with him tomorrow? Would you ask him for me, please?"

Sophia shook her head, "Mom, this is their procedure. He wants to ask you questions while everything is fresh in your mind. Do you want him to talk to me first?"

"Oh, Sophia, you are a dear, yes, please yes. You don't have to tell the Sheriff everything about our family. He doesn't need to know about the financial problems or anything to do with your brother and father fighting." Margaret squeezed Sophia's wrist, "Please just answer the questions he asks, and don't volunteer anything. I'll go out and see about Geordie. I could probably call the vet now. It isn't too early for them to be in the office. Maybe he could come right away?" Margaret hurried around Sophia to grab her jacket and head out the backdoor.

Sophia moved to the dining room table. Beautiful casseroles, plates of chocolate chip cookies, a walnut and spinach salad, and a large butternut cake were placed on the bright red and white table cloth. Sophia picked out a dark raisin bran muffin. She looked up as the sheriff's deputy walked to her. His heavy jacket with insignia sewn on each shoulder was impressive. He held his brushed cowboy hat in his left hand as he asked, "What happened to your mother, Miss?"

"Oh, I'm sorry. Her horse is ill and I asked her to go out and check on him. She will probably have to call the vet. Can I help you with something?" She held the plate of muffins to him. He put his hat on the corner of the table and plucked one off the plate. "Thank you, Miss, you are very kind."

Sophia smiled, "You're welcome and you can call me Sophia. I am a married woman with two children. What do you need to know?"

She handed him a paper napkin as he bit into the muffin and crumbs scattered on his shirt. "Oh, thank you. Yes, could we go into your father's den? I have some questions for you." As she walked beside him, he continued, "I spoke with the nurse Carol and your father's doctor. Your brother was vague with his answers and appeared to be defensive. Your mother was polite, but appeared to be mourning and unable to say much."

Sophia swallowed the last of the bran muffin only to choke on a crumb. The sheriff patted her back, "There, you could use something to drink. I'll get some water. Enough people in this house have expired from respiration failure." He did an about face to leave Sophia standing in front of her father's desk. Papa's photographs covered the wall behind his desk. Sophia remembered the stories he told relative to the photos of him at a mountain climbing event in Munich where he came in second behind a political diplomat in Greece. Her father's favorite photo was of himself dancing with a dance hall girl in Paris.

"Here you go." The sheriff handed her a mug of water. "Couldn't find any drinking glasses, but there were mugs on the table. Hope it's all right?"

Sophia took a long drink, "Yes, thank you." Pointing at the photograph next to the inner door, she laughed. "You see this photo? This is when my father was in Arabia riding a camel. He was asked to tend to a sheik that had become ill while out herding his cattle in the desert. Papa said it was a two day journey, but it took him a month to relearn how to walk without a camel between his legs!"

The sheriff pointed to an old black and white photo, "What is this? It looks like he's on a mountain with repelling gear and a hard hat?"

"Bingo! You got it. My father lived each day as if it were his last. He loved life fully. You can see from these photos all the people he knew and all the places he had gone. People loved him for he loved to tell stories, share ideas, and heal the sick." Sophia sipped her water from the mug.

"Sounds like he was a great man, what happened to him?" The sheriff continued to study the pictures.

"He lived too hard at times, I guess. He would work days and nights, taking medications to stay awake and then when he could crash he needed help with that, too. Even when he found out he had an incurable horrible disease, he tried to end his life his way." Sophia shook her head.

Getting the sheriff's attention, he pulled out his notepad. "What do you mean he tried to end his life his way?"

"It was gruesome. He knew what he had. He knew how sick he would become and how dependent he would be on his family. Somewhere he got a hold of a revolver and was going to end his life his way, out there, behind the barn." She pointed to the north. "But then, my mother was suspicious. She had my brother follow my father. My brother Granger took the revolver away from him. Then my mother and brother legally documented my father as being incompetent. They took over his accounts, his stocks, his titles and deeds, everything."

Sophia leaned against the door frame, surveying all the photos, "This vibrant man became a vegetable. It happened faster than we thought. Within six weeks he couldn't walk and then within three months he was silent. It was sad, but at least we got to say good-bye to him." Sophia wiped one of the photos near the bookcase with her index finger, "He was such a beautiful man to have such a pathetic death."

"Where was he from? The name is not from around here is it?" The sheriff studied Sophia's face.

"No, he was born in southern Italy. His father was from Spain, but his mother was an Italian princess from some small royal family south of Florence. They moved to Canada after the Second World War. She was incredibly refined, very lady like. She was an artist and a dancer. My father's father specialized in grapes. He was a vineyardist. Grandpa knew the diseases, bugs, and fungi that could destroy the fragile vines. Grandpa had his signature grape mixtures and supplements. At one point he was in great demand, but then huge vineyards developed their own medical grape staff. His diaries and recipes are over there in the brown leather volumes."

She sat down in the cloth chair beside the desk. "Grandpa's work was outsourced with the coming of the telephone and mass production. He was a good man, very quiet, very loyal to family. He died from a massive stroke when I was eleven. My father's mother didn't live long after her husband. My grandparents were a spiritual team. They were truly in love."

The sheriff sat on the short couch across from her. He put out his hand, "By the way, my name is Ignacio Cruz. I'm an investigator detective with the sheriff's department. It's standard procedure to ask the family questions when there is a home death. If you don't mind I need for you to tell me your full name."

"Ah, we are now getting down to business?" Sophia spelled her last name for him. He asked, "You and your husband live around here?"

"No, not really, we live about seventeen miles north of here at Rocoso on the east side of the interstate. We have two daughters and a fantastic view of the mesas."

Ignacio leaned back on the couch to cross his ankle over his knee. "When was the last time you saw your father?" Sophia explained how she had bathed him yesterday morning, had fed him lunch through his feeding tube, and was told to go home by her mother at five o'clock. "I wanted to stay and give him his last feeding through the feeding tube, but my mother stated she could handle it. I have full confidence in her. If she felt unable she would have called my brother Granger. He lives across the way over the ditch on Calle Paton. He would have helped her."

He wrote for a few minutes and then asked, "When did the nurse Carol Grover attend to your father?"

"Well, that's just it, isn't it?" Sophia hesitated for she wanted to be very sure he understood what occurred, "Carol has a wonderful dog named Daisy. Daisy had been playing with the neighbor's dogs next door. That would be Mr. Perkal and his wife who have the dogs. Daisy was chasing a porcupine and got quills in her nose. Carol had to take Daisy to the vet. She called and asked if I would care for Papa yesterday. The vet had to fit her in as he had a full schedule of clients. I agreed because we help each other out when there is a need."

Ignacio let out sigh, "I have a black lab that is always getting sprayed by skunks. Yes, we all need help when it comes to our dogs!" He stretched his legs out in front of him, "Did your mother understand your father's bed was not to be lowered? Was she made aware of how important it was to keep his bed elevated?"

Sophia placed her empty mug on her father's desk. "I believe Dr. Milligan had made it clear to her. As a matter of fact, Carol made a metal triangle wedge to put under the elevated part of the hospital bed. She jammed it under the back of the elevated frame. The bed couldn't be dropped. Carol takes excellent care of her patients. She's taught me a lot about healthcare and patient needs."

"Would you show me this triangle?" He stood. "It would help to understand if you could show me this device."

Sophia gulped, "You mean it wasn't there this morning?"

"I didn't say that, I just didn't notice it. Would you show me please?" He walked out of the room into the hall. Sophia felt her face grow hot as she cautiously followed him across the hall into her parent's bedroom. "Where is everything?'

He pointed to the space where the hospital bed had stood, "I believe your brother called the rental agency. They were here within an hour after we arrived to remove the bed. They had to wait for the OMI to finish his exam before they could take it. The medical examiner or OMI didn't find anything wedged in the bed frame." The deputy walked around the empty space, "We searched the room for any devices used in your father's medical care. There were no triangular metal shapes found."

Sophia started to back out of the room. He put up his hand, "Ma'am, would you show me what you were talking about, please?"

Shoving her hands into her jean pockets, Sophia shook her head, "I don't see it. I don't see it here. It must have been removed by someone else, because it isn't here." She swallowed hurriedly.

"Do you think we should ask your mother?" He moved to open the closet door.

"I'm sure my mother wouldn't know. She wouldn't be strong enough to remove it. The metal triangle was wedged in there pretty well." Sophia shook her head, "There wouldn't be anything in the closet. I think you should ask my brother or the paramedics. I don't really want to be in here anymore." Sophia turned away to hide her tears.

"Can I help you find something?" Margaret stood in the doorway to the hall.

Sheriff Cruz turned to her, "Yes, Ma'am, can you tell us about the metal triangle put in the hospital bed by Carol Granger? It doesn't appear to be here."

Margaret clasped her hands in front of her chest, "No, Sir, the paramedics took everything related to the bed and to my husband's care. I am sure they would know where it is, why don't you ask them?"

"Ma'am, I have a list here that you signed off on regarding the items removed with your husband and there is not a reference to a metal triangle of any size." He lifted the clipboard to examine it further. "No, no listing for a metal triangle."

"Sophia," Margaret focused all her attention on her daughter's face, "Did you mention this triangle to the Sheriff?"

Sheriff Cruz countered Margaret, "Ma'am, Carol Granger was the nurse who attended your husband and brought this device to be used to keep the bed from being made flat. Is this correct?"

Sophia stood firmly, staring straight at her mother without flinching. Tears fell down her cheeks, but she did not move or speak.

Margaret turned her attention to the sheriff deputy, "Yes, Carol did bring the wedge device to prevent anyone from lowering the bed by accident. She must have removed it at some point for if it isn't here, then it isn't here. I have no knowledge as to its whereabouts." Margaret slowly moved into the room. She began rearranging the framed photographs on the bureau.

Sheriff Cruz flipped the papers on his clipboard, "Mrs. Pino, do you know how your husband's bed became flat? You were aware, were you not that his bed had to remain upright? Can you explain to me how the bed was lowered?"

Margaret's hand hit a photo frame, it fell on its side, "No, I can't tell you how his bed became flat. I have no idea! I resent the fact that you are insinuating I was the one who put my husband's bed down. I will not answer any more of your questions." She glared at him, "I need some time with my daughter, if you please!"

"Mrs. Pino, I'm so sorry for your loss, but you will need to give us a statement either here or at the Sheriff's station. I can take you now in my vehicle or you could come with your daughter. You do have a choice of speaking with me here or at the station."

Margaret put her hand on Sophia's arm, "Do you mean to tell me that while I am grieving you plan to take me to jail? Please, all I need is a death certificate, the freedom to bury my husband in his favorite cemetery in Negar and the right to continue on with my life." Margaret gave a quick dramatic sigh.

Sophia studied Sheriff's Ignacio Cruz's reaction. He didn't miss a beat, "Ma'am, at the moment, we have confirmation that the death of your husband was caused by respiratory failure. We need your details of his death in order for the death certificate to be completed. The death certificate will be released by the funeral home once they receive our final information. Also, we will need to get copies of the Medical Examiner's full report before we can release the body to the funeral home. It is important for us to find your husband's cause of death."

Margaret dabbed at her dry eyes with a cotton handkerchief, "Yes, I understand. My son Granger can take me tomorrow morning around ten o'clock, is that satisfactory with you?"

The Sheriff Detective smiled, "No, this information needs to be completed now, if possible."

Margaret gave him a childlike smirk, "Oh, well, if my daughter is here, I suppose we could try to finish this now."

Sophia took her mother's hand, "Let's go back into Papa's office and sit down. Mom, you can take your time. Sheriff Cruz is a patient man and he will be gentle." Margaret glared at him.

The three of them sat in Dr. Walter Pino's office. Margaret was noticeably nervous. She perched behind her husband's desk on his executive chair. Her hands were busy with the pens and pencils. She flipped them around with an irritating and erratic movement. Sheriff Cruz sat comfortably on the wooden chair to her right and Sophia sat on the couch opposite both of them.

Margaret stuttered, "I was asleep. Sound asleep and this odor awakened me. Upon turning on the bedside lamp, I saw my husband's bed was flat. He was laying flat on his left side, facing the door to the room. His back was to me. I could see his shoulder was not moving up and down, which was a sign of his lack of breathing. He was still."

Sheriff Cruz sat studying her. "How would the bed go flat if there was no one in the room to push the button beside the bed?"

"You asked me a question and I am answering you. Don't interrupt, young man, it is very rude." Margaret sighed, pushing a black pen in a circular motion on the desk. "Once I was up and in my robe, I went over to him. He was not breathing. He was cold. His eyes were open and he was drooling onto the sheet." Margaret's tears rolled down her cheeks. "He was dead. He had been still and non responsive when he was alive for so long and then he was dead."

Sophia frowned, turning to look out the office window, she muttered, "Oh, Mom." The wind was slacking off and the trees weren't moving. "Mom, the bed could not have gone down by itself. That is logically and scientifically impossible. Think, Mom, did you hit it by accident? Was the cat in the room? Mom, there is no physical way the bed would move without help."

Margaret jutted her chin at Sophia, "Oh, you're going to accuse me as well? Fine, my own daughter is going to accuse me of killing her father. Well, I didn't do it!" She pushed her hands into a clasp on the desk, "There is nothing more I can say! God's truth, I didn't lower the bed. I did NOT lower the bed. Now leave me alone!" She jumped out of the chair, hurried out of the room, slamming the door behind her. It bounced back open after hitting the warped door frame.

Sheriff Cruz placed his clipboard on the desk. "Well, evidently your mother didn't do the deed, but someone did. Who do you think put the bed down?" He frowned at Sophia.

"I have no idea, except it wasn't me. I was at home with my family." Sophia rubbed her hands together, "Sheriff Cruz, you're the detective so perhaps you are the one who should detect this? Maybe it was the cat?" Sophia gave him a half smile.

"Oh, yes, it was the cat!" He lifted the clipboard off the desk with his right hand. "Better get back to the office and write my report mentioning the cat." He put out his hand, "Good to meet you, Ma'am." He left her alone standing in her father's office. Sophia shuddered as the cold wind rattled the side window.

5

Calavera, New Mexico
Thursday, January 15, 1988

Sophia shook her head as she heard her mother's neighbor Charlotte speak loudly to an older man in the kitchen, "Oh, yes, she has had help with her fields. She pays a local fellow and he does a good job. Dare say, she won't be alone. This fellow comes two or three times a week to help around this farm. She just wouldn't have been able to keep this farm nice what with her husband being so ill and all these last two years. Now, finally Margaret will have more than enough money to keep the place in good standing."

Picking up another raisin bran muffin from the kitchen table, Sophia turned to study her mother. Margaret sat in the sitting room by herself, waiting for the guests to come to her as the mourning queen. Most of the neighbors were standing outside the kitchen door in the cold wind, talking and sharing stories. Mr. Perkal, the neighbor from next door, had filled his plate with food. He held the plate in one hand and a mug of steaming coffee in the other. He juggled his inventory as he lodged himself onto the couch beside Margaret's red chair. The cracks in the leather couch widened with his body weight. "Margaret," his deep voice rolled out, "we're sorry about Walter. He was a fine friend and will be dearly missed."

"Yes," Margaret replied in a high pitch almost a chirp. "Thank you, Mr. Perkal. As you know, my husband has been bedridden for at least twenty-six months." She tilted her head downwards to grin as a frail ten-year old girl might. Sophia decided to sit beside Mr. Perkal on the couch. Sophia noticed Margaret's innocent behavior and smirked. Margaret gave Sophia a look of contention, "Couldn't you have dressed for this occasion, Sophia?"

"Mother, I was getting the girls dressed for school when you called this morning. It was my impression you needed me here regardless of apparel demands."

Mr. Perkal sniffed, "Cold outside today isn't it? That wind cuts a person to the bone." Margaret smiled at him as if he was demented then shifted her attention to Sophia. "Please get me a cup of tea, Sophia. Not that cheap stuff the neighbors brought, but the Earl Grey from in the cupboard. You know the one your brother ordered from England? Oh, and Sophia, get me an English muffin with some strawberry jam. I haven't eaten yet this morning what with all of the company." Margaret's hand flung out to elaborate her words.

Sophia stuffed the remaining raisin bran muffin into her mouth, letting crumbs fall on her lap. "The strawberry jam that Granger brought you from Ireland?"

Margaret nodded as if giving out orders were an everyday event. "Yes, of course."

Sophia entered into the kitchen's inner sanctum. The seventy-six year old Charlotte was busy washing dishes and handing out napkins to the guests.

"How's Margaret doing, dear?" Charlotte appeared frazzled with all of the people who had pushed into the kitchen. Her gray braids danced around her shoulders as she quickly turned to help each person. Sophia shrugged her shoulders as she reached over the stove for the famous Earl Grey tea box.

"Is the water hot in the tea kettle?" Sophia took down a china cup and saucer, no mug for her mother.

"Yes, it's hot, but I don't know how much water is still in it. Everyone has been helping themselves and as you can see, most of the folks prefer to be out on the back porch. They appear to choose the cold porch than the warm sitting room." Charlotte lifted the tea kettle and shook it, "Yes, there's plenty of water for your mother's tea cup."

Sophia returned to the sitting room with a silver tray in her hand. The tray held the china cup on a china saucer. The cup was filled with steaming water and the saucer had the bag of Earl Gray's tea. A dessert plate held two halves of a toasted muffin smothered with strawberry jam. A tiny butter knife was beside the plate. "Here you go, Mom, your tea and muffin."

Margaret nodded, "Just put them here, dear." Margaret patted her lap as she uncrossed her legs. "Mr. Perkal has been telling me about his son who is attempting to get through college. Although, he doesn't appear to be doing very well, does he, Mr. Perkal?"

Mr. Perkal sat up suddenly as if he had been electrocuted, "Not doing well? Not doing well? He is doing just fine." He quickly retrieved his fallen plate, "My son has to work and attend classes. This means he pays his own way even if it does take longer, that's all." Mr. Perkal started scrambling to stand. Sophia helped him by taking the empty plate from his hand.

Mr. Perkal frowned. "Excuse me, please. I do believe I should be getting home now." Hurriedly with mug and plate back in his hands, Mr. Perkal was gone. Sophia turned to study her mother. All the neighbors and friends were outside in the blustery wind. "Mum, why aren't your friends in here with you?"

"Sophia, this is very good, thank you," and then under her breath, "I have no idea and I find them to be intensely rude."

Margaret glanced at the backdoor which was directly across the room from her. The fire in the fireplace crackled and spit. "Sophia, dear, would you mind adding another log to the fire? Perhaps if we get the fire roaring more people will come in here for they seem to prefer being outside. "

Sophia knelt by the fireplace. Taking the scoop shovel she moved the dark coals to the side, opening the air to the flames. Two heavy logs were placed on the now roaring orange fire. "Mom, where is Granger? Shouldn't he be here to help you with things?"

"Oh, Sophia, it is so like you to blame your brother for everything. Your brother did not kill your father." Margaret delicately nibbled the last of her English muffin. "Why do you hate your brother so much, Sophia? I have never been able to understand why you two hate each other. He was the smart one. You were the slow one, but that is no reason for you two to not like one another."

Margaret wiped her lips with her handkerchief, "Why, oh, why don't those people come in here? Sophia, go ask those people to come in here. I am the grieving widow for goodness sake! Go, Sophia, go and get those people in here. I am all dressed and even fixed my hair to entertain and yet they stand out there!" Margaret let out an exasperated sigh as she pointed to the backdoor.

Sophia leaned back on her boot heels as she knelt by the fire, "Mom, we're dressed in our farm clothes. You look like you're going to the Queen's tea. Maybe they feel uncomfortable?"

"Nonsense, Sophia, get them. Don't take 'no' for an answer, get those people in here. They are people who have helped your father and me. They should be in here!"

Sophia pulled her scarf off from around her neck. She walked to the back door. Slowly, Sophia pushed the kitchen backdoor open, "Hey, guys, come inside by the roaring fire? My mother would enjoy your company right now."

Tommy Ortiz let out a snort, "You mean come in and speak to her ladyship?"

Sophia spoke softly to the crowd, "Come in and warm up. You can speak to Mom if you like or you could just come in and keep her company. What do you say?" She turned back into the house to walk into the sitting room.

She heard the door close behind her and turned. Tommy had gently shut the back door behind her. No one had followed her inside. Margaret gave Sophia a glaring disapproval as she lifted herself with her hands from the chair. She charged across the room to the back door. Margaret grabbed her winter jacket off the hook and while wrapping around her, she quickly opened the door, "Please would you come inside! There is plenty of food and Sophia has stoked the fire."

Silence ensued and then as if someone had fired a gun, the race began as people hurried around the farmhouse to their vehicles and drove away.

Charlotte's cackling laughter could be heard in the kitchen, "Sophia, there was no way to get people to move faster! Do you want a cup of tea or some food? There is plenty of food on the table, help yourself?" Sophia watched Margaret as she called after the fleeting masses, "Fine, just leave me alone in my mourning!"

Sophia took a paper plate from Charlotte, "Sure, I'll get some food in a minute."

Coming back into the house, Margaret threw her winter jacket at Sophia, "Some help you are! If your brother would have been here he would have ordered those people to come into the sitting room, which is where I will be getting warm. Sophia, you are worthless!"

Sophia returned the winter jacket to its peg by the backdoor. Margaret yelled at her, "Sophia, go into the bedroom and get me my wrap. Your fire appears to be dwindling and let's not waste anymore wood on your attempts."

Sophia surveyed her parents' bedroom. On the floor next to the bedroom door was a small piece of paper. She retrieved it. Granger Pino had signed a credit card receipt at the gas station down the road. The time on the receipt was one o'clock this morning. Sophia stuffed it into her jean pocket. "Well, life is certainly curious."

Her mother's crocheted wrap was neatly folded on her bed. Sophia walked down the hall. She heard the sound of plates clattering and then her mother's famous high pitched laugh with Charlotte admonishing her. Sophia shook her head, "Time for me to leave."

The tile floor echoed her foot steps as she went down the hall to the kitchen. She stood in the doorway of the kitchen and handed the wrap to her mother. "Mom, I am leaving now. Have chores to run shall speak with you later?"

Margaret dismissed her with a wave of her hand. She and Charlotte were washing up the tea mugs and putting the excess food in her fridge. "Yes, we'll talk, bye!"

The grey sky reflected the day's events. Everything was dull with dark clouds hovering overhead giving the appearance of an utterly smooth surface. The air was still. Still enough for there was no movement in the fields of any kind. This blustery, raw morning had allowed the air to settle into a placid peace, a great calm. Sophia bent down to pull the log holding open the oak gate into her mother's property. There was no need for it now. Then she noticed Charlotte's truck and let it drop back against the heavy gate.

"Sophia, Sophia, hey, do you have a minute?" Mr. Perkal waved to her as he loped from his opened garage to his wooden gate. Mr. Perkal's mutts ran aside him barking all the way to the closed gate at the entrance of his property. "Sophia, just wanted to let you know the Missus and I are sorry to hear of your father's passing. Even though he had been sick for over two years, just his presence gave the neighborhood a sense of peace."

"Why thank you, Mr. Perkal."

"Also, we just wanted you to know that if you hear anything about the memorial service, we would appreciate it if you would let us know. We would like to attend." He tried to zip up his winter jacket, but the zipper wasn't working. "Anyway, oh, also the Missus wanted me to tell you that when she got up last night, she gets up and down all night long with leg cramps, she saw your brother's new Mercedes driving away down the drive around four-thirty this morning. She was impressed with his thoughtfulness for he kept the lights off so as not to wake up the neighbors."

"My brother was here last night?"

"Oh, yes, he was very attentive to your mother's needs. Listen we have no problem keeping your father's dog here." Mr. Perkal reached down to stroke the black lab. "Old Blue is a good boy and is used to being with the others. Your mother gave him to us. Let her know we are proud to have him."

Sophia's voice cracked as she spoke to him, "Mom gave you Papa's dog? I thought she was going to keep him or give him to my brother?"

"No, she said your brother is in the middle of a change in his life and your mother told us your life was too busy for a pet. He's ours now and we love him." He scratched Old Blue's ears. All of Mr. Perkal's dogs as if on a secret mission turned at once and ran to the other side of his acreage. The grey-brown hound was in the lead, baying at the top of his lungs. "Ah, oh, the porcupine must be back! Better go, talk with you soon!" He scurried off with his heavy winter jacket flapping. Running to the hound, Mr. Perkal pulled the dog's snout out of the hole near the fence to wave at Sophia, "He's fine, no porcupine quills this time!"

Laughing, Sophia pulled on her worn mittens. She frowned. Seriously she hadn't purposely decided to wear her worst winter clothes. They had just been grabbed first out of comfort. Sensing movement from the side of her mother's house, she stopped.

"Sophia, Samuel Goldfarb just called?" Margaret was waving a kitchen towel wildly in the air. "Sophia, good thing I stopped you! Tomorrow at two o'clock will be the reading of the will at Samuel Goldfarb's office. You are just the person I need to speak with for Geoffrey needs to be there as well."

Sophia slowly walked to her mother. "Is his office the one on Fourth and Central downtown?"

"Yes, you can't miss it." Margaret grabbed the towel off of her shoulder where she had just put it to wrap it around her hands. "OOO, it's cold out here. Oh, and Sopha, would you be kind enough to dress in something nice as I have always wanted you to dress? Try to look like as if you were raised with some semblance of dignity!" Margaret ran back to the house, slamming the backdoor behind her.

"Well, yes, some semblance of dignity can be arranged." Sophia straightened her wool cap on her forehead. Yanking open the door to Geoffrey's turquoise truck, she noticed the rake and shovel in the back. "Hey, I even brought my own work tools, hah!"

While double choking the starter, a turn of the key brought the old truck to life. Sophia leaned forward over the steering wheel to stare into the early afternoon sky. Speaking to no one, she said, "Granger was driving away from this house in the dark, late at night, with no lights. What do you make of that?"

The clutch was pushed all the way into the floor boards as first gear was shifted in the gear box. The heater was turned high to warm the icy cold of the truck cab. She drove to the stop sign then turned right onto Calle Aspen to drive slowly down the corrugated dirt road to the Calavera highway.

6

Rocoso, New Mexico
Friday, January, 1988

Geoffrey sat up in bed to reach over and turn on the bedside table light, "What is it?" Sophia sobbed into her pillow. He pulled the sheet back from over her head, "Sophia, what is it now? Come on! I have to be at work at seven if I am going to take an hour off for the will business. Couldn't you cry about your father during the daytime when we don't need our beauty sleep?"

Sophia suddenlty pulled her knees up, "Yes, Sir!"

"Oh, come on, Sophia, enough already. Come over here." Geoffrey reached his arm under her shoulders, turned her to his chest, and hugged her. "There you go, now you are enveloped in the quiet peacefulness of your man." He leaned over her and turned off the bedside lamp. "Go to sleep, my beauty."

Sophia felt the jolt on the bed before she was fully conscious believing it to be Geoffrey getting up early to go to work, but then the jumping started. This was a herd of girls on attack. Sophia flung back the blankets and grabbed Sybil who was closest to her. "Ahhh, I am going to eat you for breakfast, my sweet!" Sybil screamed and ran into the bathroom. Donna was still trying to crawl up the side of the bed, "Mom, you can't get me. I'll eat you first!"

Glancing at the clock on her side of the bed, Sophia gasped, "Run, run, run, we have twenty minutes to be ready and out of the door. Go, girls, go!" She grabbed her underwear and her lavender sweatsuit from the dresser drawers and ran into the bathroom. The girls were giggling as they ran down the hall into the kitchen.

"I get the Sugar O's first," screamed Donna.

When Sophia walked into the kitchen she noticed that Sybil had the table set with bowls, spoons, cereal boxes, and napkins. Donna was shoveling in her Sugar O's as if she would never eat again. Sybil was busy reading the story on the back of the Shredded Wheat box. Sophia put the tea kettle on the stove, turned, reaching into the refrigerator to pull out sliced ham, whole wheat bread, mayonnaise, mustard, and some boxed fruit drinks for the girls' lunch boxes. "All right, today you both have home made lunches, but you have to tell me what drink you want?" Sophia placed the boxes of fruit drink on the kitchen table.

Donna started to sniff. Sophia quickly grabbed the dishtowel from the rack by the kitchen sink, "Another bloody nose, Donna?" Donna shook her head as blood slowly ran down her upper lip.

"Well, we are prepared!" Donna was lifted upside down by Sophia and carried into her bedroom. Sophia pushed a pink pillow under Donna's neck and shoulders letting her head fall back with the dishtowel under her nose. "We have the means to conquer this!" Sophia used her powerful voice. Sybil came dancing into the room doing pirouettes.

Sophia joyously clapped her hands as she sat back on the twin bed to watch, "Sybil, we have to get you into a dance class. You are so beautiful when you dance!"

Sybil fell into her mother's lap. "They don't have dance classes way out here in the middle of nowhere."

Sophia lifted Sybil onto her lap to be sure they both didn't get pulled off the side of Donna's bed. "We can get you into a class in Albuquerque or Rincon even if you do love to dance out here on the mesa tops!"

Sybil sneered at her mother and ran to her room, "Yeah, right! I don't like living here, Mom, I don't like it at all!"

Donna lifted up on her elbows, "Mom, I think I am all right now. Can I get up and get dressed for school?"

The girls were dropped off at their schools. Sybil went to the school in Rincon and Donna went to the school closer to the main highway to Albuquerque. Sophia hurried home to clean the kitchen, run a load of laundry, vacuum the front living room and take a hot bath.

Today she would show up at the lawyer's reading of the will dressed as a professional woman. Professor Sophia Vinder had only taken off one semester to look after her father. Two years ago, Sophia had finally earned her doctorate. She had worked on sites in twelve foreign countries and had written a profound article on the development of stronger bones once the concept of eating on a regular basis was introduced by agrarian societies. She also had published a book on the development of languages in Central Europe during the middle ages. This last book had won her an honorary award from Cambridge, England.

Her prestige and accomplishments were not going to be represented today in old jeans. Her suit made of red wool with a lining tailored in white silk would be set off by her cream colored turtleneck accessorized with the turquoise necklace Geoffrey had given her for their eighth anniversary. This would be just the ticket to impress her dear mother.

The brick building sat on the corner of Fourth Street and Central in downtown Albuquerque. The renovation of buildings was a new part of the political scene in Albuquerque. Many buildings had been redone to stimulate growth and yet retain the memory of colonialism in New Mexico. Some of the red brick buildings appeared to be boarding houses which probably were renovated brothels or large family houses. The older buildings once in stages of disrepair were now frame and stucco, painted in mustard yellow and red catsup hues the signature colors of the 1950's.

Samuel Goldfarb's office was a more modern model. It was a stucco painted white with bars on all the windows giving it the feeling of secrets well kept. There were no other buildings with bars on the windows in the area and this set it apart from the others on the immediate block. Behind Samuel Goldfarb's office was a hospital parking lot and to the far east of the parking lot was a rehabilitation center.

Sophia parked the yellow van beside her mother's silver Mercedes, which was parked to the left of Granger's green Mercedes. Sophia cautiously studied the parking lot to take inventory of who had already arrived. She could see Geoffrey's turquoise truck parked in the far corner of the parking lot. Geoffrey did that to keep others from banging into his treasured truck. There was a white Mercedes parked towards the back and two other nondescript vehicles parked on the right side of the building's entrance. Sophia tilted the rearview mirror to study her makeup. Her eyeliner was perfect. The slight touch of rouge on her cheeks gave her a healthy look and her lip gloss was glistening.

The calf- length coat of wool was pulled close to her she ran across the parking lot to the lawyer's office. The wind was still billowing from the southwest. Pieces of paper and plastic bags blew freely in the wind, slapping against the cars and the sides of the building. As Sophia ran to the steps in her laced boots the door opened. She smiled when she saw Geoffrey holding the door for her. Geoffrey quickly pulled her to his side, "Well, don't you look marvelous!" He gently took her arm as she tried to move her purse to her opposite shoulder. He yanked her into a side room.

The thickness of the red carpet buffeted their foot steps. The wall paper was a bright blue giving the room warmth, which was in stark contrast to the portraits of men's profiles framed on the walls. A round table of mahogany stood free from chairs in the center of the room. The linen drapes of glistening gold were held open with brown chords to allow visitors to view the parking lot.

Geoffrey let go of Sophia to whisper coarsely, "Sophia, there are two other men here who are evidently your father's other sons. A tall man with an ascot is here representing your half sister who lives in Canada. Granger is birthing a bovine. He has made it clear to Samuel Goldfarb that only he is the inheritor of your father's estate and they are not welcome."

A booming voice interrupted Geoffrey's quiet dialogue, "Sophia and Geoffrey, you both are here! Excellent, come in and let's get started." Mr. Goldfarb reached out his hand to Geoffrey who took it with a firm congenial shake. Sophia put her hand out, but Mr. Goldfarb was already walking out of the room and down the hall. Sophia was amazed at the thick rich carpet yet wondered why it was scarlet red. "Geoffrey, do you believe there will be a confrontation?"

Geoffrey shook his head, "We shall see. I do believe this is going to be very interesting."

Mrs. Margaret Pino, the bereaved widow, sat in the largest chair in the room. It was a Queen Anne chair with golden embroidery of flowers and birds. The arm rests on the sides allowed her to rest her arms comfortably as royalty. To her right was a wooden table graced with a tray of tea cups and a plate of biscuits. As Sophia and Geoffrey entered, Margaret pointed to the table beside her, "If you want something to drink help yourself." Margaret's right hand gently waved over the tea cups and biscuits as if giving a blessing.

Geoffrey choked down a laugh, "No, my lady, I do believe we are sufficiently fulfilled."

She shrugged pulling her suit jacket of gray linen down to her waist. "I guess Mr. Goldfarb wanted me to be the servant in the room." Margaret lowered her head to look at Geoffrey coyly.

Sophia and Geoffrey sat in two straight-back wooden chairs toward the back of the room. She quickly noticed that Geoffrey was the only person in the room wearing jeans, but at least Geoffrey's white shirt was well ironed and his turquoise bolo tie gave him a very stylish look. There were two tall men sitting in straight back wooden chairs on the opposite side of the room. Both men were dressed in nicely tailored black suits with striped ties. They nodded at Sophia and Geoffrey who returned the nod. Geoffrey quickly took Sophia's hand in his.

Mr. Goldfarb cleared his throat, "We are waiting for one other person to enter the room. I believe he is freshening up at the moment."

A hand was raised to the left of Sophia. She leaned forward to find a young man in his thirties who was smiling. "I'm back, thank you, you may proceed." The man's ascot tie of purple paisley made an impression as it was tied firmly at his neck. He had a high forehead, a brown goatee, and a warm face.

Samuel Goldfarb's short height was not noticed now that everyone was sitting. Mr. Goldfarb pulled his reading glasses out of his pinstriped suit as he walked to his desk. Granger followed and then stopped. He appeared subdued as he did not fully enter the room, but stood leaning against the door jam fidgeting with his car keys. Sophia smiled at him, but Granger ignored her. Mr. Goldfarb sat behind his desk to open a heavy brown folder. The rubber band snapped as he withdrew a thick bundle of white legal papers.

"All right, it is my duty as the legal representative for Dr. Walter Pino to inform you of his wishes in regards to the dissolving of his estate. I am going to ask that everyone please be quiet until the reading of the will is completed. If anyone has anything they wish to ask or anything they wish to define this will be done once we have completed the reading. Does anyone have any questions at this time?"

Granger coughed, "I thought we weren't to speak until you were finished?"

Mr. Goldfarb gave Granger a warning glance and continued. "This meeting of the family is not legally necessary in the state of New Mexico. However, my client Dr. Walter Pino asked in his will for the family to convene in my office for the reading of his will.

"Now this will is almost one hundred pages in length and it is not necessary for all of it be read to you today. Rather than read each request of the deceased, it may perhaps be more expedient if I outline the contents that are related directly to those of you present in the room?"

Everyone in the room made an expression of agreement and Mr. Goldfarb continued. "Dr. Walter Pino gave instructions that his estate was to be assessed, liquidated and proceeds divided after these bills had been paid. If anyone of you would like a copy of this will I have copies available to you."

Margaret put up her white gloved hand to stop Mr. Goldfarb, "Excuse me, but didn't my husband have several charities that he wished to give monetary aid?"

Papers were shuffled in Mr. Goldfarb's hand, "Yes, but before any funds can be moved or relocated I have to research for assets and liabilities. These may have occurred prior to your husband's demise and would reflect on the final sum to be distributed. These will have an affect on the bearing of funds and limitations of assets."

Mr. Goldfarb moved ahead to the decided development of property and monetary inheritance. "Starting with the youngest of Dr. Walter Pino's children is his daughter and her husband Geoffrey. The deceased states and I quote, 'the mutual property which we own together in Rocoso shall be remanded completely to Geoffrey and Sophia with no further debt being due to either my wife or my sons. The property at Rocoso Mesa shall be now placed free and clear into the name of Geoffrey George Vinder and his wife Sophia Lucia Pino Vinder. This property is the home of my daughter, her husband and my two granddaughters and the title and deed shall upon my demise be given to Geoffrey and Sophia with no further financial responsibility.'"

Granger burst out laughing, "That ain't gonna happen. We already have put the deed and the title in my name thanks to Mom. Geoffrey, there is no way in hell that you're going to get my property as long as you are married to my sister!"

Sophia felt Geoffrey's body jerk and then freeze. His jaw was set, his fingers began to jingle his change in his pocket, and his left foot started to shake. Sophia whispered, "Geoffrey, are you all right?" Geoffrey turned to give her a steely cold stare, "No," was all he said. Sophia returned her focus on Mr. Goldfarb..

Mr. Goldfarb stopped speaking to remove his reading glasses, he stared at Granger. "Sir, you are to refrain from speaking until the completion of the will has been read, do you understand?"

"Yes, but what you are reading is fiction! Mom and I have already moved properties and stocks into my name and I am her legal executor. What is the purpose of reading this piece of crap if none of it is true, Sir?" Granger left the door frame to saunter into the room with arrogance as he put his hand on Margaret's shoulder. Everyone waited for her to confirm his remark.

Geoffrey gulped air as if he was trying to swallow. He stared at Sophia. Sophia's face was beet red and her hands began to shake. Not being able to contain herself, Sophia stood, "Granger, either sit down and shut up or leave! You really enjoy being a horse's ass, don't you? If you can't respect the dead then just get the hell out of here!" Sophia started to lunge toward Granger, but Geoffrey jerked her back into her chair. He whispered under his breath, "It isn't worth it, Sophia, just let him be."

Granger had whirled around to face Sophia. His face was frozen in a smirk, "Sophia, you don't know anything. How dare you refer to your father as 'the dead?' What kind of cretin are you?"

Narrowing his eyes in anger, he gloated, "Mom and I have been busy all these months while you have been taking care of Papa. We've been busy moving, shoving, and taking control and you...you...you, Miss Pollyanna, looking after poor Papa the Helpless. Well, you chose the wrong side to hang with, Missy Prissy."

Geoffrey shook his head at him, "Granger, please just be quiet and let's get this over with for once and for all."

Margaret took her son's hand, holding it gently at her side. "Granger, please be polite. I need everyone to get along. You're the one I depend on now in my time of need. Please, try to get along."

The two men on the far side of the room watched with indifference as Mr. Goldfarb's glasses were returned to his pointed nose and the reading continued. Sophia stared down at Geoffrey's polished cowboy boots. She wasn't going to take Granger's bait again.

Mr. Goldfarb's voice rolled on and on. It appeared to never end, until he came to the part regarding extended family. "To my two older sons, I do hereby leave the sum of ten thousand dollars each. This is done out of love for them and pride in their abilities to become fine young men in a solid profession with fine families. This sum cannot be redirected nor shall it be, for the monies they inherit are in a separate account, which only Mr. Goldfarb has access to at this time."

Granger flinched, Margaret gasped and Geoffrey smiled. The two men shook hands. Mr. Goldfarb continued, "My daughter Cynthia shall receive ten thousand dollars in investments. This money has been invested for her by Thornton and Thornton and can only be removed by her and/or her family only with confirmation of identification and her birth certificate. She is to receive also five thousand dollars kept for her under Samuel Goldfarb's care for her family."

The young man with the ascot stood and nodded to Mr. Goldfarb, "Thank you for taking care of Cynthia." The man quickly sat back down. Granger glared at him, "Who the hell are you and what right do you have to be here? Obviously you are not Cynthia!"

"Oh, dear, Granger, shut up!" Mr. Goldfarb slammed the flat of his hand on the desk. "Granger, sit down. Your sister Sophia is correct. If you will not be respectful get out or be quiet. Choose one or the other, but I will not tolerate your rude abuse."

Granger smirked, "What're you going to do if I don't?"

Mr. Goldfarb's face turned bright red, "I shall call the guard and have you physically removed."

Margaret patted Granger's hand on her shoulder, "Please, son, let's be civil and continue with these proceedings. We have what we want. Just be still." Margaret whispered, "I am proud of you. Granger, you are my own personal Dr. Pino. We'll have it all taken care of, right?"

Granger walked to the back of the room, leaning on the door jam, he fidgeted with his car keys. Mr. Goldfarb's voice now rang with deep intolerance, "My son Granger shall receive the total sum of five thousand dollars for he has not decided on a true profession. He has weaseled his way out of most institutions of higher learning and if he does decide on a profession I am of full confidence that he will be able to provide for himself and his family with his own personal income."

Mr. Goldfarb concluded with the location of the cemetery to hold the funeral and the location of the memorial service. "This concludes the reading of the will. Now do we have any questions or information to add?"

Granger sneered, "Aside from the fact that my father no longer owns the property given to Geoffrey and Sophia for it is now in my name. Aside from the fact the monies given to my evidently two half brothers is now in my possession. Yes, and all the stocks and mutual funds bequeathed to anyone else are now in my control. Do you mean relevant information such as that?"

Slowly, directly and with full intent Mr. Goldfarb removed his glasses. He put them in his upper suit pocket. "Granger, you and your mother's actions have yet to be proven as legal within the state of New Mexico. What you have done is underhanded to your departed father's wishes and your actions are totally unethical. Yet, when your father was alive there was nothing we could do about what you both did." Mr. Goldfarb pushed his chair back, stood, and walked to the corner of his room where he removed a legal folder. He took it to his desk.

"As for your two half-brothers, their money is here in this envelope and shall at this moment be given to them by me. Neither you nor your mother had any knowledge of it, nor do you have the ability to touch this money for it been in my possession for the last fifteen years."

The two men in the back stood, both of them well over six feet. They both walked to Mr. Goldfarb and shook his right hand before the tallest man took the envelope. "Thank you, for your consideration, Sir."

Goldfarb nodded back, "You need to sign this legal document stating you have received your inheritance. I will notarize your signatures. Please sign here and here." A white document was unfolded and the two men signed. Mr. Goldfarb pulled a leather case from his top drawer to press a seal onto the paper. The taller man nodded to Mr. Goldfarb and then walked over to Sophia.

Both men had the facial features of the Pino family. They both had inherited their father's Mediterranean nose and warm brown eyes that radiated with a smile. "Ma'am, my name is Stuart Pino. It is a pleasure to meet you. I am a contract lawyer and would like to offer you my card. Both of us have followed your work and are very proud indeed of your accomplishments."

The man next to him put out his hand to Geoffrey, "I am Giorgio Pino from Georgia. I am a violinist with the Atlantic Philharmonic Orchestra and a retired veterinarian." Giorgio's smile filled his whole face, "Glad that I haven't met that shark before this," he jutted his thumb toward Granger, "and hope to forget about him promptly. Good luck with his ruthlessness and his mother's deviousness is beyond words."

Giorgio turned to Sophia, "Dr. Sophia Pino, what an honor to finally meet you. My brother and my family have been most proud of your work. We have been following your career. We coerced the Smithsonian to sell us your group film on the development of languages during the transitions of the Middle Ages. My children loved it as did my wife and I. What a thrill it must to have been—to be able to decipher those languages. Hope we meet again."

Abruptly Margaret wrenched her neck around to yell out, "Sophia never made a movie and she has not published articles! That is all a farce! Granger is going to write a book, aren't you dear? He will be the author of the family and as far as her being a doctor, well, we all know what a lie that is, don't we!"

Giorgio and Stuart shook their heads at Margaret but gave a nod to Geoffrey and to Sophia. As they departed the room Giorgio turned and waved to Mr. Goldfarb.

Another white envelope was pulled from the brown folder. "Mr. Voltaire, here is the check for your wife. I am sure this is a thankful welcome with all the expenses you have. Thank you for coming all this way on such short notice."

The tall man with the goatee and ascot hurried to the front desk. He took the envelope with a slight bow and then stuck his hand out to the lawyer. "Thank you so much, this should help save Cynthia's life."

Goldfarb nodded, "At least it will make her life a bit more comfortable. The numbers to her accounts and the final tally are also in the envelope. Again, I apologize for the expense of coming all this way." Mr. Voltaire turned away from the audience to fleetingly disappear out the door. A soft wind blew through the room as the front door closed behind him.

"Thank God that is over!" Margaret stroked the arm rests on the Queen Anne chair. "What right does Mr. Voltaire have to Walter's money and what was he doing here? I have a right to know as the deceased's widow."

The lawyer sank into his executive chair. His face reflected his sixty plus years. His eyes hardened as he answered Margaret, "Cynthia has terminal cancer and is in a special hospital in Montreal. He is her husband. They have a four year old son. Please leave them alone."

Margaret laughed, "Serves her right taking our money. Now let us inform Geoffrey and Sophia about the property of Rocoso."

Geoffrey walked up to Mr. Goldfarb's desk, "Yes, what the devil is going on with the ownership? Walter and I had a written personal agreement just between the two of us?"

Mr. Goldfarb focused on a spot on his desk, "Evidently, Mrs. Pino here and her lovely son Granger went to another lawyer a Mr. Costa in Santa Fe. They had all of the ownership of property, stocks, and mutual funds, which were in Dr. and Mrs. Pino's names transferred to Granger as executor." He nodded to Granger who was busy rearranging legal books on the back shelves, "They had Dr. Pino confirmed incompetent two years ago."

Granger turned, dropping a book, "No, when he tried to kill himself with his revolver that's when we got the order." He waved a black leather book at Goldfarb, "My mother took photos of him trying to shoot himself, but I'd already removed the bullets from the gun. This was sufficient evidence to acknowledge he was not in his right mind or able to retain control over his responsibilities." Spittle ran down Granger's chin.

"Come here, Granger, come here." Margaret waved her hand at him. She took a linen napkin from the tea tray and wiped his chin. She finished the thought for him, "We had no choice for we couldn't trust Papa anymore, now could we? He was going to leave poor Mom destitute."

Sophia sat stunned. Geoffrey pulled his keys from his denim jacket pocket and walked out of the room. He would go off and mull this over. They had paid all but six months of their loan to her father regarding their home and now they were no closer to owning it than the first day they had signed the agreement. Sophia looked around her, she wanted to leave the building, but her legs wouldn't hold her. Margaret and Granger were quietly whispering to one another as Mr. Goldfarb was stacking legal papers together. He glanced up at Sophia who tried to smile, but tears fell down her cheeks.

Granger was busy helping Margaret with her coat and her gloves. He appeared pleased with the situation. Sophia found a tissue in her leather purse. Mr. Goldfarb fell back in his chair to watch Margaret put her arm through Granger's as they departed the room. Mr. Goldfarb cleared his throat, "Is there something I can do for you, young lady?"

Words did not come for she felt cold and unable to speak. Mr. Goldfarb moved to sit down next to Sophia and took her hand, "I know you're in shock. Please know this is not what your father wanted for the two of you. He loved you very much and was very proud of you and Geoffrey."

Sophia studied his black polished shoes with short laces. Mr. Goldfarb continued, "I wanted to call you and warn you a hundred times about what Granger and Margaret were doing, but legally I couldn't."

Mr. Goldfarb reached to turn Sophia's face towards his, "If I were you, I would be ever so careful with the two of them, ever so careful. They are greedy, wanting to take the goodness from your father and turn it into their own benefit. If I can help you, I will. Although right now I know financially you don't have the means. You could ask your half-brother Stuart for help?"

"No, he shouldn't get pulled into this mess." Sophia pulled herself to sit straight in the chair, "There shouldn't be anyone else who has to suffer through this. Mr. Goldfarb, what did Granger mean when he said that as long as I am married to Geoffrey the house would belong to him?"

"Well, it is complicated, but the short of it is as a family member and as part of the agreement with the property, Granger holds the title. If you and Geoffrey get divorced then the property will reverse back to Geoffrey through lack of family ownership."

Mr. Goldfarb moved to the bookcase where Granger had rearranged his books. The black leather bindings on the books with gold script appeared to be heavy. "This was what they wanted. In order to control you and your daughters, the legal agreement was for you to remain under Granger's control. If you decided to divorce Geoffrey then Granger will give the Rocoso property to Geoffrey free and clear. In the legal world we refer to this as the 'Spider's Web Syndrome.'"

The tissue in Sophia's hand fell to her lap, "He wants me to remain within the Pino family as a trapped fly?"

"To put it indelicately 'yes' he wants to have full control over you and your finances, which he considers part of his estate."

Two of the black leather books were heaved out from where Granger had placed them and put in their proper order, "For some reason Granger believes that he is owed the full amount of his family's estate. He is an angry demanding man who will not rest until he has all the money he can get from everyone in the family. God help the two half-brothers. I am sure they are his next target."

Mr. Goldfarb sat down behind his desk. "What happened to your brother to make him so vindictive?"

Now the room felt hot to Sophia. She let her coat fall from her shoulders to her upper arms. "He was raised with the old adage 'Spare the rod, Spoil the child.' Both of us were. Yet somehow Granger took it all personally, very personally. Many times I stood between him and my angry father to deflect blows and words, but Granger was the victim who being vulnerable would cry, or hide, or sulk. At one point Granger even dug a dirt room under his bedroom floor to hide from my father. I received the reward from this with broken noses and bruises, but Granger didn't see what I was being put through, he only saw his own victimization."

Sophia moved to stand at the window watching the wind blow a scarf across the main street, "Granger is bitter. All of this broke him. I knew my friends had fathers who did the same. We would talk about it. But Granger crawled inside of himself. Now he denies everything to state what a lovely family upbringing we had. He thinks our painful youth is a figment of my imagination."

She turned back to Mr. Goldfarb, "Margaret promoted my father's wrath for us by her whining and suffering. She manipulated my father into his fits of anger and hitting us. The whole affair was dysfunctional to the point of bizarre. My mother was almost twenty years younger than my father. She never had a fixed father figure because her mother was divorced when she was a baby."

Reaching down to pick up the fallen tissue, she continued, "I have no idea why I am telling you this. Granger is not to be absolved of his greed or the torture he inflicts on others. Perhaps I want to protect him for somehow he is seriously sick, but when he hurts my family and those I love, I just want to throttle him myself."

"Or else," Mr. Granger studied Sophia's troubled face, "Or else, he is fully aware of what happened and has a devious plan to take all the money from your mother, from you, from whoever he can to make up for the pain he suffered as a child. This could all be an act. Personally, I find him dangerous."

"Yes, he is a conniving fellow. Perhaps because of his pain he wants to inflict pain on others." Sophia sat in the Queen Anne chair, "This really is very comfortable." She stroked the arm rests. "You are very thoughtful to provide tea and biscuits, Mr. Goldfarb. This is old world charm at its best. I commend you for your polite traditionalism."

"Thank you, Sophia. One thing you should know is a probate can be filed with the county clerk, but a probate hearing is questionable and sometimes challenged and usually does nothing to further validate or invalidate the legality of your father's will. I am sure both Granger and your mother have already covered every single legal possibility to retain what they have done. Be careful in your decisions."

The clouds hovered over the mountains like thick fat waves of whipped cream. The brown terrain was desperate for moisture as the solitary rabbit bush flayed back and forth in the wind. The van creaked and groaned as the wind pelted the driver's side. Donna was asleep in her car seat and Sybil was busy reading a book in the back seat. Sophia glanced at their quiet faces in the rear view mirror. Life was to seriously change with Granger now in control. Heavy clouds on the horizon gave fair warning of a storm moving their way.

7

Rocoso, New Mexico
Friday, January, 1988

Dinner was finished with morbid solitude. The girls were not even energetic enough to carry on a conversation. Geoffrey dragged his fork around his plate, pushing his chicken from side to side. Sophia tried to swallow some mashed potatoes, but they stuck in her throat. Donna was disappointed for after school today Sophia had stopped at the department store and bought Donna a pair of bright pink Mary Jane socks for Monday. Sybil was reading at the table, again. Neither Geoffrey nor Sophia had the desire to make her put the book down. At least she ate most of her dinner.

Geoffrey gathered the messy plates and carried them to the sink. "Come on, girls, it's time for our Friday night movies. Daddy stopped at the Movie Store. We have *Bed Knobs and Broomsticks* for the late night movie, come on!" He grabbed a giggling Donna around the middle and carried her into the family room. Sybil didn't move except to turn a page of her book on science fiction. "Sybil, you can help me with the dishes, all right?" Sybil nodded without looking at her mother.

Sophia sighed as she pushed her chair back to clear the table. The movie sound blared down the hall into the kitchen. Sybil looked up, "Did Dad get a movie?"

Sophia smiled, "Yes, he told us at dinner, but evidently we weren't interesting enough for you, right?"

Sybil raced to her mom and gave her a hug, "Oh, Mom, I love you, you know I do! Everyone was so sad at dinner. I didn't want to catch it so I read. What is going on with you two?" She pointed to the family room and at her mother. Sophia shook her head, "Go watch the movie. It's a fun movie with only a few scary parts you will enjoy it. Go!"

As Sophia washed the dishes in the deep stainless steel sink in the kitchen, she glanced up at her reflection in the dark window. She was five feet ten inches tall. She was not plump, but definitely she was not thin. She had short curly hair with walnut eyes. Her features were definitely more Mediterranean looking than Chicano. Sophia smiled, thinking about her mother Margaret who always made it a point to remark how her children were Mediterranean not Chicano or Hispanic.

The dishes were dried and the kitchen table scrubbed clean. Sophia heard the television go off and Geoffrey making 'time for bed' noises. She threw the dish cloth on the counter. She was his backup for their 'put the girls to bed' routine. Sybil was in the bathroom brushing her teeth while reading her book. Getting toothpaste on the page, she tried to wipe it off with her toothbrush.

"Sybil, really, just put the book down. Pay attention to those new permanent teeth."

Both girls satisfactorily in bed with hopes of them sleeping, Geoffrey beat her to the living room. He sat in his recliner holding a pillow against his middle as if he needed it for protection. Sophia slid into her rocking chair facing him. "Well, what do we do now?"

His solemn face frowned, "Spoke with a lawyer today at work. He gave me the skinny on what happened with your father's will or trust or distrust or whatever you want to call it." He reached over to his jacket that had been tossed on the couch. He pulled out some legal papers. "Here is the gist of what happened. I am still stunned, Sophia, totally stunned."

Sophia shook her head, studying his eyes through his thick lenses. "Aren't you industrious going for the legal side right out of the gate? Go on, I'm a big girl, I can take it."

Geoffrey gave her a wink, "The lawyer explained to me a clause in the legal world pertaining to someone who is incompetent. The definition of which I have right here."

Lifting the papers closer to his face, he read. "It describes the importance of the mental condition of a person who is subject to legal proceedings." Geoffrey glanced at Sophia as he continued to read from the long white paper, "New Mexico law describes the legal qualification of 'a person' as a person who must have the ability to perform professional functions."

Geoffrey paused as if he was waiting for Sophia to respond, then he looked at her over his glasses as he asked, "Do you understand this part?"

Sophia nodded, "But the problem is that he was not incompetent when he wrote the original will or trust. He just became incompetent when his illness progressed. So how did they make this work?"

"Well, this is just the statement that Granger gave to us at Goldfarb's office. This is not the legal ramification of it all!"

Sophia smiled, "Get down, Geoffrey, aren't we using the big words now?"

"Damn straight, evidently this was more Margaret than Granger. The legal manipulative faction they used was related to the time when your father Walter Pino attempted to change his will. Your father wanted to not give anything at all to Granger and to move the majority of his funds to the UNM Medical Research Department for the research of Prostate Cancer disease, which he was diagnosed as having. This seriously upset Margaret for she had inherited the majority of that money from her mother and considered That Money to be Hers not His."

Geoffrey held up his index finger, "All of this occurred about two weeks after he had attempted to buy a revolver and blow his brains out and Granger found him." He held his finger to his head and jerked it back, "'I'm sure your brother's attempt to thwart your father from committing suicide was seriously upsetting. This left Margaret with only one alternative, which she used wisely in her task. She found the lawyer Mr. Alfredo Costa in Santa Fe, who specializes in the elderly and mentally unstable, and went after Walter's attempt to change his will."

"Geoffrey, why did she want to move everything over all at once? Wouldn't this look suspicious to some?" Sophia took the folded blanket off the couch and covered her legs.

"Wait, let me continue." Geoffrey cleared his throat to use his professional voice as he read on, "This deals with Legal Incapacity. It requires a person to be legally competent in order to enter into a contract, sign a will, or make some other type of binding legal commitment. A person may be judged incompetent by virtue of age or mental condition. A contract made by a mentally incapacitated individual is voidable or invalid. This means a person can legally declare the contract void, making it unenforceable."

Geoffrey stopped to pick up the next page. Sophia asked, "Is this much longer?"

"Wait, this is the finish and it comes with a phrase that you will remember." Geoffrey held the paper, "A person who executes a will must be legally competent. The traditional recital in a will states that the testator or the maker of the will is of "sound mind." This language attempts to establish the competency of the testator."

Sophia shook her head, "In other words Margaret made herself guardian of her husband's will since he was in the process of changing it when she deemed him mentally incapacitated. Then she made Granger her executor to further confuse the issue and passed the properties to him thus clearing any judgment against her. This is extremely well thought out for the two of them. Do you believe it is just the two of them?"

The papers were folded in Geoffrey's lap as he answered, "Somehow this is too complicated for your brother, but your mother? Yes, she could pull this off. Remember she was made a millionaire when her mother died. All of her money became your father's money when they married. Your mother, believing the men should hold the power of the family, gave him her wealth. Your gregarious father had no problem spending her money. Your father told me how he helped his patients by giving them financial aid. He gave his patients money to fill prescriptions, to pay their gas bills and to buy food. It didn't end there."

Geoffrey pushed his recliner to recline, "Remember how your father after he retired was buying expensive fishing equipment, going to Europe, and traveling with women from all over the globe? Your mother played the role of victimized wife yet she wouldn't go with him on his trips." Geoffrey laughed, "Your mother had to stay home and grow food for the starving children of the world." He quickly put out his hand, "No, wait she had to watch the hired help pick up the horse apples. She had to stay home and monitor the horse apple pickers for if they weren't picked up correctly the world would end, right?"

"No, she had to stay home to keep the planet on course." Sophia threw her shoe at him, "You know I couldn't understand why she didn't go with him? Why didn't she go and kick up her heels, have fun, see the great museums or go to the top of the mountains in China. He would have loved to have had her with him."

Geoffrey frowned, "Sophia, your mother and father had strange attitudes toward marriage. Their commitment didn't appear to be to one another.

It was as if she wanted to suffer. Being married meant she had to be tortured or in pain."

Sophia pulled off her other shoe, "She was raised to be penitent, and perhaps she felt she had to suffer if she was happy or married or who knows?"

Jerking the recliner forward, Geoffrey stretched and stood, "You know I am bone tired after all of this. It is time we had some libation to help us appreciate our situation." He tossed Sophia the folded papers, which she caught in her right hand.

"Geoffrey, why would they go to this much trouble to change the whole of the will or did they just declare the whole of the will void, as it says here?" Sophia studied the papers.

"What?" Geoffrey was pulling on his jacket.

"Where are you going?"

"I'm going out to the truck. I stopped at the liquor store and got us some whiskey. I plan to get heavily sedated tonight." Geoffrey smiled at her as he pulled open the front door.

Sophia mumbled under her breath, "or inebriated."

The martini went down dry as Sophia swallowed. Then she started to cough, "Geoffrey, this is way too strong!"

"Just drink it. Sophia, this is medicine after getting kicked in the head by your family. Don't argue with me, just enjoy it." Geoffrey swirled his cognac in a Mickey Mouse glass that was bought at Disneyland years earlier.

Sophia winced as she sipped her drink, "What are we going to do? Are we just going to stay here and pay off the loan or can we sell the house? We could move somewhere else after getting our half from the house." Sophia tried to keep the martini glass as far from her as possible. "What does Granger gain if we are divorced? I don't understand why he wants us to live separately. Geoffrey, this seems pathological to ruin someone's marriage."

"Nothing, there is nothing, absolutely nothing that we can do. We could pay off the loan or not. Therein lies a choice," Geoffrey's eyes gleamed, "we can take out another mortgage and then another never paying off the house completely ever!"

"What good would that do? How would that get us out of this mess?"

"Ah, my sweet, we shall make Granger sorry that he ever got involved with the Vinder family. We can take out one loan or mortgage after another thus never paying off the loan, thus never giving him any authority over us in any form. We are the one's who must pay off the loan and if the loan on this property is never paid off then he has no hold over us at all." Geoffrey lifted his Mickey Mouse glass to the ceiling, "My dear, he shall regret messing with me!"

Sophia put her martini down on the side table, "Geoffrey, you are as evil as he is. I don't approve of either of you. We need to pay off this loan. We don't want to be in debt. At least I don't nor do I want my daughters burdened with a huge debt when we die. What are we going to leave them if we are so entrenched in debt there is nothing left for their college or marriage or travel?"

Geoffrey smirked, "Too bloody bad. Those girls are on their own thanks to your mother. Sophia, this is your entire mother's fault as well as your fault and if you don't mind it is the fault of the whole Pino blood line. I have no respect for any of you, not anymore!" He swigged down the liquid in the glass in one swallow. "There you go and now I'm off to bed."

Stunned with Geoffrey's remark, Sophia sat frozen. "What the hell was that all about?" She could hear Geoffrey in the hall closet pushing items around and dropping hangers on the floor. Slowly, she raised herself to stand then cautiously went into the hall. "What are you doing, Geoffrey?"

"I'm leaving. I'm taking a sabbatical just as you did from the university. I'm going to retreat into the trenches. I never signed up to be attacked by your bloody bastard of a brother. I shall drive over the mountain to my buddy Fred's cabin in Pecos. He doesn't know it yet, but by morning he'll have company." Geoffrey pulled his black suitcase from the back of the closet. "It is time to reconsider my options and my place in this clan."

Sybil's soccer ball fell from a shelf to bounce down the hall. Sophia walked back into the living room, picked up the martini glass and took it to the kitchen sink. Tossing the liquid down the drain, she inventoried her options. There was no reason for her to argue with him. He was drunk. He was angry. He had every right to want out of this mess. She wanted out as well. She would stay and be with their girls for they were the innocents in this mess. Geoffrey certainly needed more time to meditate over his options and she would give him this time.

Taking a bag from the lower cupboard she put his instant coffee, his favorite traveling black mug, some of his favorite crackers and a handful of Donna's Twinkies into it. Quickly, she hurried into the family room and grabbed his napping pillow and the lap blanket she had crocheted last winter. Geoffrey came down the hall grumbling under his breath as he bumped into Sophia. She held out the bag, "Here are some of your favorite foods, some coffee, and a pillow and blanket. Can I at least have a hug for old time's sake?"

Geoffrey took the bag of groceries and the blanket bundle from her, "No hug, but thanks for the goodies. I can't get too close to a Pino right now. My head isn't finding any forgiveness as of yet." He dragged his suitcase behind him out into the dark night.

Sophia leaned against the closed door. "Oh, damn, now we come to the part where Granger mentioned 'divorce' as an option."

She closed her eyes and slid down to the floor. "Oh, Papa, what are we going to do now? Papa, why did you attempt to shoot yourself in front of Granger! Oh, why did you have to die?"

8

Rocoso, New Mexico
Saturday, January, 1988

The television's muffled sound reached Sophia before the concept of morning was absorbed. She rolled over to touch the other side of the bed. Empty. There was no one there, again, no one. The reality of Geoffrey leaving last night was hard to accept for he was not a person who ran from a problem. He usually hit it with his hard head. Rolling over to slowly open her eyes, Sophia saw the sun was shining and had been for some time. "Oh, yes, we must endure another day of this confusion! I wonder if Geoffrey made it to Pecos."

"Mom, are you awake yet?" Sybil quietly tiptoed into the room.

"Yes, I am awake but not happy. What is it?"

"Mom, there was a phone call. Someone left a message really early this morning. Do you want me to bring you the phone and a piece of chocolate?"

Sophia burst out laughing, "First the chocolate and then the phone please!"

Sybil ran down the hall to quickly return with a large piece of dark chocolate in one hand and the phone in the other. "Here you go! Mom, we both noticed that Dad wasn't here this morning. Is everything all right?"

Sophia took the chocolate, "First let me eat this and get some joy into my blood. Then let's hear the message and we shall have a womanly breakfast of pancakes and talk. How does that sound?"

Sybil gave her mother's hand a squeeze, "All right!" Then she hurried back to the family room and the television.

Sophia sat up, brushing the chocolate crumbs off of her nightgown. The cordless phone was cold, but the message necessary. Sophia punched in the numbers to listen to the message: "Sophia, I am at the cabin. It's six thirty and stopped only once for a pit stop. Fred is here and we're going fishing. For some reason I'm not tired. Will call you tonight and speak with the girls. Hope you women have a good day, don't worry about me." Click.

She threw the phone at the end of the bed where it bounced and hit the floor. "Damn, no thought as to love or when he would be home or even if he gives a damn about any of us! He just runs away to his buddy's cabin and has a day of fishing!" Sophia threw back the covers and went into the bathroom.

The Saturday events were planned by all of them. They were off in the freezing cold weather to go to the Puerco Mountains and sled down the most dangerous of slopes. Sybil had put on her thermal pink underwear with two layers of socks. She wore two t-shirts, one turtleneck, one sweater, and her double lined winter jacket with the hood. Pulled down over her shoulder length hair was a crocheted stocking cap of reindeer pulling a sleigh and on her hands were not only one pair of mittens, but two. Her heavy hiking boots had been sprayed with water repellent, which gave off a strange odor.

Donna was more affluent in her clothing for it was all pink. She had her pink cap pulled over her ears with her pink thermal underwear, her new pink socks, her handed down cousin's pink ski pants and her pink faux fur lined snow boots. Donna also carried with her a small pink purse that held everyone's lip gloss and some band-aides just in case. Sophia wore her thermal underwear, old jeans, and two pairs of socks, sprayed hiking boots, and two turtlenecks under her heavy polyester sweater of Care Bears and her red wool cap Geoffrey had given her. She wore Geoffrey's gloves and her crocheted scarf. They were ready for the snow and the cold.

The picnic basket was a group effort as well. It was filled with peanut butter and jelly sandwiches, a bag of potato chips, and a box of chocolate chip cookies. Sophia had a thermos of hot cocoa for the girls and a thermos of hot cocoa with rum for her. Two sleds were in the back of the family van along with three blankets, one sleeping bag, and a bag of twigs and matches just in case. There was shovel and a bag of fireplace ash neatly put in the front seat on the floor in case they hit an icy patch.

"We are off!" Sophia backed the van out of the driveway while she and Sybil sang The Keeper's song. Donna was busy inventorying her seat holders for spare candy.

The glorious blue sky appeared to push away the constant wind, allowing them to appreciate the stillness of the forest snow. The top branches of the ponderosa pines reached for the heavens with fingers draped with crystallized snow. Off in the distance, the trill of a warbler gently echoed through the deep canyon. White barked aspen trees leaned under the weight of the frozen water clinging to their naked skins. Bushes of wild oak lay split and flattened by the moisture's weight. Small critters hid under their arched branches providing shelter and the earth underneath dry and warm. There were only two other vehicles parked at the sledding area both of which were Jeeps.

"Mom, there is no one else here. The snow crunches when we walk on top of it." Sybil dragged her boot over the small ice balls under her foot. "Let's make the most of this then, Come on grab a sled!" Sophia handed Sybil the round blue disc. Sleds unloaded and mittens pulled firmly on, the three of them ran through the crunching snow to the sled platform. Donna repeated her sister's words as she stared out at the great expanse of snow, trees, and canyons. "Hey, we do have this place all to ourselves, isn't this cool?"

The altitude of the cliff edge where they stood allowed them to observe Mount Taylor and Cabazon Peak hundreds of miles away. Ravens in pairs winged their way to great heights only to ride the air currents with wings spread wide. Sybil's mouth was covered with her mittened hand as she stated, "I can't see any houses or roads. Did they disappear?" Sophia hugged Sybil's shoulders, "No, this is the country of unending land. Where a person can see forever with uninterrupted beauty and appreciate nature prior to the coming of man and his technology. It is amazing, isn't it?"

Donna's soft voice asked, "Mom, can we see all the way to China?" Sophia knelt down to point to the west with her gloved finger, "You know I believe we can. It's right over there beyond Cabazon peak. If you squint your eyes just a little you can see Russia right over the ridge line there to the north."

Donna giggled, "Mom, when you talk the steam comes out of your mouth and it tickles my face." Sophia smiled, "Yes, and I can see the mist coming out of your mouth, but I can't catch it. Can you?"

Sybil chortled, "It's quiet here. You can hear the snow melting on the tree branches. Listen. Do ghosts come here? Do you think Grandpa is dancing here in the freezing forest?"

Sophia leaned forward with her arms around the girls, "We are alone here in the forest. It is too cold for those who have passed. They have been called to the Great Beyond. They're in a place of safety and comfort with views even more fantastic."

She stood and opened her arms wide, "Be cautious of the elves and the grumble bears. They are hungry in the wintertime and would just love to catch a beautiful young maiden. You two stay close to me, all right? If you hear growling or mumbling from the trees, run to me. Grumble bears and elves know mothers are deadly when protecting their young."

Sybil wanted to slide down first with her mother. Donna clapped her hands as she watched. Sophia loved the thrill of the drop, but Sybil was holding onto her for dear life. Finally at the bottom, Sophia asked her, "Sybil, what's wrong?"

"Mom, I'm terrified that I'll die. I really don't like sliding down a sheet of solid ice with no control of my own. It's not fun for me." Sybil hugged her mother's right leg. "I see myself a bloody mess at the bottom of this drop. Can I get out of sledding and just stay here and watch?"

"Yes, you can do the greeting, but don't wander off remember the elves and the grumble bears. Why didn't you tell me this before we left? We could have done something else today?"

"No, Mom, I like being way out here. It's like we're the last living people on earth. It would be more fun if Dad was here, but well, he isn't." Sybil pointed to the tops of the trees, "Look, we're totally surrounded in white with green trees watching over us. Who wouldn't want to be out here? It's like we're on our own planet."

Sophia smiled at Sybil, "Donna and I will sled down to you. If you start getting too cold let me know and you can sit in the van with the heater. You know if you brought a book you could read it while we're hiking back up to the drop point. How does that sound?" Sybil pulled her dragon book out of her parka. "I did bring my book!"

After four hours of sledding and getting wet, the three of them decided to drive up the mountain to eat their picnic lunch. The Puerco ski basin was overwhelmed with people and cars. After a quick vote, the decision was to head home. They could have the picnic on the family room floor.

Sophia studied the girls in the rearview mirror as she drove down the mountain. At some point she would have to explain the problems that involved all of them. Donna was busy smearing lip gloss all over her lower face while Sybil was again reading her book with the dragon on the cover. The book appeared to be endless.

Unloading, laughing with fresh fun memories the girls helped their mother place the food on the family room floor. The girls felt better after using the bathroom, changing clothes, and being back in the warmth of home. Sybil was the first to bring up the subject, "Mom, why isn't Dad here? Where did he go?"

Donna stared at Sophia, with her mouth full of sandwich, she said, "Yeah, where's Dad?"

Sighing, Sophia sat down on the floor between the two girls. She stuck a potato chip in her mouth, chewed, swallowed and tried to hold back tears, "We have a serious problem, girls. There appears to be conflict between Grandmother Margaret, Granger, and your Dad and me."

Sybil lifted her sandwich, "I knew it. I just knew it! Mom, it's about the reading of the will and Grandpa, isn't it?"

"How did you know, Sybil?"

Before Sybil could answer Donna spoke up, "She read the papers in the living room. She found them this morning and she read them to me. I don't have any idea what they mean, but I didn't like them."

"Oh, Sybil, what a nosey little girl you are!" Sophia hugged Sybil, "The problem is your father and I bought this property for our family, just our family. We needed some help with the money so we asked your grandpa to help us to get started." Sophia had to stop and think how she could say this simply. "When your Grandfather died, your Grandmother Margaret wanted this property. She went to a lawyer and had him put this property in her name and then she gave it to Granger, legally that is."

Donna put her drink down quickly, "You mean Uncle Granger the salamander?"

Sophia gasped, "What? What do you mean salamander?"

"That's what Dad calls him. He says Uncle Granger is 'the slimy salamander man of the Pino family who will do us all in' that's what he says, right Sybil?"

"Right," Sybil put her hand up to stop Donna from talking, "Mom, but we live here not them. Do they want to live here, too, with us?"

"No, they just want the ownership of this property to belong to them, but they don't want to have to pay the taxes or deal with the up-keep or the home owner's insurance. They just want to hold the property in their name."

The three of them ate in silence while they thought about the predicament. Finally, Sybil spoke up, "What can we do to get the ownership away from them?"

Sophia studied her daughters' fragile faces. "If I divorce your father then Granger will give the property to your father."

Donna jumped dropping all of her food on the floor, "NO DIVORCE! Carol's father and mother got divorced and all she does is cry all the time. She hates her step parents and she wants to come and live with us! NO, Mom, NO!" Donna threw her body into her mother's lap. Sophia let her tears fall with Donna's.

Sybil sat there staring at the both of them, "Divorce is not the way out of this, Mom. You know this and I know this. So does Dad. Dad loves you forever and forever and forever and he will never leave us. He just won't so we have to think of something else."

Donna snorted, "Let's kill Uncle Granger. They killed a salamander in Mr. Griego's class and cut it up for a biology lesson. We could invite Uncle Granger to my school and have him visit Mr. Griego's class!"

Sophia held Donna in a tight hug, "You know dissection might work, but he is much bigger than a real salamander. Our problem is not Granger, but the law. We need to find a way to make the law work for us not for them."

Donna wiped her nose on her sweater sleeve, "Do we know any law people who could help us?"

"Donna, you have an excellent idea. Yesterday at the reading of the will two of your half-uncles were there and one of them is a lawyer—a contract lawyer—as a matter of fact. He offered to help us. Perhaps I just should give him a call?"

She started to get up and then stopped. "He certainly wouldn't be home now although one never knows. He might live closer than his brother who said he was from Georgia." Sophia handed Sybil her napkin and sandwich. She hurried to her purse in the front room. She found the printed card. Stuart Pino actually lived in Las Cruces, New Mexico. His home address was on Las Piedras and his office was downtown off of Grand Street. "Huh," Sophia picked up the cordless phone and dialed his home phone number.

A woman's voice answered, "Pino residence this is Phyllis. How can I help you?"

Sophia was impressed, "Hello, how do you do? Is there someone there by the name of Stuart Pino?"

A groan followed, "Sorry, Miss, but we don't take business calls at home. You will have to call him during the week."

Sophia quickly interrupted, "No, no, this is his half-sister, please is he there? I just met him yesterday at a reading of our father's will and he asked me to call him if we needed help. Please, don't hang up on me."

The woman at the other end of the phone paused, "Don't tell me you are the writer? Are you Sophia, the writer who did the film on languages of Europe during the Middle Ages?"

"Yes, yes, but more importantly I am just a person who is in need of assistance. Is Stuart there, please?"

Sybil and Donna were now standing next to their mother in the kitchen. Sybil put a blank notepad on the counter in front of her mother and Donna handed her mother a red marker. Sophia studied their hopeful faces and then whispered, "His wife has gone to get him for us."

"Hello, Stuart? This is Sophia calling you for some advice. Oh, dear let me start over again. I am calling to let you know what a pleasure it was to finally meet you and to have a chance to speak with you, although the event was most unfortunate." Sophia knew she was rambling and forced the words to stop.

"Hi, yes," Stuart's voice was very similar to her father's voice, which for a moment surprised her. "If you need contract help please ask. I really don't know very much about wills and probate. My knowledge is contracts and long term business agreements either federal of state level. But if I can give you advice, please ask away."

Sophia took the lid off of the red marker writing down her questions as she asked them, "Well, both my husband and I were shocked to learn the property we held in a contract with Papa was given to Granger through arrangements with Margaret. We don't know how to get our title back or what to do to get our investments returned. Would you know how we could achieve these goals?"

Stuart almost interrupted her in mid-sentence, "Sophia, these are aspects of law dealing with possession and ownership. I don't really have any idea what you can do. I could ask some of my friends, but all of this was evidently done with full legal advice. In my opinion, and this is not legal by any means, I would ask Granger if you could sell your half to him and move. If he will not accept this offer then you're stuck to live there as long as he lives or your mother lives. The legal contract the two of them set up is legally binding. Sorry, but I don't know what else to say." He sounded sincerely unhappy.

"Stuart?"

"Yes, still here?"

"Granger did say if Geoffrey and I did get divorced that he would give the property to Geoffrey, but then wouldn't I be without a home? We have two little girls and they need a home?"

"Oh, gosh, Granger didn't put this in action. This is a 'Spider's Web' trap done usually by a parent who wants to maintain control over the family. Your mother Margaret has Granger tied to her with assets and property management. The property contract gives her control over you no matter where you go. She will offer to help you buy a property with her as co-partner and again in time this will revert to Granger. At least Geoffrey will have his money back and his property, but if you try to remarry I'm sure there is a legal clause forbidding this action."

Stuart cleared his throat, "This is all very complicated and I would recommend both of you to hire an experienced real estate contract lawyer to help with this. I have no legal knowledge in this field, although I wish I did."

Sophia took the marker to draw an 'X' through all of her questions. Sybil and Donna stared at her. Sophia said, "Stuart, thank you so much for listening and your advice. We'll go over our options again and come to a decision. This was rude of me to call and ask you for help when this isn't your field. Please have a lovely weekend. We wish you and your family our best. Perhaps sometime we could all get together to share stories?"

Stuart agreed and they both hung up the phone. Sybil took the notepad, "What, what happened? Didn't he help you? What did he say?"

Sophia pulled out a kitchen chair and abruptly sat down, "No, he couldn't help us. He isn't that kind of lawyer, but he did say Uncle Granger and Grandma Margaret acted legally. We are stuck."

The phone's ringing broke the silence. Sybil stared at her mother. Sophia shrugged to look at the clock on the wall. It was three-thirty and too early for Geoffrey to call home. Sophia pointed to the phone and Sybil picked it up, "Hello?" Sybil made a horrible face, "Yes, Grandma Margaret, she's right here."

Sybil practically threw the phone at her mother. The girls ran back into the family room and turned on the television. Sophia quickly answered, "Hello, Mother, how are things going today?"

"Oh, Sophia, there is so much to do and it would be most appreciated if you would be kind enough to come over and help me. Bring the girls with you if they are available? We could go to Applebee's for dinner, my treat?"

Sophia stared at the messy floor caused by their muddy boots, "Well, Mom, we just got home from sledding. All of us are exhausted. What is it you need help with right now?"

She heard Margaret gasp, "Right now? What do you mean right now?"

"Well, you said there was so much to do and for some reason I took it to mean right now. All right, so what's going on over there, please explain so I won't jump to conclusions?"

"Right, well, your father's hospital bed is now out of the house as you know. I wanted to move my bed back into the middle of the room and get some help with his clothes and his medical supplies. I mean what am I to do with all of his stuff?"

"Mom, you could put it in piles. On Monday call the Salvation Army or Goodwill and have them come and take all the clothes away. His medical paraphernalia is finished. Just throw pills and stuff away because no one else can use it. The oxygen tanks and the heart monitor stuff should have a phone number of the people who brought it and they can come and pick it up. You're paying rent on the equipment. If they pick it up then you don't have to pay rent on it anymore."

"Sophia?"

"Yes, Mom?"

"Sophia, you sound cold. Are you angry at me or Granger for what we did to your property? Are you still fretting over what happened at the lawyer's office?"

"Mom, I am tired. The girls and I had a lovely morning sledding, hiking and having good family fun. Evidently what you and Granger did was something you felt you needed to do although it wouldn't have hurt to talk to us about it first."

"Sophia, where is Geoffrey? Why didn't he go sledding with you and the girls?"

"Mom, Geoffrey is at his friend's cabin in Pecos. They are ice fishing or doing guys' stuff."

"Oh, did Geoffrey leave you already?"

Sophia shook her head, "Mom, what are you suggesting? Are you a fortune teller now?"

"Sophia, you have always been rude to me ever since you were fourteen years old and I still don't appreciate it. I just thought you might like to go through your father's things and take what you want, but evidently you aren't interested." Margaret hung up the phone.

The empty martini glass by the kitchen sink seemed to beckon Sophia for a refill. Sophia studied her hands as she rubbed her fingers together. She reached for the phone. It would be good to go back to the house. The girls needed to appreciate their grandfather's death. If Sophia had time alone with her mother, perhaps she could change Margaret's mind regarding the property.

Quickly dialing before she changed her mind, Sophia spoke to her mother, "Mom, the girls and I will be over there around five. We can help you with Geordie. By the way did you call the vet?"

"Yes, I did get the vet out here. He charges a fortune. Did you know it costs three hundred dollars to come to the farm? After he arrives the bill goes up considerably." Margaret paused to sip on something, "He took some x-rays of Geordie and found he has cancerous pulps in his intestine. Sophia, he wanted to put Geordie down! He said Geordie was in terrible pain and the kindest act would be to put him down! Can you imagine?"

"Mom, if the doctor feels he is in pain it would be the humane thing to do."

"No, Sophia, I can't live here without a horse! I have to have a horse here- this is a farm. What kind of farm would I have if I didn't have a horse? If you remember, we used to have four horses and now I am down to one. This horse is staying here, staying alive, and staying around to make my farm a real farm!"

"Mom, the horse is in pain. If the horse is in terrible pain you are beholden to do the right and proper thing. Poor Geordie shouldn't live his life with a disease eating up his insides."

"Well, too bad, that's all I have to say. My reputation supersedes the horse's right to die. The doc wasn't completely convincing for he left me with a hefty prescription for Geordie, which will cost a pretty penny believe you me!" Margaret was now fuming into the phone. "I am supporting his habit, the vet's not the horse's, let me tell you!"

Sophia sighed, "All right, Mom, how about we come over and see you. I will help with Papa's things and then we can go to dinner at Applebee's, your treat. Let's try to have a good time."

"Well, if you put it like that, fine. See you around five."

Sophia walked into her bedroom. Everything felt empty with Geoffrey gone. She studied herself in the full length mirror by the closet. Her jeans were covered with mud, her hair stuck straight up in the air, but her cheeks were rosy red. She called to the girls, "Sybil, Donna, I am going to take a hot bath! Then we are going to Grandma Margaret's to feed the horse."

Not waiting for a reply, Sophia closed the bathroom door to enjoy her time to relax before dealing with her mother.

9

Rocoso, New Mexico
Saturday, January, 1988

The family van reversed from the Rocoso' home with a groan. The early evening shadows outlined the black mesas against the blue sky went on to infinity. One single raven flew carelessly in the high wind. Sybil was reading her dragon book in the backseat. Donna was relating a rhyme she had read at school about a boy named Sam who had a dog that ran and ran. Sophia turned on the windshield wipers to clear the windshield of dirt smudges. The smudge smeared across the whole of the windshield. Sophia sighed for now not only did they not have a home, but the old vehicle was aging faster than they could afford right now.

At the corner gas station, the van got a full tank of gas. Sophia washed the windshield with the gas stations squidgy and wiped off the crud with the blue paper towels. The girls received a candy bar with a bottle of juice. Slamming the van's door, Sophia watched the girls share their candy bars. "Remember no mention of this candy to your Grandmother Margaret, all right?"

"Yes, Mom," Sybil sighed, "We know. If she hears we ate a candy bar she won't take us out to dinner. We've been here before."

Sophia smiled. Her girls were street smart when it came to their grandmother. No worries about these two, they would go far. The road through Rincon this afternoon was busy with traffic. Many families were going to the Range Café for dinner. A lot of vehicles had inner tubes tied to the top. They had appreciated the mountain snow. The horses in the fields were standing with their butts facing into the setting sun. Grazing Herefords with their dirty faces were huddled against the south fence on the Santa Ana reservation where remnants of alfalfa lay scattered on the ground. Their water tank had dirt dancing across the top of it. The cottonwood trees spread their naked fingers up to the evening sky as the western horizon turned a soft orange.

Following the Camino Real of the early Spaniards southward, Sophia turned onto Fourth Street. The girls became quiet. They were nearing their grandparent's farm. There was a feeling of oppression that came over Sophia whenever she turned onto Calavera Road. The life she knew and believed in was now going to shift into her mother's dimension of reality. Her mother's mantra was a child's primary duty was to their parents. This belief was above all else. Margaret's hold on this concept was pursued primarily with huge doses of guilt and spoonfuls of manipulation.

Sybil put down her book to help Donna count horses and Mustang cars as they turned onto Calle Aspen. The van bumped down the corrugated road. Cottontail rabbits hurried across in front of the van while the field to their left was densely populated with sand hill cranes pecking through the dead alfalfa stalks.

Sophia turned into the mother's driveway. Granger's Mercedes sat front center of the big double gate. She sighed. Another confrontation was certain to happen and Geoffrey was far, far away. She parked under the drooping Tamarisk tree. The girls begrudgingly unhooked their seat belts to stare at the house. Overnight it had become a grimy place of despair. Stucco chips stuck out by the fire wall on the roof. Discolored warped window frames sat framed in the stucco cracked walls. Morbid lilac bushes stuck skeleton-like fingers around the house as if pushing away anything life-like. The pasture fences were askew in the shifting sandy terrain. White paint curled and fell from the long boards between fence posts as if they were grieving tearfully. Most of the wood revealed their long boards to be gray and cracked in their uncared for and unattended demise.

Sybil kicked the back of the driver's seat, "Mom, Granger is here. He hates us. Why is he here? I thought it was going to be just us and we could feed Geordie. What is he doing here?"

Donna glared at her mother in the rear view mirror, "Mom, let's go home! I don't want to see him! Mama, please, can't we eat at Wendy's or something? Let's get out of here! Uncle Granger the salamander will spit his tongue out at us. Let's go home!"

Sophia picked up her leather purse, put the strap over her head, turned to the girls and said, "Onward! We're a team and as a team we can confront them! Come on, team. Let's go see what else they plan to throw at us. Maybe we can convince them to leave us and our home alone. We outnumber them three to two. If nothing else we can feed the horse and leave."

Just as Sophia opened the driver's door to get out, the entryway wrought iron gate opened. Halting at the gateway for a few minutes, Granger appeared absorbed in his meeting with Sophia and the girls. He held open the gate for them as if it were his diplomatic duty. Donna jumped out of her car seat to scoot over to Sybil's side. They both cautiously stood behind their mother as they approached Granger.

Granger's eyes had an element of distrust. In a raptor-like manner, he spoke softly, "Girls, why don't you go and feed Geordie before it gets dark. Be careful with the stall gate for I do believe it sticks some." Sophia pushed them around Granger, giving them the freedom to race to the barn.

Granger cinched his arm around Sophia as she went through the gate. "Well, it is good to see you, my little sister. After yesterday, I wasn't sure if you would still be speaking to me. Mom said you were rude to her on the phone this afternoon." Granger's voice was purring in her ear, "Sophia, there is no need to be rude to your mother. She is very upset after losing her husband and dealing with all of this is difficult for her."

"Granger, she didn't lose her husband. He died. She knows exactly where he is and why he is there." Sophia grabbed his hand from her shoulder and turned, pushing him away from her, "Granger, please stop touching me. I don't like it and I don't touch you. Please give me some space."

He glared at Sophia with a hardened attitude and in a polished voice said, "Ouch, someone is touchy today, huh? I'm giving you brotherly love."

Teeth bared, Sophia answered, "Well, don't."

They entered the house from the back porch. The dining room table was covered in Margaret's favorite red-checkered tablecloth. Italian teacups and saucers hand painted with spring flowers were elaborately placed on the table along with spoons and linen napkins. A plate of tea biscuits was placed as the centerpiece. Margaret was standing by the kitchen stove waiting for the large copper tea kettle to boil. There was no point explaining to her tea was to be made with hot water that had not yet boiled. Margaret was of the old school, water was not distilled until it was well boiled.

"Sophia, how good of you to come! I saw the girls running to the barn. Geordie will be pleased to have them feed him." Margaret reached out to hug Sophia.

Sophia frowned, "Oh, you mean no one else feeds Geordie but the girls?"

Margaret smacked her shoulder with the dish cloth, "There you go, always being the cynic. We need to all be friends in this time of tragedy, Sophia. Please could we have a truce? Take your coat off, dear. It is nice and warm in here unless you are planning on leaving already?"

Sophia shook her head, "Mom, I think first I'll go and see how the girls are doing with the horse. Don't you think you should listen to the vet and do what is humane?"

"Good old Sophia," Granger grabbed his heavy wool coat, "always looking on the bright side of life, aren't you? I'll go, too, and find out why everyone is having a fit about the old horse."

The two of them walked to the barn, Sophia hurried ahead of Granger. The girls were giggling, sitting on top of the highest alfalfa bale in the barn. When they saw their mother, they started to point at something up on the rafters, but then they saw Granger and flattened their bodies against the bale.

Granger went to Geordie's stall gate. Peering over he saw the feed bin was full and the grain bucket was being licked clean by the horse. "All right, Sophia, show me what you were telling Mom about, hurry, it's cold out here!"

Sophia opened the stall gate not worrying about stepping in the manure for she had on her old boots, but Granger danced around the manure piles in his fancy leather shoes. Pushing Geordie's head towards the north side of the stall, she grabbed his tail and pulled it toward her. "There, see?" She pushed Geordie's rump for Granger's dissecting eyes.

"Well, yes, I see the blood. He could have cut himself trying to rub his butt on the fence." Granger cautiously stepped over a large pile of horse apples. "Whew, it seriously stinks in here."

Indelicately, Sophia grabbed Granger's hand to have him touch Geordie's shoulder mass, "He has bloody stools and his chest has a huge knobby lump. Feel right here?"

His voice became vitriolic in tone, "Many old horses have lymphomas that are benign. He's an old horse, Sophia." Granger blew the horse hair off of his gloved hand, "He's an old horse and does have lumps and bumps and scratches. Don't think it's anything to worry about, besides the vet gave Mom some medicine for him." Granger studied the dirt floor of the stall and the dust dancing around them, "This place is just filthy. Why doesn't Mom clean it up?"

Carefully winding his way back around the horse droppings, Granger found his way to the cement floor of the barn. Using his finger tips he closed the stall door behind Sophia. "Wonder where the girls are? Do you think they are walking home in the dark?" Granger snickered at her.

"Granger, why don't you go ahead inside? I'll look for the girls? You know Mom might be worried and you calm her better than anyone." Granger walked to the barn door. Wiping his hands on his pants, he disappeared into the dark.

"Girls," She called to the cavernous barn, "are you here?" Sybil sat up to jump to the floor below. "Did Granger see us?"

"I'm not sure, but I am sure that Grandmother Margaret has tea and cookies ready for us at the big table." Sophia caught Donna as she leapt from the bale of alfalfa. "Mom, I 'm not sitting at that table. People get yelled at and put down at that table. Can we go into the guest room and play with the toys and junk in there?"

"Mom, Donna's right. If we sit at the table with you guys Grandma Margaret will be mean to us about eating or not eating, drinking tea or not drinking tea. We can't ever do anything right at her table. She will be nasty to you because Dad isn't here!" Sybil lifted her hand over her head to walk like a posh prima donna. "We didn't bring our white linen gloves did we, sister?"

Donna copied her sister only with her hand on her swaying hip, she mocked, "No, we don't have our party dresses. We're not dressed for royalty."

Sophia chased them around the barn, "Donna and Sybil, once we get inside why don't you grab some cookies and race into the back room and play with the toys?" Sophia lead the way out of the barn only to reach back and turn off the light.

Margaret sat at one side of the table with Sophia opposite her. She nodded to her son, "Now it is time for Granger to sit at the head of the table since he is the male head of the family. Granger, please tell Sophia what you told me. Sophia, I need you to be quiet and listen. There is no need to pass judgment on anyone, just listen."

Granger lifted his little finger to take a sip of his tea, "Sophia, I have decided to divorce Emily. She's in California and will be back tomorrow evening. I have filed for divorce. We have irreconcilable differences. Both of us have agreed to a friendly divorce. She will receive her car and half of my savings." Shaking his head in disgust, he added, "Even though she has never worked a day in her life. She is amenable to this." He gulped the rest of his tea.

Sophia stared at Granger. Divorce appeared to be the word of the week in this family. "She works for you at your clinic, but what brought on this divorce, oh, brother of mine?"

Granger spit tea on the tablecloth, "Sophia, you have no need to be smug! Divorce is painful! The fact is Emily and I don't have anything in common anymore. There is no point continuing on in our relationship when all we do is argue and disagree."

Lifting her napkin from her lap, Sophia wiped her lips, "Isn't your daughter Shirley a commonality between the two of you?"

Margaret inhaled loudly through her nose, "Granger, it's the time for truth. Stop pussyfooting around. Be a man and tell the truth. She will find out—time has a way of revealing all. What you're doing is trying to dodge the bullet and it's already left the gun. Tell the truth and save everyone grief."

Turning to Sophia, she said sternly, "Please, Sophia, no judgment. Let your brother say his piece and try to be polite. Goodness knows, I have tried to raise you to be polite and proper, but somehow you're like your father who was a beast of a person. Please attempt to be polite!"

Sophia turned to stare at her brother. Granger delicately poured himself more tea, "Well, several months ago, while Emily was busy with music classes and our daughter was in day care, I was left alone most of the time. Emily's best friend from California came out to visit. Emily and Katina hadn't seen each other for years. Katina stayed at the house while Emily was in class and little Shirley was in school."

Granger sipped his tea with his little finger fully erect. "Katina is a very nice person. We hit it off really well and while Emily was busy and Shirley was gone, we seriously became close."

Margaret leaned back in her captain's chair, "Oh, for Pete's sake, Granger, just tell her!"

Margaret grabbed his tea cup and set it in the saucer in front of Granger. "Tell her!"

Granger sighed, "Katina is five months pregnant with my child. I have to divorce Emily and marry Katina. There is no other honorable way to survive this. Also, I love Katina. Emily and I haven't had much to do with one another for the last six years. Well, since Shirley was born. Emily is very much into her body what with dance, diet, and even pushing me away."

Margaret interrupted him, "That's enough! You don't have to go into every single detail. Sophia, this was going on while your father was dying. Granger needs money for this divorce and it was opportune for your father to pass away when he did."

Picking up a sterling silver spoon, Margaret stirred her tea, "Now, Emily and Shirley will be cared for while Granger can start his new family with Katina." Margaret patted Granger's hand."Katina is a lovely woman filled with life and she understands your brother. This is the most important aspect of life, don't you agree, Sophia?"

Sophia sat there studying her mother and then her brother."You do know, Mother, as a professor of ethnology I find the two of you would make quite a study?"

Margaret smiled as she pressed her hand into Granger's. "Thank you, Sophia. I do believe we try to elevate the human condition, right Granger? I'm so glad you can appreciate your brother's situation. We were afraid you would belittle him somehow."

He nodded with a worried frown. "Where are you going with this, Sophia? You never compliment us. You work hard at finding ways to condemn us or to persuade others that we are your enemy. Sophia, no matter how hard you try to prove we are against you. We only look out for your best interest. Don't we, Mother?" Margaret nodded in agreement.

Granger leaned forward, "I know you are going to find a way to make it appear we are against you. Lies are all you have to throw at us, you can't prove a thing. Why can't you appreciate how much time and energy Mom and I put into you getting your life straight? You don't see the reality of your choices and the lack of opportunity you have by not being honest with yourself. "

"Well, thank you, my dear brother." Sophia pointed at him, "Do either one of you find what Granger has done to be redundant?"

Margaret grinned at her son, "You're right. She's going to say something negative about us."

"No, not negative, Mom, just something perceptive that's all." Sophia pushed the teacup to the center of the table, "Granger is sitting at the head of the table telling us of his impregnation of Katina while married to Emily.

Mom, you are the widow of a man who has impregnated many while he was married to you. Do happen to find a similar thread here?"

Margaret gasped, "You're a heartless cow! This isn't anything like what your father did to me! Your father was indiscreet and undeserving of my affection and my money. He was an animal jumping in and out of bed with his female patients. He had the gall to send their husbands' his medical bill. You cannot consider Granger to be anything at all like your father!"

Sophia heard the girls laughing and playing in the back bedroom and wished she could be with them. She calmly continued, "You may be right, Mom. Your relationship with Papa was unique and we don't know what went on between the two of you—behind closed doors."

Margaret quickly pulled Sophia's teacup and saucer over to her side of the table. "I do believe it is time to end this discussion. Everything with you, Sophia, ends up on the wrong side. How can you teach anyone anything when you are such a cynically rude person?"

Sophia ignored Margaret and nodded toward Granger, "None of this is my business, Mother. What Granger does or doesn't do is his business. I just wish both of you would have told Geoffrey and me about how you were planning to take our house, no, our home away from us and leave us with nothing."

Slamming the flat of his hand on the table cloth, Granger explained, "After your rude accusation we really don't need to explain anything. But, Sophia, we needed you to know Papa's money wasn't free to you or Geoffrey."

"Free! What are you talking about Free! Geoffrey and I didn't take any money from him. We borrowed it and we paid it back with interest. There was no Free involved in this equation, not at all!" Sophia pushed her chair back to stand. "Granger, you can stick your dipstick wherever you want, but to take money Geoffrey and I earned to ensure a future for our family was not just immoral but wrong!" Sophia threw her linen napkin on the table.

Margaret shot out of her chair, "Sophia, sit down. Sit down this instant! How dare you refer to your brother's dipstick! How dare you accuse us of stealing! This is a family and we look out for one another!" Margaret pointed at Sophia's chair, "Sit down now, young lady! Sit!"

Sophia perched. Her chair was a foot from the table. Granger cleared his throat to state in a dictatorial fashion, "Sophia, we feel that you and Geoffrey are not good for one another. I know, I know, you're going to tell me to mind my own business."

He brushed his linen napkin over his moustache, "We didn't do anything wrong here. This money is Pino money whether it came from Papa or it came from Mom. It stays in the family, that's all I am saying." Granger smiled into his napkin, "Besides, Katina and I are going to have a boy. We need male children in the Pino family to carry on the family name."

"Ahhh," Sophia smirked, "since Geoffrey and I have only girls you want to dump him and the girls by the wayside as you are doing to Emily and Shirley? What a bunch of shallow losers the two of you are! How dare you judge someone by their genitals? Is this how you gauge people? The two of you are horribly pathetic."

Granger sat straight in the chair and pointed his finger at Sophia, "Now you listen here, little sister of mine, you may believe that your degrees or diplomas make you into something special, but they don't! Men rule the world. Father's family was from Italy, don't you forget that!"

Sophia scrunched up her face, "Italy? Papa's family was from a Latin Patriarchal Society, what does Italy have to do with anything? Granger, I have taught in Italy and done research in Italy. Believe me they accepted my degrees. You're the one with the problem. Is it because you don't have any degrees or diplomas? Is it?"

Margaret put her hands over her plate, "Time! Time out! What is the matter with the two of you?" She brushed invisible crumbs off the tablecloth, "Sophia, you have degrees and diplomas, but they aren't as important as having a male child. You know this is true, why are you making such trouble over this?"

Sophia gasped, "What about Geoffrey's money? What about my husband who I love and has worked hard right beside me to buy our home? What about him? Is he disqualified?"

"No, if he divorces you then the property is his and Mom and I will help you buy another home for you and the girls. The girls are Pino's, too, you know? You can change their names if you want." Granger leaned back in his chair. "You can still remarry and have a male child. You can't adopt one though and you can't marry someone who has a male child, the male child has to be of Pino blood."

This time Sophia stood. She walked around Granger to the back bedroom, calling out, "Girls, come on we're going home now. Time's up!"

"Sophia, no, we're going to take you three out to dinner. I mean Geoffrey is gone now, right? Let us help feed you and the girls? Come on, don't be so hasty!" Margaret tried to block Sophia and the girls from leaving the hall.

Sybil moved under her mother's arm, "Grandma Margaret, we are tired from sledding today and we really really, really, want to go home."

Donna hustled her little arms forward to her grandmother, "Grandma Margaret, how about a hug before we go?"

"Oh, all right!" Margaret gave the girls a hug while Sophia took their jackets down from the backdoor coat rack. Granger was standing in the kitchen staring out the window into the night. They left without saying goodbye to him.

Sophia sighed once the old van was cruising down the corrugated road of Calle Aspen. "Girls, now we can go home to a good movie and some popcorn. Truth is stranger than fiction! In my whole life I never would have thought to hear words such as those that came out of my mother's mouth tonight!"

"Mom," Sybil waved her hand about in the dark, "Mom, what did Granger mean when he said Dad wasn't part of the family? He's our dad, isn't he?"

"He certainly is, but as far as Granger and Grandmother Margaret are concerned anyone who isn't bred and born a Pino is inferior to the rest of the human race." Sophia watched the traffic at the stop sign.

Donna sniffed, "Mom, what's the rest of the human race?"

Sophia laughed, "Everyone else on the planet and especially those who are female!" The three peered through the dark at the lights, the traffic, and the road home. Sophia drove through the Burger Barn to buy everyone dinner. The girls were put to bed promptly at nine o'clock. She waited for Geoffrey's call, but gave up at eleven-thirty.

It was after midnight when the phone rang. Sophia rolled over to lift the cordless phone from Geoffrey's pillow. "Hello?"

"Hey, it's me."

"Geoffrey, the girls were seriously disappointed they couldn't say goodnight to you earlier."

"You and your mother are good at the guilt treatment, aren't you?"

"Geoffrey, we all miss you. We love you. When are you coming home?"

"I don't know yet. Sophia, there is much to think about regarding money, home, and future."

"I am devoted to you regardless of my crazy family."

"What's that supposed to mean?"

"Oh, Geoffrey, while you have been gone developments have happened you would not believe! Seriously, bizarre events have occurred which hurt the mind."

"Sophia, I don't want to know! Right now my soul is in agony and I don't know what to do to fix it. All I know is when I am with you and the girls, I feel helpless when it comes to your family. They castrate anyone who comes near them."

"Geoffrey, listen to me, Granger is divorcing Emily and Shirley. He knocked up Emily's best friend who came out here to visit her. Granger is going to marry this friend Katina and dump Emily and Shirley. He needs money evidently and lots of it. Our loan or our money to Papa appears to be Granger's saving grace to live with Katina."

Silence prevailed across the miles. "Geoffrey, are you there?" The phone went to dial tone. Sophia swore, "Oh, no, too much too soon! I should have waited and told him in person, damn!" She buried her face in the pillow trying to hold back the tears.

10

Rocoso, New Mexico
Monday, January, 1988

Monday morning found Sophia loading the girls into the yellow van by herself. Geoffrey had not called or come home on Sunday. Sunday had passed quietly what with homework to be done, clothes washing, and eight games of Slides and Ladders. Sophia was tired. The girls were somber as she dropped them off at school. They were assured she would be there to pick them up on time perhaps even go for a treat before going home later.

Desperate not to cry, Sophia turned up the radio and tried to sing along with the Oldies. On a regular day she would be washing and caring for her ailing father. The girls would be happily working at school and Geoffrey busy with his work. Sophia pulled into the front drive at home to turn off the van's engine. Staring up into the heavy winter clouds, she said, "Now Papa is dead. Geoffrey is gone, and the girls and I are falling off a cliff with a hole in our hearts."

Dragging the vacuum cleaner along the main hall, Sophia had not heard the front door slam. Suddenly, she turned to find Geoffrey standing behind the vacuum cleaner. She dropped the vacuum hose to run to him. He didn't move. Sophia froze to stare at him, "What are you doing home?"

Geoffrey put his suitcase on the couch, "I live here, too." Sophia felt the tension rise, "Why are you angry at me? What have I done to make you so cold and hateful to me?"

He walked into the kitchen. His black plastic coffee mug was emptied and washed out in the sink. "Sophia, I do believe this marriage is over. Your family has ordered it over, haven't they?"

Sophia's knees went weak, quickly she pulled out a kitchen chair and sat, "My family wants a lot of things, but they aren't in control of us or our dreams. What about the girls? What about our love for one another? Are you just going to roll over and play dead?"

Geoffrey leaned against the counter, "I knew what you would say. I know what you are doing. You're playing me for a sap like your mother and your brother. Well, I'm not going to play. Sophia, my love for you was real, really real. But when you sat here and cried upon hearing of your father's death just a few mornings ago, I knew somehow, just somehow that your loyalty is more to them than to us."

"Geoffrey..."

He put up his hand, "No, wait, Sophia. You said that you loved them. Sternly you told me that you knew your brother and mother killed your father and there was nothing you could do or would do about it, right?"

"Well, yes, but..."

"Hey, that's all you have to say. Your loyalty is to them not me and probably not even to the girls—although if you follow the family lineage through the women in the Pino family they are more Pino than Vinder, right?"

"Geoffrey, let me..."

"No, I am getting some of my things and moving into town. I found a place to stay for two weeks. Then you and your mother and brother can find you another place to live. This is my home. I paid for this place after working for twelve long hard years. I know you put money into it, too. I will give you some in case you want to have full guardianship of the girls, but I get to see them, too, all the time." He walked around the table, stepped over the vacuum cleaner to go into the bedroom. Sophia didn't move.

After four trips from the house to the truck, Geoffrey closed the front door and drove away. Sophia didn't move for two hours. She sat at the kitchen table trying to breathe. Her growling tummy averted her to the fact she hadn't eaten since the night before. There were girls to care for and plans to be made. There was no time for self pity.

The University of New Mexico dean's secretary offered Sophia a bottle of water. Sophia winced at the thought of carrying around a plastic bottle. Dr. Alaire smiled as he came around the corner of his office, "Dr. Sophia Vinder, please come in, what a delight to see you again! Are you planning on teaching this summer? Come in, come in and have a seat." The tall French American dean pulled out a grey plastic chair for her.

"Yes, I would like to teach. Would you happen to have any openings for this spring semester? If you have some eight week openings toward the end of this spring semester, I am available." Sophia pushed her bangs back from her forehead.

Dr. Alaire typed on his computer. Studying it for awhile, he smiled, "Yes, we do have two eight week classes in Early Eastern Ethnology. Both are available to you. The man who was going to take those classes decided to get married. You would be doing us a favor if you could take them. There are about fifty students in each class and both classes are on Tuesday and Thursday. One is at nine in the morning and the other is at one o'clock which should give you plenty of time to get the girls to school and to pick them up afterwards."

He turned to see her reaction, "These classes will start the first week of March. Do you want me to draw up the contract?"

Sophia tried to smile, but a frown was the best she could do, "Yes, that would be wonderful. I can come next week and sign it if you would like?"

Dr. Alaire jumped out of his chair, "No worries. Let me get Eloise to print a contract right now and you can sign it. You might want to take a card from the Anthropology Department and get the textbooks now at the bookstore. Then you can have your syllabi ready and have your class schedule prepared."

"Yes, yes of course." Sophia watched him hurry out the office door.

The contract signed, copy in her valise along with the textbooks, she retreated to the yellow van in the parking lot of UNM. She checked her watch. It was time to leisurely get the girls.

The world felt ethereal as she drove. Everything around her appeared to be foreign. Sybil was waiting for her, standing alone by the school bus stop. The buses were already gone. Sybil liked to go to the school library after final bell to get books to read. This way when she went outside to wait for her mother it was peaceful and quiet. Sybil threw her backpack onto the backseat and jumped in to fasten her seatbelt. She thumped on the back of her mother's seat, "Ready to roll, driver!"

Sophia smiled. They were quiet as they turned down the main street to Donna's school. The parked parade of parents' vehicles fumed as they waited patiently in the cold for their children. Donna's teacher waved to Sophia as he ran beside Donna down the long sidewalk to the van. Donna's teacher Mr. Dillon pulled open the passenger's door, "Mrs. Vinder, can I speak to you for a moment? Why don't you park? The girls should be fine in the vehicle, we can talk right here."

Sophia studied Donna's face as she stumbled into her car seat. Donna didn't say a word, but her eyes were puffy and her nose was red. The van was parked. Sophia ran through the waiting cars to the teacher. Mr. Dillon took Sophia's elbow, "I'm not sure what is happening at home, but all day today Donna cried. She cried uncontrollably at times. Is everything all right or is there something you should be telling me?"

Sophia gasped air, "I apologize for Donna, but we are all in shock right now. My father died last week and it appears the family is having difficulty." Sophia tried to stop the tears, but they flowed freely down her face. She wiped her face with her mittened hand since she had left her purse in the van, "I'm sorry. I can't, just can't seem...I don't know what to do?"

Mr. Dillon pulled a tissue from his pocket and handed it to Sophia. "Would it help if you kept Donna home for a few days until you can figure things out? She is not doing well in class. She can't focus, isn't paying attention, and it is distracting to those around her."

Taking the tissue, Sophia tried to smile, "Well, school is the only normal thing in Donna's life right now." Sophia pushed a laugh, "That and her pink socks are keeping her sane, I think."

"Well, you think about it, all right? You can call the school in the morning if you want to keep her home. I will write up a report about her family problems. The administration will understand if she doesn't come in for a few days. We are not a cold hearted group here." He lifted his left eyebrow.

Sophia stood and stared at the man. "What do you mean? Certainly Donna's education is primary, regardless." Mr. Dillon shook his head and walked into the wind away from Sophia. Tears kept flowing down her face, turning she saw both girls watching her from the van. Gathering up her courage, she walked to them. "All right," she swung open the driver's door and sat in the driver's seat, "we need a treat! We all need a super treat of gigantic proportions! Where do you suggest we go?"

Sybil burst into tears, "Mom, I hate this town. I hate these people! Mom, I want to move somewhere else where we are a family again!"

Not to be out done, Donna started crying, "Mom, I want to go home and hug my pillow pet. I don't want to go anywhere, but home."

"All right, we shall go home." Sophia waited for the cars behind her to leave before she backed out of the school property. Right before she took the turn off, she pulled into the Baskin Robbins's store. "I just have to have a chocolate almond ice cream. Who wants to join me?"

Ice cream cones dripping on mittened fingers, they silently made it home. Sybil ran into her room and slammed the door. Donna went into the family room to turn on the television and watch Sesame Street. Sophia went into the kitchen and began preparations for dinner. The blinking light on the cordless phone on the wall finally got her attention. She pushed the buttons and listened, "Sophia, I will come by this evening for dinner. I want to tell the girls myself about my plans. You have your own to work out, but I have made my plans and feel it best if I tell you and them in person. Shall be home around seven this evening." Dial tone followed.

Talking to the dial tone, Sophia said, "Fine, if you don't want to work with me on this. Only a human would attempt to work as a team!" She fled to the bedroom and closed the door.

When the door bell rang, the table was set and the girls were dressed in their dressy clothes. Sybil answered the door. Donna hesitantly hid behind her mother. Sophia had on her nice pants, her Christmas sweater that Geoffrey had given her, and she was trying desperately to stay calm. Geoffrey walked in calling, "There are my girls!" Donna ran to him, letting him lift her to his shoulder for a hug and a kiss.

"Dinner is just about ready. Would you like a cold beer?" Sophia pointed to his favorite beer mug on the table.

"No, I don't think a drink would serve me well tonight. I just want a glass of water and a good home cooked meal." Geoffrey pulled out his kitchen chair and sat down with Donna on his lap. "So, how's my girl doing here?" He touched Donna on the nose.

"Daddy, we need you to come home. Mama and all of us miss you! I can't do anything at school except cry and today my teacher had a meeting with Mama outside the classroom and Mama stood there crying. Sybil and I are frightened. Daddy, please come home and be with us like we used to be?" Donna started to cry again.

Geoffrey studied Sophia's face, "Maybe I will have that beer after all." He reached out to take Sybil's hand for she was standing right beside them. "Sybil, what do you think of all of this?"

Sybil shrugged her shoulders. Tears began flowing down her cheeks.

"Daddy, what did we do wrong? Mama and Donna and I love you forever and forever and you just left us alone. Daddy, Mama cries all the time and Donna and I feel like you hate us. What's going on?" Sybil ran into her bedroom and slammed the door.

Sophia stood at the other side of the table, leaning forward to hand him his cold bottle of beer. "Here you go."

Donna wiggled out of her Daddy's lap to run into Sybil's room and slam the door. Geoffrey took a swig from the beer bottle, "A lot of door slamming tonight, huh?"

Sophia turned to the stove, stirring the mashed potatoes, she shrugged. She heard Geoffrey move behind her. "Sophia, I'm sorry to hurt you and the girls, but there doesn't appear to be any other way out of this mess. What do you want me to do?" Sophia kept stirring the potatoes with the wooden spoon. "Sophia, talk to me."

Geoffrey took her shoulders and tried to turn her to face him. Sophia let her body go rigid as he tightened his grip, speaking more to the potatoes than to him, she said, "Geoffrey, we are all willing to work with you on this as a team. You are the one who has decided to leave, to bail out and abandoned ship."

He stepped back from her, "Sophia, all right, I acted hastily but I don't feel I have a choice here. Tell me if you think I'm wrong, tell me."

She turned off the potatoes. "Geoffrey, what can I say? This family is being ripped into pieces. This family of yours, no one else's, is in such pain. Donna and Sybil love you with all of their being as do I, but for some reason you have read into things we don't understand. If you decide to come back to us, we are scared you will leave again. If you leave us, we are afraid we will die from pain. I don't know what to say or do...I don't!" Sophia stood staring at him with tears falling once again down her cheeks.

Geoffrey took a long pull on the beer bottle. "Hell, what are we to do?" He walked to the other end of the kitchen table.

Sophia took a deep breath, "Geoffrey, dinner is on hold. Why don't we sit down in the living room and would you please tell me what happened with Fred at the cabin?"

In the living room, Geoffrey sat abruptly in his recliner. The pillow was held in his lap as was his fashion. "When I got up there I was jazzed with hatred for the Pino's. The concept of them taking twelve years of our money away from us was beyond immoral or unethical standards. People kill for less."

He punched the pillow, "My fishing buddy Fred is getting a divorce from Eve. She found another lover and wants to leave the boys with Fred to go off and start a new life with her new man. Fred and Eve have been married for twenty-three years. He's devastated beyond belief." Geoffrey took another swig from the beer bottle.

"Well, we drank. We drank a lot and I listened to Fred. We both decided the women in our lives were not to be trusted. He listened to me tell him about Granger and what happened at Sam Goldfarb's office. He just couldn't believe it."

Geoffrey rubbed the top of his bald head, "When you told me about Granger getting divorced and dumping Emily and his little girl, well, I knew this is what would happen to me next." Geoffrey put the beer bottle down on the coffee table.

"It felt at the time, life was divided between you and your Pino family and you and the Vinder family." Geoffrey sat forward still hugging the pillow, "Sophia, your family is ruthless and blood thirsty. How and where are we to live? They have taken everything from us. Twelve years of mortgage payments are gone! Twelve years of monthly payments, close to one hundred thousand dollars just gone, zapped and disappeared!" Geoffrey fell back in the chair letting the pillow fall to the floor.

Sophia rocked slowly in the rocking chair. "Geoffrey, whether it is you, just you, or all four of us, we're all in this. You aren't alone. If you leave us what are the girls and I to do? Where are we supposed to go?" She swallowed hard, "We still love one another. This won't change if you leave or you stay. I still love you. I love you major more than the Pino group. You are my husband. You are the father of my children, my rock, and my man." Tears poured down her face, "Oh, Geoffrey, how will we live separated?"

Sybil came into the living room holding Donna's hand. "Daddy, shouldn't we have a vote? You always said if we don't agree we get the chance to vote, right?"

Geoffrey let out a loud laugh, "If only it were that easy!" He scooped up the girls into his lap. "I don't know about you guys, but I'm starving."

Dinner finished and the girls were put to bed with some semblance of calm. Sophia wiped down the counter in the kitchen while Geoffrey sat at the kitchen table working on a graph. "Sophia, if we can get at least half of our money back from Granger this would give us a substantial amount for a down payment on another property. If he doesn't go for it, well, what do we do?"

Sophia draped the dishcloth over the side of the kitchen sink. "Geoffrey, what if we do get divorced? Well, not really divorced, but divorced enough for Granger and Margaret. You would get this property free and clear is that correct?"

Geoffrey unfolded the papers to his right. "According to the copies that Goldfarb and Costa have drawn up, yes, if I divorce you and I have to be the one who does this then the property becomes mine free and clear. There are no more required payments."

"So, what if we get divorced, you get the property, sell it and we remarry? What happens if we do this?" Sophia sat down to lean forward on the table.

"No can do, sweetheart. The Costa file states if we divorce we're not allowed to remarry each other or cohabitate or this property reverts back to Granger Pino. If we sell it and remarry, I am obligated to repay the amount designated by the appraiser prior to the sale of the house."

Sophia slapped her forehead, "Are you serious? Let me see that document!" Geoffrey pushed the papers to her. Sophia brushed them open to read each line out loud. When she finished Geoffrey coughed, "Your family is thorough if nothing else. Now what do you recommend we do?"

The phone interrupted their conversation. Sophia jumped to answer it before the girls were awakened. "Hello?"

Granger spoke hurriedly to her, "Sophia, Mom has sold her Mercedes and bought a used Toyota truck! She never asked me! She needs to talk to me about these things! She went out today and traded in her Mercedes for a used truck, of all things! Did you put her up to this?"

Sophia almost laughed, but held herself in check, "Granger, I have never been able to influence mother in any manner. No, I had nothing to do with this. Why did Mom want a truck?"

Geoffrey sat at the table twirling his fingers near his head to sign crazy. Granger's voice was becoming exasperated, "Sophia, you and I have to work as a team here. Mom said she wanted to help Emily and Shirley move to Negar into the old house. Mom has decided to sell the old house in Negar to Emily. Can you imagine?"

"Granger, settle down or you're going to have a stroke. What do you mean Mom is selling the old house in Negar to Emily? I didn't know she still owned the old house. Didn't she turn over all of the properties to you?" Sophia sat down to wait for his answer.

"No, she wanted to keep one. She gave me some cock and bull story about how if anything were to happen to us she would need a place of her own. She kept Negar house, but had me paying the taxes and the insurances on it from her account. Sophia, I can't believe she is going to sell it to them! This is a family property! Emily and Shirley are no longer family!"

Sophia raised her eyebrows, "Emily and Shirley are always family, Granger. You can't disown your own daughter because you impregnated another woman. Shirley is your daughter for life."

Granger was getting angrier for Sophia was not agreeing with him, "Fine, Sophia, take her side, but this doesn't change anything with you and Geoffrey! You have to divorce him if Geoffrey wants the Rocoso property." Granger slammed down the phone. Sophia quickly pulled the phone away from her ear.

Geoffrey tapped his pencil on the kitchen table, "Well, you don't have to tell me what he said. I heard it all. So, now what are we going to do with the slimy bastard?"

Sophia set the phone on the table, "You mean with the salamander?" They both burst out laughing. "Oh, dear, I have to go and visit a friend." Sophia ran down the hall to the bathroom. Geoffrey sat back to study his graph. As he picked up his pencil to add something to it, the phone rang. He glanced up at the kitchen clock. It was only nine-thirty, but felt well after midnight.

"Hello?"

"Hello, Geoffrey, this is Enid calling to find out if Sophia is available? I wasn't sure when you put the little princesses to bed."

"Yes, Sophia is here, but right now she's in the bathroom."

Enid burst out laughing. Geoffrey could envision her long blond hair tied up in a knot at the nape of her head and her blue eyes accentuated by her pink lipstick.

"Geoffrey, you don't have to tell everything you know! Listen do you know what is going on in the Pino family? I mean aside from the fact the dear doc died, what is going on around here?"

Geoffrey waved to Sophia as she walked down the hall to the kitchen, "Here, here is my wife. She can let you know all the details. Good to speak with you, Enid, here is she."

Sophia took the phone frowning at Geoffrey, "Enid? How are you tonight?"

"Well, Sophia, this is exactly why I am calling you. By the way, please have my sympathy with the passing of your father. He was so ill, but as long as a person is alive there is always hope. When I lost my father I was devastated for months, but each person's situation is different."

Geoffrey shook his head at Sophia as she responded to Enid, "Yes, that's true. We really thought we were making headway with the new meds the doc was trying. But what is it that you need to know?"

She heard Enid sigh into the phone, "Tonight, this evening really, Emily came into the store as she usually does. I was expecting her to help with the stocking and cleaning and such." Enid stopped talking for a moment to get her second wind, "She was a wreck. Her hair was in her face. Her eyes were red and her nose running. She was as pale as my grandmother's sheets. When I asked her what was wrong, Emily burst into tears and fled to the back of the clinic. I followed her. I was worried she was ill or something, but she was in the back stuffing her personal items into brown paper bags."

Sophia could hear Enid walking around, moving things, "Sophia, she packed her white clinic jacket she wears to make appointments for Granger. She took all the small photos off the wall. Her tears were endless and finally with her hands full of bags, she whispered she loved me and my family and she was leaving town and taking Shirley with her."

Geoffrey handed Sophia a torn piece of graph paper. On it he had written, 'am staying here tonight, going to take a shower.' Sophia smiled and gave him thumbs up.

Enid's voice was becoming raspy, "Sophia, what is going on? What did Emily mean when she said she's moving away?"

"Enid, oh, dear, how can I put this delicately without influencing your perspective of anyone?" Sophia moved to the kitchen sink to get herself a glass of water. "Well, Emily and Granger are getting a divorce, did you know that?"

There was a gasp on Enid's side of the phone. "No. What happened? They were working here just fine and little Shirley was happy. There didn't appear to be any problems, oh, wait! Yes, the woman from California was in here all last week while Emily was having her music classes. Is she the instigator of this?"

"Well, she is impregnated. Katina and Granger evidently hit it off. She is pregnant with Granger's child and Emily and Shirley are out."

Enid snorted as she laughed, "Sophia, you were never one to mince words! You and Geoffrey are so refreshing!" Enid's tone changed to somber, "This is not a laughing matter. Now what will happen to the clinic? Henker and I are partners with Granger and Emily. If Emily leaves I guess we will have to buy her share out of the agreement."

Sophia interrupted her, "Enid, does Emily actually own stock or assets within the clinic or firm? I thought Henker was the main holder of the clinic and Granger went in with him?"

"No, no, we all put money in the pot equally. Emily's family helped her with her fourth of the investment. She invested her money into the office supplies, examining tables, and state of the art equipment. These were expensive."

Enid's voice was becoming harried, "Granger and Henker made an agreement to buy into the business. They both pay the costs for licensure and the insurance. Henker holds the degree as a doctor of Chinese Medicine and Granger is the licensed Back and Pain therapist who has no degrees at all. I was left to put in my two cents for the inventory of herbs, supplements, and vitamins. These are replenished from the income of the clinic. In the beginning, my family helped me to take out a loan for we were already maxed out financially. This was our dream come true."

"Do you know if Granger has already given Emily the money she invested back?"

Enid took in a breath. Her voice was quivering, "No, I didn't know any of this until just now. Wait until Henker finds out. We haven't been doing well financially for the economy is rocky what with the new overpass near Belen."

Sophia frowned, "Yes, but don't you have regulars who only come to see you?"

Enid's voice softened, "The new highway has folks moving out of the area due to lack of jobs. Many clients' insurances won't pay for Granger's work and he refers them to Henker to cover overhead. We have regulars who come in for supplements and vitamins and their insurance will pay for much of these.

The doc's recommend them and the insurance will pick up the tab. The forms and paperwork were all done by Emily. She knows the insurance company rep's and has an in with so many of the doctors in the area, this is going to be devastating!"

Geoffrey walked into the kitchen with just a blue towel around his middle. He came up to Sophia, who was leaning against the kitchen counter. He put his arms around her. Sophia smiled at him, pointing to the phone. "Enid, listen, I really have to go now. I would advise you to let Henker speak with Granger and the two men can work this out. Granger is very much into male dominance as you know?"

Enid attempted a laugh, "Oh, yes, the weaker sex is to take the backseat. Henker is at home with four year old Alistair right now. This is the only time they have together since Henker is at the clinic at six in the morning. I get there around nine to work the day until three-thirty when I get Alistair from pre-school. This is going to shake the very foundations of the H&G Clinic, let me tell you! Good night, Sophia, be well." Enid hung up.

Sophia turned to embrace Geoffrey as they moved down the hall to their bedroom.

11

Rocoso, New Mexico
Tuesday, January, 1988

The peaceful early morning was quickly broken with the loud voices of the girls jumping on the bed. "Dad, Dad! You're home again! Yeah! Daddy, we love you!" Pillows were thrown to try and get them off the bed as their little knees poked the adults' long legs. Geoffrey finally grabbed Sybil around the middle. Sophia rolled over to pull Donna under the covers with her. Geoffrey growled in his bear voice, "These little goblins must be eliminated!" He let go of Sybil, chasing her down the hall into the kitchen. Sophia heard him running the water and filling up the coffee maker.

"Well, my little goblin, what shall I do with you?" Sophia hugged Donna tighter around her middle.

"Mom," Donna squirmed, "now I have to go to the bathroom! Let go of me!" Donna crawled from under the covers to run out of the room to the girls' bathroom. Sophia balanced on her elbow to look at the bedside clock. It was almost seven-thirty. Time to rock and roll for everyone had somewhere to be this morning and it wasn't lying in this bed. Slowly, she lowered her legs over the edge of the bed to groan, "Oh, dear, back to the old grind of running, driving, and worrying."

The girls decided they wanted their Dad to drive them to school. Sophia had the truck and Geoffrey took the van. Sophia was relieved for now she could work at the University's library later in the afternoon. Geoffrey could gather the girls after school. There were blessings in being married, working as a team, and loving one's family just the way they were.

This morning, Sophia was busy outlining the chapter on Eastern Ethnology at the kitchen table. The phone rang. She reached over the counter and picked it up, "Hello?"

"Sophia, this is Granger." His voice was harsh.

"Yes?" Sophia impatiently thumped the pencil's eraser on the table.

"Why did you tell Enid that Katina and I are adulterers?"

Sophia tried not to giggle, "What? I don't understand the question?"

Granger's tone became terse, "Sophia, I am coming over there right now to have it out with you! Right now, don't leave the house, don't try and get out of this. I am going to be there in thirty minutes!" He slammed the phone down.

Sophia shook her head, "Adulterers? What the heck? I never said any such thing. If the kettle wants to call itself black then what's the harm, but I never referred to him as an adulterer." She went back to her outline, then grumbled, "If he wants to come over here, fine, but he should be able to take as good as he gives."

Granger threw open the front door with a bang. The wind and his fury followed him down the hall and into the kitchen. "Sophia, damn you, what right do you have to pass judgment on someone else? I have been trying to help you and Geoffrey and this is how you show your appreciation?"

The chair Sophia was sitting on was jerked out from under her as Granger flung it into the hall. "What the hell were you thinking, woman!" Leaning her upper body on the table, Sophia kept herself from falling to the floor. Cautiously, she turned to be met with Granger's glaring brown eyes. The light from the hall revealed a presence standing in the kitchen doorway.

"Granger," Sophia pushed back with the kitchen table against her thighs, "Granger, why don't you introduce your companion?"

Whirling around Granger yelled, "I thought I told you to wait in the car! What the hell is the matter with you women! Huh, what the hell is going on with you?" He stood with his finger pointing at the woman at the door and his other hand held up to stop Sophia from moving forward. "Go to the car!" His voice echoed in the house.

The woman in the kitchen doorway quietly replied, "No." Her voice was soft, "Granger, it would be impolite of you to not introduce me to your sister. After all, we wouldn't want to be impolite now would we?"

Admiring the woman's impertinence to her brother, Sophia cautiously ducked under Granger's outstretched arm, "Hello, I am Sophia, Granger's sister. Welcome to my home."

Granger sucked in air. He retrieved the kitchen chair to carry it into the kitchen. Abruptly, he sat on it. "Well, hell, why not? Sophia, this is Katina my fiancée and soon to be the mother of my son. Katina, this is Sophia my disappointing and unfortunate sister."

Not dropping a beat, Sophia asked, "Would you like a cup of tea?"

Katina smiled, "Love one, thank you so much." Granger mumbled something neither of the women heard and went down the hall to close the front door. Katina established herself at the kitchen table, taking off her heavy coat and gloves. Neither woman said anything. Sophia watched Katina study the kitchen.

Sophia studied Katina. She appeared to be older than Sophia. Katina's hair was blonde with streaks of gray. Her hair was thin and hung unevenly to her shoulders with fringed bangs to her eye lashes. The woman was extremely thin. Her long limbs were covered in bright natural fibered clothing. Katina wore no makeup and was pale with no hint of tan. The kettle whistled and Sophia put the mugs, the hot kettle, tea bags, and spoons on the table.

"Help yourself." Sophia sat down to face Katina.

"Thank you, it has been incredibly cold as of late. Don't you think?" Katina plopped a tea bag into her mug. "Sophia, I know this must be very difficult for you to appreciate. The relationship between Granger and myself is rather sudden," she stirred her tea with the spoon, "but we do love one another. We didn't ask to fall in love, it just happened. One thing lead to another and here we are. I hope you and I can be friends. There is no need for hostility between you and Granger. Don't you think we can all be friends?" Katina took a sip of her tea. Her blue eyes peered over the mug at Sophia.

Sophia sat with her hands in her lap, staring at her. "Well, hum, there is just one tiny problem with what happened between you and Granger. The problem being Granger is already married. He is married to your friend and they have a child together. This is something to consider, don't you think?"

Katina clenched her jaw. The skin on her face stretched taut, "Yes, that was a problem. Emily and Granger weren't in harmony. Emily didn't complete Granger like I do. He completes me. No one can foresee the emotions of the human heart, don't you agree?"

Granger could be heard walking around the house. Sophia stood up, "Excuse me, my brother appears to be rifling through my things." Sophia scurried to her bedroom where she found Granger rummaging through Geoffrey's bureau drawer. "Granger, can I help you?"

He jumped, "What? No, this is my house after all. I wanted to see what goes on around here." He smirked as he walked out of the room and down the hall to the kitchen. She closed the drawer. Taking a deep breath she followed him into the kitchen.

Sophia stood at the table with her hands on her hips. "You have no right to go through our things, Granger! I don't go to your house to take inventory of your stuff, what are you doing?"

"Get over it, Sophia. My house isn't your house. This house is my house. What is there to understand? Where is my mug for tea?" He started to open the cupboards when the mugs were hanging right beside the kitchen sink. Sophia pushed him aside to hand him a mug with a fish on it. "Here, help yourself. The hot water is in the kettle and the bags are on the table."

Granger shoved his kitchen chair close to Katina's, "We are in love, right?" He kissed Katina on the cheek. She smiled at him revealing two lower black teeth. He pushed her hair behind her ear as he tried to kiss her again.

She lifted her hand and shoved him away. "We want you to know we're going to get married on top of a mountain at Yellowstone National Park. Granger says he will rent us an airplane to fly there. He wants to sky dive out of the plane with the minister, but how would we get the witnesses in the circle if we are all flying through the air?" She chuckled to herself.

Sophia grimaced, "How lovely for you both. I suppose Margaret would need to be flying in the air beside Granger when this happens, right?"

"Well," Granger put his arm around Katina, "We were just dreaming. Probably we will marry in California. Katina's family can attend and Mom and you can come. If you want to bring the little rug rats, they will be invited of course."

Katina whirled around to face Granger, "What did you call her children?"

Granger blanched, "My father used the term rug rats. He thought it an endearing phrase."

"Oh, right, and he beat the tar out of you and your sister, right? If we have children and you so much as touch them in anger I will personally castrate you to your back bone and don't you forget it, dear." Katina patted the side of Granger's face with the back of her hand.

He reached for her wrist, "I would never harm one of my own. Katina,

I am cut to the quick for you to even suggest I would hit or hurt my child especially my son." He kissed her fingers.

Feeling like throwing up, Sophia chirped, "Oh, yes, a mother will protect her offspring with her life, Granger. You better remember this or you will lose body parts. Katina, how far along are you in your pregnancy?"

Patting her flat abdomen, Katina shook her head, "The first time we made love I knew I was pregnant. I could feel the egg begin to hatch into a spiritual being. The rush of electric energy flowed through my veins. I, myself was reborn with spiritual strength. Brightness filled my soul with such warmth I cried. I cried, didn't I, Granger?"

"Yes, my love, you cried and I cried." He put his hand on her emaciated abdomen. "She is around five months pregnant, right?"

Katina pulled his hand off of her body, "Yes, I bel.eve I am about five months along. The baby should be due around the middle of April. We met in late July and it was a spiritual bonding immediately."

Granger blushed, "We couldn't keep our hands off each other. It was difficult."

Sophia rested her elbow on the table and cupped her jaw in the palm of her hand, "Do you feel the baby moving?"

Sitting up straight, Katina glared at Sophia, "No, the baby doesn't move until the seventh month. You know things are different with pregnancy now!" Defensive venom poured out of Katina's mouth. "Hundreds of years ago women felt their babies move when they were just two or three months along. Probably you felt your babies when you were five months, but this is modern times and pregnancy has changed. We feel our baby's presence. We are patient for him to move and let us know he is here. He told us he is male and will be strong like his father." Katina shoved the sleeve of her sweater up to her elbow clearly revealing scars of punctured skin in circular patterns around her vein.

Sophia bit her lower lip, as she asked, "Who is your OBGYN doctor? Is he someone in the area that I might know?"

"No, Granger and I decided we don't want to get involved with Western Medicine. I have an appointment to see his friend Henker at Granger's H&G Clinic in Belen. Isn't it cool how they named their clinic using their first initials? I trust Granger to take care of me and our baby."

Not wanting to be thoughtless, Sophia questioned further, "Katina, it is important to see a dentist regularly when you are pregnant. I couldn't help but notice your teeth and an infection in your gums or bad teeth can affect the unborn little fellow there."

Granger and Katina stared at her. Granger cleared his throat, "No worries, Sophia, I will take good care of my wife with my insurance once we are married. No need for you to fret over every little thing."

Katina remained motionless, "Do you have any honey?"

Reaching into the cupboard for the honey, Sophia cautiously remarked, "Granger, how do you know for sure Katina is pregnant?"

Katina pushed her tea mug to the center of the table, "You know I don't really feel like tea. I believe I've had enough of your sister for the day, Granger. Another time we can try to get together after everyone has gotten used to the idea that we are a couple." She fumbled with her winter coat on the back of the kitchen chair. "I am pregnant, Sophia. A woman knows when she is pregnant for God's sake!"

Attempting to find her coat sleeves, Katina gloated, "There's too much negative energy in this house. Granger, when they leave this house we will need to have it purified." Katina struggled with her coat, "Granger, be a dear and help me here."

He put his mug in the sink and hurried to her side. "Katina's weak from the pregnancy. I believe she has prenatal edema. We have to watch what she eats and drinks." Lifting the coat over her shoulders, he rested his hand on Katina's lower back.

Katina gave a nasty smile to Sophia, "I can understand why your brother is trying to help you get away from your husband. The spiritual energy in this house is dark. You should be very careful."

As the couple ambled to the front door Granger turned to Sophia, "Don't tell people we are adulterers, for we aren't! We are two people who are deeply in love. Emily is better away from us, away from this."

Katina brushed her white bangs from her face as she asked Granger, "Did you tell your sister about the Memorial Service?"

Granger wiped his moustache with the back of his hand, "Oh, yes, we had Papa cremated and we've hired a twin engine Cessna. Mom and I are going to drop Papa's ashes over the Grand Canyon. We have this scheduled for next Tuesday. I know you are too busy to participate, so we didn't include you. Mom really doesn't want a Memorial Service. She is putting a notice in the paper for people to give donations to their favorite charities in Papa's name instead." Katina and Granger disappeared out the door and this time it was closed quietly.

Sophia stood at the kitchen window watching the green Mercedes back out of her driveway. Katina appeared to be laughing. Sophia shook her head, "Papa is being cremated when he wanted to be buried and has already paid for the site. Go figure that one?"

In the afternoon, the university library was blissfully peaceful as Sophia researched the early anthropologists' stories on Eastern European digs. She loved to teach through stories rather than just the dry bones. This was her M.O. and the students appeared to love her style for it helped them remember the dates and cultural transitions. The early struggles of anthropologists and their families brought the excitement and information to life. Sophia was pleased to find a donated library book at the library from a retired anthropologist in Wyoming. She was miles away in her head when she heard her name being softly called. Geoffrey was standing in the middle foyer of the library searching the tables for her. Sophia had to smile.

Many times a person could be standing right in front of Geoffrey and he wouldn't see them. She waved and kept waving, finally he noticed. Grinning from ear to ear he tip toed to her table and sat down opposite her. "Hey, professor, do you have time for an interested student?"

"Sure, but what do I get out of this intercourse?" Sophia coyly smiled.

"Whoa, you use big words in this sacred chamber of books. Do they allow you to use words like that in here?" Geoffrey glanced around them.

"Why, yes, verbal intercourse is pursued in these institutions of higher learning and of course there are the quiet relationships between authors and their works." Sophia tapped the thick book in front of her.

"Oh, my, these are things outsiders would never guess." Geoffrey leaned forward to whisper, "You do know I love you, Professor, and would like for you to come with me to the world of reality where two young girls await your company."

"You brought the girls here?" Sophia pushed the chair back to make a scraping sound on the wooden floor. "Ah, oh, must be quiet. Where are they?"

Geoffrey nodded his head toward the door, "They are out in the open park climbing the statues. Come on, we have more to discuss. Today at work, I received a certified letter from Mr. Costa's law firm in Santa Fe. He is giving us thirty days to file for divorce or Geoffrey will take over our property."

Sophia's brown eyes widened, "What? Can they do that?"

"Let's get out of here. I can't talk when everyone is so quiet." He watched Sophia slide her notebook and books into her valise.

He lowered his voice, "Also, Granger accused me of manipulating your mother into selling her Mercedes to buy a used Toyota truck."

Geoffrey shrugged his shoulders, "This is beyond my comprehension. Your mother doesn't even speak to me. How could I convince her to buy a truck?" Geoffrey trailed behind Sophia as they departed through the doors of the library. Sophia heaved her valise into her arms as they marched to the open park. The girls were running around yelling at each other with their coats zipped tightly. Students walking to class either glared at the girls or smiled.

Geoffrey proffered Sophia a seat on the cold concrete bench at the edge of the park. "Sophia, we have to do something for doing nothing is going to lead down a very dark road. The only choice I feel we have is to walk away from the property and make a new life with nothing. We have nothing now. All the money, all the years of hard work and all of our energy we put into the house in Rocoso is gone. Let's just pack up and move."

Sophia studied his sad face as he continued, "Granger can have the house. He can stick it up his shiny ass for all I care, but I don't want to do this anymore. I love you and the girls."

Donna came running up to her parents, "Did you see what Sybil did? She climbed up the giraffe and she didn't even fall. Daddy, can you lift me onto the giraffe so I can be with Sybil, please, Daddy?" Geoffrey tickled Donna and with one arm he carried her to the giraffe.

The sky filled with heavy snow clouds and the wind started to blow as Sophia in the truck followed Geoffrey with the girls in the van. They drove to Rocoso, to a place that was supposedly their home.

12

Rocoso, New Mexico
Wednesday, January, 1988

"Mr. Goldfarb what an unexpected surprise," Geoffrey opened the front door. "It is very early in the morning. Please do come in, for this is a most excellent visit!" Geoffrey quickly pulled the rope tie on his striped terry cloth robe tightly around his waist. "Let me get your coat. Sophia is in the other room. Just have a seat here in the living room, just a minute."

Mr. Goldfarb loosened his long gabardine coat, took off his wool hat, and followed Geoffrey into the living room. "I...I...I am sorry if I am intruding. I just wanted to get here before everyone took off for work or school or places unknown. If it is inconvenient we can talk later?"

"No, no, let me get Sophia. She will be very pleased to see you." Geoffrey took the heavy coat from Mr. Goldfarb. "Have a seat."

Geoffrey retreated into the bedroom where he jerked Sophia's shoulder back and forth. She rolled over and stared at him, "What do you want? Do you know how irritating that is?"

"Sophia, Mr. Goldfarb is in the living room wanting to speak to us."

"What? What time is it?" Sophia struggled to sit. Her eyes were bleary and her hair stuck straight up in the air. Her nightgown was wrapped around her legs. "Dear God in Heaven it is quarter to six in the morning! Not even the angels are up yet! What is Mr. Goldfarb doing in our living room?" Sophia tried untangling her legs.

"He's waiting for you, my beauty. Get your act together. I shall put the coffee on and make small talk." Geoffrey stood back to appraise her. "What do you do in the night to make your hair go straight up in the air?" Sophia threw a pillow at him.

Within seconds, Geoffrey hurried into the walk-in closet in his robe and pajamas. He turned to come out in blue jeans and a flannel shirt while Sophia was struggling to pull her underwear out of the drawer. Geoffrey hurried to the kitchen, calling out, "How about some coffee, Mr. Goldfarb? We have some of the best Hawaiian blends you have ever tasted!"

Mr. Goldfarb followed Geoffrey into the kitchen. Geoffrey smiled, his wife always left the kitchen spotless before she went to bed. Mr. Goldfarb studied the girls' drawings stuck on the fridge with animal magnets. "You have some real talent here." He pointed to Sybil's watercolor of a tall tree with bare branches reaching skyward under a winter sky.

"That's Sybil's. She is nine years old and lives to draw tree branches. Her interest is in the 'veins of life' as she calls it. Sophia believes Sybil will go into medicine, probably something to do with the circulatory system."

Mr. Goldfarb studied the finger-painted pink hands below the tree, "And who did this one?"

Geoffrey turned, "That's Donna's painting. She's six and a half and loves everything pink."

"Oh," said Mr. Goldfarb, "she's into the aesthetics of life and knows what she likes?"

"Yes, Donna definitely knows what she wants and always figures out a way to get it."

The coffee percolated, giving a healthy aroma to the kitchen. Mr. Goldfarb strolled back to the living room to retrieve his black leather case. He placed it on a chair at the kitchen table.

"Hello!" Sophia danced into the kitchen. Her face was scrubbed to a glowing pink and her lips were dazzling with lip gloss. Her green sweater was accentuated with dangling turquoise earrings and her eyeliner was of matching green. She had on her nice jeans and hiking boots. "Mr. Goldfarb, you certainly are an early riser. What brings you to the top of the mountain here in Rocoso?"

"The views here on the mountain are outstanding. I stood outside for a good fifteen minutes admiring the panorama of dark mesas, soft clouds, and soaring ravens before knocking on your door. The shadows of the mesas and the depth of the canyons are glorious in the early morning light. My wife used to paint New Mexico scenes until she lost her vision to macular degeneration." Mr. Goldfarb stood at the kitchen window staring out at the broad expanse.

Sophia turned to Geoffrey who shrugged his shoulders, "The coffee is ready if you would like some? We only have mugs, but believe me they are clean." Geoffrey reached for the mug with the American flag on it. Sophia hit him on the shoulder. "Geoffrey, of course the mugs are clean!"

Mr. Goldfarb moved from the kitchen window to the kitchen chair. He took the steaming hot mug from Geoffrey to smell the aroma. "Oh, this is wonderful." He took a small sip and put the hot mug on the table. "Actually the reason I'm here is because of my wife. She was your father's patient and friend. When she heard what happened with Granger, Margaret, and the property, it seriously upset her."

Sophia sat opposite him, "Your wife did a drawing for my father. Didn't he have it hanging over his desk at the clinic?"

Mr. Goldfarb nodded, "Yes, the drawing of Negar falls done in pen and ink on Japanese rice paper with the walnut frame."

"I remember your wife," Sophia closed her eyes, "she had golden hair braided around her head. Her green eyes were kind and gentle."

Mr. Goldfarb smiled, "She still has golden hair in braids around her head. Her eyes are still green but now they don't see much, which is sad." He lifted his leather case to the table. "Therefore, with my loving wife's push your case has been researched in regards to the legality of what Margaret and Granger did to void your father's will."

Laughing, Sophia remarked, "You are right about voiding my father's will! He probably would have used the same term only with a medical perspective, hah!"

Two sets of papers were placed on the table. "These are for you to read. Keep these close to your chest. We don't want the others to know what we're researching. Right now it appears they feel confident in their statutes, but the judicial system is a public system. When there is a change done to wills without the judicial system being made aware of the change and without it being given to the clerk to file, then things become murky and questionable."

Geoffrey placed his kitchen chair closer to Sophia and sat down. Sophia held the papers in front of both of them. Mr. Goldfarb continued, "It is important to notice section 46A-3-303 states the importance of there being no conflict of interest between the representative and the person represented of among those being represented with respect to a particular question or dispute and there follows the details of dispute as you can read further."

He took a savoring sip of his coffee. "Sophia, aren't you having any coffee?"

She shook her head, "No, caffeine plays havoc on my nervous system. Please continue."

Mr. Goldfarb put the papers down on the table. "The short of the long of this is there was and still is a conflict of interest in the changing of your father's will. The primary will, which was completed five years prior to your father's death is the will filed in the county court house. It is insitu. This is the Latin term for being 'held in place' or 'is in position' with the judge of the court. The will transfer done by Margaret has not been filed nor has it been accepted by an acting judge to be law as is necessary in our judicial system."

"How can we find out if anything Margaret and Granger did is legally accepted by the judge and is filed with the clerk?" Geoffrey was sitting up straight holding the paper. Sophia put her hand on the paper to help hold it still.

Mr. Goldfarb smiled, "This is where I come into the picture. If you hire me as your attorney, I will represent you to defend your father's primary will in front of the standing judge." He held up his hands, "I know you cannot afford my services. I am doing this gratis for I am doing this not only for you, but for your father and my lovely wife."

He sipped his mug of hot coffee, "Margaret and Granger have abused the legal system to manipulate the law to their favor with no consideration at all for my dear friend Dr. Walter Pino. Your father trusted me to carry out the requests of his will. Right now I have failed him. It's not a good feeling at all." He rubbed his chin, "This gives me a clear conscious as well. I can't promise you anything, but we can give them a run for their money."

Geoffrey had hurriedly left the room to return with legal papers. "These were delivered to my office yesterday through certified mail. From what I can gather they state that I have thirty days to file for divorce or vacate the premises."

Legal papers were handed to the attorney. He unfolded them flat on the table, picked up his mug of coffee and read. Every now and then he mumbled. Finally, he pushed the papers to Geoffrey, "These papers have no legal standing. Mr. Costa is losing his grip or else Granger typed these on Costa's letter head.

Nothing has been filed with the county clerk and nothing has been petitioned within the judicial system as of five o'clock last evening."

Mr. Goldfarb studied Geoffrey's face, "Do you want to divorce your beautiful wife?"

"No, divorce is not even considered."

"Sophia, do you wish to divorce Geoffrey?"

"No."

"These papers are an idle threat. These have no legal ramifications. Granger or Margaret may not be aware of this property being within Rincon County. Geoffrey, those papers are listed as being filed in Sandoval County. This would make their legality invalid. If Margaret and Granger have issued these papers representing property owned within the Sandoval County jurisdiction when this property is indeed in Rincon County—their papers are completely invalid." He handed the papers back to Geoffrey. "Keep these worthless documents for we can use these against them if we need to go to court. These papers, Geoffrey, have no authority."

Geoffrey paced back and forth behind Sophia, "So, what do you recommend we do?"

Mr. Goldfarb lifted his hand, "Hold tight, and don't do anything. Let them believe they have you by the short hairs. I have found cocky people often make mistakes."

He pointed to the papers he had brought, "You need to read through these papers fully. They describe the purpose of representatives, the judiciary, and the validity and termination of a will or trust. If you read the law right here on these pages, you will find where Maragret and Granger acted hurriedly and without due process. A probate will not help you, but understanding the definition of the law will." Mr. Goldfarb patted the legal papers on the table.

He took his empty mug to the sink, "Thank you for the coffee. Right now it is seven-thirty and I have to be at work by eight-thirty." Nodding to the back bedrooms, he said, "Certainly you have beautiful girls to get off to school. Therefore, I shall not keep you. Please make a list of the questions and call me Friday. Friday is two days away. I shall be free after two o'clock in the afternoon. In the morning, I have court cases. Make sure your list of questions is precise. This will make it easier for me to answer them. Thank you, for the coffee." He walked into the hall, "Now, where is my coat?"

114

Geoffrey hurried to the bedroom to retrieve his coat. "Here you go." He held it as Mr. Goldfarb put it on and buttoned the front. "All right, we shall speak Friday afternoon."

As the front door closed, the screaming began. The girls ran into the living room yelling at the top of their lungs as if the ghosts of the banshee had arrived. Geoffrey grabbed Sybil who was racing straight for him. "Girls, please! Mr. Goldfarb just left. He'll think we're skinning you two alive!"

Sophia hugged Donna, "Come on, group hug! We may win this war after all. The first battle they believe is theirs, but we have the warriors and the brains to outsmart them!"

Geoffrey hugged his girls with tears in his eyes, he whispered, "Who would have figured Goldfarb would be at our door this morning like an angel delivering us from the wrath of evil?"

He straightened to clap his hands. "All right, everyone to their battle stations! Time to get dressed, eat food, and get on down the road to celebrate the rest of the day! Go, troops, go!" Geoffrey chased Donna into her room to help her find the pink socks.

The girls were dropped off at school. Geoffrey was on his way to work. Sophia drove to the neighborhood grocery store in downtown Rincon. The sky finally cleared to allow the sun to shine through the air of cold crystals. Flocks of birds circled the small town as Sophia parked. Many of the older population braved the cold to come out for supplies. Sophia needed to get Donna gluten free baked goods to keep her nose bleeds down to a minimum. The pediatrician had explained how the gluten dried out her nose, clogged her tear ducts, and made her throat dry.

When the house was gluten free the nose bleeds were scarce, but lately with all the chaos the gluten had been put on the backburner. Pushing her cart down the baked goods aisle, Sophia searched for the gluten free flour. It was usually between the white flour and the sugar bags.

"Sophia, is that you?" A short plump bouncy blonde called out from the bakery department. Sophia pushed her cart around the aisle. An old man with oxygen was wheezing his way to the meat department. He almost ran into her cart. Sophia peered over other customers' heads to see the nurse who cared for her father waving at her.

"Carol! How wonderful to see you again. What are you doing here?" Sophia embraced her round friend with a big hug.

"Oh, you know, I have to have my sugar fix in the morning or I'm a bitch all day long." Carol pointed to the large box of jelly doughnuts in her cart along with a fifty pound sack of dried dog food. "Sophia, I wanted to tell you how badly I felt after out last conversation at your parent's house when your father died." Carol shook her head allowing her curls to bounce, "I had no right to accuse you of participating in their scheme."

"Carol, the past is in the past. We can leave it alone, all right? Tell me what you are doing now? Who are you caring for way out here?" Sophia patted the bag of dog food, "How's Daisy dog doing? We miss seeing her everyday."

"She's still with me. We go everywhere together, as you know only too well. Right now I'm actually house-sitting. I haven't been able to brave the emotional fury of caring for the terminally ill, at least not yet." Carol smiled weakly, "Also, I have been in contact with your brother. He can be quite evasive when he doesn't want to admit guilt, have you noticed?"

Sophia turned her cart to be even with Carol's, allowing the other customers to reconnoiter around them. "Are you referring to my brother Granger?"

"Absolutely, he has been on my radar since that fateful day in Calavera. He has not taken my calls. He has returned my last three letters. Yesterday he called the foundation to say I'm unqualified and unprofessional. He even tried to get me fired."

"What!"

"Oh, yes, Sophia. He is a real piece of work, but I'm a dog with a juicy bone. I'm not letting go of him. I'm not giving up on my cause. I went to the M.E.'s office and got a copy of the autopsy along with the report on chemical samples in your father's blood." Carol pushed back her bouncy bangs as they pushed their carts to middle of the vegetable department. "Say, Sophia, how about if we go somewhere and talk? Maybe have some brunch? It's too crowded in here to actually talk. Are you free?"

They both burst out laughing. They had taken that quote from her father's favorite British comedy program *Are You Being Served*. Still smiling, Sophia nodded, "Sure, I need to grab some gluten free flour for Donna and some pork chops for dinner. Why don't we meet at the Range down the street?"

"Perfect. They have the best sausage and green chili burritos in the world. I'll go check out my goodies here and hightail it over there to save us a table." Carol pushed her cart to the cash registers.

Sophia stood staring at the different sized bags of gluten. The larger bag was less expensive than the little bags, but the smaller bags had a sugar derivative in them. She finally chose a five pound bag, picked out the pork chops and a head of fresh lettuce. Standing in line gave Sophia time to worry about Carol's relationship with Granger. Anyone who tried to get the best of Granger usually failed miserably.

The Range Café doors were pushed open to a variety of aromas. The most predominant smell was that of roasted chili and garlic. Sophia walked the wood ramp to the front desk where she was met by a young woman holding menus in her hand. Sophia explained she was meeting someone. As she walked past the baked goods of éclairs, cream puffs, freshly made pies and cakes to the central area, Carol waved. Sophia joined her at a table in front of a plate glass window looking out on Main Street.

"You got here quickly." Carol handed her the extra menu. "The hostess just sat me down. Look they have fresh raspberry ice tea unsweetened and the special today is a green chili chicken chimichanga. So, what will it be?"

"Well," Sophia perused the menu, "I think I will have a green chili omelet with two bits of bacon on the side."

"Ah," Carol placed her menu on the table to wave at the waitress.

The food arrived in quick order and after they had eaten a few bites, Sophia asked Carol, "You do know Granger is dangerous, right?"

"I do now." Carol mumbled while she chewed, "He's a scoundrel. There's no denying it. He really can't do anything to me. I'm not family." She took a sip of the tea. "Also, I have my pit bull Daisy with me. She's my great protector. You remember my Daisy dog, right?" Sophia nodded.

Swallowing, Carol said, "The swabs from your father's feeding tube proved to be most interesting."

"What do you mean? We were the only ones authorized to use the feeding tube. Why would there be anything unusual about the tube?" Sophia wiped her mouth.

"If you remember, Sophia, we did show Margaret how to use it. Your father had the tracheal tube. He couldn't swallow or talk. The feeding tube had to be administered with nutrients and proteins every six hours. The feeding tube is a good way to introduce foreign substances into the body, right?" Carol pushed the Spanish rice around her plate.

Sophia nodded. "Yes, but Margaret didn't appear to be interested. Her reaction to the human body was gross. She was repelled from any interaction with the feeding tube, the Foley's catheter, the eye drops, everything."

Carol's round face smiled broadly, "She told us to take the evening, the night, and the morning off, remember? Who was going to help with the feeding tube if not her?"

Sophia's face froze studying Carol's face. Carol shrugged, "Two plus two equals four, right?" Reaching into her large beige purse, Carol retrieved typed medical papers, "Here, take a look at these. These are the results of the chemicals found in the feeding tube at the lab."

"What? Why would they swab the feeding tube? Are they allowed to do that?" Sophia took the papers.

"Remember when the paramedics were in the bedroom?"

She nodded, "Yes."

"Well, they take everything. They remove the tubes, the catheter, the medicines, the sheets, the pillow, everything. The medical examiner examines the body. The paramedics examine the location, collect samples, and paraphernalia relative to the death scene. Their job is to collect proof of fact regarding the death of victim."

Sophia gulped her ice tea, "Victim? Papa was the patient."

"Anyone who dies is a victim of something—whether it's natural causes, poisoning, or disease. These are the facts of life, my girl." Carol patted her hand. "Now, the proof is in the facts. The chemical analysis found powdered traces of Pentobarbital sodium dried in the feeding tube."

"What?" Sophia put her fork down on her plate. "What is Pentobarbital sodium?"

"Ah, the best way to do someone in is to give them high doses of sodium or potassium. This is a medical fact. You can take this information to the bank. Potassium chloride can be bought in most drugstores or grocery stores. Given in high doses it will kill someone very dead and leave behind no trace for it is absorbed into the body within minutes."

Sophia shuddered, "But what about the Pentobarbital sodium?"

"Sodium is poison. Simple table salt will kill you if taken in large enough doses. In some cases in the Middle East, salt was found to be the suicide chemical of choice. Using regular table salt though, would be crazy for you'd need to use a full cup in four ounces of water in order to poison the body." Carol made a face, "It would taste terrible, hard to swallow!"

Sophia sat back, "Where would anyone get Pentobarbital sodium?"

Laughing, Carol stuck her hand in the great beige purse. She pulled out an envelope of developed photos. "Your father's closet has an inventory of deadly goods. Here, take a look at these." Carol pulled a small magnifying glass from her purse and handed it to her.

The photographs were of a closet shelves in her parent's bedroom. The photos revealed boxes and boxes of medications, stacked on the numerous shelves next to her father's hanging clothes. Sophia studied the boxes. The most prevalent box was a white box with dark writing. Clearly legible in large print was the name Nembutal Sodium Capsules 100 mg. on four of the boxes. Under the large print was written pentobarbital sodium USP. "Are these they?"

Carol smiled, "You are a fast learner. When I first started working for your dad, I scooped out the joint. It's important to take photos of what is around the patient. If someone accuses you of stealing or moving things, you have the photos to prove nothing unnecessary was touched or moved. "

"But why did you photograph the stuff in Papa's closet?" Sophia put the photos on the table between them.

"His closet was filled with outdated drugs, syringes, and numerous medical paraphernalia. Most people don't have large quantities of outdated drugs in their closet. Most people don't have syringes, bottles of outdated insulin, morphine, cortisone, or cracked blood pressure machines just laying around for anyone to find." Carol's voice continued, "These items should have been thrown out when your father retired from medicine some twelve or fifteen years ago."

Sophia frowned, "Mom said they cost good money. She believed that the expiration date was exaggerated."

"And you're a professor? You believed what she said?" Carol stared at her. "Was your mother going to administer these drugs or was she going to give them to Granger? Your father certainly was unable to continue his practice after his last stroke. What was your mother going to do with them?"

"Who knows?" Sophia shook her head as she handed the photos back to

Carol. "So they found residue in the feeding tubes, what do you make of it?"

"Very simply, not only did they put the bed down allowing your father to aspirate, but they put pentobarbital sodium in his feeding tube to assist in stopping his heart and his breathing. In an elderly man it wouldn't take much to kill him. A small dose would have influenced his weak body. Perhaps anywhere from two to ten grams of the stuff would have stopped his breathing and his heart without needing to put the bed down at all."

Sophia pushed her plate away from her, "What does it do? How does it affect the body?"

"This is a barbiturate otherwise known as salt or ester. It can also be used in psychiatry as a hypnotic drug. Barbiturates cause mood alterations from excitability to mild sedation. In high enough doses it will prove to be an anesthesia. Barbiturates depress the sensory cortex, which in turn decreases motor activity. In large doses such as grams, for instance, this causes death. The body shuts down."

"Death?"

"Yes, death, but we don't have any idea how long they may have been grinding up the pentobarbital to mix it with the Ringer's lactated saline solution to inject into your father through his feeding tube." Carol took another bite and then said, "Although the dextrose in the Ringer's would have slowed down the decomposition, it didn't show up in his blood work."

Sophia rotated her tea glass in front of her, "How do you know they actually injected this potion into him?"

"Oh, come on! The residue was inside the feeding tube! It didn't get there by itself. Sophia, remember both sodium and potassium are untraceable in the blood stream? But they found it inside the tube!" Carol lowered her voice, "Remember how important it is to first push a clean syringe of Ringer's into the tube to clean it? This was to be sure there weren't problems with the tube and to be sure pathways are clear. Then the nutrients and supplements along with the antibiotics were pushed through the cleared tube into his stomach. Finally, the tube was flushed with another sterile syringe of Ringer's to keep the tube clean. You were doing this all the time, right?"

Sophia nodded, "Yes, but they put his bed down and then they also poisoned him? Their attempt was certainly overkill, don't you think?"

Carol wiped her mouth with the linen napkin, "Yes, sadly. Granger and your mother are efficient in their choice of actions. This is unbelievable to me, really, unbelievable."

"Carol, what did you tell Granger?" Sophia studied Carol's face. "You didn't tell him all of this did you?"

Carol shook her head. Her curly bangs bounced. "I sent him copies of these photos of the closet shelves and the medical boxes in your father's closet prior to and after your father's death. I added the photo with the open Nembutal boxes lying on the shelf that I found the day your father died. Nobody noticed me. The paramedics were busy taking the tubes out of your father and Granger was in the kitchen with your mother." Carol gave a coy smile, "I didn't take anything but photos. Hah!"

"Oh, Carol, you do know you're dancing with the devil if you try to blackmail Granger? You know this right?" Sophia stared out the window. "They could say you messed with the box and you took the pills. Margaret will protect Granger with her life and accuse you of doctoring the scene and making it appear Granger was involved. It would be your word against theirs. Granger won't go for blackmail."

Waving her fork in the air, Carol shook her head, "Sophia, blackmail is such a dirty word! No, I'm not blackmailing him. I'm threatening him. I want to ruin the slimy sucker for I can turn the evidence over to the police. I have the power to prove your father's feeding tube was compromised by someone caring for him the night prior to his death and it wasn't us! I have the power!"

The two women sat and looked at one another. The waitress noticing the pause hurried to the table. "Would you ladies like some dessert?"

Carol glowed as she mixed the whipped cream with mousse in the tiny bowl at her place setting. "You know, Sophia, dark chocolate is better than an orgasm?"

Sophia smiled. Carol licked the spoon to continue, "Granger has nothing on me. I have an excellent reputation with all of my patients and my supervisor. He can't touch me, but I have him." She lifted up her spoon of mousse in a salute.

"Carol, no one is invincible as far as Granger is concerned. Did he return the first couple of letters you sent him? Does he know where you live?" Sophia wiped the table in front of her with her linen napkin.

Carol gave a gutsy laugh, "Hell, no! The return address is to my work place. He can't trace me from there. Everything in the office is confidential. He has no idea where I live. My name isn't in the phone book and as of this month, even if he did find my home address, I am house-sitting for a friend. He's in the dark as to my location." She took another spoonful.

Sophia quietly groaned, "Carol, this isn't good. This is terrible. What exactly is your reason for getting involved with Granger?"

"Simple. People who are evil need to be punished. I can punish him."

"How, what are you going to do to him?"

Carol swirled her concoction in the little bowl, "I have thought long and hard on this, believe me, Sophia. As of right now I'm not sure. I want him to burn in hell or at least never work with patients or people again. He knows I am out here and he knows I have proof. Maybe this will give him sleepless nights."

Sophia looked at her watch, "Carol, I have to go. Please be careful. Oh, by the way there isn't going to be a memorial service. Margaret and Granger cremated Papa and they're dropping his ashes over the Grand Canyon. Mom, put a notice in the paper." Sophia waved at the waitress for the bill.

Carol winced, "They cremated him? I thought he had a burial plot?"

"Yes, he did, does, whatever. It isn't like he has a choice now, is it?"

Carol reached for the bill from the waitress, "I'm paying for this!"

Sophia peeked to see the final amount, "Let me leave the tip? Carol, how is your diabetes?"

Carol pulled two twenties from her wallet and placed them on the bill. "My diabetes is still a problem because of my weight. I need to watch what I eat, but it's so lovely to see you that a celebration was in order." She handed the money and the bill to the waitress, "Please, would you bring back the change?"

The waitress nodded, racing to the cash register in the front of the restaurant. Pulling pink lipstick from her purse, Carol delicately colored her lips. "Sophia, I'm doing water aerobics. The house I'm staying in has an indoor pool. I swim every morning and evening and am determined to bring my weight down. You, just watch in two months I will be as thin as Cher!"

Sophia laughed, "Carol, I believe you. Call me later and let me know what your decision is regarding Granger? Do you still have my phone number?"

Carol picked up the change from the waitress. She pulled a torn prescription paper and I crayon from her purse, "Here write it down because I can't find anything at the house where I am sitting. I'll call you tomorrow." Sophia wrote her phone number in large print on the scrap paper and gave it to Carol.

The two women went their separate ways as they drove out of the parking lot to Main Street. Sophia turned north to Rocoso and Carol turned south in the direction of Albuquerque. Neither one of them noticed the green Mercedes idling on the corner of Calle Blanca and Main Street. The green Mercedes turned onto Main Street to follow Carol's VW bug southward.

13

Rocoso, New Mexico
Wednesday, January, 1988

Sybil ran into the kitchen for a snack. Donna ran into her bedroom, slamming the door behind her. Sophia quietly closed the front door, carrying the girls' backpacks. "Donna, you get back here and tell me what happened today at school? Your behavior is unacceptable!"

Sybil leaned out into the hall with a handful of crackers. "Did she tell you?"

Sophia handed Sybil her backpack, "No, and I do believe you have homework. Isn't there a spelling test tomorrow? You need to ace this test, young woman."

"Mom, I hate spelling." Sybil took her backpack into her room.

Sophia knocked on Donna's bedroom door, "Come on, Donna, we don't keep secrets in this house. Open the door."

The door slowly opened. Sophia pushed it open to find Donna hiding behind it. Donna had a *Big Hunk* candy in her hand. She slowly smiled as her mother stared at the candy. "It's mine. Sybil doesn't get any."

"Where did you get such an obscene candy bar?" Sophia knelt down on the floor to be at eye level with Donna.

"The teacher had a treasure box at school. Anyone who had a clean area was allowed to stick their hand in the treasure box and pull out their prize." Donna smiled, "I got this! No one else got a candy this big. This one's mine." She sucked on the end of the candy.

Sophia fell back to sit on the carpet. "Donna, if you eat that whole candy you won't have any room for dinner."

Donna smiled as she took a lick, "That's all right."

"You won't have any room for one of your favorite pork chops."

Donna took another lick, "That's all right."

"You won't be able to sleep tonight because you're going to be so full of sugar."

"That's all right. Mom, I really want this candy because it's mine."

Sophia put out her hand, "Can I just look at it for a moment. I won't steal it, promise."

Donna glared at Sophia, "Mom, you expect me to believe you?"

Nodding, Sophia put on her serious face, "Yes, I am your mother who never lies to her girls. Now, please let me see it?"

"Oh, all right." Donna quickly shoved the candy in front of Sophia's face. "Here you can see it, but you can't hold it."

Sophia grabbed the white gooey bar and ran with it into the kitchen. Donna screamed behind her. "Mama, Mama, you promised you wouldn't take it!"

Donna reached up to grab the candy out of her mother's hand. Sophia broke it into two pieces. Donna let out a wild high pitched wail, "Noooooooooo!"

"Donna, you cannot have this whole candy before dinner! You can have half now and the other half tomorrow after school." Sophia let Donna have the half she had already licked. "Here, take this, but the rest of this is going in a safe place."

"Mama, you said you didn't lie." Donna pouted as she licked her broken candy.

"I didn't completely lie. You have half of the candy. My first priority is for your health and well being. You may have to get a job if we move. You need to be in your best physical health. Eating this huge candy will rot your teeth and make you lazy. We can't have that, Miss Donna!" Sophia took a clear sandwich bag and dropped the other half of the candy in it.

"Where are you going to put my candy, Mama?"

"Oh, this candy is going in a place where you will never find it!" Sophia smiled at Donna, "Now go and finish your homework. Try not to get everything sticky while you eat that thing."

Donna frowned as she walked to her room. Sophia took the candy in the sandwich bag and placed it in the high cupboard with the Christmas platter and silverware. "There, now we have treasured the treasure!"

Geoffrey walked in the front door. "Well, at last it appears the weather is warming up some. How's everyone doing here? I don't hear any screaming or door slamming."

He dropped his work bag on the couch and walked into the kitchen. At the sink he opened his coffee container to dump out the stale coffee. Washing the mug, he asked Sophia, "So did you get to read any of the legal papers Sam Goldfarb left us?"

Sophia was bending over the kitchen counter peeling carrots onto a paper towel. "No, nothing like yesterday when Granger called and then arrived to accuse me of accusing him of being an adulterer."

"Hah!" Geoffrey shook his head, "The old saying—I will shoot the horse for leaving the barn after I forgot to close the door routine, huh?"

"Absolutely," Sophia smiled at him, "I never had the chance to tell you."

"Well, did he bring the illusive Katina with him? Is she as mysterious as everyone makes out?" Geoffrey grabbed some carrot stems between his fingers to munch on them.

Sophia smacked his hand, "Yes, and she doesn't appear healthy. She has the emaciated look of a prisoner or a drug addict. She's thin, pale, and her blue eyes are flat with no sparkle. Her hair is blonde with streaks of white and has no resiliency. She needs a cheeseburger and some sunshine on her face."

"Oh, dear, the ghost of Granger's desire may just be a ghost after all?" Geoffrey reached for the place mats and put them on the table. "Do you think she's into drugs? It wouldn't surprise me at all what with Granger having the clinic and the availability for drugs."

Sophia gave him a frown, "There is something else of intrigue going on here. Evidently Papa has been cremated. Mom and Granger are going to fly over the Grand Canyon and drop his ashes from a plane. I wasn't invited. Obviously I am too busy to participate." She opened the refrigerator and took out a head of fresh lettuce. She put the lettuce in the colander next to the sink. Looking out the kitchen window, she saw the tumbleweeds blowing across the front yard. The yucca and rabbit bush whipped back and forth desperately clinging to the dried earth around the cottonwood tree planted in front of the tool shed.

"All the orange in the sky out there, makes you wonder about pollution, doesn't it? We seriously need rain, for our whole world will just blow away with your father's ashes." Geoffrey stood behind her, putting his arms around her waist, he said, "The airplane flight to drop your father's ashes over the Grand Canyon is a good thing, my dear. I have heard when a plane door opens while it is in flight high in the air everyone gets sucked out through the door. Whoosh, this may solve all our problems!"

Sophia quickly turned to push him away from her, "Geoffrey, what a horrible thought!"

"Not at all, my dear, we should take our blessings where we can find them. By the way, how do they drop ashes from a plane in flight? Certainly the open door would cause suction and thus would suck everything and everyone out of the plane, right?" Geoffrey danced away from her as she tried to smack him with the dish towel.

Glaring at him, Sophia said, "I have no idea, but you have a problem daughter who needs your help."

Geoffrey watched Sophia wash the lettuce in the sink, "Just a minute, why did they cremate the old man? What about the famous plot he bought? He was going to be buried in the military cemetery in Santa Fe, right?"

Sophia washed the lettuce under the sink faucet, "No, he decided to not be one of thousands, remember?"

Geoffrey walked to the fridge to grab a bottle of his Near Beer. "Ah, yes. Your Dad changed his mind and wanted to be buried in the Negara cemetery. Didn't he pay some local artist to sculpt an angel for him, an outstretched angel with wings to hover over his grave site while he rests in eternal sleep? Wasn't that the plan? Margaret certainly was livid when she found out he paid for it." He opened the drawer to get the beer bottle opener. "Who is going to get the plot in Negara?" Geoffrey popped off the metal beer bottle lid to throw it into the garbage can in the corner of the kitchen.

"Oh, Geoffrey, how should I know?" Sophia tore lettuce into the bowl with the chopped carrots.

"All right, which one of my daughters needs help? Which one would that be? Ah, don't tell me. Is it Donna?"

"No, It's Sybil. She refuses to study her spelling and tomorrow is the spelling test! She barely passed the last test. Her interest is in art not spelling, but she has to pass this test."

Sophia unwrapped each of the pork chops to wash in the sink. "Can you help her now before dinner?" She nodded her head toward the hall.

Geoffrey took another swig of his beer. He placed the bottle at his place at the head of the table to call out, "Lady Sybil, where are you?"

Donna sat at the table sucking on her candy. She had an empty plate in front of her, which she chose to ignore. Sybil and Geoffrey were quietly eating their pork chops and salad. Sophia studied her family. Donna was definitely contrary. May this be a trait she would soon out grow of to become more tolerant of those around her. Sybil was fastidious in everything she did. She read with passion, she drew with passion, and she refused to study her spelling with passion. Geoffrey was home. This made the world work and somehow they would survive as long as they were all together.

Sybil glanced at her mother, "You aren't eating? Is the food bad?"

Sophia laughed, "No, I'm just sitting here admiring my beautiful family. It is lovely having all of us together." She stabbed a piece of lettuce.

Donna frowned, "Mom, can I have a pork chop, please?" She put her sloppy candy on the edge of her plate. Geoffrey dumped a pork chop on her plate. "Eat, my treasure hunting princess, for you need your strength to get through the treasure chest candy!" He burst out laughing. Donna gave her father a dirty look, "Dad, that's not funny. Don't laugh at me!"

After dinner, Donna stood on the wooden stool in front of the kitchen sink. She was wrapped in her mother's flowered apron. Sophia and Donna worked together washing dishes.

Sybil was following Geoffrey in and out of the front door. They were bringing in his possessions from the rental apartment. Each time Geoffrey and Sybil brought in a suitcase or a box, she was asked to spell a word out loud. If she couldn't spell the word, she had to stay outside until she could spell it correctly.

"Dad, it's cold out here!"

"Sybil, how do you spell 'submarine'?"

"Dad, I don't know. I don't want to do this anymore!" Sybil's voice was firm.

"Well, if you want to spend the night outside, I guess I better get you a blanket."

Donna asked, "Is that how you learned to spell, Mom?"

Sophia shook her head, "No, I loved spelling. Words fascinate me. Words are beautiful in the way they are put together with sounds and letters. Each word is rounded and curved. I love words for each one has its own meaning and sound."

Donna yelled at Sybil, "Sound out the word!"

Sybil screamed, "You little runt, what do you know?"

Geoffrey stood in the doorway. "Sybil, think about the word. Submarine is made up of three syllables, right? Can you sound out each part of the word?"

Sybil put her hands on her hips, "Yeah, and I'm going to sea, right? This is a word I really need in my vocabulary, right?"

Geoffrey called into the house, "Sophia, Sybil wants to build a submarine and go to sea! This way we won't have to pay for her college!"

Sophia burst out laughing, "Geoffrey, let her in the house!"

"Dad, all right, you made your point." Sybil took a stick and wrote 'submarine' in the dirt. "There are you happy?"

Geoffrey picked her up and gave her a big hug. "You knew all along! Now, let's have a spelling test! Onward!"

Sybil sat at the kitchen table writing in cursive each word Geoffrey dictated to her. She spoke under her breath, "Dad, I want to be a marine biologist. Do they have to go in submarines?"

Geoffrey paused between spelling words, "Sybil, you can do whatever you want to do and be whoever you choose. If you want to go in a submarine you can. At least now you know how to spell it, right?" Sybil bared her teeth at him.

Sophia and Donna tried to ignore the emotional tension in the room. Finally, the test was completed. Geoffrey took the paper from Sybil. "Wow! You have each one of these words dead on correct. What's the problem with you doing this in class?"

"I don't like spelling. This is a fact pure and simple. I love to read, but I don't want to write or spell, or be tested all the time. I don't like tests or people who give them!" Sybil grabbed her spelling test out of Geoffrey's hand. She ran to her room and slammed the door.

"Ah, life is back to normal around here. The door slamming has resumed and the world is well." Geoffrey walked over to Donna. "It's time for bed, my treasure hunting princess." He lifted her off the stool. "Come let's get you out of these servant's clothes and into bed clothes. Tonight you get to pick the book we read." The two of them disappeared down the hall.

Sophia wiped down the counter. As she wrung out the dish cloth, the phone rang. "Now who could be calling at this hour?" She hurried to the wall phone, "Hello?"

"Is this Sophia Vinder?" A man's deep voice asked apprehensively.

"Yes, how can I help you?" Sophia sighed, praying this wasn't a phone survey.

"Yes, Ma'am, this is A.J. Salazar with the Rincon County Sheriff's office. We found your phone number beside one Carol Grover. Ma'am, I need you to come down to the sheriff's office in Rincon as soon as possible." His voice had a tone of authority.

Sophia leaned against the counter, "What? What do you mean beside Carol Grover? What has happened to Carol? What's the problem?" She heard her voice crack at the end.

"Ma'am, it's best not to answer any questions over the phone. Please would you come down to the Rincon Sheriff's office? We're on the corner of Main Street and Calle Cordova."

Sophia swallowed hard, "Just a minute, can you hold the phone a minute?"

"Yes, Ma'am, if this will expedite matters, I will hold." He didn't sound terribly patient, but Sophia put the phone down on the counter anyway. She hurried to Donna's room, "Geoffrey, please, can I speak to you for a quick minute out here?"

Frowning, Geoffrey placed the open book down on Donna's bed next to her and followed her into the hall, "What is it? It's not Granger again?"

"I hope not. The sheriff is on the phone and he wants me to come down to his office right now! He's down in Rincon. He said he found my phone number beside Carol Grover." Sophia hugged him, to whisper, "Do you think she's been attacked by Granger?"

He hugged her back, "Doesn't sound good, not at all. Do you want me to go with you?"

"What about the girls? We can't just leave them here alone not with all the evil floating around in the world." Sophia stood back to peer at Donna reading the book by herself in her bed.

Geoffrey kissed her cheek, "No, I suppose I better stay put. You go, but tell Sybil you are going or she may think I locked you outside." Geoffrey tried to smile, but he frowned instead.

Sophia opened Sybil's door, "Sybil, I have to go out on some business would you keep an eye on your father and sister while I am gone?"

Sybil was in her flannel nightgown. She had her dragon book resting on her bent knees in front of her. "Sure, bye, Mom."

Sophia warmed the van as she pulled her wool cap over her head. The night was dark with no moon. The shadow of the mesas gave an ominous glow. The wind blew gusts of dirt across the front of yard. The van jerked with a groan as she backed out of the driveway.

The road to Rincon is two-lane, light gray concrete. On either side of the Calle Rocoso rise small banks of eroded clay, finely crumbling down to the main interstate of white lights moving at high speeds. Sophia's van lights illuminated the broomstraw waving between the short juniper trees and dark pines. Occasionally deep gullies appeared, filled with small stones holding impenetrable branches and twigs mixed with tumbleweeds.

She crossed the bridge spanning the six lane interstate below her. The road began its descent toward town, as the hills surrounding spread wide to envelope the small town of Rincon. Main Street was quiet with no other cars. There were six signal lights in Rincon, Sophia knew Calle Cordova was at the third. The Sheriff's department was on the right next to the Family Dollar Discount Store. All the signal lights on Main Street were green.

The family van sat alone in the parking lot. Sophia pulled her purse strap over her head, grabbed the keys, and after taking a deep breath walked to open the office doors of glass. There was no one at the front counter inside. She could hear phones ringing in the back, but no one was there to appreciate her presence. There were wooden chairs lined up against the inside wall. The linoleum floor was well polished. The only interior door was to the left of the front counter. It had a narrow view into the waiting room from a window placed at eye level. Sophia decided to knock on the door.

She put her van keys in her pants pocket to knock on the door. There was no response. Not wanting to be arrested for yelling in the sheriff's office, she quietly tried the door handle. It moved. The door opened. She craned her head around it to see if anyone was there. The door was jerked out of her hand, flinging her forward. "Opps, we have a curious perpetrator entering the premises, Sir." A nearsighted woman with glasses in a brown uniform stepped back allowing Sophia to regain her balance.

"No," Sophia blurted as she balanced herself, "I was called down here and found no one at the front counter."

A formative man with graying hair at the temples promptly stood. His office was partitioned by a glass wall at the far side of the large room. The room was filled with gun metal desks of gray. Quickly, he strode forward to greet her. "Are you Mrs. Sophia Vinder?"

"Indeed, I am, Sir." Sophia felt her mouth go dry.

"Please follow me, if you will?" He stood erect as if he was retired military and indulged in social etiquette and expected respect.

The woman stepped back, allowing her to enter the room easily. Sophia followed the Sheriff down the hall. The young woman picked up her stride to fall into step beside Sophia. "Do you want me to come with you?"

Sheriff A.J. Salazar stopped abruptly at a heavy metal door. "Trisha, you need to stay on duty at the front counter, please." He nodded to the young woman who retreated. Punching in a code, the door of massive size popped open, "Ma'am, I need you to come with me. I'm going to be driving you to the scene of the crime. Is there anything that you need to bring with you from your vehicle?"

Sophia patted her purse, "No, Sir, but couldn't I follow you?"

"No, Ma'am, we will return here to do the follow up." He pulled the door to him, and nodded for Sophia to go through it to the outside. Wind blasted dirt into their faces. He wiped his face with his gloved hand, "Ma'am, please go first. My name is A.J. Salazar. I'm the detective on this case. Please follow me."

The door to the back passenger's side was opened for her. The front seat was filled with a myriad of debris including paper forms in clipboards, a radio in the dash, and what appeared to be a megaphone. The backseat was clear of debris, but smelled of stale vomit and urine. Sophia tried not to touch the seat. She crouched more than sat, clutching her purse in front of her. The Sheriff drove silently, listening to the drone of the radio. They drove south through Rincon, turning left onto a dirt road. There was no street sign on the corner. The cruiser bumped down the road of pot holes only to stop at two adobe structures that flanked a wrought iron gate. The gate was closed. Sophia was about to offer to open the gate for the Sheriff when she noticed there were no door handles in the back seat.

The driveway to the large house was neatly manicured. All leaves and dead tree branches had been removed. The front drive was raked in a pattern and the front light illuminated the wooden door. She followed detective Sheriff A.J. Salazar down a path to a side door. He lifted his hand to pull a key from the top of the doorframe. The side door revealed a room of modest proportions. The kitchen was small and cramped. The main bedroom had only one double bed, a dressing table and a tall wardrobe that was freestanding. Sophia noticed Carol's large purse hanging from the wardrobe's corner. They continued to walk through to the living room and dining room. The rooms felt cramped by the furniture.

The house reminded Sophia of the new development houses for sale. The show houses had overstocked furniture in every room inviting the buyer to buy one and get one free. As if the king sized bed would fit into the twin bed sized room.

This house was sterile everything was neatly kept. Everything was in its place. The only thing out of place was a wet towel thrown on the floor at the far side of the living room. Sophia sniffed. She could smell wet dog and chlorine more strongly as she followed the detective Sheriff around the wet towel and into another room. He slid open a thin white partitioned wall to reveal a moderate swimming pool encased in a warm room with large windows. Sophia was surprised to see four other people at the far left side of the pool with cameras, measuring tapes, and note pads.

"This way, Ma'am, would you please be careful where you step." The Sheriff pointed to the tile of red, polished to gleam with the overhead lighting. "Please keep to the right of the yellow tape." He pointed to warning tape stuck to the sliding doors where they entered to the people at the other end of the pool. Sophia hesitantly moved forward until she came to a chair of yellow plastic. Suddenly she sat down, "Sir, I'm afraid I can't go any further until you tell me what this is about. Please, talk to me? Carol Grover was my dear friend and I have no idea what I'm doing in this strange house."

The detective turned to answer her, "Ma'am, please it is important for you to follow me. We need to go to the sight."

"No, don't think so. You're going to have to arrest me first. I don't want to go over there. I don't know why, but my gut tells me something horrible happened over there. I really don't want to see who or what is going on until I know why I am here." Sophia's eyes glistened, "If you would at least tell me what's going on I would appreciate it!"

Sighing, he knelt down beside her chair, "Ma'am, everything will be explained to you if you would just follow me."

"Nope, I'm not moving until you speak to me about all of this." Sophia waved her arm.

Someone called out to the Sheriff. He stood, staring down at her trying to read her emotions. "Stay here, I have to go and talk to my associates." He hurried to be with the others. Sophia wanted to run, but she had no idea where she was in relation to her home. She would have to find the Sheriff's office to retrieve her van unless she found a phone and could call Geoffrey. She stared into the water of the pool.

"Excuse me, Dr. Sophia Vinder, right?" A man short in stature with a receding hairline waddled his way to Sophia. "Yes, I do believe I am correct in my assessment." He stuck out his hand dressed in purple latex. Noticing his hand, he said, "Oh, my goodness, where are my manners?" He pulled off the glove, wadded it into a ball and stuffed it into his brown suit pocket and tried again. Sophia took his hand for a moist handshake.

"You must excuse the Sheriff. He's a knock down the perpetrator, slap on the handcuffs, and into the cruiser." The man pushed his heavy glasses up the bridge of his nose. He sat on the chair next to her. "My name is Dr. Brimley. I am the pathologist for Rincon County. We were called this evening by the housekeeping woman. She happened to come by to retrieve some frozen strawberries your friend Carol Grover had for her. Upon entering the house, the housekeeper searched for Carol Grover."

Dr. Brimley pointed to the area of focus, "The housekeeper found her there on the tiles. Carol Grover was not moving, but was breathing and alive."

Dr. Brimley turned back to Sophia, "The housekeeper is a fast thinker. She called 911 and had the ambulance here within minutes. Unfortunately, the housekeeper had already left the premises by the time the ambulance arrived. Evidently, she had family who needed attending to and could not wait." He shook his head, "They have taken Carol to the emergency room where she is now. She's in surgery and listed in critical condition. We don't know if she will make it or not at this point."

Sophia held her breath while he was speaking. He put his hand on her shoulder, "You might want to exhale here at anytime or we will be taking you in as well."

She asked, "Do you know what happened to her?"

"You were brought here with high hopes. Do you know the name of her housekeeper and do you know who else she might have met with here tonight? All the doors around the pool are locked." He waved his hands around the room, "The intruder must have been invited in through the front door. That is why you were brought in by the rear door." He pulled the latex glove off of his left hand. "Ms. Grover must have known her attacker. The housekeeper said Carol always kept the house locked for she was fearful of someone who might want to hurt her. There is evidence of all the windows locked with wooden dowels in place to be sure they couldn't be opened." He sighed, "Ms. Grover was conscientious about locking the house so it is bizarre to find her attacked. The housekeeper had a key."

Sophia shook her head, "To be honest, Sir, I have never been in this house before in my life! I don't have any idea who the housekeeper is or why she would even have a housekeeper. Carol never told me the name of the people who owned the house or where the house is or was." Sophia's eyes grew wide as she tried to manage her emotions, "I feel completely foreign to all of this and want to know why I was called. Do you know why?"

He tilted his head to study her over his thick glasses, "Yes. A torn paper with your phone number on it was discovered near her body. There were no other clues around her." He pointed to the area, "You can appreciate how clean this place is with the tile polished to perfection. There are no other props, no other papers, nothing else here for clues aside from the one piece of paper revealing your phone number."

His intimidation and the oppression of the situation brought tears to roll down her cheeks landing on her hands. Her leather purse was clutched to her chest. "Dr. Brimley, was there anything else on the paper?"

The tired doctor shook his head, "Sorry, I can't really tell you anything at this point. Everything collected is a being kept quiet until further investigations can be made. It is early yet. Surely you understand?"

Sophia noticed Dr. Brimley's cumbersome glasses were equally as thick as Geoffrey's. Dr. Brimley's lenses were smeared with fingerprints. She observed his unsophisticated foot wear of flip flops. "Sir, I would really like to leave now. My head hurts and I don't feel very well."

Standing, he waved to the group of men at the far side of the room, "Let me get one of the deputies to take you back to the Sheriff's office. Someone there will need to get a statement from you. Where were you this evening between five and seven o'clock?" His voice was calm, professional.

Sophia swallowed her agitation, "I was at home with my family. We had pork chops, salad, and Donna and I washed the dishes." She was going to continue, but he interrupted her by calling out, "Carl, can you take this woman back to the station to get her alibi for tonight?"

Carl hurried to them. He was a man who worked out with weights. His muscles bulged through the sleeves of his jacket. As he walked to them, he frowned, revealing dimples on each side of his face. His effeminate walk was decidedly exaggerated. Sophia followed him outside as he opened the backdoor to his cruiser. Once she was crouched on the seat, he slammed the door firmly. They drove back silently to the office. The odor of his cologne infiltrated the whole of the car's cab.

Following him through the backdoor of the Sheriff's office, Sophia breathed in the fresh air. Carl pointed to a metal chair with gray padding on the seat and back. "Have a seat." Sophia perched, still hugging her leather purse to her chest.

He pulled out a clean piece of white paper from a bottom drawer in his desk and rolled it into an ancient typewriter. "What is your name?" Sophia spelled it for him.

"What is your address?" Sophia told him as he clicked the typewriter keys.

"Where were you this evening between five and seven o'clock?" Dramatically Sophia described her evening events at home.

"What was your relationship to the victim?"

Sophia frowned, deciding to wait until he gave her eye contact. He continued to ask as he stared straight at the paper. "Ma'am, what was your relationship to the victim?"

Cautiously, she began to walk to the door. Carl was in front of her before she had taken two steps. His voice tersely stated, "Ma'am, you are not permitted to leave until you have answered all of the questions."

Defiantly Sophia snapped at him, "I will not be goaded by your interrogation. Let me contact my lawyer."

Carl lifted his shoulders in exasperation only to drop them with a sigh, "Ma'am, I am not arresting you. You are a person of interest. You will be allowed to leave as soon as you have answered all the questions."

Sophia was now indignant, "No, I don't want to answer any more questions. I have no idea what happened, when it happened, or why I am here other than you find me as a person of interest of which I am not. I have children at home who need me more than you do. I am leaving now unless you arrest me."

She stepped around him. Mustering courage, she walked out the side door, through the front room, and into the parking lot. She allowed herself to breathe once the van's doors were locked. Sophia pounded on the steering wheel, "Damn, how dare they accuse me of being a person of interest!"

Main Street was illuminated with only a few street lights. The green signal lights beckoned her through town, up the hill, and across the bridge to home. Sophia studied the silhouette of her house. The light was on by the front door. Geoffrey was waiting for her at the kitchen window.

"Sophia, what happened? Where have you been?" His outstretched arms enveloped her. She fell into them with tears flowing down her cheeks. "Oh, Geoffrey, someone tried to kill Carol and I have a good idea who it was!"

"Come, sit down, and tell all while I fix you a mug of tea with brandy." He placed her in a kitchen chair. Sophia told him about her lunch with Carol and what Dr. Brimley had told her. Geoffrey drank the mug of tea, listening with his eyes wide open.

"Why did they take you to the house?" Geoffrey swallowed the last of the tea. "I can understand wanting to speak with you at the Sheriff's station, or whatever they call it, but why take you to the house?"

She smiled at him, "Do you think I could have a mug of tea now?"

"What? Oh, did I drink it all? Sure, here let me put the kettle on the stove." Geoffrey filled the aluminum kettle and placed it over the glowing gas burner. "Sophia, what did you notice about the house? There must have been something that caught your eye. You are a compulsive addictive neat person, what looked out of place?"

"Am I supposed to take that as a compliment?" She frowned at him with her empty tea mug in hand.

The mug was put beside the stove. "Yes, I meant it as a high compliment. Tell me about the house? What was it like in there?"

"Well, the house itself was too small for the amount of furniture in it. The bedroom had a queen sized bed and was only large enough for a single bed. The house was a contradiction to Carol. She's a large lady and she needs a lot of space. The house was not large and was overwhelmed with bulky items. The furniture, the lamps, the pictures on the wall—everything in the house felt impersonal as if it was bought for show not for comfort."

Geoffrey handed her the mug filled with steaming hot water and a tea bag. He reached to the high cupboard and pulled out a small bottle of brandy. "Here, put this in with your spearmint tea."

Sophia poured a drop of brandy into her tea. She continued, "The kitchen was off somehow. Everything was put away. The large box of jelly doughnuts Carol bought this morning was not out on the counter or anywhere to be seen."

"Maybe it was in the fridge?" Geoffrey took down a mug to make himself some tea.

"No, that's just it. Carol was the one who told me to never put doughnuts or cakes in the refrigerator. The Freon in the cold air dries out pastry. She told me twice at Mom's to leave the doughnuts out on the counter for the moisture in the air and the room temperature would keep them fluffy and more digestible." She took a sip of her tea.

"Won't they go moldy faster?"

"No, not if they are eaten within a day or two. They weren't on the counter at that house this evening. Maybe she gave some of them away. Although," Sophia held her mug to her lips and blew on the hot water, "Dr. Brimley told me the housekeeper came by to pick up some frozen strawberries. Geoffrey, people with diabetes wouldn't buy strawberries. Papa couldn't eat strawberries because of the fructose. Fructose throws a diabetic's insulin level out of whack. The whole setting was off, very strange."

"Did Carol tell you she liked strawberries?"

"No, the subject of fruit never was a discussion with us. Although there was something else that caught my attention. Oh, yes, I know, it was in the bedroom."

Geoffrey pointed to the brandy bottle and Sophia shoved it over to him. "The bedroom was barren of clothes and items that would be lying around if someone was living there. Carol is flamboyant with colorful clothes, scarves, boxes and boxes of costume jewelry, and shoes, oh, my goodness, Carol loves shoes. They would have been all about for she was house-sitting. The wardrobe would have the owner's clothes in it, right?"

"Wardrobe, isn't a wardrobe rather old fashioned? What happened to the closet?"

"Geoffrey, that's it, you got it!" Sophia stood next to their tall refrigerator with the freezer on the bottom. "The wardrobe is about the height of this fridge. Carol is around five feet two inches tall. How could she put her heavy purse with small straps way up here?" Sophia demonstrated using a plastic bag.

Sophia squatted down and tried to lift her arms over the edge of the refrigerator. Geoffrey came to her aid. "Geoffrey, you can't help. You're about six two, right? This is easy for you, but Carol is down here. How could she lift her purse, with twenty pounds of stuff in it, to hook over the edge of the tall wardrobe?"

"Someone who is as tall if not taller than I am must have helped her." Geoffrey shrugged, going back to his chair and his mug of tea and brandy.

"Right, someone put her purse up there and maybe someone put her purse there after they took something out or put something in it?"

"Yes, but why clean the room? Where are her clothes, her boxes of jewelry, her shoes, and why would anyone take all her stuff?" Geoffrey sipped his tea.

"All of the removal would take time, planning, and by someone who is familiar with her character, right?" Sophia sat down next to him.

"Right, who knew her as well as you do? Who knew about her style and her habits?" Geoffrey handed Sophia a napkin.

Sophia shook her head, "My mother knew Carol well. After all Carol took care of Papa for almost two years and was there everyday. Margaret is such a puritan not wearing any jewelry, no makeup, being demure and helpless. Carol is resilient. I am sure much of what Carol did was conspicuous to my mother and probably Granger!"

Geoffrey shook his head, "Granger would notice. He absorbs everything. He was incessant with interest in what Carol did. He watched her take her insulin injections, and studied her watch, everything. At one of our family dinners I remember his smugness in telling about Carol purchasing a watch from Avon. Carol told some folks she inherited it from her great aunt. Granger was disgusted at Carol's feral shopping with Avon."

Sophia laughed, "I believed her! She told me a long drawn out story about her aunt and her famous watch!" She sighed, "Wait, you said he knew about her insulin injections? How would he know about those?"

Geoffrey pointed to their refrigerator, "The inside door of the refrigerator at your mother's had two bottles of insulin. Carol had color coded each one. The one with the pink sticker was hers and the one with the blue sticker was your Dad's. She had to take her insulin an hour after each meal, whereas your Dad only needed his in the morning since you were tube feeding him." Geoffrey went to their fridge and opened the door. "She kept them inside on the door, under where one would keep the butter dish." Geoffrey closed the refrigerator door.

Sophia rotated her mug of tea in front of her, "So, Carol sent him the photos of Papa's closet with all the bottles of meds and insulin with the hopes of scaring him. What if she did scare him?" Sophia blanched at the thought.

"You know, dearest, you may not be able to protect him anymore." Geoffrey stood behind her, rubbing her neck and shoulders. "It may be time to let the devil out of the genie bottle. You can't keep turning a blind eye to what he does, even if he is your brother."

Sophia jumped, pushing his hands away from her, "I know Granger, Geoffrey. I don't believe he would try to kill someone who is perfectly healthy!"

"Oh, he only kills people who deserve to die or are too sick to live? Is that what you're saying?" Geoffrey picked up the tea mugs and put them in the kitchen sink.

Sophia leaned on the far counter. "No, that's not what I meant. Anyone can kill if they have enough reason, but Carol and Granger? What an odd duo? How would he get into the house? How would he hurt her?"

Geoffrey frowned, "Sophia, you explained Carol's obsession with the photos. Do you believe she was trying to goad Granger into something? Granger isn't someone who is swayed by blackmail, as you clearly stated." He studied his list, "So what did happen to Carol? Do you know? Did anyone there tell you if she was drowned, shot, stabbed, or poked with insulin? Did they tell you what happened to her?"

She shook her head, "You know for some reason I felt I could see her lying there on the cold tile trying to breathe. Geoffrey, I was terrified for her. The thought of what had happened never crossed my mind!" Sophia pushed her bangs from her face. "I was totally stupid not to have asked the sheriff or Dr. Brimley!"

Geoffrey grabbed a notepad from the counter by the phone. He sat at the head of the table and took his black pen from his shirt pocket. "We're going to make a list. You're a research writer and have seen more than enough bones and bodies in the jungle, deserts, and basements of higher learning to know how to begin a research study. Let's begin with where the house is located?"

Sophia sighed and rubbed her eyes. "The house is an old adobe house on the southeast side of Rincon. It has two adobe structures holding a wrought iron gate. It was latched when we drove up and didn't appear to have a lock or chain. "

"Good, now who does the house belong to, did they tell you? Did Carol tell you?" Geoffrey hurriedly wrote his questions down and Sophia's answers.

"I have no idea. No one told me and I never thought to ask. I feel so stupid right now!" Sophia stared at the ceiling as if the answers were above her.

"Hey, no problem, we're trying to get through this with logic not emotion. Did the house appear to be owned by a single owner, a married couple, a guy or a girl? What was the mood of the home?" Geoffrey held his pen in midair waiting for her answer.

Sophia outlined a wet mark on the table with her finger, "The front room had dark adobe walls. It was stark. There were large Mexican pots gorged with dried pampas grass. There was a green Buddha in an adobe crèche by the front door. The statue was about yea high." She stood placing her hand at her waist.

"A waterfall the size of our blender was next to it. A frayed rug-runner led into the living room. The living room had chairs made out of wood. The couch was a wooden frame. None of the furniture appeared comfortable. Maybe they were Danish or Scandinavian. They were sculpted of white branches."

She closed her eyes and continued, "The hard backs of the furniture were of barren wood. The seats had foam cushions an inch deep, not enough to give much comfort and they were covered with Southwestern designs. The white walls bestowed sterility. There were no personal photos or paintings. The framed photographs of outdoor scenes appeared to be from magazines. There were no photographs or paintings of a personal nature on either the side tables or on the fireplace hearth. A manufactured clock of black plastic, probably from a department store, was set on the fireplace hearth. It was a strange place for anything plastic. Certainly plastic would melt if there was a fire in the fireplace."

Geoffrey dutifully wrote every word she said. Sophia paused to let him catch up to her. Geoffrey rubbed his fingers with his left hand, "Well, you are observant that's for sure. I would never have caught the plastic clock idea."

"Oh," Sophia opened her eyes, "The smell was of wet dog. Geoffrey!" She jumped from the chair, "Geoffrey, what about Carol's dog Daisy? The dog wasn't there! There was no sign of Daisy. I didn't see a dog dish. Where was her leash? Carol dressed Daisy in small outfits or whatever they call dog clothes and they weren't there either."

Sophia nervously walked around the kitchen table. "We need to call someone about Daisy dog. She could be out there lost in the cold."

Geoffrey tapped the pen against his left hand, "No, Sophia, we have to leave it alone. The sheriff may have picked up the dog. They won't reveal anything anyway. It's very late right now. Let's finish our list and call someone in the morning."

Sophia leaned her hands on the table, "Oh, dear, the dog could roam miles by morning. You're right, though, I can't see wandering around in the dark calling a dog who doesn't really know us. She could be frightened and alone, lost and hungry."

Smiling, Geoffrey said, "The dog might be at the Sheriff's department, fed, happy, and asleep. Don't blow this out of proportion. Daisy will have to wait until morning."

"All right, no hysteria." She sat back down. "What more do you need for our list?"

"The house evidently had issues for you. Define each one and we'll write them down for later thought."

Sophia closed her eyes, "The hall floor was unfinished. The flagstone or tile floors were polished. The rough bricks in the hall were incomplete. In the center of the dark hall bricks were missing. Suddenly the floor became sand. It was if it had been leveled, but no bricks were in place. When you're walking along not watching where you're going, all of a sudden your step drops onto sand. This is disconcerting for you feel like you're going to fall."

She took her mug out of the sink to put it back on the kitchen table. "Push me the brandy, would you?" Geoffrey removed the lid. "Here you go. This should help stimulate the gray cells."

Yawning, she poured the brandy straight into the mug, "The bedroom was sterile and cold. The whole house had an impersonal air to it. The bedroom was no exception. There were no photos on the walls, no doilies on the bureau, no boxes of personal items lying around and the bed was flat, the pillows untouched with dust on the ruffle over them. It felt like a room in an old hotel where no one ever visited, as if it were only a temporary shelter from a storm."

"Maybe the house belonged to a hermit?"

"No, a hermit is too busy in his head. The house would have been a mess." Sophia grinned at him.

"Touché, Sweetheart. Maybe the owners put everything in storage especially if they were going to be away for a long time and didn't want anyone to steal their personal items." Geoffrey tapped the pen on the legal pad.

"Hey, that's a thought, but where's Carol's stuff?" Sophia shrugged her shoulders, "The room must have been cleaned, maybe by the housekeeper?"

"You mean the woman who found Carol? Now, wait a minute, why would the owners maintain a housekeeper if they were letting the house to a single person?"

"Why indeed? But then we are projecting now. There was only one messy item in the house," Sophia stretched her arms out over the table, "The towel on the floor in the living room was thrown haphazardly in the doorway by the hall."

"But I thought she was found by the pool? Why would her towel be in the living room if she was swimming in a different room?" Geoffrey pushed the notepad to Sophia, "Here draw me a picture of the room with the pool."

Sophia took the pen. She drew the house from an omnipotent view. She added the pool under her main house drawing, putting an 'x' where the body was supposedly found. "You know the housekeeper leaves a question for sure, Geoffrey. Why was she there and why would they have her coming regularly if Carol didn't work?"

Geoffrey smiled at Sophia, "Yes, did Carol mention a housekeeper? A housekeeper in my mind would make Carol crazy for she is a take charge type of person. She always cleaned your father's area. She kept your parent's bedroom in ship shape. A housekeeper and Carol are a conflict of interest." He shook his head, "The two conflicting points are the housekeeper and the dog."

He drew a line on the paper with a dip in it, "Do you think someone could have removed the bricks in the hallway? What if they had blood or evidence on them and were removed along with Carol's possessions?"

"Conflicting points bring us back to the question of how she was hurt or if she was attacked, poisoned, or someone attempted to drown her." Sophia opened the cupboard behind her. She put a box of crackers on the table. "Hey, I'm hungry."

Geoffrey frowned, "It is getting late almost midnight now. How do you think she was hurt? You said the doctor told you she was in surgery, which means she is repairable."

The box of crackers was returned to the cupboard. "You're right. It's too late to eat." Placing her index finger on the 'x' in her illustration, Sophia added, "This is where Carol was found by the housekeeper who called 911 and possibly saved her life. If the housekeeper saved her life then she hadn't wanted to kill her, right?

He sighed, "Unless, the housekeeper believed her to be already dead or in the process of being dead. What did the housekeeper tell the sheriff?"

"Dr. Brimley told me the housekeeper had already left when the ambulance and the sheriff arrived. Evidently she told dispatch, or someone, she had to go home to her family. No one has met her or knows about her." Sophia pushed the legal pad back to Geoffrey. "My head hurts. I think we should go to bed and call Samuel Goldfarb in the morning."

Geoffrey shoved the legal pad back to Sophia, "Where was the towel found? Why should we call dear Mr. Goldfarb?"

Sophia put a circle where she had seen the towel on the living room floor. "Because they believe I am a person of interest."

Geoffrey leaned over to study the drawing. He smiled at her, "Now, I know why they took you there. They wanted to see your reaction to the crime scene. Ten to one they wanted to see if you were eager to go to the scene or if you were repelled by it."

"You mean the old cliché about the murderer always returns to the scene of the crime, right?" Sophia put the ballpoint pen down. She rubbed her tired eyes.

"Yes, and you were frightened. You didn't want to have anything to do with the place. That was probably your best defense." Geoffrey put his arm around her shoulders as they quietly walked down the hall.

Sophia whispered to him, "I still want to call Goldfarb. He's our personal angel." Geoffrey smiled as he reached back to turn off the light in the kitchen. "You didn't do it. You have witnesses."

14

Rocoso, New Mexico
Thursday, January, 1988

The phone woke them early in the morning. Geoffrey sprinted to the kitchen to grab it before it woke the girls. "Hello?"

A woman's voice inquired, "Hello is this Mr. Geoffrey Vinder of Rocoso?"

Sybil walked past him to the refrigerator.

Geoffrey watched his dutiful daughter of nine years put a carton of milk on the table. "Sir, are you still there?"

"Yes, yes, what is it you want and who are you?" Geoffrey felt redundant.

"This is the Santana Daily Journal and I am Clarisse Montoya. I would like to ask you some questions regarding the attack on Carol Grover." Her voice held the tone of grand inquisitor.

Geoffrey proudly observed Sybil take out four bowls, four spoons, and three boxes of cereal and place them on the table. "Ms. Montoya, I have no idea as to what you are inquiring. Would you to please explain to me how Carol Granger was attacked?"

Sybil froze with her hand holding four napkins. She stared at her father. The female voice continued in Geoffrey's ear, "Sir, are you familiar with the brutal attack on Carol Grover?"

Geoffrey responded, "No, I haven't a clue as to what you are insinuating. I would love to learn more. Please educate me." Geoffrey pointed to the coffee maker. Sybil turned to where his finger directed and nodded. She put the napkins down and filled the coffee maker with water. Geoffrey smiled and pushed his thumb down in the air. Sybil stared at him with a laugh. "What? What do you want me to do now, Daddy?"

Geoffrey mouthed, "Turn it on." Sybil shook her head and ran to the bathroom. Geoffrey turned back to the phone conversation, "If you want me to answer your questions you need to answer mine first." The phone hummed a dial tone. "Ah, yes, the old I get to interrogate and you have to cough up the answers routine. Well, two can play. It's too early for twenty questions with no answers."

While the coffee maker percolated, Sophia made sandwiches for the girls and Geoffrey. Each lunch box was given an extra treat for Thursday was the last day of the week for packed lunches. Friday school got out early and Geoffrey ate at his company's favorite watering hole. Sophia glanced at Goldfarb's legal papers on the counter under the phone. Today she would need to make her list of questions.

Donna dragged her backpack into the kitchen. Her six year old face was filled with worry, "Mom, where are my pink mittens? Did you wash them last night?"

Sophia slapped the counter, "No! Oh, Donna, it was so busy around here last night! Your pink mittens completely slipped my mind."

Donna pouted, "What mittens can I take to school if my mittens are dirty? I don't think I can go to school without my pink mittens."

Geoffrey came down the hall and scooped her up into his arm. "No school today? We have to have school today or we all go to jail. No mittens, just like the kittens that drowned? Why we have to have mittens!" He set her down on her feet. "Sophia, where are Donna's mittens?"

"Here's your lunch box. The pink mittens are in the washing machine. Miss Donna dropped them in the mud yesterday and ensconced them in mud and grime. I was informed by her majesty here of the need to wash her filthy mittens."

Sophia knelt down to at Donna's eye level. "Since we were busy trying to figure out life and death matters the mittens were not washed. Thus, Donna has no clean pink mittens."

Geoffrey handed Donna his leather gloves, "Here, you can use these today, Donna. Just do not ensconce them in mud, please."

Donna pushed her father's gloves away from her. "I didn't sconce anything in mud, they fell. Mom, I'll wear the muddy ones no one will notice anyway. Everyone at school is clueless when it comes to fashion." Dejected Donna sat on the edge of a kitchen chair with her backpack on her foot.

Sybil held open the front door as everyone filed out of the house. Geoffrey helped Donna with her car seat buckle. "Those pink mittens are beautiful,

Miss Donna. No one will notice the mud unless you show them." He gave her a kiss on the cheek.

Walking around to the driver's side of the van he opened Sybil's back passenger door. "Dad, I don't need a kiss. I'm a big girl, no coffee face." She put out her hand to stop him, but he pulled her hand down and kissed her on the forehead. "There, now my morning duties are almost complete." He closed the door and jiggled it to be sure it was tightly closed.

Sophia leaned forward out of the driver's window, "Hey, good looking, where's my candy?" Geoffrey put his hand around her neck and gave her a juicy kiss. "Onward troops, I shall see you later. Be well, be safe, and pass spelling tests!" He waved as they backed out of the driveway.

The girls were dropped off at their respective schools. Sophia drove to the sheriff's department on Main Street. Her confidence was stronger in the daytime and her concern for Daisy dog made this visit important. She parked in the same place she had last night. The parking lot appeared much smaller. There was a young man at the counter. His short hair accentuated his deep set eyes. "Hello, may I help you?" He was shorter than Sophia, but his professional demeanor gave him an air of importance. He wore the usual uniform, but didn't have a gun or fancy black belt.

"Yes, I am here to see A.J. Salazar. This is concerning an ongoing investigation. I was called in last night as a person of interest." Sophia laughed.

"What is your name, please?" The inquisitive young man was no longer smiling. Sophia told him. He moved to the desk behind the counter. Turning away from her, he dialed a number. "Yes, sir, this is Henry at the front. We have a Sophia Pino here to see you, yes, sir."

Gently he put the phone back in the cradle. Walking back to the counter, he informed her, "He will be right with you, if you care to take a seat?" Patiently, Sophia occupied the corner metal chair in the front room.

Twenty minutes passed before Sheriff A.J. Martinez opened the side door. He nodded at her hesitantly, "Mrs. Vinder or is it Dr. Vinder?" He waited for her to come to him.

Sophia held her head high and put out her right hand, "It's Dr. Vinder, but you can call me Sophia. Please can we start over again?"

He shook her hand, "Perhaps we should start over. Last night did not end well for either one of us." He offered her to go through the door first.

"Please, go back to my office at the left of the water faucet."

A.J. Salazar's office had glass framed military decorations hanging on the walls. He had photos of himself in his army military uniform receiving metals, giving metals, and one of him with the President of the United States and four other gentlemen Sophia didn't recognize. "Wow," Sophia sat on the chair opposite his desk, "This is impressive." She waved at all of his photographs.

He smiled, "Yes, all of those were taken some time ago. Time has a way of moving on and not necessarily in the direction one had hoped. My wife wanted to move back home here to Rincon. Since she is the love of my life, I came with her." He pulled out his office chair and sat facing her. "Now, what happened last night that spooked you so badly you had to leave?"

Sophia lifted her purse strap from around her head and placed her purse on the floor beside her. "When I found out my dear friend was hurt it made me angry. The accusatory way you drove me over there without any explanation was unkind. Then you dragged me through a strange house to a crime scene without any consideration for my emotions. You were heartless in your attempt to intimidate me."

A.J. Salazar didn't say a word, but let her continue. "Finding out that my friend was attacked put my mind in an emotional state rather than a logical one. I hope you can understand?"

He picked up a file to toss at her side of his desk. "Here, these are the preliminary findings. You might want to take a peek."

Sophia opened the file to find photographs of Carol lying on polished tiles beside the indoor pool. Blood oozed from the right side of her head. Carol's swimming suit was ripped to reveal her endowed right breast. Blue lips were opened in the shape of a '0'. Carol's brown eyes were open. Sophia gasped, "Is she all right? Did the surgery save her life?"

A.J. Salazar crossed his ankle over his knee, "It was touch and go until about four o'clock this morning. The doc realized she was going into a-fib. He caught it in time and with medications and fancy medical speak he saved her. Right now she is in a coma. The doc felt it best to keep her in the coma and not try to bring her out of it because of the head trauma. They're watching her brain for bleeding or swelling, whatever."

Turning the top page of the file, Sophia found the first report; 'Victim found with severe head trauma, needle marks found along inner left and inner right thighs. Possible drug addiction or medical injections, victim was not wet, but found in bathing suit. Hair was not wet, makeup was intact, and there were no signs of forced entry or struggle.'

Sophia closed the file and put it back on his desk. "Don't need to read all of this, thank you. I just needed to know she is in recovery. Although, I thought you should know her dog was missing last night from the area. There was so much going on and it wasn't until later that I realized her dog wasn't there. Do you know where the dog is?"

A.J. Salazar lifted the phone to punch in three numbers, "Carl, come in here." Sophia frowned. Carl would not be pleased to see her. The young man entered the office unaware of its visitor.

Sophia tried to turn her head away from him for the smell of his cologne was overwhelming. A.J. Salazar appeared to be immune to the odor and continued with his questions, "Yes, Carl, do you remember Dr. Sophia Vinder from last night?" A.J. Salazar nodded in Sophia's direction. Carl stepped back to see her, "Yes, sir, I do. How may I be of help?"

"Dr. Vinder says the victim had a dog with her last night. Did you find the dog or find any evidence of a dog at the scene?"

Carl stared at Sophia. His lips bent down into a frown and his eyebrows hovered over his eyes trying to remember, "Ma'am, a dog?"

Sophia nodded, "Yes, a yellow pit bull, female, named Daisy. She is a dog about three years old with a red rhinestone leather collar and black eyelashes. Carol had her chipped and fixed. The dog was always with Carol. Carol even brought the dog with her when she came to work at my father's house."

Carl studied the front of A.J. Salazar's desk. "No, Sir, no dog was found at the scene. There were no signs of a dog at the residence. I am sure Dr. Vinder is mistaken." Carl cautiously lifted his hand to pat his blonde hair.

A.J. Salazar glared at Carl, "Dr. Vinder has no reason to lie. She has known the victim and has a history with the victim, you do not. Please find out if any of the neighbors remembered seeing a dog with the victim. Also, check her home in Albuquerque. Find out if the dog is there. We don't want it to starve to death because of our own inadequacies." Carl nodded and departed the area.

The file was opened again as A.J. asked Sophia, "Do you think we could finish the report?"

Leaning forward with her elbows on her knees, Sophia smiled, "Certainly, I am ready to answer your questions. As you know there are many people of interest involved."

A.J. Salazar pulled out a half-typed page and inserted it into the typewriter beside his desk. "One step at a time, please, Dr. Vinder."

Sophia grimaced, "You know I have doctorates in philosophy not medicine? Please can't we agree to use my first name and work together on this?"

Surprisingly, A.J. Salazar looked right at her, "Definitely and you can call me A.J. since we have all these sheriffs and all these deputies. If you ask for me by my initials everything can be expedited with ease." Studying her eyes, he elaborated, "Only my wife is allowed to call me by my proper name." Turning back to the typewriter he continued to ask her questions.

Basic questions answered, A.J. turned his full attention to Sophia. "You mentioned other people of interest. Would you please elaborate as to whom you are referring?"

Studying her hands, Sophia felt a knot in her stomach, "Sir, this is difficult for most of the people who knew Carol and knew of her habits were the people of my family."

"Certainly," A.J.'s tone softened, "We are discrete when it comes to an informant's confidentiality."

"My husband Geoffrey Vinder felt I should be forthcoming with you since Carol was my friend."

He nodded in agreement, "When we are early on in the investigation it's best to gather all information possible as soon as possible. Please continue?"

"Carol and I met for lunch at the Range yesterday. Was it yesterday?" She searched his office for a calendar, "Yes, wow, it feels as if it were years ago. Anyway, Carol showed me photographs she had taken of my father's clothes closet. She had taken them while he was alive. The photos revealed an impressive inventory of drugs placed in plain sight on a shelf above his polished shoes. The day he died, Carol returned to take photos of drugs removed or used since the first photograph."

Sophia rubbed her fingers together in her lap. "Oh, dear, maybe I'm wrong. Perhaps Carol was misinformed. I don't want to send you on a wild goose chase."

A.J. clasped his hands on the desk, "Let me decide, please continue."

She studied the small cubicle. "Well, Carol felt my brother Granger possibly used the drugs on my father. She showed me the lab report from the pathologist. She explained how dried Pentobarbital sodium powder was found inside my father's feeding tube."

He nodded in agreement, "Yes, we have the same report. Please go on."

"Carol and I were not there the night Papa died. My mother or my brother may have put something in the feeding tube. The drug has serious consequences. Maybe they weren't aware of the drug or its purpose?" Sophia felt her mouth become drier as she spoke, "I really feel uncomfortable talking about this behind their backs."

"Understandably, but the facts will come out one way or another." His chair squeaked as he leaned back to stretch his arms over his head.

Embarrassed by the sheriff's movement, she said, "My brother Granger does work with medicines and supplements. He may have thought he was helping my mother or my father with this injection of Pentobarbital sodium. Anyway, Carol was convinced their actions influenced the early demise of my father." Sophia squirmed in her chair. "Did you find anything about this?"

A.J. brushed off his sleeve, "We're doing a follow up on the drugs used by your father. There are many inconsistencies in his death. I'm sure you're aware of his doctor's interest as to the bed being lowered. We have many issues with your father's death. Did you ever find the wedge put in the hospital bed? Our very own Ignacio Cruz has been searching for it at your mother's house."

Sophia's voice cracked, "The wedge? No one found it yet? Wasn't it with the items taken by the paramedics at the time they removed my father's body?"

"No, no one has found a wedge. Ignacio Cruz did speak with Carol Granger about the wedge and she confirmed your statement of it being made by her, placed firmly between the bed frame and the movable part of the bed. She was surprised someone was able to remove it from the area. She told him she had completely forgotten about it until he questioned her. She gave him the name of the young man who had welded the wedge for her. Ignacio is still following up on this missing piece."

A.J. Salazar lowered his voice, "You believe these two incidents are related?"

Sophia studied the floor, "Well, everyone knew everyone in both situations. I can't imagine anyone wanting to hurt Carol for just being a nurse. Somehow I'm concerned someone who felt threatened by Carol attacked her." She lifted her purse into her lap, "Did anyone find the housekeeper?"

Laughing at her, he said, "Now you're going to be our own Agatha Christy? Information will be given out as needed. This is still early on, too early to be free with our findings."

He patted Carol's file, "Right now our concern is Carol Grover. Her attack occurred within the last twenty-four hours. It's in everyone's best interest to follow the leads promptly in order to catch the perpetrator or perpetrators. Certainly you can appreciate our urgency in finding information, please do go on with your list of suspects." He opened his top desk drawer and handed her a piece of bubble gum. "Would this help?' He took a piece for himself. The unwrapped gum was popped into his mouth. "Go ahead, no worries here."

She lifted the pink gum from its wrapper. Chewing cautiously, she said, "Carol was sure my brother Granger was behind Papa's death. She was confident enough in her findings to send Granger her photos. When I asked her if her intent was blackmail, she flat out told me 'no.'"

A.J. smirked, "Maybe she knew he had the wedge. What did your brother have to gain from your father's death?"

"Oh, God, " Sophia felt her face get hot, "Granger has money problems. He stood to inherit a large sum upon the death of my father."

The file was flipped through until A.J. found a page of interest, "We don't have any information on your mother's history. Would you be able to help me fill in some gaps?"

"I'm not sure what I can say, but I'll try." Sophia's hands began to sweat.

"Where was your mother born, who were her parents, where did she meet your father, and how did she come to hire Carol Granger to be his nurse?" He frowned as he continued to inventory the gaps on the page in front of him.

"Oh, is that all!" Sophia rubbed her palms on her jeans. "My mother was born Margaret Vivian McBride in Big Springs, Texas. Her father was a dentist who worked for the Public Health Department. Grandpa had divorced my grandmother when my mother was a baby. He lost his fortune gambling. My mother felt sorry for her father, who lived in the same town, and assisted him in his dental practice. When she got older she chose to go to the Dentistry College here in Albuquerque."

Sophia waited for A.J. to catch up to her monologue. "My father the doctor was working with the Federal Government to care for the railroad employees, receiving a government paycheck. As a medical doctor, he gave physicals to the workers and my mother worked with a dentist who worked on their teeth. The railroad men were modernizing the electric tracks from Loamy to Bella. My mother worked in the government health program the same year as my father and many times they shared the same office."

"Your mother doesn't have a southern accent. I thought she was raised in the northeast among the upper aristocratic class. Just goes to show you can't tell a book by its cover, huh?" He winked at her as he flipped to a new page in the file, "What year did she meet up with your father, do you know?" He wrote the answers on the page with a pencil.

"I believe it was around 1947. He was nine years older than my mother, but she told everyone she was ten years younger than he. Vanity is a big part of my mother's personality. She thrives on compliments. If you need more information from her, I would recommend starting the interview with a compliment."

Nodding, he shifted in his office chair, "Where did they get all their money?"

"Oh, dear, I knew this was going to rise to the surface." Sophia crossed her legs and pushed her bangs to the side, "My grandmother Sophia Bethany, who I was named after, was quite the femme fatale. She loved men to love her and she made it a habit of marrying rich men throughout her life. She was a beautiful woman, well educated, and was raised in Louisiana. She lived her life to the fullest. Men took her on cruises, on safaris, and she even lived with an artist in Greece for six years. When he died he left her all of his money for he didn't have any children."

Lifting her head, she spoke proudly, "If there were two people who grabbed hold of life with both hands, it would have to be both my grandmother and my father. They didn't like each other, but they both loved life."

Taking another pencil from his top desk drawer, A.J. asked, "About how much money are we talking about here?"

Sophia frowned at him, "About how much? I would say my grandmother was worth a couple of million dollars. She was also married to a man who had a Cuban cigar company in Havana, but she never went to Cuba. She continued to live with him in Shreveport, Louisiana, until his death. She paid her taxes, kept her nose clean, and kept right on marrying elderly men who didn't live very long. My grandmother died when I was twenty-eight years old. She was my idol, although I only love one man and I'm married to him."

A.J. was writing furiously to keep up with her. "We're getting there. Now how did your mother find Carol Granger and come about hiring her to care for your father?"

"Mom was given a list of home health caretakers from Dr. Milligan my father's doctor. He recommended three nurses and Carol was the only one not employed at the time. My father had always enjoyed beautiful women and Carol is plump and efficient. I think my mother hired her for her down to earth attitude. She knew my father wouldn't have approved, hah!"

Resting his hand, A.J. continued with his interrogation, "Why would Carol go after Granger? If she didn't want to blackmail him, what did she have to gain by threatening him?" A.J. pulled another piece of gum from his drawer.

Sophia shrugged, "I have no idea what she wanted from him. Carol explained to me she was confident Granger wouldn't be able to find her. She was house-sitting and no one knew where the house was. She didn't even tell me where the house was or how long she would be there."

A.J. swiveled his chair back and forth, making it squeak "It wouldn't be difficult to find or follow her. The yellow bug she drove was an eyesore. Anyone would be able to hunt her down easily. Do you know where your brother was last evening?"

"No. I was at home with my family." Sophia took the sweet gum out of her mouth and placed it in its paper. "Do you know where Granger was yesterday afternoon?"

"We're in the process of trying to track your brother down. He disappeared into the wind. Although, we did find out his intended bride was the housekeeper. She was befriended by Carol who had met her at veterinary clinic." He took his gum out of his mouth and dropped it in the wastebasket beside his desk. "Katina Simmons was investigating r edication for your mother's horse when she met Carol. They were both at Dr. Gallegos' office. Dr. Gallegos is both a large and small animal vet."

Sophia frowned, "Katina was investigating medications for the horse? Did the vet give her anything? My mother's horse is older than Methuselah and seriously in need of medical care. Dr. Gallegos felt the horse had terminal cancer in the intestine and recommended the horse be put down, but my mother refused. Wonder why she dragged Katina into this issue?"

He shook his head, "Ignacio spoke with Dr. Gallegos this morning and was told no medication is given out to a third party. Also, he would need to visit the horse again and get an update on the horse's health before administering any new medication. Dr. Gallegos doesn't handout prescriptions to anyone for another person's animal. Actually, Dr. Gallegos was not pleased with Katina's aggressive behavior. But we can come back to her once we find her."

Flipping through Carol's file, he stated, "Katina Simmons' fingerprints were found at the house Carol was house-sitting. Katina Simmons was identified as the 911 caller. She is also a person of interest. Her ties to your brother make our interest in her obvious." A.J. pushed a yellow pencil to the front of his desk, "Your brother holds our interest with many issues. If you hear from him would you ask him to call our office?"

Sensing the interview was coming to an end, Sophia stood, "Yes, certainly. Please let me know if you find Carol's dog. Her dog's name is Daisy."

A.J. accompanied her to the front room, "We will be sure to let you know if Daisy appears. Please stay in touch with this office. If you have any other ideas or suggestions call me immediately."

15

Rincon, New Mexico
Thursday, January, 1988

Sophia ran through the hard blowing wind to her van. She had Sheriff A.J. Martinez's card in her wallet with his home phone and car phone numbers written in pencil. Driving southeast of downtown Rincon, Sophia was determined to find the house of the attack and possibly Daisy dog. She took the first left after the last signal light. The road was paved and dead ended at a trailer park. All dogs were noticed, but no Daisy dog appeared. Sophia turned around in the driveway of a faded green trailer.

Back on Main Street she noticed the street name signs. Last night she hadn't seen a street name sign when A.J. brought her to the house. She was almost to the interstate turnoff when she found the road. It was dirt with potholes and ended at two large adobe structures on either side of a wrought iron gate. Beyond the house was the interstate with cars racing past in both directions.

Sophia groaned. If Daisy dog got out onto the freeway her life was in serious jeopardy. Sophia pulled the van to the left of the adobe gate structure. The wrought iron gate had yellow police tape running from one side to the other. Behind the adobe structures was open land to the house. There were no fences. Grabbing her purse, she jumped out of the van and proceeded to the house. There was more yellow tape blocking the front door. A white paper listing the legal contacts was firmly tacked to the doorframe. Muddy prints were on the front steps with footprints moving to the right side of the house. Sophia followed them to the side door. She lifted her hand to feel along the frame. Her fingers touched the key.

Suddenly, Sophia felt a chill. Shivering, she withdrew her hand from the top of the door frame, leaving the key in its place. She stood solidly thinking out loud, "If I go in then I am returning to the scene of the crime. I'm here only to find Daisy dog." She tugged the leather strap of her purse higher onto her shoulder. She turned toward the front of the house, calling out in a strong voice, "Daisy dog! Daisy dog, where are you, puppy?"

Sophia crouched down searching for paw prints. "Ah-hah, a dog has been here!" She bent down to push through some dried lilac branches. Leaning against the outside wall, she duck walked to the back of the house. There sitting next to a doghouse was Daisy. She was wagging her whole bottom for her tail was only a stub. Barking and jumping up and down, Daisy greeted Sophia as a long lost friend. "Daisy dog, what are you doing back here? How did you get here?" Daisy was released from the metal chain holding her to the dog house. Leaping and dancing backwards, Daisy moved to a porch with a door. "Is this the door Carol used?"

Daisy swirled around and jumped on the door. The door pushed open with a bang. Sophia flinched at the sound, then called out, "Daisy dog, come here, girl, come here!" Daisy disappeared inside the room and didn't reappear. Quickly, Sophia opened her purse and pulled out her wallet. Holding A.J.'s official card she slowly crept into the room. Daisy was nowhere to be seen. There was a black phone on a secretary table by a wooden bookcase. Using the phone to call A.J., Sophia kept her eyes on the pet door leading into the main house.

"Hello, may I speak with Sheriff A.J. please, it's an emergency." Sophia tried to sound calm, but her voice kept trembling.

There was a short pause and then, "This is A.J., how may I help you?"

Sophia explained where she was and how she found the dog. He told her to stay put, he was coming directly. Just as Sophia was about to hang up she heard a loud splash. "A.J., are you still there?"

"Yes, what is it?"

"I think the dog just jumped into the swimming pool."

He burst out laughing, "Well, please don't join her. I'm on my way. Stay where you are. Please don't enter the main house." He hung up the phone.

Hearing his voice calling out for her only a few minutes later, Sophia walked outside to direct him to the backyard. "Wow, we had no idea this area was here. Of course we searched in the dark of night. Why isn't this attached to the front of the main house?"

A.J. hurried into the room from the patio. There was a high bookcase, the secretary table with the phone, behind the door was a clothes closet filled with bright wild clothes. He pushed on a partition painted with oriental birds only to have it fall over with a clang. They lifted and moved it to the middle of the room. There, behind where the partition had been, was another bedroom. It was small with a twin sized bed. The wall around the bed was lined with shoes of various shapes and styles. Scarves were thrown on the bed. At the foot of the twin bed was a doggy bed covered with fur and filled with half eaten chew bones.

"Bingo," Sophia smiled with tears in her eyes. "This is the Carol I know! She's big on having her things all over the place. The other bedroom is sterile and empty. Whoever did attack her didn't know about this room. Remember her purse on the wardrobe in the other bedroom? Well, it didn't belong there." A.J. listened as he continued to search the room.

Sophia gloated, "The wardrobe is too high for her to hang her purse." She jumped when she felt something wet push behind her right leg, "Daisy dog, here you are! Daisy dog, please met A.J. He is the hero of the hour!" Sophia knelt down to give Daisy a hug, but Daisy pulled away to dance around A.J.

Daisy dog crouched down on her front legs to smile at him. When he reached out to pet her, she jumped up onto his leg and tried to lick his hand. "Friendly little thing, isn't she?"

"Yes, and she's supposed to be a guard dog. Poor thing hasn't been fed since yesterday, but she did have plenty of water. Feel her, she is soaking wet."

Sophia backed away from the wet dog. "You know yesterday when we walked into the living room? The first thing I smelled was wet dog. If Daisy dog had knocked Carol down how did she get attached to the doghouse in the back? Someone would have had to take her there. Do you think Carol had already put her there for the night?"

A.J. was studying papers on the small bureau. "Sophia, you should join the force. You're much more inquisitive than Carl and he's on my team. I can't believe we didn't find this room last night." He walked back into the big room with the floor to ceiling bookcase. Searching the adobe wall all they could find was the small dog door cut out of the adobe wall. "How did Carol get to this room? She wouldn't have crouched under the lilacs each time she came and went. There must be an easier way."

The two of them went outside. The lilacs were close to the house on the south side, but the north side of the house had rose bushes all along the wall. This made it impractical and dangerous as a path. There was open space around the dog house, but it only led down to an arroyo of rocks. Across from the arroyo was a neighbor's wood slatted fence.

A.J. stood with his hands on his hips. "The only way to get to her bedroom would have been through a passage in the house. She parked in the front. We found her yellow VW bug parked directly in front of the house. Why is there no obvious way in from back here?"

Sophia stood behind him studying the landscape. There were no footprints in this area. The rains of last week hadn't dried for the weather hadn't warmed up enough. "We need to watch the dog. The dog will know how to get in and out of the room." Sophia bent down and took Daisy dog's collar, "Let's take her into the main house and watch how she gets back here." Daisy dog jumped around not happy about being pulled. Sophia quietly asked, "You know how to get into the main house, right?"

A.J. laughed, "Yes, and you do, too." Shaking his head he crawled under the lilacs. Sophia followed him holding tightly to the dog by her collar.

Daisy dog ran through the house barking. She raced into the kitchen to dance around in front of the stove. The humans followed her only to stand and stare. Believing them to be totally stupid, Daisy dog raced down the hall and then came to a dead stop. She started sniffing the sand as she walked round and round in circles. Then she started to squat. A.J. moved with lightening speed. He grabbed her collar, "No! Bad dog! You're not allowed to pee in the house!" He jerked her out of the sand and into the living room.

Daisy leaped up and twisted. A.J. cried out in pain. Daisy raced out of the open partition into the swimming pool. She dove into the water without a thought. A.J.'s face was white as he turned to show Sophia his finger, "Look what she did to me?" His finger was bent at an unnatural angle. "I bet it's broken, damn dog!" He hurried to the kitchen sink to flush it with running water. Blood slowly gushed out of his finger, into the sink, and down the drain.

Sophia called out to him, "Don't worry, Carol was a nurse. She must have a first-aid kit around here somewhere. Hold on, I'll find it." Sophia hurried to the bedroom and then remembered this wasn't Carol's room. Pushing her way into the main bathroom, she opened the medicine cabinet only to find it empty. She pulled back the shower curtain. Potted plants lined the bathtub. A floor to ceiling closet door was behind the bathroom door. Sophia had to close the bathroom door to open the closet door. There it was! The door opened to the back room.

She had to seriously push the door open to get through into the back rooms that were used by Carol. Once the door was shoved open, Sophia realized the restraint against the door was the oriental partition that had fallen over when they were in the room earlier. Lifting the oriental partition and pushing it against the wall, allowed the door into the room more freedom to swing open. Quickly, she found the back bathroom. This was Carol's for it was filled with hair products, makeup, colognes and sprays. A bright orange bathrobe hung over the shower curtain. Sophia searched for Carol's white metal first-aid kit. Opening the cupboard under the sink filled with lipsticks, Sophia found the medical kid sitting on top of a pair of sneakers.

Racing into the kitchen, Sophia held up the white metal case. "Here, A.J. and I found the door to the backroom. It's through this bathroom. The oriental tapestry was in front of the actual a door. I found the medicine kit. Here let me see your finger?"

A.J. was sitting at the kitchen table with his finger in his mouth. Sophia shook her head, "You know your mouth is filled with bacteria?" She took hold of his hand. His crooked middle finger bent into the air. "Oh, dear, this needs more than what I can do. There is a broken bone sticking out here." She pointed. A.J. groaned and looked at her with sad eyes. "Should we call an ambulance?"

Sophia burst out laughing, "No, I can drive you to the clinic. You aren't in a life or death situation. But we should probably call someone to come and get the dog. They will need to lock up the house, or search for more clues."

He stared at her with his lips pinched. Sophia cracked a smile, "Oh, yes, you're the sheriff. What do you want to do?" He pointed with his good hand to the white phone placed on the kitchen wall, "Call Carl. He can come and get the dog. While we're gone he can search for more clues. We can leave after he gets here."

"Yes, sir, I will call Carl. What's his phone number?" Sophia punched in the numbers. Carl arrived in short time. While A.J. called the Urgent Care, Sophia gave Carl a tour. She showed him the door from the main bathroom to Carol's part of the house. The pet door was cut out of the adobe wall, which pushed open easily for the dog. The illusion of the floor to ceiling enclosure was amazing. Both men were as impressed as Sophia had been when she first found the movable openings. The homeowners appeared to enjoy using partitions stretched over two-by-four frames.

Daisy dog was placed in the back of Carl's cruiser. Carl agreed to wait at the house and look for clues until A.J. Salazar returned. Although, Carl did not appear pleased to have a wet slobbering yellow pit bull in the back of his cruiser, he didn't say anything. Sophia was surprised A.J. wanted her to drive him to the clinic, but then he probably didn't want to leave her there with the dog and the house filled with evidence.

One hour later, A.J. walked into the sunshine proud of the white bandage enveloping his right middle finger. As told to do by the doctor, he held his right finger proudly above his heart as they walked to Sophia's van. Driving down main street back to the suspect house, A.J. rested his hand on the window frame. His extended middle finger was in plain sight to those they passed. He gloated as he showed off his hurt finger to the general public.

When they entered the house they found Carl sitting on a wooden couch in the living room. He jumped to attention when A.J. strode into the room. "Sir, how's the finger?"

"Hurts like hell, if you must know. Now what did you find after we left?" A.J. plopped down on one of the wooden chairs only to jump, "These aren't comfortable at all, are they?"

Carl turned to study the couch's wooden structure, "They take some getting used to, sir." Carl led the way down the sandy hall to the bathroom. "I didn't find anything suspect in the victim's room. Her things are strewn all over the place. She has boxes of jewelry on the floor under the bed. There is no way for me to know if anything was stolen. She has lots of stuff everywhere in here."

As they followed him into Carol's bedroom, he pulled out the top drawer of the small bureau. "Sir, she has over fifty different kinds of lipsticks, eye shadow cases, and nail polish colors. Her curlers and hair dyes are in the bottom drawer. Her underwear drawer is the second drawer. I didn't dare go through all the different types of thongs, full sized cotton briefs, snap briefs, and front closing brassieres and her girdles."

A.J. turned in a circle studying the room. "Where did she hang her clothes beside the closet in the outer room?"

Sophia answered for him, "More than likely she would bring the clothes she needed for a short period of time here from home. Most of her own clothes would be at her house in town. She has no reason to bring everything she owned here. She probably takes trips home and gets what she needs for the following week. If she's like most women, she only brings her temporary winter clothes here."

"All right, let's lock up and talk about the dog." A.J. slammed the backdoor from inside. He locked the door knob. He led the way through the bathroom into the main house. Carl was mumbling under his breath. Finally, A.J. stopped in the living room, "Speak up, man, what do you want to say?"

Carl's face turned scarlet, "Sir, I put the dog in the backyard. She was trying to dig through the upholstery in the backseat of my vehicle."

A.J. clenched his jaw, "Go and get her. You can go around the house under the lilacs on this side." He motioned with his good hand. Sophia moved out of Carl's way as he hurried out the front door, ripping off the yellow tape. The white paper fluttered to the ground. "Oh, Carl, look what you did?"

Sophia hung back as the men discussed how to reattach the tape. The tack, used to hold the white legal paper, was lost in the bushes. A.J. stuck the paper into of the crease of the door as he shut it. "I'll get Carl to come back and nail this to the door." He shook his head.

Daisy dog was retrieved with broken branches stuck in her leather collar. Carl's hair was mussed with dried leaves and small bits of fauna. A.J. was sitting in his cruiser, talking on his radio phone. Daisy dog ran to Sophia and sat down on her left shoe. "I think she should come home with me, Carl. We have an enclosed backyard and can keep her safely until Carol is out of the hospital." Sophia reached over to take the leash from Carl's hand. "Unless," She looked up at Carl, "Do you want to take the dog?"

Carl pushed the leash into her hand. "No, Carol's your friend. You take her dog."

A.J. waved to Carl with his bandaged hand. The radio phone was placed on the dash board of his cruiser, "You need to go back into the house and get Dr. Vinder the dog food. This way she won't have to buy a bag. You can retrieve the dog bed, the dog bones, and the water dish in the backyard. Carl, go get this for her. You know where the key is by the side door. We'll wait for you."

Sophia opened the passenger door of her van. Daisy jumped right into the seat. Sophia lifted the seat belt, wrapped it around her, and clicked it in place. Daisy dog shook in happy anticipation. "Wait here, girl, wait for us to load up your stuff. Stay!" Daisy smiled as Sophia closed the van's door.

Carl returned with his arms filled with dog items. He had loaded everything onto the dog bed. The empty bowls, the dog chews, and the twenty pound bag of dry dog food were stacked precariously one on top of the other. Following Sophia to her van, he dropped everything in the open space behind the backseats. "There, you should have everything. I looked for canned food, but I couldn't find any."

Sophia shook his hand, "Thank you, Carl, you certainly are animal friendly." Carl barely let her take his hand before jerking it away. "Yes, Ma'am, now we best be going." He wiped the dog hair off of his sheriff's uniform as he retreated to the driver's side of his vehicle.

A.J. Salazar backed his sheriff's vehicle out of the driveway first. Carl moved his cruiser to be behind his boss. A.J. waved Sophia to go ahead of them. As he rolled down his window, he called out, "Had to make sure you'd leave. I don't want any more noses getting out of joint. Good luck with the dog!" He rolled up his window, waving her ahead of him.

Daisy dog sat like a proper passenger. Sophia stroked her furry head, "Daisy dog, my girls will be so excited to have you at home." The dog just smiled and wiggled her rear end.

Daisy had no problem following Sophia into the house. Daisy's dog bed was placed in the corner of the living room. Her water bowl was filled and the feeding bowl was put on the counter. The dog chews were scattered around the living room for her to find. Sophia took the dog into the backyard and let her sniff around on her own. Closing the backdoor, Sophia hurried to the kitchen to call Geoffrey at work.

Geoffrey answered on the first ring of the phone. Sophia explained her morning adventures. Geoffrey listened quietly. Frustrated at his lack of response, Sophia asked, "Is there someone in the room with you? I'm sorry I should've asked instead of just running off at the mouth."

There was a moment of silence before Geoffrey answered, "Your brother is here. He heard about Mr. Goldfarb's assisting us. We're in the middle of a discussion. Would you like to speak to Granger, Sophia?"

Sophia gasped, "No, I don't think I have anything positive to say to him.

You can tell me about his visit later. Why don't you ask Granger to call Sheriff A.J. Martinez? The sheriff is anxious to speak with him. Did you tell Granger about Carol?"

Geoffrey was quick to answer, "The roses we ordered haven't come in yet have they? I hope not because we don't have the back garden fertilized. No, I didn't buy the fertilizer. I thought you did?"

"Oh, good, we can keep our news to ourselves. I'm going to fix myself some lunch, read the Goldfarb papers and make my list. Are you going to lunch with Granger?"

Geoffrey laughed, "Oh, you need to me to buy more pink mittens? Yes, being six years old is a serious age and Donna is certainly focused on her mittens. I can go right now on my lunch break. I have half an hour. We have a big meeting at two o'clock. I'll go right now." He hung up the phone.

Sophia heard a howling coming from the backyard. She ran down the hall to the backdoor. Daisy dog was scratching the outside of the wooden door. Quickly she opened it. Daisy ran into the kitchen to her water bowl. She lapped almost the whole bowl of water only to lie down under the table and take a nap.

Dinner had been a busy affair what with Sybil pleased she passed her spelling test with a 'B.' Donna made friends with a new student in her class. This young girl appeared to have an awareness of clothes and auxiliary wearable's. Daisy dog was adopted by everyone. Even to the extent of allowing Geoffrey and the girls to take her for a walk before dinner. This gave Sophia some time to cook with her own thoughts.

Geoffrey was quiet throughout the dinner, although after his busy day, he had good reason to be. Sophia tried to keep the momentum going until everyone had taken their bath and was tucked gently into bed. Geoffrey had opted out of reading tonight for he said he had work to do in his office at the back of the house.

Sophia pushed open Geoffrey's office door. He was drawing detailed work on his drafting table. He appeared to be totally engrossed. Quietly, she closed the door. Pleased at having time for herself, she went into their bathroom and closed the door. Sinking into the sweet bliss of a lavender bubble bath, she let the soft warm moisture engulf her body. The white puffy bath pillow was placed behind her head as she lifted her novel from the bathroom floor. "Ah, sweet luxury of life, there is nothing as fine as a quiet bath in a peaceful house."

A soft knock on the bathroom door roused her from her novel's plot. The door squeaked open, as Geoffrey whispered, "Can I come in or is this private time?"

"You may enter, my slave, just don't let the cold air follow you." Sophia waved her hand in the air.

"Oh, we're back in ancient China are we? How's the novel going? You've been reading your mystery for at least three months." Geoffrey put down the toilet seat and sat.

"Well, life around here is never dull. You may have noticed the intrigue and high suspense of every day. What can I help you with, my fine fellow?" Sophia put her bookmark in the book.

"Sophia, you do love me, right?" Geoffrey's face was pensive.

"Absolutely, I love you. There is no question of my love for you. We are united against the common enemy, whoever that may be." Sophia pushed the bubbles closer around her.

"You wouldn't be angry with me if I told something to Granger—something that might make him volatile?" Geoffrey lifted his hands to rub his bald head.

"What? What did you tell Granger?" Sophia sat up, the bath pillow dropped down into the bath water behind her. "He isn't one to be toyed with as we found out with Carol. He may not have been involved, but it's not good to anger the dragon."

"I told Granger there was no way I would divorce you or leave the girls. The only way we could be separated was if I was dead." Geoffrey leaned back against the bathroom wall. "I was clear about my love for you and our loyalty to one another. He stared at me as if I had l lost my mind. Then he asked me if I understood the importance of having sons."

Geoffrey crossed his arms over his chest. "What could I say? I love our girls. Sons or daughters, children are children, and when they are your own you love them with your life."

He started to pace back and forth in front of the bath tub. "Sophia, I swear your brother is insane. He went on and on about family lines and the importance of longevity and the ability to live forever through male children."

Finally, he stopped pacing and stared down at her, "What does gender have to do with longevity? We are who we are. What we do and what we choose for our own lives makes our lives important not our children! Sophia, he really scared me. Granger refused to sit down. His eyes glowed when I told him I would never divorce you. He got a flat look as if someone had hypnotized him."

Sophia couldn't look at Geoffrey. She studied her feet sticking out of the bubbles instead. "Geoffrey, Granger has been brainwashed by my mother for as long as I can remember. All of the child abuse he suffered he blamed on Papa. He never realized she was the voice behind Papa's actions."

Geoffrey knelt down next to the bathtub. His knees popped as he continued, "Sophia, I meant it. I meant every word. I am totally devoted to you and our girls. I would rather die than leave you or the girls."

Sophia put her wet arms around his neck, "Geoffrey, you don't have to die to prove your love for us. You have to live to prove your love. We need you and want you in our lives for as long as we possibly can. I don't want to live without you either, but when it comes to my daughters' survival versus our own—I will pick their survival. We can make it. Even if we have to live separately this doesn't mean we aren't still in love. This entire threat means we have to play their game until they disappear."

Abruptly, Geoffrey grabbed her arms to push them from her embrace. He rocked on his heels to lean back against the sink console cupboards. "No, I need to live with you and the girls. Separation isn't an option. I made it perfectly clear to Granger we would not separate. Separation would be over my dead body." He walked out of the bathroom and closed the door quietly.

Sophia pulled the bath pillow from behind her. "Damn, now what are we in for?" She closed her eyes and prayed.

Towel dried and powdered, Sophia pulled her gown of blue flannel over her head. Her nightgown clung to her damp body as she climbed into bed next to Geoffrey. "Hey, you're still awake. Do you know it was last Thursday when all of this horror began? Papa died one week ago, today. How do you feel about our crazy life right now?"

He grunted as he lay flat on his back with his hands across his chest. "I'm feeling restful. Although the phone has been ringing off the hook while you were in the tub, I feel like your answering service."

"Who called?" Sophia cuddled up to him. Geoffrey put his arm around her to pull her closer. "Enid called said she was worried about Emily. Emily appears to have gone off the deep end as far as Granger is concerned. Enid wanted you to call Emily."

"Oh, dear, and I am remiss in not calling her. We were never close, but she's family after all, right?" Sophia put her head on his chest.

"Yes, rather remiss, but then Emily called right after Enid. Emily was terrified. Margaret is helping her move into the house in Negar. There is too much furniture for the small house. Margaret suggested they put some of Emily's boxes in the old barn behind the house. Granger came to help move the boxes. At least he didn't bring Katina with him. Anyway, Granger came across some sticks of dynamite which freaked out Emily."

Sophia grunted as she put her arm around Geoffrey's waist to give him a hug. "What is she afraid of?"

"Evidently several years ago, Granger bought some dynamite to blow out a tree stump in the field behind their home in Calavera. He set it with a timer and didn't tell her. Shirley was outside riding her bike after Granger had gone to work at the clinic. About an hour after Granger was gone, the stump blew out of the ground leaving a huge crater in the center of the field. Shirley got cut with some flying tree shrapnel."

Geoffrey yawned, "Emily made it sound horrible. She thought the world was ending at the time." He kissed the top of Sophia's head. Her hair smelled of lavender. "Emily said after the explosion she didn't trust Granger at all. She became paranoid and wouldn't eat anything he cooked and wouldn't let him drive them anywhere. The divorce appears to be a good move on her part."

Sophia lifted on her elbow to study Geoffrey's face, "Granger always loved to invent new stuff. He especially liked dangerous inventions. Once when we were in our early teens he made cages for black scorpions out of toothpicks. He had cages of them in his room. They scared Mom's cleaning lady something terrible."

"Sophia, Emily believes Granger is going to blow up the Negar house with Shirley and her in it. She asked for Goldfarb's phone number. She wants to get a restraining order against Granger and maybe even Margaret." Geoffrey turned to put his arm around her. "Did you write your questions for Goldfarb?"

Sophia kissed Geoffrey's cheek, "Yes, they are folded in my purse."

"You could have left them on the kitchen table for me?"

"Geoffrey, I didn't want those things that go bump in the night to steal my questions."

"Things that go bump, you mean the bumpkins?" Geoffrey hugged Sophia with his right arm as he kissed her on the lips.

"Yes, oh, dear, I just thought of something. The Daisy dog will be up before dawn." Sophia rubbed her feet against Geoffrey's warm feet.

He jerked, "Hey, those are cold! Why would the dog get up early?" Geoffrey rolled over on his side to face Sophia. He kissed her again on the lips.

"Geoffrey, you taste good! Is that bubblegum on your breath?" Sophia giggled.

"Ah, good guess, yes. I used Donna's pink bubblegum toothpaste in the girl's bathroom. Someone was hogging our bathroom and I couldn't get in there to brush my teeth."

Sophia scrunched up her face, "Whose toothbrush did you use?"

Geoffrey shook his head, "I'm not dumb. I have no idea where those toothbrushes have been. I used my finger." He lifted his index finger to show her.

"I knew there was a reason I married you! You're one smart man!"

"All right, now tell me about the dog getting up early with Carol, what's that about?" Geoffrey pulled the quilt higher over Sophia's shoulder.

"Carol comes from Texas trailer trash train tracks." Sophia kissed Geoffrey's chin.

"What do Texas trailer trash train tracks have to do with anything?" Geoffrey kissed her on the forehead.

"It means trains in Texas roll around five in the morning through the trailer parks, thus Carol always gets up bright and early before the sun shines." Sophia smiled.

Geoffrey groaned, "Then we better get busy or the dog will be in here before we know it."

Sophia closed her eyes, "Where is the dog now?"

"The dog is lying flat on her back in her dog bed, snoring."

Sophia pushed her bangs from her forehead, "Did you ask Granger to call the sheriff?"

Geoffrey laughed, "I'm not stupid. You can tell him yourself." Geoffrey reached over and turned off the bedside light. "Good night, my love." Sophia didn't answer.

16

Rocoso, New Mexico
Friday, January, 1988

The panting woke her. Sophia opened her eyes to locate the cause of the fast breathing. In the dark of early morning, she made out the outline of the short dog sitting next to the bed. Daisy stared at her, drooling. Sighing, Sophia lifted on her arm to glance at the clock on her bedside table. It was five fifteen and the sun wasn't up yet. She whispered, "Oh, Daisy, you're ready to get going aren't you, girl? We'll certainly have to get you back with your Mommy sooner than later." Geoffrey rolled over pulling his pillow over his head.

Quietly, Sophia slid out of the bed, grabbed her fuzzy terrycloth robe, pulled the belt firmly around her middle to quietly let Daisy out the backdoor. Daisy gleefully raced into the cold dark. She twirled as she ran back and forth from one side to the other of the backyard. Suddenly she stood still, listening. Down the road a car was revving its engine. Daisy lifted her head to howl at the sound. Sophia danced in the cold air, she seriously needed to go the bathroom. "Come on, Daisy, let's go in now."

Daisy dog glared at her to continue running frantically around the back of the house. She danced just out of Sophia's reach. Frustrated Sophia walked into the house and closed the backdoor. "Fine, just stay out there." She hurried to the bathroom.

The girls straggled into the kitchen one by one. They were awakened by the smell of bacon and fried eggs. "Mom, what's the matter?" Donna rubbed her eyes, "Are you sick or something?"

Donna pointed at the stove, "Mom, you have bacon, eggs, and pancakes? Are we having a breakfast party?" Daisy raced from the living room, where she had been chewing on her rawhide bone to leap onto Donna. Donna turned, pushing her down. "Ouch, Daisy, get down now!"

Sophia laughed, "Donna, since the dog is an early riser I thought we should have a fancy breakfast for a change. What do you think about down home food for this morning's breakfast?" Before she could answer, Sybil came into the kitchen. She was holding her book. The right side of her face was still pressed in from sleep.

Sybil sniffed the air. "Wow, what smells so good?" Donna told her what their mother had done. "Cool," Sybil sat down at her place at the kitchen table, "When do we eat?"

Sophia frowned at her, "We can eat as soon as you set the table, young lady. You are nine years old and don't need me to wait on you!"

Geoffrey waltzed into the kitchen, holding a pair of his old cowboy boots. He had shaved, showered, and dressed in his blue jeans. He had on his white shirt with snap buttons and the high black socks. "This kitchen smells like a real farmhouse breakfast. What's going on in here?" He hugged Sophia's waist as she put the pancakes on a large round serving plate. "Time to celebrate life, my love, we're going to eat well this morning for it is Friday. This is a day to celebrate. Samuel Goldfarb is assisting us with our life's dream!" She turned and kissed him on his cheek. "Oh, you smell delicious."

"Yuck!" Donna was holding her fork and spoon at the ready. Geoffrey took the plate of pancakes and placed it in the middle of the table. "Here, you girls, help yourselves. This is an informal meal." Sophia gave each of them a plate with two fried eggs, three pieces of bacon, and a wedge of orange. Sybil smiled, "Mom, this is like going to a fancy restaurant." Sophia gave her a wink, "Don't forget to leave the tip."

Geoffrey turned in his chair. "You know I have to get these old cowboy boots to the boot repair? They have nails sticking into my left heel. I planned to wear them today. This is informal Friday and I want everyone to see what a real farmer looks like." He pulled off his left boot and stuck his fingers into it. "Yep, two nails sticking out, but I can wing it until this afternoon. I'll just not walk very much."

Sophia laughed at him, "Some cowboy! You're going to sit around on your butt all day?" He threw his white linen napkin at her. The girls were too busy eating to notice. They made happy noises as the syrup was passed around the table. Sybil didn't even look at her book. She kept her focus on her food. Donna's main concern was to not get syrup on her pink pullover with white kittens on the front.

"Did you find my list for Samuel Goldfarb that was in my purse?" Sophia wiped her mouth with her cloth napkin.

Geoffrey pulled his left boot back onto his foot, "Yes, I have both of our lists. Yesterday when Granger was at the office, I was honest with him. I told him I was going to see Goldfarb today around one o'clock and there was nothing he could do about it. Personally, I believe your brother is a flake. What kind of man only marries women who will give him sons?" Geoffrey cut into his pancakes. Sybil snorted into her milk glass, "You can say it, Dad. You can say he is a salamander!"

Sophia smiled, "Well, Henry the Eighth wasn't exactly a firm supporter of wives who couldn't have sons. He killed his wives with a vengeance."

Sybil nodded at her mother, "Yes, but he got sick from all the women he dabbled with on the side."

Geoffrey almost dropped his coffee cup, "What did you just say?"

Sybil blushed, "Dad, I'm in third grade and I do read as if you hadn't noticed!"

Sophia shook her head, "Yes, perhaps we should monitor what you do read." Sybil bit into her bacon and ignored them.

Sophia gathered the dishes, putting them in the sink of hot water while the girls retrieved their backpacks. Geoffrey searched for his father's Stetson hat in the hall closet. Sybil helped Sophia dry the dishes and put them away. Donna walked Daisy in the backyard before locking Daisy in the house. The kitchen cleaned and the girls already to go, Sophia grabbed her coat and ran outside to get into the van.

Geoffrey gave each of the girls a hug and a kiss. Whispering to Sophia, he said, "Why don't you call your brother and tell him to see the sheriff?" Before she could respond he quickly ran to his truck.

Sophia and the girls backed out of the driveway. Sophia checked her rearview mirror to see if Geoffrey was following, but he had hurried back into the house for something. The girls were dropped off at their schools. Sophia decided to return home. It was time to call her mother and find out how Emily was doing with the move. Turning into the driveway, she was surprised to see Geoffrey's truck still in the driveway.

Sophia entered the unlocked front door, "Geoffrey, where are you?" She heard a groan from the back of the house. Running into the bedroom, she saw Geoffrey lying on the bed with his hand wrapped in a white wet dishtowel. "What on earth happened?" His left boot was black with soot.

He lifted his head. His face was bright red as if it had been burned. His eyes were watering, "Thank goodness you came straight home. Would you drive me to Urgent Care?"

Sophia hurried to his side, "What happened! What's wrong with your hand?" Geoffrey moaned as he tried to sit upright. "Something in the truck shorted out. I was electrocuted when I put the key in the ignition. We really should get floor mats for the old truck, the metal flooring didn't help, and I got a charge of electricity through the nails in my left boot!"

Daisy sat next to the bed with her chin on Geoffrey's side. She watched him cautiously with her large brown eyes. Geoffrey fell back onto the bed. "My head hurts, my hand hurts, and my whole body feels pain. I can't feel anything in my left foot. Don't ask anymore questions, let's go get help."

They leaned against one another as they toddled through the house. Sophia grabbed her purse off the couch when they moved through the living room. "Daisy, you stay here and guard the castle. We'll be back soon, be a good girl, stay!" Sophia let Geoffrey lean against her right side as she locked the front door.

Geoffrey sighed, "You know these locks are an illusion of security? They really don't keep people out. If someone wanted to get inside, they could. Oh, I shouldn't speak, it hurts."

They drove silently through Rincon and up the hill to Rio Grodno's Urgent Care Clinic. Geoffrey had pushed the seat all the way back and down. He groaned with his eyes closed as Sophia brought the van to a stop in the Urgent Care parking lot. Sophia asked him to stay in the van. The stark cold reality of the medical facility reminded Sophia of how fragile their lives are. She asked a young male orderly with a high and tight haircut for a wheelchair. He pushed it for her out to the van. Geoffrey wasn't looking any better. The odor of burnt skin mixed with burnt leather wafted out of the van as the orderly lifted him from the passenger's seat to the wheelchair.

The Urgent Care doors automatically opened for them. The orderly called to a nurse who pulled the locked interior doors. Geoffrey was pushed into an examining room. The nurse asked Sophia to remain at the front desk with her in the entry to give necessary information. Sophia pulled out her wallet. Sheriff A.J. Martinez's card fell to the floor at her feet. She picked up the card and stuck it into her jean pocket.

The energetic nurse handed a clipboard to Sophia, "Please fill out these pages and return them to me as soon as possible. Frank has gone to get the triage nurse. You can take these with you to your husband's room. Please hurry for I need this information in order to get approval for him to receive medical care." She lifted the top page, "This last sheet is the insurance form. Put his card numbers and the expiration date here on the third line."

Sophia found the examining room. Geoffrey was being prodded and poked by a tall woman with red hair. Her medical jacket barely covered her low-cut dress. The woman's six inch heels were set off with glittery hose. The smell of perfume permeated the small room mixing with the odor of brunt leather and burnt skin. Geoffrey appeared to have rallied with this woman's attention. Sophia quietly studied the forms and filled out what she could, sitting in the plastic chair beside Geoffrey's gurney.

"Sir, you say you have been electrocuted?" The tall woman sat back on the medical stool to the right of Geoffrey. She had her own clipboard of questions to ask.

Geoffrey closed his eyes and sighed, he didn't attempt to speak. Sophia spoke up, "Geoffrey told me he had been electrocuted. I found him lying on the bed." Geoffrey carefully turned his head to stare at Sophia.

Again the question was directed at Geoffrey, "Sir, do you know how you were electrocuted? Was it in the house or was it from digging a hole outside?"

Geoffrey winced, his lips were dry. Sophia lifted her hand, "Could he have some water?"

The woman shook her head, "We would prefer to watch him for awhile before we give him anything to eat or drink."

Sophia patted Geoffrey's unhurt left hand, "Oh, let me answer for him. He put the key in his truck's transmission and was electrocuted." Sophia nodded her head toward her husband who attempted to smile.

"Your truck shorted out? Do you usually work on your own vehicles?" The woman kept focusing on Geoffrey. It was obvious Geoffrey didn't want to speak or couldn't speak.

Sophia lifted her hand again, "No. He drove home last night and the truck was fine. This morning he went out and the truck tried to kill him." Geoffrey rolled his eyes at her. She glared at him, 'What? Isn't that what happened?"

The examining room door opened and the nurse from the front desk reached her hand out to Sophia, "Have you finished the forms?" The clipboard with the completed forms was handed to her. "Thank you!" The nurse disappeared. The door closed for a moment only to open once again.

A booming voice entered the room, "Well, well, well. Who do we have here?" The assisting woman stood as the formidable man entered the room. He had thinning white hair and was rotund in physique. The woman pressed against the wall as the doctor moved to the head of Geoffrey's gurney. The woman gave the introductions, "Dr. Baker, this is Geoffrey Vinder. He says he was electrocuted while attempting to start his truck this morning."

Dr. Baker studied Geoffrey's face as he grabbed the medical stool. The doctor's medical jacket was not wide enough to button. He was handed the clipboard, his stethoscope was around his neck and his reading glasses were perched on the end of his Roman nose. Reading from the clipboard, Dr. Baker asked, "Geoffrey Vinder is it?" Geoffrey stared at the man.

Sophia stood, "Yes, this is my husband Geoffrey. I'm his wife Sophia."

The doctor frowned at Sophia. "Good thing for men to have a wife. Wives take good care of their men, well most of them do. Tell me, Sophia, did you see what happened?"

"No, sir, I backed out of the driveway before him to get our daughters to school. I wasn't sure why he wasn't following us. When I came home I found him on the bed in severe pain."

Dr. Baker looked down his nose through his reading glasses at Geoffrey, "Are you in much pain?"

Geoffrey nodded. The tall woman hurried out the door, "Let me get his chart from Rosie. I'll be right back, sir." She disappeared.

The doctor leaned back on the medical stool. "I believe this might have been an attempted murder, young man. What do you think?" Geoffrey closed his eyes. The doctor frowned. "Yes, I do believe we need to contact the authorities. Where is the truck at this moment?" His question was directed at Sophia.

"It's still in the driveway at home. We didn't move it. I'm amazed he got out of the truck and into the house with the jolt he must have received." Sophia touched Geoffrey's left hand, but this time he jerked it away.

While Sophia explained the condition he was in when she found him, Dr. Baker moved down to Geoffrey's left boot. He carefully prodded Geoffrey's ankle. Removing medical scissors from his pocket, the doctor began cutting away at the leather boot. Geoffrey's eyes widened as he lifted his head from the pillow to see the boot fall apart without even being cut. The leather crumpled like dust and fell to the floor.

Dr. Baker sniffed the black sock. "We need to care for burns." Dr. Baker rolled purple latex gloves onto his hands. Cautiously, he lifted Geoffrey's black sock. It disintegrated revealing Geoffrey's discolored skin.

The doctor stared at Sophia, "Ma'am, we need to have a specialist check out his truck. It may still have problems. What are you driving?"

"I drive the family van," Sophia fought back tears, "For some reason our lives have been very complicated lately."

Ripping open the pearl snap buttons on Geoffrey's cowboy shirt, the doctor put his stethoscope to his chest. He shook his head. The doctor opened a large cabinet and pulled out a metal scope. He carefully removed Geoffrey's black framed glasses to study his blue eyes, his mouth, and look up his nose. "We need to admit your husband and find out how badly he was injured. The problem with electricity is it can affect the heart, the nervous system, even the brain and we need to run extensive tests. The body is a network of nerves, electrical impulses and delicate tissues."

Dr. Baker jerked the plastic front off of the scope and threw it into the garbage can. He examined Geoffrey's thick lenses in the black plastic frames. 'These got a bit heated, didn't they?"

Showing Sophia the tiny hair-like cracks all throughout the frames, he asked, "Why don't you get your husband admitted with Rosie? She'll get your husband a room and have more forms for you to fill out." He opened the examining room door for Sophia.

The two of them walked side by side to the entry counter. Dr. Baker signaled Rosie. "We need her husband admitted for tests. His burns are not life threatening, but have the potential for infection. Also, we need to call the sheriff's office and have them examine the truck." He turned to Sophia, "Please don't leave without seeing me first. We'll take good care of your husband. His injuries appear to be minor, but without tests we won't know for sure." He took Sophia's right hand. "Make sure your husband's truck is no longer dangerous. Call the officers, please."

Rosie handed Sophia another clipboard of forms. "I'll call the sheriff's office and see if someone can help you. Do you know of anyone at the sheriff's office?" Sophia reached into her jean pocket and handed Rosie A.J.'s card. Rosie dialed the phone number, but did not hand Sophia the phone. She asked, "Yes, is this the sheriff's office. We have a possible attempted murder. The victim is here at the Rio Grodno's Urgent Care Clinic. Do you have time to speak with the wife of the victim? Yes, they are both here in the Urgent Care."

She handed the phone to Sophia. "Hello? Yes, this is Mrs. Vinder. Is A.J. Salazar available please?"

Sheriff A.J. Salazar stood tall behind Geoffrey's truck in their Rocoso driveway. The Dodge Dakota truck was a vibrant turquoise with white trim. Sheriff A.J. had spoken with the Rincon Bomb Squad and it was decided to leave the interior of the vehicle alone. The bomb squad would examine the truck thoroughly once it was in their impound lot. There was still a strong smoky smell emanating from the cab. Geoffrey's truck key was hanging in the ignition with his Star War's key ring insignia. When they were first married, Geoffrey told her he preferred to carry several small sets of keys. His reasoning was one large key chain put a bulge in his pant's pocket.

Sophia watched A.J. She leaned back against the passenger's side of the yellow van that was parked about twenty feet on the south side of the truck. The warm sun felt good on her face now the wind had stopped. When she left Geoffrey in his hospital room, he had been sleeping soundly in a bed of clean white sheets. Medics had x-rayed him, taken his blood, scraped his skin and finally let him sleep after three hours of probing. Sophia glanced at her watch. It was almost one o'clock and she needed to call Dr. Goldfarb and let him know Geoffrey would not be making his appointment.

The gray tow truck backed slowly down the driveway. It was beeping with every moment, following A.J.'s directions. Sophia smiled at A.J. Salazar. He was becoming a good friend. After her call to him from the hospital, he was at the house within the hour. He even brought the Rincon County tow truck.

A car horn honked behind her. She turned to see their neighbor Patsy wave as she drove into the driveway on the next hill. Patsy and her husband lived on the quarter acre of land due west of them and loved to come over and sit the girls. Patsy called out, but Sophia wasn't able to hear her over the noise of the tow truck. Sophia turned her head to listen when she heard a clicking sound. Cautiously, she began to move forward toward the sound. The clicking was barely audible over the loud tow truck's beeping.

A.J. put his hand up stopping the tow truck. The tow truck wasn't even close to Geoffrey's truck. Suddenly Sophia felt A.J. shove her. In one mighty sonic boom shrapnel flew through the air. A.J. hugged her around her waist as he threw her to the ground. His body pressed firmly against hers. His gloved hand held the back of her head, shoving her face into the dirt. Sophia tried to lift her head as she gasped for air, but A.J. had a death grip on her. She could feel his body jerk on top of her. Something wet dripped down onto her cheek and into her right eye. Her hands were trapped under her with A.J.'s weight heavy on her back. Suddenly there was a deafening silence.

Sophia shut her eyes and then heard a truck door slam. After a few minutes, a gruff voice with a thick Spanish accent called to her, "Lady, you get up?" Sophia tried to open her eyes against the dirt. All she saw were black work boots. "Lady, let me get him. No, he's no good. He no move, do you have phone in house?"

Sophia tried to lift her body, turning her head to the right her skin was raked in the dirt. She whispered, "Yes, there's a phone in the kitchen! Call an ambulance. Please hurry!" She could feel sticky blood on her face. A woman didn't have to give birth to know the feel of blood. "A.J., are you there? A.J., are you awake?"

Sophia felt her right leg cramp and then her back went into spasm. "Oh, please, be alive. Please, God, let him be alive!" Sophia desperately wanted to free her arms and hands, but his weight and the concern for his health kept her flat against the ground.

She heard footsteps running to her. "Lady, ambulance coming, I give your address from order sheet. The man coming now, here no time. No move. The man he's no good." The speaker knelt next to her. Sophia mumbled through the dirt, "Can you help me? My right leg has a cramp. Can you pull my foot toward the house, just give a gentle pull, it hurts."

"No, is blood. I no hurt you more." The man stood and walked away from her. Sophia was worried he might leave. Frantically, she called through the dirt around her lips, "Sir, can you stay by me? Come back and stay with me? Tell me what happened, please?" Dirt wedged between her teeth. Blood kept dripping down her cheek.

The man moved closer to her, "The truck went boom! Metal all over. Truck ka-boom, man in truck bleeding, no move." She heard the man sigh as he lit a cigarette. "Good I use side mirror. My head in truck, truck no good. Tires gone, metal here, dog in house is good dog."

Sophia closed her eyes, poor Daisy. She had been removed from one murder scene to another. The sound of sirens filled the air. Sophia closed her eyes and let the darkness surround her. Somewhere in her brain she knew she was being moved, jostled, and placed on a moving bed, but she couldn't open her eyes. Sounds of voices and smells of alcohol filled her senses. She felt someone cutting off her clothes and tried to come back to the light. The darkness wouldn't let her go.

"Try again, maybe this time she'll wake up. Just gently nudge her onto her left side." A soft voice spoke from across the room.

Sophia felt her arm move. Carefully, she opened her eyes. The room was gun metal gray. She started to close her eyes. "Sophia, hey, Sophia, open up. It's time to wake up. Your sister-in-law is here and your mother wants to talk to you. Come on, open those big brown eyes."

Slowly, Sophia lifted her eyelids. Her voice was barely above a whisper. "Are you an angel?" The woman leaning over her had a flowing mane of red and gold. The woman's emerald eyes were evenly placed around a straight nose with a few freckles carefully scattered on the tops of her round cheeks.

"No, it's me Emily. I came when Margaret called me. We're both here. We were scared for you when we heard about the explosion. Granger picked up the girls from school. He has them at your house in Rocoso. We thought it best if the women of the family were here with you." Emily's soft voice comforted Sophia.

Sophia jerked forward, "Granger has the girls!" Her throat hurt. The left side of her face felt as if it has been sandpapered. "Emily, we can't leave Granger with the girls, he'll kill them! My God, Donna is only six years old and Sybil is nine! He could do horrible things to my girls!"

Margaret was now standing behind Emily. "Sophia, now listen here, your brother had nothing to do with the explosion! Your brother would not hurt your girls. He loves them as if they were his own. I will not have you saying such things." Margaret shoved Emily out of her way to face Sophia, "Family does not hurt family! I will not put up with your paranoia. Why do you hate your brother?"

Margaret brushed Sophia's hair off of her forehead, "We're here to help you! Do you understand? Your brother cares about you and loves you. He would never hurt you or the girls!" Margaret's voice got higher in volume as she spoke as she glared at Sophia.

Emily interjected, "Sophia, don't worry about anything right now. You need to rest and get better." Emily turned her attention to Sophia's mother, "Margaret, weren't you going out the door to help Granger with the girls? Remember Granger called about Donna's nose bleed and you told him you would be right there? Weren't you leaving to help him?"

Margaret smirked, "Yes, I guess I am. Donna only gets nose bleeds for attention, she doesn't fool me. I will set her straight and Granger is a complete wuss for a medical man!" She gave Sophia a firm pat on her shoulder, "Sophia, I love you. You are my beautiful daughter. Your Mama loves you, don't you forget it." Margaret grabbed her heavy coat off the back of the plastic chair as she circled the hospital bed to give Sophia a kiss on her right cheek. Carefully, she wiped her pink lipstick off Sophia's cheek, "There, there, you rest and don't worry about the girls. We're here to step in and help out." Margaret shoved her purse under her arm, "Emily, I'll talk to you later. Try to get to Rocoso no later then ten o'clock because I have to get home to feed the horse."

"Wait!" Emily's flowing India print top billowed around her as she disappeared around the corner of the hospital door. She called out to Margaret, "Why don't you get Granger to feed Geordie? He knows how and it's close to where he lives."

Slowly, Sophia took in her surroundings. The hospital room had another bed in it, but it was unoccupied. Tan curtains separating the beds were pushed back against the wall of gray. A television was screwed into the wall straight in front of her. The television screen was black. The windows to her right had tan Venetian blinds, which were lowered to the bottom of the window frame. The floor was gray linoleum. Ceiling squares of white were placed in metal frames.

Sophia wiggled her toes and then she moved her feet. The only intense pain she felt was in the back of her right calf muscle. There were tiny pinpricks of pain up and down the back of her right leg, but one place felt as if she had been stabbed with a knife. She moved her fingers up to her face. The left side of her face burned when she touched it. This cheek was the one that had been pushed into the dirt.

Carefully, Sophia pushed her fingers through her hair. Her hair was sticky on the right, but there were no cuts or sharp painful areas on her head. She was trying to pull the sticky stuff from her hair when Emily walked into the room. "Your mother doesn't believe Granger wants to mess with Geordie. Evidently Granger finds horses to be dirty and he was raised on a farm! Margaret obviously knows what's best for her horse, right? Well that's the Pino family for you!"

"Oh," Emily hurriedly pulled Sophia's fingers out of her hair. "There's blood in your hair. We tried to get it out using a warm washcloth and some soap, but you really need to have your hair shampooed. Don't mess with it. You're only making it worse."

Sophia pointed to the plastic pitcher on the side table, "Could you get me some water? My throat's dry."

Emily took the plastic cup into the bathroom with the door open she explained, "It's amazing you survived the explosion. The television has been running news about it since four o'clock this afternoon. Evidently even the adobe walls around the front of your house have metal or steel shrapnel stuck in them. On the television it looked like a porcupine sculpture. The noise alone was heard all the way into Rincon." Emily brought the cup to Sophia. "Here, take a drink of this. There isn't any water in that pitcher."

Sophia carefully swallowed the gloriously cold water. It tasted of chlorine. Emily continued, "The Rocoso fire department, the Rincon fire department, and the Rincon Sheriff's department all descended on the scene within minutes. Your nice neighbors Jim and Patsy took the dog to their house. They called Samuel Goldfarb who gave them Margaret's phone number. I guess you had Mr. Goldfarb's card on the kitchen counter. Patsy gave the ambulance crew all your information. She was great, evidently." Emily pulled a plastic chair close to the hospital bed.

Emily combed her flowing mane of hair with her long fingers."You gave everyone a horrible fright. Evidently houses shook up to several miles away and we were thankful there was no fire." Shaking her head, she brushed the knees of her black leotard leggings. "The sheriff saved your life. If he wouldn't have pushed you to the ground, you would've been cut in half with all the flying debris. The poor boy in the tow truck didn't make it." Emily shook her head, "A piece of glass from the tow truck's back window ripped right through his throat. He was turning to stare out the back window. Mr. Torres the tow truck driver is an emotional wreck. He was the one who called the ambulance."

Pushing buttons on the remote beside the bed Sophia finally got the bed to rise, allowing her to sit upright. "Emily, does Geoffrey know what happened? Is he all right?"

Emily stared at the floor, "Geoffrey is in trouble. They have him under house arrest for the explosion. The State Police believe he electrocuted himself when he was setting the bomb. They won't listen to anyone. They're convinced Geoffrey is the mad bomber."

Shaking her head, Emily said, "They have a guard at his door down the hall. There was a big guy from the State Police with a black uniform and a gun keeping out the television people and curious groupies. Now I think they have a cop who just sits out there reading magazines or something. He won't let any of us into see him." She pointed to the south side of the room. "Of course Geoffrey was terrified when he saw the news on television. They won't let him out of his room and he isn't allowed any visitors. They won't even let him use the phone. I'm sorry, Sophia, this is all a horrible mess."

Sophia let her tears fall, she wiped them with the top of the bed sheet, "This isn't your fault. You didn't do this, did you, Emily?"

"No. You and I both know who did and we have no proof to show for it." Emily brought her a tissue box from the dresser on the other side of the hospital room. "Here you go, the last thing you need is a red nose to go with your red cheek." She laughed and then shook her head, "Poor Geoffrey is in horrible pain. His foot is wrapped in creams and sterile bandages. We don't know if he is going to lose his foot or not. Then this happens." Emily shook her head.

Sophia took another sip of chlorine water, "Do you know what happened to A.J.?"

"Who? Here let me move the pillow for you." Emily gently removed the pillow from behind her back to place it behind her head. "Your poor hair is a mess. There, are you feeling better? Are you more awake now?" Emily perched on the edge of the plastic chair.

"Yes, thank you. The sheriff is A.J. Salazar. How is he?" Sophia rolled her stiff shoulders.

"Oh, yes, he's in the critical care unit. His wife and son are there with him. Last time I checked, the nurses weren't letting anyone see him. He was in surgery for almost three hours earlier. His wife is in shock. She kept saying, 'nothing like this happens here,' over and over again. His son is a clerk at the Bank of Rincon. He's trying to get his mother to go home and rest, but she won't leave."

Emily reached under the chair to pull a woven bag into her lap. "Would you like me to wash your hair? I have some shampoo in here. What with the moving and all, I put all of our necessaries in my traveling bag." A small bottle of shampoo appeared. "Here is the two-in-one shampoo and conditioner hair treatment bottle. This is found in every hotel across the country."

Feeling weak and unsure, Sophia whispered, "Sure, I would love to have my hair washed, but how can we do it?"

Emily pointed to the open hospital room door, "The bathroom has towels and its right behind the hospital door. You were watching me wash out the cup, remember? We can take this chair in there, lean it back against the sink and you put your head back and I'll wash." Emily pushed the chair into the bathroom after closing the main door to the room.

She returned to help Sophia sit straight in the bed. "All right, let's get you sitting up with your feet over the edge of the bed. What do you think? Do you think you can do this?" Emily folded back the hospital sheet and white blanket. She rubbed Sophia's legs with her cold hands.

"Emily, your hands are as cold as ice! They feel good, but do you think I am allowed to get up?" Sophia was hesitant, her throat still burned and her heart was beating quickly. "I want to go home where I can sleep and not be weak or stupid!"

"You're not weak or stupid. You were attacked by flying metal and have been through a horrible shock. Sophia, take your time. We can do this slowly." Emily hugged her. "Please don't feel pushed, if you aren't ready to get up right now, we can wait."

"I feel so weak and sad, Emily." Trying to sound strong and not whine, Sophia persisted to explain, "Everything's going wrong. I know I need to be brave, but for some reason right now I feel so tired. I'm tired of being attacked by Granger and my mother. If only my girls were here or Geoffrey then I would do better, I promise." Sophia leaned her head against Emily's shoulder. "I am glad you're here--can we wash my hair, really?"

"Sure, the I.V. is out, the catheter is removed and the doctor said you could probably go home tomorrow." Emily handed her another tissue, "Wipe your nose and let's give it a go. Here, I will sit next to you and you put your arm around my neck. This way if you feel faint I can catch you."

Slowly the two of them worked to have Sophia standing. "I never realized how tall I am. This feels very high for me." Wavering, she held tightly to Emily. "This is wild, I feel like I grew."

"Hey, you're smiling!" Emily laughed, "Imagine the basketball players who are seven feet tall? I wonder if they get altitude sickness when they get up in the morning." Emily lifted Sophia's right leg away from the hospital bed, "You have a deep gash in the back here. See the bandage? Try to not hit it on anything because it will hurt." They slowly moved into the bathroom.

Two pillows were placed under Sophia's bottom as she tilted in the plastic chair. Sophia's neck nestled on a rolled towel at the edge of the sink. The back of her head was held in Emily's cupped hand. Emily was testing the water to be sure it was warm, when the nurse came into the room. "Hey, where's my patient?"

Emily called out, "We're in the bathroom, in here." The nurse's smile brightened her face and her brown eyes, "Why you have your own hairdresser, how lovely. Maybe you can do my hair when you finish with hers?"

Laughing at her, Emily replied, "We thought we would get the sticky blood out of her hair. Is it all right if we do this?"

The nurse leaned her shoulder against the door frame, "Sure, I came in here to see if she could walk down the hall with me, but this works." The nurse disappeared for a moment only to return with two more thin towels. "Here, I'll put these on your lap, okay? Also, are you hungry? Do you want me to bring you some soup or a sandwich? We have some supplies at the nurses' station and I thought you might be hungry?"

Sophia tried to turn her head, but Emily had a firm hold on hair. The nurse interrupted her thoughts to say, "When you finish with the hair washing she needs to use the toilet. We need to measure her output. Be sure to use the catch tray, all right?"

Thinking she better speak, Sophia asked, "Some soup would be great and do you have any crackers? Oh, and do you know how my husband is doing? Can you tell me anything about his foot?"

"The soup and crackers are no problem, but the information about your husband will not be forthcoming. Would you like something to drink? We have fruit juices and bottled water?" The nurse moved closer to watch Emily pour the shampoo mixture onto Sophia's hair.

Closing her eyes for protection, Sophia answered, "How about some apple juice with the soup and crackers?" The nurse patted her shoulder and disappeared out the door.

"They have good room service here at this hospital. How funny for her to think I was your hairdresser, right?" Emily gave her head a firm scrubbing. "Sorry about the news being withheld regarding Geoffrey."

Toweled dry and safely back in bed, Sophia sighed. The soup and crackers had been quickly eaten. Emily pulled a container of Baby Lotion from her purse and rubbed the pink lotion on her hands. "You must have been hungry you ate all of that in a heartbeat!" She pushed the moving table away from the bed. "Here, let me rub some lotion on your legs and back. I can give you one of my deluxe massages."

The bed was put flat as Sophia rolled onto her stomach. Emily's massages were famous. Emily and Granger had started their relationship at massage school nine years ago. They had fallen in love and both decided to stay in the same field, but in different specialties. Granger studied back and muscle pain therapy. Emily continued to study massage and became a specialist in Shiatsu deep muscle manipulation.

They had their own business for a time. Emily became more in demand than Granger and their lives changed. When Emily was pregnant with Shirley, they decided to go into the associated business with Henker and Enid. Emily continued as a freelance masseuse out of their home in order to have enough money for Shirley's preschool. This gave her some independence and time to be with her daughter. As she became better known among the professional dancers, Popejoy Theater paid her to come twice a week to work on their ballet troupes' sore muscles. Emily fell in love with ballet and dance. She followed the dancers not only in their performances, but she also took classes with some of them.

Sophia groaned in delight as Emily worked on her back. "Oh, that feels so good."

"You need to rest now. Tomorrow you're going to be alone with the girls for the weekend. They're probably scared and concerned." Emily pushed her thumb into a tight muscle in Sophia's back.

Emily explained, "The girls and I worked this afternoon at picking up a bunch of metal so when you come home tomorrow it won't be all over the place. The flatbed of the truck is still intact and the tires are fine. They look brand new." Emily rubbed more lotion into Sophia's back.

Speaking out of the left side of her mouth, Sophia explained, "Granger's accusations have put my marriage into a conundrum. Emily, do you know Granger said he's going to take the Rocoso home away from us if we stay married? What does he expect us to do?" She let her body relax under Emily's professional instructions. "Oh, yes, the tires are only one month old."

"Granger really is a dirt bag, Sophia. No offense to you. You and Granger are as different as day and night. Of course you never followed Margaret around as if she were the saintly mother of God." Emily pushed on a knotted muscle, "Wow, you really are tight. The sheriff must have landed hard on your back. He should be given a hero's medal. Just breathe through this, Sophia, this is going to hurt." Emily covered her body with Baby Lotion, "Sophia, for what it is worth, Granger isn't the sharpest knife in the drawer. He is easily manipulated by your mother with promises of money and materialistic wealth. Be careful what you say to either one of them in regards to the property or Geoffrey. My experience with Granger is that whatever you tell him hits his mother's ears before he is able to cognate what was said." Emily patted her on the back, "There you go. Now I better wash my hands and get out of here."

Emily lifted the phone on the bedside table, "Sophia, I am going to call Margaret to let her know I'm on my way. It is after nine o'clock and she will be frantic to get home."

Hanging up the phone, Emily placed a brush on the side table. "You look fantastic. Too bad we couldn't visit Geoffrey." Emily grabbed her woven purse and flung it over her shoulder, "I'll be here tomorrow around eleven with your girls to take you home, right?"

Sophia smiled, "Right, but Emily, where is Shirley? I'm sorry I forgot to ask."

"No worries, she's with Enid and Henker at their house. She's having fun with Alistair. This is a vacation for her. I'm glad she's with them and having some fun, times have been tough lately. See you tomorrow, hope you feel better." Emily disappeared into the hall.

Sophia pushed the nurse's button. The nurse who eventually answered her call was Hispanic, all gangly limbs, thick brown hair, with enormous eyes and apprehension, "You rang?"

"Yes, I would like to walk. My legs are stiff and some exercise might limber them, what do you think?" Sophia pushed away the sheet and blanket.

The nurse came to her side, "It would look good on your chart if we had a walk. Here let me help you. By the way, my name is Stacy." The nurse lifted Sophia's legs to the side of the bed. "There you go, just hop right off the old bed."

"Whoa, you're a tall one aren't you? Don't lean on me or I will fall over!" Stacy let Sophia find her equilibrium. Sophia put her arm through Stacy's as they slowly ambled down the hall. The smell of pine cleaner was stronger in the hall. She noticed the policeman sitting in a cafeteria chair similar to the one in her room. He had his back to Geoffrey's door. As they moved closer, she noticed he was reading a magazine on foreign weaponry. When they came to him, Sophia stopped. "Excuse me, but do you think I could see my husband?"

The policeman didn't even look up from the magazine. He grunted, "No one is allowed in there, good night."

Stacy gave Sophia's arm a gentle pull, "Come on, he's a stickler that one. He won't even let us take in the food tray. Just leave him alone."

When they finished their walk, Stacy helped Sophia to the bathroom and back into bed. "Honey, you just have to let things work themselves out. There's nothing you can do with the cop sitting there. Just let it be until tomorrow." She pulled the sheet and the blanket over Sophia. "When you get out of here go talk to the bomb squad. They have some specialists from Kirkland Air Force Base examining the wreckage. It was on the news. You go to sleep and let the world find the truth."

Sophia leaned back on the soft pillow as she put the bed flat. Closing her eyes she could envision Geoffrey in his bed down the hall. Saying a quiet prayer she went to sleep.

17

Rio Grodno's Hospital
Saturday, January, 1988

There was a soft knock on the hospital door. Sophia was preoccupied with her soupy oatmeal, cold tea, and dry toast on the tray in front of her. Glancing up, she said, "Come in." A tall man dressed in a Navy uniform strode into the room. Dropping his duffel bag on the floor, he moved quickly to Sophia. She was out of the bed and in his arms in one movement. Her voice squeaked as he squeezed her tightly against his uniform. "Stephen, when did you get here? Where have you been?"

His arms firmly held her against his chest, "No one is to know where I've been. If I tell you then I'd have to kill you and there is enough of that around here, but I'm here now." Gently, he set her down. Her bare feet were on his big boots. Stephen placed her onto the bed. "My superior received a telegram stating Geoffrey was at death's door. Later I got a call that you were blown up and the girls were left to the devices of a wicked grandmother. Here I am!"

Lanky fingers reached to pick out a dried piece of toast. He drank down the half cup of tea and moved to the chair by the window. "All right, you have some explaining to do."

Sophia covered her legs with the sheet as she leaned back in the bed, "Stephen, we are at war." She related to him all the events of the last two weeks, including Carols' confrontation at her father's the day he died and Carol's attack by the swimming pool. Carefully, she explained the problems with the truck. Shaking her head, she outlined the events of how Geoffrey had told Granger about being at the lawyer's office at one o'clock, which was the exact time the truck blew up in their driveway.

Stephen kept sneaking the food off her tray, slowly eating as he listened. "Wow, you are under attack. You do know who all of this is pointing to, don't you?"

"Yes, my brother, but we don't have anyway of proving his involvement with any of this." Quickly, Sophia put her hands around the soupy oatmeal and pulled the bowl away from him. "This is mine."

"What about the sheriff A.J.? Did he find any evidence that pointed to your brother? Did you two talk about Carol and her condition the day the truck blew?" Stephen knelt beside his duffel bag forging for something as he listened to her.

"Stephen, A.J. is my hero. He's the one who listened and cared about what I said. He knew for a fact Geoffrey wouldn't hurt his beloved truck. Stephen, we worked for four years to buy Geoffrey's truck. Remember how we were driving the old yellow family van for years as our only vehicle? I would drive everyone to school, hurry to get Geoffrey to work, rush to the campus, only to turn around and do the same thing in the afternoon. It was crazy."

Sophia pushed her bangs from her forehead. "A.J. was someone who cared about people. I miss him and pray he is all right up there." She pointed to the ceiling. Stephen pulled a pair of worn jeans, a white shirt, and yellow windbreaker out of his mystery bag.

Another soft knock rapped on the door. Both of them turned to find an older Hispanic woman hunched over in the door's opening. Her soft voice was barely audible, "I'm glad you believe my husband is your hero." The woman fell against the door frame. Stephen hurried to her side holding her as he led her to the chair. He kicked his duffel bag out of the way, "Here, please sit down."

Her soft brown eyes were red rimmed. Her face was pale and made more so by the sadness she held. "Are you Mrs. Vinder?"

Sophia slid off the bed and knelt at her side, "Yes, I am. Are you A.J.'s beautiful wife?"

The woman attempted a smile, "Yes, I am." Gulping for air, she took Sophia's hand. "A.J. is in a coma." Tears fell down her delicate cheeks. "They don't know..." She shook her head, "They don't know if he will be with us much longer." Stephen handed her a handful of tissues he had pulled from the box by the bed.

Sophia noticed the woman was much younger than she appeared, "Mrs. Salazar, if I know A.J. and I only met him two days ago, I believe he will be with us for a long time. He isn't one to give up on you or anyone. He survived many tests in his life and this is just another one. He'll pull through. I know it!"

They both heard Stephen go into the bathroom. He closed the door and a loud stream of water ensued followed by the flushing of the toilet. Both the women stared at each other and then burst out laughing. At the same time they said, "Men!"

Mrs. Salazar wiped her eyes. "You know you're right. I am so tired of waiting for him to wake up. I think I'm just tired." She put her hand on Sophia's shoulder. "How are you feeling?"

Sophia stood, "I'm fine, but worried about your husband, what is happening in our lives and what we should do next. I'm going home later this morning, which doesn't seem fair with your husband fighting for his life. Do you think I could go and see him with you?" Sophia reached behind her to pull her hospital gown closed. "Then maybe you should let your son take you home for some sleep. You have to take care of your health if you're going to be taking care of A.J. later. Both of you need to lean on each other."

"Mom, what are you doing in here?" A young man in his twenties with dark hair, a full beard, and a rumpled brown suit rushed up to Mrs. Salazar. "Sorry, I didn't mean for her to come here and bother you."

The bathroom door opened and six foot eight inch tall Stephen appeared. He had replaced his uniform with his less formal clothes. His shiny dome of a head was well washed as was his shaven face and his blue eyes appeared to be refreshed. The duffel bag was dropped at the foot of the bed. "Hey, we're having a party! See what I miss when I'm off trying to save the world? All this good stuff happens wherever Sophia goes." Stephen stuck out his enormous hand, "Stephen Vinder's the name, brother-in-law to this beautiful woman right here. How do you do, Sir?"

The young man's hand disappeared in Stephen's big hand, "Marcus Salazar at your service, Sir."

Stephen burst out laughing, "You were in the military?"

Marcus smiled, "I was in ROTC in high school several years ago. The officers beat respect into you, Sir."

Stephen slapped him on the back, shoving him into the bed, "Good job! Now, we have a situation here. We may need to be working together in order to solve these mysterious threats. There is a rat in the cupboard who believes himself safe and invincible. Our purpose, men and women, is to prove him wrong. Are we willing and able?" Stephen stood erect as he spoke.

In response, Mrs. Salazar lifted her frail body from the chair, "I am Rosa and if I'm going to be part of the team, you need to call me Rosa." She saluted him with her hand and a smile.

Stephen saluted her, "Yes, Ma'am, we shall do so."

Marcus grinned, "Mom, you are finally smiling! Let's get some chairs and come up with a plan, if this meets with your permission, Sir?"

Stephen wrapped his arm around Marcus," You know, Marcus, you're going to go far. Let's go get some chairs." They disappeared into the hall.

Rosa resumed sitting, "This brother-in-law of yours is something. Does he solve problems in the military?"

Smiling, Sophia said, "Well, he thinks he does and sometimes he believes he does it all by himself."

Rosa nodded at the door, "He is a ray of sunshine on this gloomy day. I hope he can help us figure out who is doing all these murders. My husband could use the help now that he is in the hospital, although, A.J. did tell me you were quite the Miss Marple."

"Miss Marple?" Sophia frowned, "He told me I was a want-to-be Agatha Christy. Wish he would get his characters straight so I know who to be!"

Stephen came into the room carrying a chair. Another man in a uniform followed him with two more chairs. Pressing her hospital gown closed, Sophia put out her hand in greeting, "Ignacio, it is good to see you! We are sorry about your boss."

Ignacio twisted his sheriff's hat in his hands. "Yes, Mrs. Vinder, sorry you were hurt. I went up to see Sheriff Salazar and they told me his family was here. The office feels empty without him being there."

Rosa delicately lifted her hand to him. Stephen bellowed, "Howdy, you must be the new sheriff in town! I am Stephen Vinder—just rode in here to help solve the predicament of the day." Ignacio's hand disappeared in Stephen's as they shook hands. "Now, I believe your boss A.J. had facts relevant to this case. The State Police have my brother under lock and key up the hall there." Stephen nodded to his right, "They won't let me see him and I'm an admiral in the United States Navy. The cop outside isn't even a deputy." Stephen shook his shiny head, "Sad state of affairs when they hire a rent-a-cop to keep an admiral from doing his civil duty."

Ignacio laughed, "You know I like you!" Then he turned to Sophia, "A.J.

found some evidence at the scene where Carol Grover was attacked. There were empty vials of double strength insulin in the garbage bag outside her neighbor's house. The neighbor called A.J. to tell him someone had put their garbage bag in his receptacle. The man is very possessive about his receptacle because once he found loose syringes in it and was sure Carol's landlords were drug dealers. When A.J. brought the bag to the department we found the vials. They were outdated and old, but the pharmacist at the Walgreen's Pharmacy told us they were potent."

Stephen slapped Ignacio on the back, "You know what this means don't you?"

Ignacio regained his balance, "Sorry, don't know much about chemistry. What does it mean?" Taking a pencil from his inside shirt pocket, Stephen pulled the menu paper from Sophia's food tray. "Here let me show you."

Rosa was now standing beside Ignacio. Sophia was sitting on the bed with Stephen next to her. Stephen drew a diagram on the paper, "Here is the normal level of glucose in the body. This happens when someone takes too much insulin. See how this line dips way down?" He drew a straight line then a dip. "The human body cannot function without some glucose. The brain, the kidneys, every major organ in the human body needs a supply of glucose or sugar to be fully capable of supporting the life system." Stephen drew dotted lines straight across the paper.

Ignacio stepped back, "What happens if there isn't enough glucose?"

"The human body shuts down. It ceases to function within minutes. The kidneys fail, the brain ceases up, and the heart stops pumping, the person goes into a death spiral. Death is almost instant. Most diabetics have sugar in their pocket or know when they are in trouble. The person will start to shake, sweat, and have difficulty breathing. They know immediately what to do. Unless, they're in a swimming pool and can't reach any sugar."

Rosa put her hand on Stephen's arm, "Is this what happened to your friend?" Stephen drew a stick figure lying on its side, "Yes, this happened to Carol Grover and your husband figured it out. He knew about the insulin and I bet he knew about the photos."

Turning to Ignacio, Stephen asked, "Did your boss find any photos at Carol's crime scene?" The diagram paper was wadded up and thrown into the wastebasket across the room.

Ignacio shook his head, "No, we searched because of what Mrs. Vinder told us, but we didn't find anything. Mrs. Vinder did explain to us that Miss Grover's purse was out of place, but we didn't find anything in Carol Grover's purse."

Shaking his head, Stephen stared at Sophia, "Mrs. Vinder, huh? Her first name is Sophia, but maybe you didn't know? Or are we to refer to her as Mrs. Vinder from now on?"

Ignacio turned his round rimmed hat around in his hands, "Yes, Sir, did know her name, but my boss prefers we show respect to the persons of interest. In the line of duty and all that is important."

Sophia reached for the phone, "I'm going to call Carol's hospital in Albuquerque and find out how she's doing."

Ignacio leaned against the bed, "They didn't tell you?"

Sophia put the phone down, "What?"

"She died last night in the intensive care. Both of her kidneys failed and there was nothing anyone could do. I sat next to her, holding her hand until they declared her dead."

Rosa promptly fell onto the chair. She pulled the tissues to her face as tears quietly fell. "Por Dios, more people die."

Ignacio turned away from them. Pulling the chord on the Venetian blinds, he allowed the bright daylight into the room. "A.J. sent me there when he got your call for help with the truck. He told me to stay with her until she was out of danger. He was worried someone might try to make a second attempt on her life. I stayed right beside her. I sat and watched her until eleven-thirty-four last night. I was there when they declared her dead. I walked her body to the morgue. Then I went home and crashed." He turned to Rosa, "I came this morning to see you and find out about A.J."

Giving him a confirming welcome, Rosa nodded to him. "A.J. is still not able to speak, he is in a coma. But tell us about your friend Carol"

Ignacio's his voice cracked as he spoke, "You get to know someone when you go through all their history. Carl went through all of her drawers and he even inventoried her makeup. I spent hours searching for her next of kin or someone who would come and be with her. There is no one in her family left alive. She shouldn't have died, not like that, not so young."

Clasping her hands in front of her, Sophia asked, "She had no family at all?"

"No, no one to contact and perhaps no one to go to her funeral or have her buried properly." Ignacio's face was becoming redder.

"Ignacio, no, she does have family. She has us and we will see to it she is not forgotten. She will have a proper burial, although, she did write up a will. It must be somewhere. Oh, we will have to go to her house in town and find it. Will you go with me?" Ignacio silently nodded at Sophia.

Marcus dragged two chairs into the room. "Hey, Ignacio's here. Now we have a full team. Ignacio how goes it, man?" Marcus placed the chairs around Sophia's bed. Everyone was focused on Ignacio and ignored Marcus.

Marcus put his hands up, "What did I miss?" His face was solemn with concern. Rosa waved at him with her tissues, "No, Marcus, Ignacio is speaking of Carol Grover. She was the woman your father was investigating. She's dead." Marcus put his hand on Ignacio's shoulder, "Sorry, man, sorry to hear she died. Was she special to you?"

Surprisingly, Ignacio answered, "Yes, she was real special. She was a bright spirit with a reason to live. I interviewed her about Granger Pino's fiancé and the horse. She had a really cool dog that never protected her, but she believed her dog was her spirit guardian." He stared out the window into the light. "She was really upset over Dr. Walter Pino's death and Mrs. Vinder's strange relationship to her family." He kept rotating his hat in his hands.

Stephen coughed, "We need a plan. First, we have to spring Sophia from this place. Then somehow communicate with Geoffrey. He knew his truck better than anyone. He would know who and how to rig the truck." Turning one of the chairs backwards he straddled it, "The problem is we need proof. In order to get proof we have to catch the bad guy in the act. Any suggestions, people?"

Sophia nodded, "Somehow we need to let Geoffrey know we're trying to help him. Stephen, he's safe in here with the rent-a-cop, isn't he? At least a certain person can't get in there and hurt him, right?"

Stephen looked at her through his eyebrows, "Sophia, Geoffrey can take care of himself. Evidently, he wasn't seriously hurt by the jolt he got from the truck. Somehow he knew the truck was rigged when the key went in rough. The damage could have been much worse if he hadn't been aware of trouble." Stephen cleared his throat, "Geoffrey is probably safer in here with the rent-a-cop outside of his door. Geoffrey would know how to trap the culprit."

Marcus frowned as he sat down in the chair to the right of Stephen, "You both are speaking as if you know who the guilty person is. Do you?" A woman's voice announced from the loudspeaker in the hall that the time was ten o'clock and all visitors were to leave. Visitors would be allowed later at six p.m. this evening.

Ignacio pulled the Venetian blind chord to let the blinds fall, "Yes, we all know who the culprit is." He kicked Stephen's chair, "Tell him."

Stephen glanced down at Ignacio's polished boot, "It's Sophia's family. More precisely it is more than likely her brother Granger."

"What the hell is going on in here? Why are you talking about me?" Granger charged into the room reeking of cologne. His moustache was well coiffed, his brown hair slicked back with pomade, and his red satin ascot neatly knotted. "I don't know what you think you're doing here, Stephen? I'm here to take my sister home." Granger glared at Sophia, "Stephen, you should go back to protecting the country with your bombs and secret codes. You're not welcome or wanted here."

Granger's icy eyes studied each one of them. "I'll be waiting for you in the hall, Little Sister! Oh, Mom is here with your clothes. You don't appear to be bothered entertaining with your butt flapping. Here she is." Granger walked out as Margaret hurried in breathless.

"Oh, my, all these people are here!" Margaret carried a small pink suitcase. "Hello, Stephen, how nice to see you. How thoughtful of you to visit your sister-in-law. How sad you weren't here to help with your brother yesterday. You know he was almost killed?" She took inventory of her audience, "Goodness, I wasn't expecting so many people to visit you, Sophia. Who would have thought you were so popular? Why don't you introduce to me your new friends?"

Margaret flung the suitcase onto the bed, "Sophia, here are your clothes. You might want to dress in the bathroom, unless you want to make a spectacle of yourself, which we all know you like to do. I just keep hoping someday you will become the woman I always wanted you to be." Before Sophia could introduce anyone to Margaret, she turned on her heel and departed the room.

Nodding at Sophia, Marcus said, "Wow, that's your mother-in-law?" He stood and lifted two chairs. "No," Stephen tersely answered, "That's her mother also known as the Great and Almighty God Mother. Here, Marcus, let me go with you. Sophia, we'll leave you to dress, come on, guys." The men emptied the room carrying chairs back outside of the room. They closed the door behind them. Rosa blew her nose on a tissue. "Sophia, can I call you Sophia? You have such a beautiful name. I only had one son and he is a dutiful son, but I always wanted to have a daughter. "

Opening the suitcase, Sophia nodded 'yes.' She pulled out a sports bra, a pair of white cotton underpants, and a pair of black socks. She placed her jeans and a green sweater next to them on the bed. Shaking her head, Sophia lifted her hiking boots from the bottom of the suitcase. "She packed them with the mud still stuck to the bottom treads. Go figure?"

Rosa reached into her purse and pulled out a plastic comb, "Here, for your hair." Sophia took the comb, grabbed her clothes and went into the bathroom.

When she came out, Rosa was smoothing down the sheet and blanket on the bed. Sophia smiled at her thoughtfulness, "You know they're just going to strip the bed when I leave?"

"Yes, but at least you have a neat room. It's important to leave the room in order." Sophia reached over to the bedside table, "This was under the sheet by the foot of your bed." She gave Sophia a small piece of faded blue paper. She set the suitcase by the door. "The pencil is difficult to make out. Did you read it?"

Rosa took the small piece of paper from her. She held it close to her face, "It says, 'the battery was wired to the starter Granger too stupid.'" She handed it back to Sophia.

Whispering loudly, Sophia hugged the paper, "It's from Geoffrey! How in the world did it get in here?" She took Rosa's hand, "It's from my husband!" She hugged Rosa's shoulders in her hands, "How in the world did this get in here, Rosa? I miss my husband so much!" Tears fell from their eyes as they hugged.

Rosa moaned, "It hurts! It hurts all the way to the heart!" Rosa held Sophia just as tightly as they tried to comfort one another. "Damn, damn, damn, we have to get our husbands back!" Sophia straightened, "Rosa, we can't fall apart. Those men out there are counting on us to find the clues. Men are helpful, but let's face it, they need us women." Sophia lifted her suitcase and opened the door, bowing as she offered Rosa to go through into the hall first.

Laughing as her tears fell, Rosa wiped her nose on her ragged tissue, "Yes, you're right. Come on." Rosa followed Sophia out into the hall. Granger and Stephen were having a heated debate by the stairwell door. Margaret was harassing a nurse at the nurses' station.

Marcus was leaning against the wall next to Ignaci who was speaking to the rent-a-cop outside Geoffrey's room. The rent-a-cop stood and shook Ignacio's hand. Stephen and Granger both stopped talking to watch as the rent-a-cop let Ignacio enter Geoffrey's room. Stephen stiffened while Granger's face fell as they watched the door close behind Ignacio. Marcus said something to the rent-a-cop who was shaking his head 'no.'

The two women stood side by side watching from the hall outside Sophia's room. Marcus hurried up to them, "The cop let Ignacio see Geoffrey. He won't let anyone else in though, he has his orders. Ignacio is a sheriff's deputy and has permission to interview the suspect." Taking his mother's arm, Marcus said, "Mom, I think we should go see how Dad's doing. If he's still in a coma then you need to go home and get some sleep." He pulled her with him to the elevator doors.

Sophia ran to catch up with them. The pink suitcase was held close to her side to avoid hitting her bad leg, "Wait, I'm coming along." Margaret was oblivious to her family's actions for she was busy lecturing the nurse on the importance of her husband's influence over medical health care. Stephen appeared to be arguing with the rent-a-cop. The elevator dinged. Rosa, Sophia, and Marcus disappeared into it. Sophia watched her mother gesticulate as the nurse desperately tried to move away from her.

The elevator opened into a hall of beeping monitors. The air felt stagnant and tight. The smell of hot metal permeated the odor of pine cleaner. Marcus strode ahead of the women as he marched into a square room of green linoleum tile. The only occupants in the room were empty chairs against faced green walls and a small table with a black telephone. A silver coffee percolator quietly hummed next to the phone. Picking up the phone, Marcus punched in five numbers. "This is Marcus Salazar and I would like to know the status of my father Alejandro Jesus Salazar."

He was quiet as he listened. Slowly, his face smiled, "Yes, Ma'am, my mother's right here. Yes, the double doors on the left. The button is on the right of the double doors? Yes, Ma'am."

He returned the phone to its cradle. Sophia could sense Rosa holding her breath as she listened to her son's quiet words, "Mom, he's out of the coma. He's in extreme pain and they have him doped up, but he's asking for you. They will let you see him for five minutes, no more. Come with me."

Rosa gasped for air, "Oh, Dios, he is alive!" She crumpled into Sophia's arms. Sophia tried to catch her as they both ended up kneeling on the floor. Sophia pulled the small woman into her embrace as she cried out, "Thank you, thank you, thank you, God and all the Spirits of the Universe!" She rocked back and forth as the two women held one another. .

Marcus stood and stared at them unmoving. His tears dropped onto the linoleum floor as he held his hands together in front of his chest. "Por Dios."

Sophia wiped her nose with the back of her hand, "Oh, dear, it doesn't take much for us to fall to pieces, does it? Rosa, come on, you need to see your husband. Drugged or not he's still your husband and he needs you." She helped Rosa to her feet. Rosa's exhausted eyes and ashen face reflected how long she had gone without sleep. Marcus took his mother's other arm as they stumbled to the double doors. He pushed a red button on the wall and slowly the doors opened. "Go," Sophia handed Rosa to the nurse on the other side of the opening.

"Are you Mrs. Salazar?" The nurse took Rosa's arm. Rosa glanced back at Sophia and Marcus. "Yes, thank you for letting me see my husband." The doors jerked and then shut. Sophia grabbed Marcus' hand. "We need to sit down and wait for her."

Stephen's voice was heard echoing down the hall, "Sophia? Where the hell did you go? You disappear faster than a corpsman in a bar fight!" Marcus jumped out of the chair and rushed out of the waiting room, "Hey, Admiral, we're in here. My Dad is out of his coma and Mom is in with him. Mrs. Vinder and I are in here waiting for her. Do you want to join us?"

Stephen entered the room with his duffel bag flung over his shoulder. "Do they have coffee in here?"

Marcus pointed to the tall silver coffeemaker on the short table. "Over there, but who knows when it was last made?" Stephen dropped his duffel bag on a chair as he reached for a Styrofoam cup. "My hours are catching up with me. Four hours in a bus, ten hours in a plane, and another two hours in a car have brought me to this place without one cup of coffee." He pushed the cup under the spigot of the coffee maker. The coffee came out steaming. He sniffed it, "Not bad, maybe it was just made." He took a sip, "Yep, it's not half bad. Anyone else want some?"

Sophia laughed at him, "I forgot your duffel bag when I left the room, good thing you remembered it! The nurses are good at getting you the right stuff." Stephen gave her a grimaced face as he tasted the coffee.

Marcus stood as Rosa came into the room. Her face was flushed and her eyes were sparkling, "He knew me. I gave him a kiss and he knew me." She fumbled with her purse, "He's bad, Marcus. He's cut up all over his back and his legs. Something hit him on the side of his head and left a deep gash. He lost a lot of blood. They're worried about his right eye and his right arm has some nerve damage, but he is alive and he knew me." Her attempt at a smile was sad, "Now, I'm ready to go home."

Sophia put her arm around Rosa's shoulders and gave her gentle hug, whispering, "He is a hero, a hero who shall live to fight another day."

The light of day almost blinded Sophia as they stepped out of the hospital. Stephen opened the rental car door for her. He threw his duffel bag into the back seat next to Margaret's pink suitcase and slammed the door. Backing out of the parking place, he said, "I asked Margaret and Granger to leave. I won't tell you what your mother said to me. Granger just stormed off saying I was nothing but a jerk. Your mother tried to cry, but she couldn't find the emotion. They said they would call you later." Stephen pulled the sun visor down, "Oh, and I asked Margaret when we could eat her horse."

He straightened the rental car forward as they pulled out of the parking lot. "You need to tell me how to get to the Rocoso from here." Patting the dash board, he added, "I got this vehicle in adobe brown to avoid showing the dirt, what do you think?"

Sophia sighed, "Stephen, you're just causing more trouble, you know this, right?"

Checking his rear view mirror, he mumbled, "Tough, you're my family. By the way I spoke with Ignacio when he came out of Geoffrey's room. He wanted to know if you received Geoffrey's message. What's that all about?"

Reaching into her jean's pocket, she pulled out the crumpled paper, "Here it is. Rosa read it to me because the pencil barely shows up on this blue paper. Geoffrey wrote, 'the battery was wired to the starter Granger too stupid.' What do you think he meant by this?"

Stephen shrugged, "Where did the dynamite come from do you think?"

Explaining further, Sophia said, "This has to do with Emily. Granger and Emily were married for nine years and now they're getting a divorce. Granger impregnated Emily's best friend Katina with a male child. Emily called Geoffrey to tell him Granger found some dynamite in the shed or the barn in Negara."

"What, this is too much information too fast. You mean Granger is going to marry the adulteress and dump his ever loving wife?" Stephen put his blinker on at the intersection.

"Yes, that's what I just said. Margaret is going to sell the house in Negara to Granger's wife. It was there the dynamite was found and extricated and possibly used in an attempt to blow us all to kingdom come." Sophia tilted the sun visor down to protect her eyes.

Stephen pushed the seat back, allowing his legs more room. "Why would Margaret sell a house to Granger's ex-wife? Don't Granger and Emily have a kid together or something?"

Sophia pointed for Stephen to turn left at the stop sign, "Margaret is moving Emily to the house in Negara because she likes to keep everyone close. If Emily buys the Negara house then she will be indebted to Margaret."

Stephen yawned, "All this daylight is tiring. New Mexico has way too much sunshine." He put on the blinker at the red light. "Ignacio said Geoffrey told him to check the explosive wrapping. Why would Granger, who is busy impregnating women, go around trying to bomb his family? This makes no sense and Geoffrey loved that truck. He practically cried when I told him it was demolished."

Sophia pointed to the right, "Here, turn here and go across the bridge and up the mountain. We turn right at the first turn at the top of the mountain."

They drove in silence for a time. Stephen pulled over to the side of the road before turning right into Rocoso. "Sophia, please promise me you will never put a web around the girls? Please, because if you do, I will have to take them away from you."

She put her hand on his arm, "Stephen, you have my word. My girls are being raised to be independent, self sufficient and self reliable. There is no way I want to control them. I want to admire and respect them as independent human beings with their own minds and their own choices. I love them too much to suffocate them. Besides you, Geoffrey wouldn't allow it either." Sophia shook her head, "I know my mother loves me. She is devoted to me and has helped me so much in my life in her own way. She is a beautiful person, she just was raised in another time zone, in my own way I dearly love her."

Stephen stared at her, "There is nothing more one can say about daughters and mothers. Your two girls of only six and nine have had so many traumas in the last three days to last a life time. I just want to make sure nothing bad comes their way anymore." He turned to observe the view, "This place is spectacular. Do you think the girls will be pleased to see me?"

"They will be absolutely delighted! What worries me is the sight we will see when we pull into the driveway. I hope Emily is still with the girls. You will like her, Stephen."

"Now, don't get me hitched. I'm here to solve a mystery, not get hung up on some woman. My life is the military, besides the more I know about women the less I understand them."

Sophia chortled, "No worries there. I think Emily feels the exact same way. She has probably had it with men."

Stephen turned onto the Rocoso road. As they got closer to the house, Sophia hurriedly said, "Stephen, someone was killed in my front yard. Do you think the tow truck and the debris are still there?"

"We shall see, here we are." Stephen stopped the rental car behind the old yellow van. All the windows where shattered or spider webbed in the van. The tow truck was gone. There was only a blackened area where Geoffrey's truck had been. Sophia's eyes searched for the area where she had fallen. There was a small pool of blood about four feet from the van's passenger door. Someone had placed the wheelbarrow by the north side of the outer wall. It was filled with small metal fragments.

Stephen patted her hand, "Don't look, Sophia, let's go and see the girls. Come on, don't go over it again. You will have time to remember when the investigators ask their questions. Come on, let's go in. Take your mother's suitcase with you in case someone tries to blow up this car." Stephen gave a hollow laugh as he grabbed his duffel bag.

Sophia sat there staring, her body started to shake as tears fell from her eyes. "Stephen, they blew holes in my van. The old family van that has held us together through the years is now a wreck. God, Stephen, do I look like that old van?"

He put his arm around her shoulders, "Sophia, what happened was not your fault or Geoffrey's. You are alive and unscathed pretty much, now we have to appreciate the fact that your home is still here and the girls are safe and untouched. Geoffrey will be all right. One small step at a time, please. You need to hold it together for the girls. They are as freaked out as you are and their perceptions are going to need warmth and love. Come on, get out of the car, here come the girls." Stephen pointed to the front of the house.

As soon as Sophia stepped out of the car, she was attacked. "Mama, you're home!" Sybil wrapped her arms around her mother's legs. "Mom, don't go away again! I can't take care of Donna anymore. Mama, please don't go away again." Sybil's eyes filled with tears. Donna raced to her Uncle seconds later. He grabbed and flipped her upside down, "Uncle Stephen, put me down! Put me down this second!" Donna beat at his back with her small hands. "I want my Mommy! Put me down!"

"Uncle Stephen!" Sybil turned, "Have you come to help Daddy?" Sybil dragged the pink suitcase beside her as she followed them into the house. She firmly shut the door behind her. Emily quickly embraced Sophia in a warm hug. "We missed you."

Emily took the suitcase from Sybil. "I tried to pick you up this morning, but Margaret insisted she and Granger retrieve you." Emily studied Stephen as he carried the girls down the hall. "He's a nice improvement from the Pino clan. Where did you find him?"

Sophia walked to Geoffrey's recliner chair. She fell into it. "Emily, I miss my husband, but if I had to find a man who could be as helpful it would be Stephen Vinder. He arrived at the hospital this morning right before Granger and Margaret. He told them to leave us alone. Oh, Emily, the problems keep stacking up one on top of another." She reached down and picked up Geoffrey's favorite pillow. "What a mess. Emily, what are we going to do with my mother and my brother?"

Emily sat on the couch, grabbing a cushion to hug, she said, "Sophia, we're going to survive this and they will have to admit their guilt." Emily threw the pillow at her. "Now, how would you like some lunch? You both must be starving? The girls and I made grilled cheese sandwiches and minestrone soup from scratch."

Donna wandered into the room, "Mom, Uncle Stephen is sound asleep and snoring!"

Sophia put out her arms, "Come here, Miss Donna, your mama needs a hug from you." Donna ran into her mother's arms for a tight hug. "When's Daddy coming home? Mama, you both scared us. We thought the slimy salamander got you both! Sybil and I cried all night. Good thing Emily was here to read us all those books. Mama, don't go away again, please!"

Emily took Donna's small hand, "Let your mother have some of our fancy lunch, okay? You worked hard on it and we don't want it to get cold, huh?"

The women sat around the kitchen table. Most of the food was gone. They had made a plate for Stephen and it put aside for him. Sophia was tapping the eraser end of a pencil on the table, "We need a plan as to how to straighten out our lives. Who has some ideas?"

Emily lifted her hand, "I believe we should take Daisy over to Mr. Perkal's. Carol used to let Daisy play with his dogs while she cared for your Papa. I did call Mr. Perkal yesterday afternoon when we found out about Carol. He said to bring Daisy over anytime. They would love to have her, the more the merrier."

Sybil stared at her mother, "Mom, what happened to Carol? She was Papa's friend, right?"

Sophia studied her daughter's deep green eyes, as she explained, "Carol died from an overdose of her medication. She didn't over medicate herself, someone helped her. There is nothing more to say."

Emily pushed her soup bowl away from her, "Are they going to have a funeral for her? She was one special lady as far as I am concerned."

Donna piped up, "Me, too. She let us use her makeup and she even put my hair up like an adult. We should have a big old party to remember her with marshmallows and cake."

Sybil asked Emily, "You mean she's dead? Really dead and we won't ever see her again?"

Emily reached for Sybil's hand, "Yes, we won't see her again, but she's up there in the great beyond watching us. I think a party would be a good idea and then we could remember her at the party with balloons and festivities. We would have Daisy dog there, too, don't you think?"

Sybil started stacking the soup bowls and plates, "I'll wash the dishes. You guys can figure out the plan." Sophia grabbed Sybil around her small waist, "Hey, I'm proud of you for taking charge, Sybil. We had nothing to do with Carol's death, but we may have something to do with catching whoever did. You will help us, right?"

Sybil leaned against her mother, "You bet! I read all kinds of books about catching bad guys. I have some really neat ideas."

Donna leaned back in her chair, "Auntie Emily, can you stay? It's nice and if Mom takes off again, you'll be here for us?"

Emily smiled, "I'll stay as long as I can, how's that? I have Shirley to think about and she's staying at a friend's house. She probably misses me, too."

Donna sat up straight, "Bring Shirley over here! Mr. Perkal said 'the more the merrier.' If we're all here no one will bother us!" Donna burst into tears. "I want Daddy to come home!"

Sybil groaned, "Mama, Donna is scared. We both were taken out of class and told the house was blown to pieces. Our teachers kept us in the office until Uncle Granger picked us up and he wasn't nice. He said we'd have to come and live with him if anything happened to you. Donna almost threw up in the back seat of his fancy car she was crying so hard." Sophia pulled Donna into her lap and held her.

Catching her breath, Sybil continued, "We were scared 'cause Uncle Granger stayed here with us. He went into Dad's office and closed the door. He was opening and closing drawers and yelling. Donna and I didn't know what to do."

Sybil reached over and turned off the water in the sink, "Then Grandma Margaret showed up here with pizza and it had tomatoes and weird stuff on it. We wouldn't eat it. She yelled at us and sent us to our rooms. Mom, she's not nice. She said she'd have Granger beat us if we didn't do what she said." Sybil wiped her nose on the back of her sweater sleeve. "Mom, if you go away again, Donna and I are going to run away and live with strangers."

Her nine year old body started to shake, "Mama, it was so horrible the school nurse, at each of our schools, took us out of class and stuck us in her office." Sybil put her arm around her mother's shoulder. Sophia put her arms around her daughter and gave her a hug. Sybil continued, "Granger didn't even have a car seat for Donna. We were both scared, but I was the bravest, right Donna?"

Holding onto her mother tightly, Donna cried, "Mama, I hate Uncle

Granger. He's a salamander! A mother salamander wouldn't even like him!" She cried even harder.

Emily smiled at Donna. "Well, aren't I the lucky one. I get to move far away from him and his mother." She leaned over to take Donna out of Sophia's lap. "Donna, if I were to stay here where we would all sleep? This house is only big enough for five."

Donna wiped her nose on a napkin, "You could sleep with me in my bed?" Emily frowned, "No, I think I need to go and get my little girl. She needs to know her mother loves her and won't let her be taken away by the slimy salamander also known as her father." Donna ran into her room and slammed the door.

Emily helped Sybil wash the dishes and Sophia dried them and put them away. They spoke of the weather and how to make chocolate chip cookies using gluten flour.

The phone rang interrupting their productivity. Sophia picked it up, "Hello?"

"Sophia, my darling daughter, how are you feeling now that you are home?" Margaret's voice flowed with cheer.

"Fine, Mom, I 'm just fine. Emily has everything in order and the girls are doing great. How are things with you?" Sophia tried to stay calm. Sybil gave her mother a dirty look as she stepped away from the sink.

Margaret answered, "I'm worried about your brother, dear. He seems so fidgety lately. He's running all over the place, trying to set up a meeting with Mr. Goldfarb. I keep telling him not to worry everything will be all right. Sophia, what legal action did you and Geoffrey file against Granger or me?"

"Mom, I'm sure I don't know why Granger is upset. Mr. Goldfarb is a dear friend. As far as I know we haven't filed anything against you or Granger. Mom, I just got home from the hospital!" Sophia felt herself getting testy.

"Well, Granger is a mess. Poor Katina is here vomiting in the bathroom. I can't tell if it is because she's pregnant or stupid. Maybe albino people vomit all the time. She's a confusing woman. Did you know she won't eat anything that can run from her? She's a vegan or some such crazy thing." Margaret's voice whispered, "Sophia, what do you fix for dinner when someone won't eat anything but dead vegetables and tree bark?"

Sophia pushed positivism, "Mom, you'll think of something, you always do. Just ask her what she eats. The Health Food Store is right down the road from you at the corner strip. You could ask her to go with you and shop together as a bonding experience?"

"No, I don't think I want to be seen with her out in public! She's so thin. She keeps vomiting on things. She isn't very pretty, not like Emily. And in all confidence I don't think she's very bright. I mean she is completely loyal to Granger. What kind of a woman does that make her?" Margaret's cynicism was actually refreshing.

Emily and Sybil put away the last of the washed dishes. Donna was pulling Sophia's hand to go outside. Sophia put her finger to her lips and pointed to the phone, "Mom, I have no advice for you regarding Katina or Granger and I have to go. We have a lot to do around here. We're going to take Carol's dog to Mr. Perkal's later this afternoon and maybe we will stop by and see you. I hate to promise anything with Stephen here. He wants to spend as much time as possible with the girls."

Margaret didn't waste a moment, "You're going to cut me off after all I have done for you and those spoiled girls of yours? Fare thee well, good bye." Sophia gently hung up the phone.

Emily smiled at her, "We heard Margaret all the way over here on this side of the kitchen. Katina is vomiting because she's on drugs not because she's pregnant. I seriously doubt she's pregnant. Her butt isn't even fat, did you notice?"

The two women burst out laughing. Sophia took Donna's small hand, "There, now let's go outside and inventory the damage done."

The front adobe wall had hundreds of metal fragments stuck in the stucco. The metal reflected in the sunlight, making it almost beautiful. Sophia grabbed a pair of pliers from Geoffrey's tool box in the garage that he had made into a workshop area. The adults pulled the pieces of metal out of the wall and the girls dropped the pieces into the wheelbarrow.

The pool of blood by the old van was constantly in Sophia's field of vision. Finally she grabbed a shovel and went to the back of the property to load it up with sand. She dumped the sand over the dried blood. "There now the bad memory is buried in the past."

Sybil pulled her father's work gloves over her small fragile hands, as she scavenged the property for metal shards. Donna stood behind Emily, helping her with the metal wall debris. Sophia studied the family van. The side windows needed to be replaced. The front passenger tire was flat and the front grill had collapsed. The radiator wasn't leaking. The front windshield was cracked, but still in place.

Sophia hurried past Emily and Donna to the front porch, "I'm going to see if I can start up the van. Maybe it runs and isn't as bad as it looks?"

Emily spoke right away, "Sophia, No. What if the van is rigged? What if the van explodes like the truck? I think we should wait. Have Stephen check it out first. No one wants anymore explosions or flying metal, especially your neighbors." She jerked her head to the front of the driveway.

Patsy strode towards them down the driveway. She was being pulled by Daisy dog. Donna dropped the metal she was carrying and ran to meet them. "Daisy, you're home!" Donna fell to her knees and hugged the yellow pit-bull mix. The dog's short tail was wiggling with joy. Patsy called out, "Hey, how are you feeling? How's Geoffrey?" Patsy gave the leash to Donna and walked up to Sophia and Emily.

The seventy-year old woman had a mop of gray hair on her head. She wore a brown winter jacket and leather gloves. Her blue sweatpants were tucked into her boots. Her soft gray eyes watched Donna with the dog. "Jim and I loved having Daisy with us, but she is ready to play at early dawn. Neither of us are early risers. I'm glad she has a place to go for her pre-dawn tactics."

Patsy put her hand in her coat pocket, "Here are the phone messages that came in yesterday. The explosion was yesterday, right? It feels like eons ago now that you're home."

Some of the papers fell to the ground. Sophia gathered them as Patsy continued, "A bunch of people from Geoffrey's work sent flowers to him at the hospital. The police thought they had weapons in them. Some florists tried to put them in your hospital room, but your mother routed all flowers to the OBGYN ward. I guess your mother paid the florists to take the flowers to the nursery."

She handed pink notepapers to Sophia. "Oh, and all the newspapers called. The television crews want to interview you and there are some messages from the bomb specialists who need to interrogate you as well. Your step-brothers called. One of them named George called from Georgia and another from Las Cruces wanted to know if you were all right." Patsy tapped the papers held in Sophia's fingers. "Oh, and a woman named Rosa Martinez called over and over again while you were being taken to the hospital. I think she is the wife of the sheriff."

Patsy turned to watch Donna chase Daisy. "You do have a place for the dog, right? I wouldn't want her going to the pound!"

Sophia smiled, "No, she's going to my father's neighbor's home. He has five dogs and already knows Daisy. She has spent time at his house and he wants her." Sophia started to read the telephone messages. "This one's from California. Do you know what it was about?" Sophia handed the paper to Patsy.

"Oh, yes, this was a strange call. The man wanted to know how much your house was selling for and when he and his family could come and take a look at it. He asked me if the price was set or if he could talk you guys down. I told him the house wasn't for sale as far as I knew. He said the advertisement was in the Wall Street Journal. The contact person was Granger Pino. He was persistent. I was equally so right back at him! He was disappointed, but I gave him Margaret's phone number. I figured they could fight it out amongst themselves." Patsy frowned, "This is your property, correct?"

Emily interjected, "Patsy, we really want to thank you for keeping Daisy. We didn't know where else for her to go in such short notice. I hope the explosion didn't damage your property?"

Patsy pointed to her house, "The windows on this side of the house shook, but only one cracked. It was a perfect crack straight up and down in the guest bathroom window. We felt the ground shake. Sophia, it is amazing you survived. When I came over here with Jim it looked like Armageddon." She shook her head, "That poor sheriff, there was blood all over you and him. The young man in the truck..." She shivered, "He was very young to die such a dreadful death."

Turning back to Emily and Sophia, she said quietly, "Did you know the young man was an illegal? He hadn't been here but a few days. Mr. Torres the tow truck driver just hired him to help with the tow truck business. Mr. Torres is from Chihuahua, too." Patsy sighed, "So much trouble for illegal aliens. They don't have any rights. They can't get any insurance or help. I feel for them. Can you imagine his mother back in Mexico learning about her son's death and there is nothing she can do about it?"

Sophia shook her head, "I had no idea all of this was going to happen. Geoffrey was electrocuted, which was terrible. We thought there was nothing worse and then Boom!"

Patsy pulled a plastic bag out of her coat pocket, "Here are some dog treats for Daisy. I bought them to use as bribes. I better get home. Jim and I have to go grocery shopping. Did you know pork chops are for sale at the grocery in town?" She hurried up the drive and disappeared around the pine trees along the road.

Emily shook her head, "Wow, Patsy is a big help. Who else gave you a call?" She returned to pulling pieces of shrapnel. Sophia reviewed the papers. Emily wiped her forehead with her gloved hand, "Sophia, you do know I have to leave in a little while and get Shirley? We need to get to Negara now that it's our home. All our stuff is there."

Sophia's frightened eyes stared at Emily, "Oh, Emily, you can't leave! There is so much to do here and now I don't have a vehicle. The girls appreciate you and have loved their time with you. We are going to miss you! Thank you for being there when I woke up in the hospital and washing my hair. It is good to know that we are friends now that Granger is out of your life, right?"

"Sophia, Granger has said some horrible things about you and how you treated him and his mother, but now I see for myself that all of his focus was on getting you away from the family's money. It is sad that a man such as Granger is only focused on money, not on his duty to the community or to his family, but only on making more and more money." Emily threw a piece of shrapnel into the wheelbarrow. Sophia leaned against the adobe wall and stared out at her yard.

Emily came over to her, "Sophia, you're going to be fine. Stephen will wake up eventually, I'm sure. The girls will help you, they're great. By the way, you do need to go to the grocery store. As for taking Daisy to Mr. Perkal's—don't go alone. Take Stephen with you."

Emily lifted her jacket sleeve to check the time on her watch, "As a matter of fact, it's after three o'clock. You might want to wake him so he'll sleep tonight." Emily jerked another piece of metal out of the wall. A piece of stucco came with it. "Good thing you have property insurance, right?"

Calling the girls, Sophia moved under the porch roof out of the sun, "Sybil and Donna, I need you to wake up Stephen. He needs to rise and shine for we have work to do. He's been asleep now for almost four hours. Go get him!" Screaming the girls ran into the house, slamming the door behind them.

Pulling Emily aside, Sophia asked her, "Do you feel safe in the Negara house? Geoffrey told me about the dynamite."

Shedding her gloves, Emily stared at the dirt at her feet, "I don't know if I feel safe anywhere with Granger running around. What Patsy said about this house being for sale? I knew Granger did it. He talked to me about it, but I never thought he had the gall to actually try to sell the house out from under you."

Emily knelt down leaning her back against the wall, "Granger did take the dynamite. Margaret insisted he remove it from the property. He put it in the trunk of his green Mercedes." Emily gazed out across the mountain, "I knew about the insulin, too."

She wouldn't look at Sophia, "Granger bragged about taking the insulin from your Papa's closet. He said the expiration date was a farce." Emily looked into Sophia's eyes, "Granger is dangerous. He knows as long as we are married I can't testify against him. My word has no value. Sophia, he is after money. His greed is for himself, his new wife and baby boy. Be careful, be very careful around him. I'm glad Stephen is here. Granger is afraid of Stephen. Stephen is smarter than Granger and Stephen is another male who is twice his size. Granger likes to intimidate women, but men make him nervous."

Emily unzipped her tan jacket, "It's warming up for January. Sophia, I'd better go. I am worried sick Granger may try to kidnap Shirley. Every minute I'm away from her I get more anxious, you understand?"

Sophia nodded, 'yes.' The two of them walked arm in arm into the house. Comfort engulfed them as they found Stephen sitting at the kitchen table being pampered by the two girls. Stephen greeted them holding a cold grilled sandwich, "Hey, my two favorite grownup women! How's the metal business going outside?"

Donna cautiously carried a hot bowl of tomato soup from the microwave to Stephen with a hot pad. "Here, don't hit it." She placed it in front of him on his big dinner plate. Stephen was dressed in a black turtleneck, dark pants, and a red scarf hung loosely around his neck setting off his bright blue eyes.

Emily laughed, "Well, don't you look good enough to eat! I could gobble you right up! No wonder you have these two youngsters eating out of your hand."

Sybil spoke up, "No, Aunt Emily, he's eating out of our hands, look?" Stephen was shoveling a spoonful of soup into his mouth.

Everyone laughed. Emily pulled the hair band from around her long hair, letting her golden red tresses fall around her shoulders, "Stephen, I have to go and get my daughter. She's staying with some friends."

Emily knelt down next to Sybil, "We have to go back to Negara tonight. I want to thank you two girls for your hard work, your courage, and your love. You are terrific people!" Emily gave each of them a hug. Standing, she gave Sophia a hug and before she could let go Stephen was hugging both of them. Emily pushed away, "Long good-byes are dreadful. Let me get my stuff and get out of here." She ran into the backroom, grabbed her backpack and was out the door before anyone could stop her.

Stephen finished his meal. He studied the list on Sophia's paper, which was sitting on the table in front of him. "We're taking the dog to Mr. Perkal this afternoon?"

Donna was leaning against the table next to him, "Yeah, and Mom told Grandma Margaret we might stop by and see her. I almost threw up."

Stephen glanced at Sophia who was staring out the kitchen window at her van. "Stephen, do you think the van will run? I can't stand the thought of our family van being dead."

Stephen moved next to her as he finished eating his grilled cheese sandwich. "Well, it does look sad, doesn't it? Let's go out and check the engine. We will need Star War's suits. Where's the armor?"

Tears fell down Sophia's cheeks as he spoke, "Stephen, you sound like Geoffrey and I miss him. We can't call him, can we?"

Stephen put his arm around her, "No, we can't, but we do have Ignacio. Why don't we give Ignacio a quick call to find out what's happening at Geoffrey's end of this equation. Then we can check out the van. We best do it before it gets dark."

The phone was held in Stephen's left hand as he wrote frantically with his right. "Yes, okay, when? The fragments of lose material? Yes, the girls have been picking up debris. Yeah, where is this place? Do we need to go there right now?"

Stephen motioned for Sophia to read what he had written. She peeked over his shoulder. Just as she was making out the words, Stephen started writing again, "Ignacio, what do you mean fatalities? Oh, those two, yes, do you have any news on your boss? Yes, oh, do you have the phone number? Yeah, we'll do it right away. Are you coming by later, yeah, what time?"

He finally hung up. "Well, A.J. is out of critical condition and is in a special medical unit. They're going to move him to UNMH. There is a medical treatment he'll need around ten tomorrow morning. If you want to go and see him at Rio Grodno's Hospital he said you should do it before eight o'clock tonight."

Taking a deep breath, Stephen said, "The scraps of debris investigated by the bomb squad found paper from dynamite dated circa the 1960's. Evidently there was a particular color and type of paper used during the '60's. No fingerprints were found."

He walked to the sink to get a glass of water. "The problem with explosives is they decimate any trace of who placed the dynamite. It was rigged with a timer. Not rocket science by any means. The bomb was wired to the starter, which was the source of Geoffrey's shock. Anyone who took eighth grade science could figure out this bomb."

He drank down the water, putting the empty glass in the sink. "The State Police will not release Geoffrey. Well, they can't. Plus he's still under medical care for his burned foot. Ignacio spoke with Dr. Baker and found out Geoffrey's burn is only second degree, but he may need a skin graph."

Stephen smiled, "Your lawyer Samuel Goldfarb did get to see Geoffrey this afternoon. He evidently is representing Geoffrey. Ignacio wanted to know if you had spoken to Goldfarb."

Donna and Sybil ran inside, slamming the front door behind them. "Mom, Daisy does tricks. Look what she found down in the arroyo? We threw the ball for her, but she came back with this. Look!" Sybil held out a button of yellow braided leather. Sophia smiled, "This is a button from Granger's jacket. He only wears camel hair with yellow buttons for informal events."

Taking the button in his big fingers, Stephen tilted his head, "Informal events like setting bombs?" He knelt down and looked into Donna's blue eyes and then into Sybil's green eyes, "You two girls have a habit of slamming doors, did you know that?"

They both nodded. He knelt down to be at their level, "When there has been an explosion near the house and there is a possibility of more explosions it is not a good idea to make shock waves. When you slam the door you cause shock waves. Please stop slamming doors or the next door you slam may be your last." He stood up and patted the top of their heads. The girls stared up at him with their mouths open. He smiled at Sophia, "Now, what's our next step?"

Sophia took the button into the kitchen and placed it in a sandwich bag. "We can keep this as evidence. Girls, where's Daisy?"

Donna whispered, "She's back down in the arroyo. We couldn't get her to come with us."

Sybil's question was quietly spoken."Daisy may be a trained sniffer dog. What do you think, Mom?"

Stephen grabbed his pea-jacket from the side of the couch. "Let's go find the dog. Check out the van and then hightail it to Rio Grodno's Hospital. Daisy dog has been volunteered to be part of the team. Does she get sick in the car? I do have a rental."

Donna laughed, "No, she doesn't get sick anywhere. Come on, I'll show you where she is." Stephen and Donna disappeared out the front door.

Sybil leaned against the side of the couch. Her face was wrinkled with worry, "Mama, can we talk to Dad? I really miss him. I know he misses us. Can we talk to him?"

Sophia took her daughter's hand. "You may be nine, Sybil, but you have the heart of a wise woman. Come on, let's go with them. Your Uncle Stephen is a magnet for trouble even more than your father. Let me get my heavy jacket."

The four of them followed the dog's lead into the deep arroyo. The early evening cooled with the setting of the sun. The western sky was ablaze with pinks and oranges. A slight breeze chilled the air as they foraged their way through juniper bushes and scraggly pinion trees. Daisy sniffed every rabbit bush and every rock. Donna shadowed the dog's every move. Stephen decided to check the van while they were safely far away from anything that could explode. Sophia and Sybil searched for more evidence. After an hour, they decided to see Stephen.

Stephen's butt was sticking up in the air while his head was down in the engine. He had Geoffrey's mechanical pack unrolled on the far front bumper. There were two oily cloths hanging on the other bumper. Stephen was mumbling under his breath.

212

Sybil skipped up to him, "Hey, Uncle Stephen, how's the surgery going?"

"Well, hell, the hose from the radiator to the main is cut. The carburetor has issues. Valves on the manifold were probably sticking. This van is in poor shape even with the explosion." He jumped down from the front bumper, "Sophia, this van is shot. She ain't going to run no more. You need a new one. If there is time, you should call the insurance company. They need to help out with a new vehicle." He wiped his hands on the cloths. There wasn't a speck of oil on his clothes.

Sophia hurried into the house to call. Donna kicked the front flat tire. "This van has been the only van I've ever known. She's like a member of the family. Do we bury her in a cemetery?"

Sybil patted the passenger door, "Donna is only six she doesn't know about dead cars yet. They take old vans to the dump with the rest of the garbage."

Kneeling down to be Donna's height, Stephen contradicted her, "Well, now, they don't take her to the dump, Sybil! She will go to a car parts place where they sell her good parts to people who need them. She will be recycled. She's a love and has many parts that other folks could use."

Donna stared up at him hopefully, "You mean like an organ donor?"

"Exactly, an organ donor is what she will be." Stephen pulled open the passenger door. "Let's get your car seat and put it in my rental car. We have to go out and we're all going to stay together. Do you think your mother will let Daisy stay here? I'm not ready to see your grandmother again."

Sybil jumped into the van to unhook the car seat for him, "Donna and I don't like Grandma Margaret. She's mean and hates us. She says 'hate' all the time because she hates everybody."

The car seat was finally extracted. Donna held the straps as Stephen carried it to the brown car. Sybil hooked it to the car frame while Donna sat in it. Daisy suddenly jumped in next to her. "Well, the mystery dog returns." Stephen straightened to stretch his back. "Did she bring anything with her?"

Sybil ran around the rental car to him. "Look, at this? It's a brown bag." Stephen peeked into the bag. There was a faded yellow paper inside of it with the name of a company and the type of dynamite caps sold. "Yes, I do believe we need to keep this dog. She knows about explosives."

Sophia hurried to them, "The news is not good. He didn't know if they could help with a new van because our van is over twelve years old. The man said they will send an adjuster tomorrow afternoon between noon and five. He wouldn't give a definite time. It's a special assignment to come out on a Sunday."

She glanced at the burned ground where Geoffrey's truck had stood, "He knew about the truck. The adjuster was out here yesterday with the television crews. He said the truck is definitely totaled. They will reimburse us for the full cost of the truck and the price Geoffrey paid for it new."

Stephen stepped back, "We got the car seat in and Daisy is a keeper. She found the original bag the dynamite was kept in with the receipt from the store." He handed the dirty brown bag to Sophia who pushed it away, "Stephen, we need to keep these things in plastic bags and not touch them. There may be fingerprints on this. Although, my brother wears gloves, but you never know?"

"Right, you never know?" Sybil parroted her mother. "Now what do we do?"

Stephen spoke over his shoulder as he walked into the house, "Now, we're off to Rio Grodno to see friends. The dog is going to have to come with us. Then we will go to dinner with the dog, or something?"

"Wait," Sophia caught his arm, "The dog is staying with us? We can't keep the dog! She'll have to be with us all the time. This won't be good for her. Daisy needs to be with people who don't' get blown up or die." Sophia felt her eyes well up with tears as she stared at the ground, "My mother gave Mr. Perkal my father's dog. The two dogs can comfort each other with the loss of their owners."

Stephen reached out to hold her. Sophia pleaded with him, "Stephen, we can't keep her. She is promised to Mr. Perkal and he is waiting for her. Please, let's take her there on our way to Rio Grodno? Please."

He studied Sophia's face, "All right. We'll take the dog to Mr. Perkal. Sorry, just thought the dog would guard the girls. The dog found evidence. I thought she would be a valuable part of the team. If you want her to go to Mr. Perkal's, fine, we'll take her." He walked around her into the house. Sophia saw her daughters' faces in the dim light of the evening. Donna had tears in her eyes. Sybil just glared at her. Daisy sat in the back seat of the rental car, panting. Sophia went in the house and got her purse.

18

Calavera and Rio Grodno
Saturday Evening, January, 1988

Everyone was quiet as Stephen drove down Calle Cottonwood to Mr. Perkal's farm. Stephen's square jaw was set in a stubborn clench. Sybil was reading her book on dragons with a handheld flashlight. Donna was quietly stroking Daisy. The setting sun illuminated the world around them in an orange red hue. Birds pecked away in the alfalfa fields, stabbing at the ground for their evening meal of bugs. The road of corrugated dirt led them to Mr. Perkal who was standing at his property gate with a pair of wire cutters. The car's headlights illuminated his work. He was repairing a lose fence line attaching it to a metal 'T' post. He lifted his hand to protect his eyes from their headlights and then to greet them.

Donna leaned over Daisy, "Mom, we don't have to see Grandma Margaret do we?" Sybil turned off her flashlight, "Yeah, Mom, we don't have time to see her, right?"

Sophia opened her door, "Girls, we will see how long this takes. If we have time we may see Grandma Margaret, but we're on a tight schedule. Come, bring Daisy."

Mr. Perkal's dogs were milling around his ankles as Daisy jumped over Donna and out of the car to greet them. Mr. Perkal squinted through the darkness now that Stephen had turned off the car lights, "Howdy! It will be good to have Daisy here. The wife and I want to do something in remembrance of Carol. We enjoy having Walter's dog and now we can share our lives with Carol's pup. The more the merrier as I always say."

He opened the gate for them. Daisy took off at a dead run with the other dogs beside her. They barked, ran, jumped, and finally settled by the garage door to sniff one another.

"Mr. Perkal, this is Geoffrey's brother Stephen. He came to help us. Stephen this is Mr. Perkal." Sophia nodded to each of them. Stephen took Mr.

Perkal's work gloved hand and gave it a firm shake. Mr. Perkal laughed, "You have one fine brother, Stephen. Geoffrey's wife and girls are great friends of ours. Howdy, girls, how's your Dad doing?"

Sybil stood tall to answer, "Dad is still in the hospital and they won't let us see him. They think he blew everybody up, but he didn't. He doesn't blow people up. Sometimes he makes Mom climb the wall, but he doesn't hurt people."

Stephen and Mr. Perkal smiled at her. Donna was focused on the dogs, "Do your dogs like Daisy?"

"Oh, yes, they get along famously. As a matter of fact, every afternoon they're out here waiting for her. Usually Carol came in the afternoons, right?" Mr. Perkal lead them to the house. "We were glad when she agreed to house-sit. Our friends had to go to Europe for six months and desperately needed someone to watch their home. The wife and I encouraged Carol to get away from caretaking. She was depressed after your father passed. Somehow she took it personally." Mr. Perkal walked with them down the driveway. "Please come in the house."

Sophia took Sybil's hand, "Yes, Carol told me she wanted a change. The house she stayed in is beautiful with the swimming pool and with the back room she had plenty of privacy."

Mr. Perkal opened the door to the kitchen. "Her death was such a shock to us, but no more talk of this. The wife has fixed some hot cocoa and made homemade chocolate chip cookies." Stephen closed the door behind him.

Mrs. Perkal greeted the girls with big hugs. She was no taller than five feet, wore her white hair in a bun at the nape of her neck. Her rosy cheeks and a big smile highlighted her round eyes of opaque blue. Her dress was neatly protected with a pinned on apron of purple paisley. She had on house slippers. The kitchen was filled with the delicious smell of cookies right out of the oven. "Here, girls, have a seat at the little table. It has all the fun crafts on it. The big table is boring. Come on, I'll sit with you and we can make a card for your father."

The girls followed her to the small table in the corner of the kitchen by the window. There were packets of colored paper, colored pencils, crayons, watercolor paints with paint brushes in yellow plastic cups. Sophia watched as Mrs. Perkal wrapped aprons around both girls. Sybil's eyes lit up when she saw the pencils of neon colors in an unopened packet. Donna grabbed a paint brush and a cookie at the same time. The plate of cookies was in the middle of the menagerie.

"I wish I were shorter," Stephen stood behind Sybil. "This is a wonderful place to just let go. You know I used to do watercolors before the Navy got me involved with nuclear missiles."

Mrs. Perkal jumped at the sound of his voice. Stephen bent down to take her small hand, "How do you do, I am Stephen Vinder, Geoffrey Vinder's brother. Don't believe we have met?"

She put her left hand on top of his right hand. "Oh, I should have known someone else was in here. Todd, you didn't warn me!" Stephen stood still as he let her touch his arm, move up to his shoulder, and feel his face.

Sophia smiled at him, "Stephen, Kara was born blind. Most people would never know for she has an uncanny ability to see things other people miss completely."

"But how can she know about colors, painting, drawing, and all of this?" Stephen pointed to the small table where the girls were sitting.

Mr. Perkal grumbled, "Who knows? I believe she can see just fine and likes to keep the rest of us in the dark. Here, who would like some cocoa?"

Mugs of cocoa were passed. Cookies were eaten. The girls drew on paper to make four cards for Geoffrey. The dogs were let into the house. They promptly went to sleep in front of the floor heater on a braided rug. Sophia glanced at the clock on the kitchen wall, "Oh, my, we had better get a move on it. We need to be at the hospital before visiting hours are over. Thank you, so much for your kind hospitality, but we need to run."

In the car, the girls had their cards neatly placed in large plastic bags on their laps. Donna fell asleep as they drove up the hill to Rio Grodno. Sybil stared at the lights from the houses. "You know, Mom, if anything happens to you and Dad, I think Donna and I should live with the Perkal's, but not tell Grandmother Margaret."

Sophia prayed the girls would be able to see their father tonight. Both of them were in low spirits. Stephen broke the silence, "Do you want to go on up and see A.J. while the girls and I check out the gift shop?"

"Let's see if we can't get everyone into the hospital. They have to let the girls see their father." Sophia turned around to tell Sybil, "Your father and I aren't going anywhere, Sybil, we are going to be beside you until you grow up regardless of how crazy or strange life may become. We love you and want to spend our lives with you and your sister, don't ever forget that, all right?"

Stephen parked in front of the hospital. "Here we are. Do we have a plan?"

"Yes, we're going to conquer the hospital bureaucracy. Sybil, please wake your sister. Bring your bags with the cards and put on a happy face." Sophia patted Stephen on the back, "Admiral Vinder can lead the light brigade. We take no prisoners and shall achieve our goals with the minimum of danger."

Stephen laughed, "Now you've got it!"

The bright lights and floors of polished green linoleum in the hospital were blinding. The smell of pine cleaner clung to the air with a vengeance. They walked straight to the information desk with determination. The woman dressed in pink at the front desk informed them of A.J.'s new room on the third floor. She expressly stressed visiting hours were over in forty-five minutes and there were no acceptations. exceptions

Stephen held Sybil's hand. Sophia took Donna's and without a thought they marched down the ramp to the elevators. Family and visitors were sitting on the benches along the far wall. Some were in hospital garb others still had on their jackets and coats. Small babies cried while grandparents spoke in hushed voices. Gurneys moved in and out of elevators along with the mixed cultures of the area and different languages were spoken.

Sybil pushed the elevator button. All four of them entered to watch the doors close. Sophia took a tissue from her purse. She handed it to Sybil who quickly wiped off her elevator finger. "Thanks, Mom, I don't want to catch any cooties from anyone, right?" She handed her mother back the tissue.

Stephen nudged Sophia, "Does she do the hand wiping often?"

Sophia shook her head, "Sybil is very conscientious when it comes to medical diseases and bacteria. Being nine years old and an avid reader has brought many concepts her way. Humoring her is best."

The theme song from Ghost Busters hiccupped from the sound system overhead as the elevator slowly rose. When they departed the elevator there were no people in the hall. The foursome marched astride straight to Geoffrey's hospital room door. No one sat outside. No one stopped them.

"Dad, we're here!" Sybil gleefully raced into her father's room to jump full force onto the bed. The bed squeaked and moved three inches toward the far wall. Groaning, Geoffrey put up his hands. "Whoa! Sybil, I'm in a state of recovery, no need to attack!" The six year old Donna was right behind her sister, only she didn't get enough momentum to make the leap to the bed. Sophia lifted her six year old Donna into Geoffrey's arms.

The girls sat, one on either side of Geoffrey. Sophia stood at the foot of the bed with a huge smile. "Wow, you are finally free. Where are the State Police when you need them, right?"

Geoffrey stared at her, "You're a sight for sore eyes, my beautiful wife! I have missed you beyond your wildest imagination. Each night, I lay here thinking of you." He hugged the girls to his chest. "Each morning I envision you with your hair leaping straight up in the air." Sophia squeezed his good foot.

"Ouch! Was that really necessary?" Geoffrey glared at her. Sophia frowned, "Yes, your brother is here." She turned. Stephen was not in the room. "Girls, where did your Uncle Stephen go?"

"Don't know," Sybil snuggled closer to her Dad. "We had Daisy dog staying with us today. She found Granger's button in the arroyo and she found a dirty bag full of bomb stuff."

Donna dangled her feet over the edge of the bed, "Yeah, we took her to Mr. Perkal's house. She's happy there. Mama said Daisy needed to be with people who didn't explode or die." Donna gave Sophia a dirty look. "We made you some cards, Daddy, here."

Geoffrey took the plastic bags of colored cards. "Thanks, girls, do you think I could speak with your Mom for a minute. Can you two get down and give me some breathing room, please?" Sybil rolled off the bed, landing on her feet. "Sure, Dad, if you and Mom want to kiss we won't look. Come on, Donna, we can sit over here."

Donna hopped off the bed to join Sybil by the window. The Venetian blind was green in this room. It was all the way up, revealing the city lights. Sybil reached into her coat pocket, "Donna, remember Mrs. Perkal gave us masking tape. We can tape Dad's cards to the wall."

"Come here, you," Geoffrey reached for Sophia. She bent over and kissed him. His lips were dry and rough. He tasted of Colgate toothpaste. "I seriously missed you. You are my partner in crime, don't you know?"

"Geoffrey, shush, you don't want to say things that aren't true. The walls may have ears." She hugged him gingerly. "What are they going to do with your foot?"

"Dr. Baker believes the skin on my foot will heal in time. They have a new medical product that promotes natural skin growth. He was telling me they tested it on dogs burned in house fires. Here, look at this strange bandage stuff they put on my foot. It breathes, but it inhibits bacteria from growing. The Scots figured this out, I guess they have lots of fires over there."

He pulled back the sheet to show them a translucent filmy bandage. "The bad part is I can't walk on it. I have crutches." He pointed to the tall wooden sticks beside the bed. "They want me to walk up and down the hall five times in the morning and in the afternoon. By the time I get back to bed, the foot is throbbing like a base drum at a football game."

Sybil touched the bandage, "Does this hurt, Dad?" Donna felt the edge of the filmy material. "It feels like a butterfly wing, doesn't it?"

Sophia placed the sheet back over his foot, "What did Dr. Baker say about your heart and any nerve damage?"

Sighing, Geoffrey said, 'They put me through a battery of tests. They had me lifting weights and then I pushed myself in a wheelchair up and down a ramp with all kinds of wires attached to my chest. They had me in a breathing chamber, which is something I never want to do again. Finally, they gave me a clean bill of health. The one good result was my eyesight has improved. When I get out of here I can get a new pair of glasses." He handed her his glasses.

"These are slightly melted on the nose bridge." She ran her finger over the middle piece, "Does this hurt your nose when you wear them?" She handed them back to him.

He gingerly placed them on his face, "No, I try to sleep most of the time. The doc said the more sleep the faster the repair. I feel drugged being stuck in here. They won't let me outside or off this floor." He held Sophia's hand, kissing her fingers. "I have been frightened for you and the girls. When they told me Granger was sitting the girls after the explosion I was desperate to get out of here. Then Margaret insisted she bring me some pajamas."

Geoffrey lifted his arm to show off his cotton pajamas with blue and white stripes. "Your mother made the guard bring these to me. She practically thrust him through the door. At first, I was sure they were covered in some kind of poison, but Stacy the nurse said she would wash them for me." He patted down the sleeves, "They work. They weren't soaked in poison and actually it was very nice of your mother to be so thoughtful. Don't you think she was thoughtful?"

Before Sophia could answer him, the bedroom door burst open. Stephen and Ignacio charged into the room. Stephen had his arm around Ignacio's shoulder. Ignacio was dressed in his sheriff's deputy attire. Once in the room, he pulled away from Stephen.

Stephen leaped forward to take his brother's hand, "Geoffrey, hey, how're you doing, my big brother?" Then he grabbed Geoffrey into a bear hug. Ignacio shook Geoffrey's hand.

Geoffrey lifted his left eyebrow, "Stephen, you aren't hitting on my beautiful wife are you?"

Stephen stared at the polished floor. "Geoffrey, you know what a ladies man I am? Actually Sybil and I have been working together on the old yellow van. She is an expert on car seat mobilization and has found her way into my heart."

Sybil ran over and kicked him in the shin. "Uncle Stephen, I don't mess around with older men!"

Stephen feigned pain as Sybil returned to taping cards on the wall. Sophia studied Ignacio and Stephen. "What have you two been up to?"

"Granger isn't as smart as he wants everyone to believe." Ignacio lifted his left hand to reveal a clipboard. "The Admiral here asked me to look into the possibility of anyone seeing a green Mercedes at your house the night prior to the explosion."

Geoffrey laughed at Stephen, "Are you going by Admiral now?"

Stephen chuckled, "Hey, if you've got it flaunt it, right?"

Ignacio ignored them continuing with his evidence find, "Guys, we hit the jackpot. Bingo. The gas station attendant at the Chevron station remembered Granger's green Mercedes. The surveillance camera focused on the cars at the gas tanks. We have a green Mercedes there dead to rights the night prior to the explosion."

Ignacio studied the clipboard again. "Then we have a photo taken by the camera that monitors the speeders leaving Rincon at the hill by Rocoso at nine forty-five p.m." He turned to Sophia, "At ten-fifteen that evening you were with us reviewing the evidence where Carol Granger was attacked."

Scrolling his finger down the clipboard, Ignacio put his finger on the list, "Then, the Mulholland's came home from a theater production at Popejoy. They noticed a green Mercedes parked beside some juniper bushes in front of your house at quarter to eleven. Mr. Mulholland was familiar with the vehicle because he sells supplements to H&G Clinic and recognized the vehicle as belonging to one Granger Pino from the license plate."

Ignacio pulled out a piece of photograph paper, holding it up to show everyone a license plate; 'NMDRPN.' Geoffrey burst out laughing. Stephen slapped Ignacio on the back, "Good job, old man, good job!"

Sybil stared at the paper, "What does that mean? It doesn't spell anything!" Geoffrey pulled her into his arms, "Come here. It is short for New Mexico Doctor, what?"

Ignacio smiled, "Pain or Pino, or whatever you want I suppose."

Sophia shook her head, "It reads No More Doctor Pino to me." Breathing deeply, Sophia collected herself, "You do know we are talking about my brother Granger? He is my flesh and blood as I live and breathe. This is a terrible situation and I believe I need to go find A.J. and listen to his side of the story."

"Wait," Stephen took the license plate paper, "Sophia, is your brother really a doctor? I thought he was a therapist or someone who is only practicing?"

"He has a license to practice therapy as long as he works with someone who has passed the exam with the medical board. Granger is allowed to work under M.D. supervision. He himself does not have a degree in medicine just a license to do his chiropractor and give advice. The medical doctor he works with is the one who writes the prescriptions and gives a diagnosis. Carl Henker is the medical doctor on his team."

She put up her hand, "I know he likes people to believe he is a doctor of medicine maybe because his father was a medical doctor or perhaps because I have my doctorate in philosophy. For some reason he feels safer behind the illusion. I know it's sad, but there it is."

"So, now we have him, right?" Ignacio put the clipboard at the foot of Geoffrey's bed. "Certainly the State Police have this information? They were on top of this within minutes after the explosion. Why aren't they arresting Granger?"

Geoffrey frowned, "We need verifiable proof. Everything we have could be argued. He may have needed gas on his way to see Sophia. When he got to our house and saw her van wasn't there, he may have left. I was putting the girls to bed in the back bedrooms. A vehicle in the front of the house would be out of our field of vision. We don't know how long Granger was in the front yard and we don't know what he was doing there if anything?"

Ignacio moved to the window. He stared out at the city lights, "Maybe we should just ask Granger what he was doing driving to your house late Friday night? He might have a good answer."

Sophia lifted the clipboard off of Geoffrey's bed before it fell, "What about Friday at one o'clock? Geoffrey, you had an appointment with Mr. Goldfarb, right? Didn't you tell Granger about the appointment? The timer was set for that time and would have solved Granger's problems if the truck would have exploded in the parking lot."

Geoffrey studied her expression, "No, Granger would have problems if the truck exploded in Goldfarb's parking lot." He rubbed his bald head, "Goldfarb was in here earlier. He's the one who had the State Police remove the guard. Samuel Goldfarb told me Granger had asked to meet with both of us at one o'clock at his office. I had no knowledge of Granger's desire to meet at the lawyer's office. Why would Granger want to blow himself up along with the rest of us?"

Stephen sat down in the plastic chair. He straightened his long legs out in front of him, blocking the girls from leaving the corner of the room. "Both of you have made excellent points. We have hypothetical information, which isn't doing us one bit of good. We must compile what we have and put together the final noose to catch this sucker."

Geoffrey smiled at his brother, "Is that how the Rear Lower Half Admiral in the Navy speaks to his men? You talk of nooses and traps as if you are familiar with ambushes?"

Nodding, Stephen said, "I am, but usually I use nuclear missiles. Now I have to dumb down to catch this bugger. What's the plan?"

Sophia laughed as she reached for the door handle, "Guys, I am going up to see A.J. before visiting' hours are over. You figure this out with the girls, bye."

Walking down the long hall to the elevators, herds of people surrounded

Sophia pushing their way to the doors. She waited for the elevator to empty and quickly stepped inside. "Hey, Mrs. Vinder, is that you?" Sophia turned to find Marcus standing in the back corner of the large elevator. He was holding two cups filled with steaming coffee. "Marcus, how's your father?"

Marcus peered over the shoulder of a tall man with a fuzzy beard who stood between the two of them in the elevator. Marcus' voice whispered, "He's anxious to speak with you. Tomorrow they're moving him to UNMH. We hope they can save his right eye and help him with the nerve damage in his right arm. Of course, his splinted middle finger gives everyone his final comment, but he's doing better, much better." The two of them exited the elevator.

Sophia walked beside him down the hall, "How's your mother? Did she get some rest?"

Marcus shook his head, "You know when her head hit the pillow she was out for six hours. I couldn't wake her or move her. She's here now, looking at least twenty years younger. You won't recognize her." He pushed open the hospital door with his hip and stood aside.

"Wow, look who is sitting up and almost human!" Sophia stood in the door frame and stared at A.J. He was smiling at her, "Come on in here. How's your husband?" A.J. lifted his left hand out to her. Sitting beside him on the bed was Rosa. Her hair was curled and fluffy. Her eyes sparkled and her red lips appeared to be permanently placed in a smile.

Marcus gave Sophia a gentle nudge on her arm, "Go on in, you're blocking the door here." She grasped A.J.'s hand, he squeezed her hand with force, "See, I am alive and well, no thanks to you! Why didn't you drop with me when I pushed you down?"

She retorted, "What? Why didn't I drop with you? You were on top of me, I could hardly breathe and you almost suffocated me with all your blood dripping on my face. You have no right to yell at me, Sheriff? Sir, I was the victim."

Rosa put up her hands, "Enough, you two, time out here. What is with you?"

A.J. snorted, "She's the cause of my pain and suffering." Then his face lightened, "How is your husband?"

"He's better. The State Police no longer have him under lock and key. Your sheriff deputy Ignacio Cruz has been a great help to us. Did you put him up to being our sole help in law enforcement or did you want him to keep an eye on us?"

A.J.'s voice was gravelly, "Could be, I knew Geoffrey didn't set the explosive or the timer. Your husband isn't an idiot and only an idiot would set a timer with a battery and then try to start the engine. It would be suicide."

Rosa handed A.J. a cup of water with a straw. After a long drink he continued, "Your husband was clever enough to jump out immediately with only minor burns. He would never have left the truck rigged in your front yard either. Doesn't take a rocket scientist to figure out the evidence either, by the way how's Ignacio?"

Rosa interrupted their conversation, "Ignacio took Carols' death to heart. You could see it in his eyes when he told us how he walked her body to the morgue. His heart was hurting." Rosa reached up to hold her husband's hand.

Marcus pushed a green cafeteria chair to Sophia. She sat beside Rosa, "Ignacio and Geoffrey's brother Stephen are working on a plan to catch the perpetrator. They have the suspect in their sights, which puts me in a difficult situation as you know? If you could give me more proof maybe I won't feel so guilty."

"If you believe this has something to do with your brother, perhaps. Although I believe there is another aspect of the problem no one has addressed. It's too easy to blame Granger. He is an obvious victim. Don't forget everything points to him. There are witnesses everywhere who have seen him at both crime scenes. There is verifiable proof of his capacity and capability to perform both crimes. This alone makes me suspect he is being set up."

Sophia sat up straighter in the chair, "Who else could it be?"

A.J. winced as he shifted his weight in the bed, "That's the problem. No one has done a serious investigation into Carol's death. Her high levels of insulin were serious enough to kill her, but how did the insulin get into her body? Her skull was hit with a blunt instrument not found at the scene. The dog was chained to the dog house, but everyone said she always had the dog with her." A.J. lifted his splinted middle finger, "That damn dog may have the answer. Everything we've seen has had an element of overkill. Your father not only aspirated, but was poisoned. Carol was not only given too much insulin, but she was hit on the head. There may be more than one perpetrator in each of these."

Rosa lifted the cup of water with a straw in it for A.J. to take another sip. He went on with his thoughts, "Then, we have the issue with the bomb in the truck. In my opinion the bomb should have gone off at Mr. Goldfarb's office. This had the potential of killing numerous innocent people including Geoffrey. Granger wanted Geoffrey in your house and he wanted Geoffrey to live in it without you or the girls. Granger wanted you two to suffer being separated. I don't believe he wanted Geoffrey dead. "

A.J. lifted his bandaged right arm to elevate it on a pillow beside him, "Granger had a reason, maybe to teach you some kind of lesson. He and your mother already have a house in mind for you to live in and they have given a bid for property closer to them. According to what the State Police found Granger explained to the real estate agent that he and his mother wanted to buy the property for you and the two girls."

Sophia cleared her throat and then said, "Wait a minute. Emily told me this afternoon about Granger putting the Rocoso house up for sale with a notice in the Wall Street Journal. Why would he do such a thing if he wanted Geoffrey to live in the house?"

The nurse charged into the room, carrying a tray with pills and a syringe. "All right, everybody out. I have to change a bandage and spoil the Sheriff."

Then the nurse turned to face Sophia, "Mrs. Vinder, is that you? I'm Stacy remember me? I hope you found the blue paper I stuck in your bed. Your husband wanted me to give it to you, but the police kept checking on you and I wasn't sure if you'd find it. Did you find it?"

Sophia put her hand on the nurse's arm, "Thank you, I had no idea how it got into the bed. You're very clever. I'll let my husband know your scheme worked."

As they walked out into the hall Sophia thought of A.J.'s comments. Her concentration was interrupted. "Mrs. Vinder, can you stay longer?" Rosa hurried to catch up with her. "Do you have to leave now?"

Holding out her arms, Sophia hugged Rosa. "Yes, I have to go and retrieve my daughters. I want to speak with my husband and then we should probably get home." Letting her go, Sophia continued, "A.J. is certainly something, isn't he?"

Rosa and Marcus spoke at the same time, "Let us know if you need help?" Marcus grinned at her, "I'll be with my dad everyday from now on.

They gave me time off at the bank. If you need to know information or how to get it, just ask. Give our best to your husband." Sophia smiled at them as she took her leave, "Bye and thank you."

Marcus walked with her down the hall, "Mrs. Vinder, my dad wanted you to know Carl is working on finding out more facts on your mother." He stood in front of her, "Dad hopes you don't mind. Carl has gathered information regarding her finances and her sale of the Mercedes. It might be wise to have someone contact Carl." Marcus winked as he left her in the hall and returned to his father's room.

Geoffrey's room was filled with silence when Sophia entered. The girls were on the bed next to their father. Donna was asleep in the crook of his left arm. Sybil was drawing on the back of one of the cards with a pencil. Ignacio was pacing at the foot of the bed and Stephen was still sprawled out sitting in the chair. They all looked up when Sophia entered the room.

Ignacio quickly spoke, "How's the boss doing?"

Sophia nodded, "He's doing well. He told me something I never thought of and perhaps you should hear. He feels that Granger is being setup as the fall guy. A.J. said all the evidence, all the witnesses point to Granger. A.J. doesn't believe Granger is that stupid nor does he believe Granger would be careless enough to hurt others or put himself in such a position. A.J. mentioned Carol was hit on the head with a blunt object, which wasn't found at the crime scene. There is also the fact of Daisy being leashed to the back dog house. Carol never left Daisy outside at night. Daisy was her alarm clock." Sophia leaned against the wall of the room, "Also, folks, no one has found the wedge that was shoved into my father's hospital bed. This is making me crazy! Where could it have gone and why would someone take it?"

Ignacio leaned against the wall beside her, "You know I have been curious about Carol's crime scene. There was blood everywhere, but not in the water. A.J. had the water in the swimming pool tested. The towel on the living room floor was used on the dog. It had dog fur all over it and smelled of wet dog." Ignacio's face became somber, "Why would Carol take too much insulin? She would know it was dangerous, right?"

Stephen groaned, "Civilians are messy and complicated. In the Navy we have everything compartmentalized. Ignacio, we need to go back and review the evidence at Carol's crime scene. Do you think we could get into the house without a warrant?"

"Sure, we can, the key is by the side door. What do you hope to find there, though?"

Geoffrey interrupted them, "I knew when I heard about the truck exploding Granger was not the bomber. There were two things in the truck out of place."

He leaned back and closed his eyes, "First the floor mats were piled on top of one another on the passenger floor. We need new mats, sure, but the old ones were on both sides when I came home the night before." He lifted his head, "The gloves on the seat were not mine. I noticed them before I slid the key into the ignition. I was going to warm up the truck and then examine the gloves."

Stephen was standing next to the bed, "What about the gloves? What did they look like?"

Geoffrey smiled at his younger brother, "Oh, let me see? Ah, yes, they were gloves from an Admiral in the Navy!"

Stephen put his head back and laughed, "Good one, now what did the gloves look like?" Geoffrey sighed, moving Donna up and down with the heaving of his chest. "The gloves were mechanic's gloves. They were the heavy duty material with blue stitching, red around the wrist, and had padding where the finger tips would be. There was blue writing on one of them, but I didn't catch what it was. Ah, now I remember, the gloves were small. They looked like gloves a child would wear. Also, they were very clean. There were no obvious wear marks. They looked brand new, unused, as if the price tag might still be on them."

Ignacio took his clipboard off of the side table, "I'm going up to see A.J. He told me he made a list of what was inside the cab when he was there that morning. I bet he saw the gloves. Nothing gets by A.J. he has the eyes of an eagle. Be right back!" Ignacio disappeared down the hall.

Stephen stretched his neck and shoulders, "I admit Granger is the perfect patsy for this, but who else in the whole wide world would be interested in killing Carol? Who else would blow up the truck, and want to destroy your lives? Can either of you think of anyone?"

Sophia moved to Geoffrey's side. She held his hand. Sybil shifted her weight, allowing her mother to be closer to Geoffrey. He looked at her, "Sophia, who do we know that would want to kill Carol? Who do we know who wants to harm the family?"

She shook her head, "Granger wants all the money from the family. He's in the process of getting a divorce, having a son, and helping his mother spend all her money. He's intrinsically selfish. I pray he is not behind this, for in my own way I do love him and want him to be happy."

Geoffrey squeezed her hand tightly, "There are others involved here. Margaret is not happy with the arrangement of the lawyers. She and Granger found the lawyer in Santa Fe to move everything over into their pockets. Do you think Margaret is involved in this?"

The intercom announced Visiting Hours were over and for all visitors to please depart. Sybil kissed her father on his cheek. "Daddy, you smell good. Do you use after shave?" Geoffrey kissed her back on her forehead, "Yes, I knew you were coming."

He lifted Donna to Stephen who gently hugged the six year old, allowing her head to fall on his shoulder. Stephen gently touched Geoffrey's hand, "Good to see you, brother. Get out of here soon. I don't trust this place."

Geoffrey pulled Sophia into his embrace. He kissed her long and hard on the lips. "I love you, woman of mine, take good care of our treasures. Let Stephen spoil you and please don't do anything without checking in with me. I couldn't live without you and the girls." Tears welled up in his eyes, "I mean it. I love you beyond life itself. Now go and feed the herd."

The table at IHOP was filled with dishes of partially eaten food. Stephen had inhaled his pancakes, sausages, bacon, eggs, and hash browns within seconds. The girls were busy in a scientific experiment, trying each one of the different syrups. They had fixed a plate for each pancake and each pancake with different syrup. Stephen was drawing on his napkin, "Let's make a family tree with everyone's name on it. We will put Walter and Margaret at the top. Now who are the children and what is the order in relation to age?"

Sophia ignored him. "Geoffrey looked good didn't he? Girls, what did you think of your father's mood?"

Donna poured half the pitcher of blueberry syrup on one of the pancakes, "He is fine. Dad's fine, he needs to come home. They don't have enough for him to do."

Sybil wiped strawberry syrup off of her chin. "He smells good."

"Ah-hem, am I speaking to myself? Come on help me with this. Who is in the family Pino?" Stephen tapped his pen on the napkin.

Sophia took a deep breath, "You know, Stephen, I am tired. My brain is tired. I just think we need to go home and let it be for a time. If we can rest, recoup and find our balance the path may become clear. Right now I can't think anymore about anything. I just want to bask in the knowledge that the people I love are alive and healing. Can we just appreciate the moment?"

The pencil was carefully placed on the table. "Yes, we can let it be for tonight." Stephen took his fork and tasted Donna's blueberry syrup. "I forget we're here in the Real World, not the world of scheming and masterminding. Forgive me. Sophia, you're right, we need to be in the moment with Sybil and Donna."

Sophia handed Stephen the bill, "Here, you can pay this, Admiral. We're done for the day. Come on, girls. Let's go home to sleep perchance to dream."

After the girls had their bath, books were read and the lights were put out in each of their rooms. Stephen spent his time on the telephone speaking with someone in the Navy. Sophia sat in her bedroom with her yellow legal pad and paper. Everyone related to them was listed and as she read down each name, she wrote their relationship to her family and their relationship to Granger. She turned her head, listening to Stephen's serious questions being asked over the phone. Sophia tried to figure out what the point would be to kill her husband or the death of Carol.

Stephen had hung up the phone. He knocked quietly on her bedroom door. "Can I come in?" Sophia nodded at him, "You can, but I need a hot cup of tea. How about it? Would you like some tea and a list?"

Sophia and Stephen met in the living room just before ten o'clock. Sophia sat on her rocking chair holding a glass of white wine. Stephen stretched out on the couch with a can of beer. They stared at the empty fireplace filled with powdery ash. Stephen dropped the pad of paper with the list onto the floor beside him. "This list gives us some idea of who is where and their relationship, but there is something missing. Someone has a direct line to the effect of what Granger is doing. We need to figure out who the person is and why they are so threatened by Granger and your family."

Sophia stared at the dead ash in the fireplace, "Geoffrey's job is to empty the fireplace." Sophia lifted her glass in the air and took a drink.

"Ah, the ashes of life are left to my brother, how contemptuous." Stephen sipped the beer and rubbed his nose.

"Stephen, don't talk about it. We promised we weren't going to talk about it tonight, right?" She leaned down to unlace her boots. She nudged off her right boot with her left foot. "Oh, now heaven has come to my body."

"Your foot bothering you, is it? You want a foot rub?" Stephen didn't move.

Sophia wiggled her toes, "No, just need my foot to breathe. It's been a long confusing day. I do want to thank you for helping us take Daisy to Mr. Perkal's farm. She will love it there. Daisy enjoys being with other dogs. Also, I can sleep late."

Stephen let his head lean against the back of the couch, "Yes, his wife is an incredible woman. At first she fooled me. Wasn't she good with the girls and all the colors and paper? You would never think she couldn't see color."

Sophia coughed, "She told me once that she can feel and smell colors. Gives you a whole new perception of what is around you, doesn't it?"

"Yes, and they knew Carol and Daisy well. How thoughtful of them to help Carol with their friend's need for a house-sitter. Life is certainly serendipitous, isn't it?"

Sophia stretched out her arms, "Stephen, do you want to sleep in here on the fold-out couch or do you want to sleep in our bedroom? It doesn't matter to me, but it will matter to the girls. If you sleep in our bedroom you can use our bathroom. The girls will not take kindly for you to use their bathroom. Where is the best place for you?"

Stephen yawned, "I'll sleep here and use your bathroom with you. My brother wouldn't appreciate me sleeping with you in his bed. At least I don't believe he would. Is that what you're asking?"

Sophia flung her boot at him. It fell short to land on the floor. "You know what I mean! Now, do you want to sleep in the living room alone or in the bedroom alone?"

Stephen rolled over on the couch. "We need our space. The couch is good and I can use your bathroom. I already checked out the girls' bathroom, it's definitely too feminine for the likes of me."

They made up the couch bed. Sophia gave him the extra pillows and escaped to her own room while Stephen stripped down to skivvies ready to get into the couch bed. Once the lights were out, Stephen cautiously moved to the front door. He moved in a crouch as he opened the door. Outside, he took care to stay lower than the height of the rental car. Stealthily, he moved to the driver's door. The folded paper he had placed in the door frame was lying on the ground. The air was cold and quiet. Stars lit the crisp night sky.

19

Rocoso, New Mexico
Sunday, January, 1988

Quiet steps moved around her bed. Sophia kept her eyes closed. A small voice whispered, "Mama, time to rise and shine." Sybil put her hand on her mother's shoulder. "Mom, your hair is going straight up in the air, just like what Dad said."

Sophia leaned up on her elbow, "Hi, Sybil my sugar plum? What's going on out there in the world?" She glanced at the bedside table clock. It was almost ten-thirty. The sun shone in through the windows.

"Mom, there is another bomb. You need to keep your voice down. Donna and I have been creeping around waiting for you to come and see. People have been calling all morning. We didn't want to wake you because Uncle Stephen said you needed to sleep."

Donna tip-toed into the room, she whispered, "Mom, there's another bomb. You better get up because a whole bunch of guys are here with uniforms and they're talking with Uncle Stephen." Donna carefully climbed on the bed and scooted to her Dad's pillow.

Sophia fell back on the bed, "Oh, shit!"

"Mom, that's a nasty bad word!" Sybil jumped on the bed to be with her sister.

"Bombs are nasty, bad and men in uniform are even worse. A nasty bad word was needed to express my feelings." She rolled over to hug both girls, "I am so tired of all of this. Dead tired of this! Why can't people go away and leave us alone? Huh? What did we do to cause all of this angst and trauma?"

Sybil tried to stroke her mother's hair down, "Mama, you didn't do anything wrong. It's the other guys who are messed up and crazy. We're the good guys."

Sophia smiled, "Your Uncle Stephen has been giving you both pep talks, huh?"

Donna rolled over her sister to be closer to Sophia, "Mom, you really need to get up! The men are in the kitchen making a mess. They ate the French toast we made for you already and they're drinking coffee from Dad's coffee maker! They're going to eat us out of the house if they keep munching!"

"Oh, all right, let's get going. How many men are in the kitchen, Donna?"

"There must be about two forty and they have on some strange uniforms with metal chests and helmets, but they took those off when they came inside." Sybil started to pull on Sophia's arm. "Mom, come on!"

The kitchen was empty when Sophia arrived. The dishes were washed and in the drain board. The coffee maker was sparkling clean and stood proudly on the counter. She heard voices in the living room. After making herself a cup of tea, she joined the voices.

Stephen jumped up from Geoffrey's recliner, "Sophia, this is the Kirkland bomb squad. They removed the bomb from the rental car this morning."

Quick to stand at attention, the men put out their hands to shake Sophia's. No one gave their name, just a smile, a nod, and a handshake. Sophia nodded back to each one of them, "Thank you, gentlemen, for your fast response and expertise. I am sure we all appreciate not being blown up once again. Did you find any evidence or anything different from the other bomb?"

The shortest man of the group stepped forward. His voice barked out, "Ma'am, if you please, Ma'am?"

Sophia stepped back to look at the man. Stephen smiled, "Please go ahead and speak?"

A short man of compact stature stared straight at Sophia as if she were an immovable object, "Ma'am, the bomb in the rental vehicle was made with the equivalent dynamite but from a different year. There are obvious signs of evidence. The technique was similar. The breaking into the vehicle through the trunk reveals the person or persons who set the bomb were familiar with this type of vehicle. There were traces of material retrieved from the spare tire lying in the wheel bed of the trunk. We vacuumed a large quantity of dog fur." He stepped back to be even with his fellow crew.

"Oh," Sophia took a sip of tea, "You are very thorough, aren't you?"

The youngest member of the crew broke into a smile, "Ma'am, we assure you the vehicle is now safe to drive. We do have information, which we cannot reveal at this time for we are working with the State Police and the local

Sheriff's deputy. If you need to gain information, it would be wise to speak with them directly."

Stephen interrupted, "Thank you, men. Better let you get on your way. It is Sunday and even though you don't have the day off, I' sure you have things to do on base. Again, the Navy thanks you for saving one of their own."

The dark green uniformed men marched single file out the door. Each picked up their helmet and equipment. Stephen accompanied them to their military Hum-V. He saluted as they drove down the road.

Sophia abruptly sat in her rocking chair. "Wow, all those men. Geoffrey will be sad he missed all this macho stuff." She heard the girls giggling in Sybil's bedroom. Stephen gently closed the front door and came into the living room. 'The bomber struck last night while we were putting the girls to bed. After lights out, last night, I went out to check the vehicle. My safety paper in the car door had been dislodged. Someone had entered and set devices."

"Stephen, you're speaking like those guys. Who do you think broke into the car, ripped it all up, crawled through dog hair, and did what they did?"

"Hell, I don't know, I'm just a Navy man. What do I know?" He walked out of the house.

Sophia heard the rental car's engine start. Hurrying to the kitchen window, she saw Stephen back up and drive away. She sighed, "At last, it's just me and the girls. Look at this kitchen?" She wiped her finger along the counter top, "Someone could do surgery in here."

Sybil and Donna ran into the living room. "Mom, can we watch a movie? Donna wants to watch Bed Knobs and Broomsticks again?"

"Me? You do! We both do, can we, Mom?" Donna shoved Sybil aside.

"Girls, you can do whatever you want to today. We are free agents. Uncle Stephen just drove off into the great unknown and we are free to do as we please. Help yourself to cookies, drink your soft drinks, and watch your movies. We are alive and we are home. No one could ask for more?"

Sybil frowned, "Except for Daddy to be here, right?"

Sophia hugged her daughter, "Right! Now get what you need and go and enjoy! I plan to do laundry, vacuum the floors, and read. Off with you two!"

The laundry was started. The vacuuming was accomplished. Another cup of warm tea in hand, Sophia sat at the kitchen table and dialed the hospital.

She had two telephone operators to go through before Geoffrey answered the phone. "'Geoffrey, how are you, sweetie? We miss you, what's going on over there?"

Geoffrey sighed and said nothing. Sophia frowned, "You have visitors and can't talk now, right?"

His voice was cautious, "Exactly. My brother Stephen is here visiting me. I am sorry, Mr. Goldfarb, would I be able to call you later in the morning?"

Sophia lowered her voice, "Yes, later is appropriate." She hung up the phone.

The girls fixed their own lunch and decided to eat it in front of the television. Sophia made a fried egg sandwich with tomato. The last of the potato chips were dribbled across the top of the kitchen table. Sophia swept them up and dumped them on her plate. Just as she was going to join the girls, the doorbell rang. She jumped dropping the potato chips on the floor. Groaning, she grabbed her jacket and moved around the couch to answer the front door. A young woman in blue work pants, a shirt of red flannel, and a heavy jacket stood at the door holding a clipboard. Her hair was hidden under a red skull cap.

"Mrs. Vinder, is it?" Her large brown eyes questioned Sophia. The rich smell of lavender floated in the air around her as she stood close to Sophia.

"Yes?" Sophia slid on her jacket.

"I'm with your car insurance company. They sent me out here to review the damage on your family van." The young woman turned to point at the old yellow van. "Is that your van there?" There was disdain in her voice as she stared at the open hood, the flat tire, the destroyed windows and the sagging frame.

Sophia closed the front door behind her to keep the cold outside. "This is my van. Yes, it suffered in the great explosion of Friday. Evidently your man came out and investigated the truck but was remiss in reviewing the van." The two women went to the van. The young woman peered into the gapping engine. "Wow! This is a mess. Did someone try to work on it or was this what happened in the explosion?"

"Most of the damage was from the explosion. Obviously the hood wasn't up when the truck exploded. It was down. I drove here to meet with the Sheriff. He told me to park while the tow truck backed to the truck."

The young woman stared at the black dirt where the truck had once parked. "Wow! There isn't much left is there?"

"No, the truck has been removed for investigation. The whole truck didn't blow up, if that is what you are thinking. They county sheriff's department team took the truck for evidence. All that's left are the pieces of scattered metal. We have been picking up the metal everyday to try and remove the horror of the situation." Sophia waved to the area in front of the house. "What about my van? We have had it for just less than twelve years. My husband took good care of her." Sophia wanted to protect the van from this young woman's examining eyes.

"This is my check list, here." She showed Sophia her clipboard. "Why don't you give me some time and I'll come in and we can talk after I inventory everything? Sometimes it's better if you aren't hovering while I do this."

Sophia stood under the roof of the porch watching. She said under her breath, "Hovering? If Stephen were here he would be hovering. Not me, I don't hover."

"Mama, are you talking to yourself?" Sybil poked her mother in the back with her finger.

"Yes, I am. What do you want?" Sophia didn't turn around.

"Donna and I wanted to know if we could have a Popsicle. Can we?"

"Sure, eat whatever you want, Sweetheart. You both deserve rewards."

"Mama, who is that woman and what's she doing to our van?" Sybil pointed at the young woman.

"I'm sure she has a name, but she hasn't told me yet. She's going over the van to give us an estimate. She will tell us how much damage was done and how much money they will give us for her. Right now we don't have a vehicle. We can't go anywhere."

"Oh, Mom, the old van smells liked something nasty has burned up in it. I hope she can fix the old van cause if she can't what would we live in if the house blows up? We will be stuck out here in the cold?"

Sophia knelt down to her nine year old daughter, "Sybil, we're in hard times right now. Granger and Grandma Margaret are trying to take our house away from us. Someone is blowing up all our vehicles. Your Dad is in the hospital and your Mom feels strung too tight. Uncle Stephen is running around. I need you and Donna to enjoy yourselves and be happy. Don't think anymore about bombs, can you do that for me?"

"Sure, Mom, we can. Does this mean we don't go to school tomorrow? We can't walk that far!"

"No, you are not going to school tomorrow. Someone may try to blow up the school. We appear to be a magnet for trouble. Go inside, stay warm, you don't have your coat on and it's cold out here." Sybil raced into the house to share her good news.

"Mrs. Vinder?" The young woman waved at her.

"Yes?"

"The windows are all blown out as you can see. The rubber seal around each window has cracked probably from age not explosion. The tires are well worn and probably all of them need to be replaced." She took a dime out of her pocket and placed it in the tread of the back tire. "See, the dime rolls off if I don't hold it. You have no tread on these tires."

She walked to the back passenger door. "The runners on the doors are shot. The rubber is worn and well used. This happens with age and use. Now, let's look at the engine and the frame." Pointing to the engine, she continued, "The valves have been tampered with and this was done by human hands. The radiator is in good shape, just old and probably needs a good cleaning. Carburetor and battery are still good, although the fuel pump and oil pump are old."

Kneeling on the ground, she said, "Here, you'll need to get down on the ground with me." She rolled over on her back. Sophia groaned as she knelt and rolled under the van. Her mind raced back to the explosion with A.J. lying on top of her. She gulped air as she moved closer to the insurance adjuster. The young woman continued, "The van's basic body frame is solid. It isn't bent or cracked."

Her index finger rubbed the long metal frame, "The insurance company will try to get out of paying you anything for this vehicle. When the frame of the vehicle is safe enough to be driven, the insurance company will want you to repair or rebuild the vehicle yourselves." She scooted in the dirt to move closer to the underside of the engine. "Here you can see the wear and the leakage from badly worn valves. This van was on its last leg when it got hit from the explosion." She crawled out from under the van to sit up, leaning against the tire. Sophia rolled on her side, placing her head on her hand.

The young woman picked up the clipboard from the ground beside her, "If the frame isn't declared totaled or beyond repair, the insurance company will weasel out of paying." She checked off items on the clip board. "It would be in your best interest not to report this van. If you do claim it on your insurance—there's a chance your insurance policy will go up even more. You already have a totaled truck. This won't look good on your policy even if you get a different insurance company." She put her hand on her knees and stood.

Sophia let the young woman give her hand as she was pulled upright. "Okay, then the van is totaled, but not by your company. She's just finished?"

Shaking her head, the young woman took copies of papers from the clip board, "I'm going to give you this copy. Talk it over with your family. It's in your best interest to not file, but this is my opinion. As a single mother of two boys, I always try to give my best opinion. The van was probably not going to last much longer anyway. It would be wise to sell it to a car parts place, take your profits and buy a used vehicle. This way your insurance company will not be upping your monthly bill."

"Would the car parts place give me much for it?" Sophia patted the van's frame.

"In my opinion and this is all it is, I might actually think you would get more money if you took it to a metal recycling place. There is one over off of I-40 and State Road 35. Get a tow truck or call them, they may pick it up for free. They will weigh the metal and give you top dollar for the metal weight." Pushing back her red cap, she added, "Do what you can afford to do. That's my motto."

Sophia stared at the paper. There were red check marks, illustrating the death of her van. "What would you do if this was your van?"

Walking to the engine, the young woman pointed to the open hood, "I would sell the engine to a mechanic. He might give you a good price for the engine and he may be able to rebuild it and sell it himself. The rest of the van is junk. If you find a mechanic who will buy the engine, he may have a tow truck. Take it to the car part's place and get money for parts."

She peeked into the window. "I see you have kids and it would be better for them to know the van was recycled rather than demolished. Try to sell off the parts and let this old girl live on helping out others."

The young woman handed Sophia a card. "Here, this is my card. I am Geraldine Slade. You can call me at either number and let me know what you want to do. Just call me within the next twenty-four hours. The window to file a claim is seventy-two hours and we are almost there."

Not waiting for Sophia to respond, she hurried to her black Dakota truck and drove away. Dark clouds were gathering on the horizon. Starlings flew in groups to the arroyo. The juniper and pine trees began to dance in the wind. Dust swirled around, pelting everything in its path.

"Well, a storm is brewing." She stared at the card, "There you go." She opened the van's passenger door and gathered old school papers, torn candy wrappers, and Donna's traveling doll. Dirt blew against her legs as she ran to the house with her arms filled with cargo.

Dropping her goods on the kitchen table, she noticed the throbbing red phone message light. On the counter under the wall phone was a school paper with a list of five people whose calls she had missed earlier in the morning. Samuel Goldfarb had called twice. Geraldine Slade had called around ten o'clock. Margaret had called and Granger wanted her to call him back promptly. After checking on the girls, Sophia called the message answering service. The girls were on the floor coloring and the movie was playing quietly.

Back in the kitchen, she listened to the messages, "Sophia, this is your mother. It's now almost two o'clock and I have not heard from you. I'm coming over there. When you left the hospital yesterday, I forgot to give you your prescriptions and the discharge papers. Why don't you answer your phone? I hate it when you don't answer your phone!"

The next message was from Geoffrey. She dialed the hospital and was put right through to his room. "Hey, how's it going over there in demolition alley?"

"Geoffrey, you're not funny. What's your brother up to? He took off in a huff this morning." Sophia tried to fold the laundry from the dryer and hold the phone between her shoulder and ear.

"He said you were short with him. He's never lived with women before, be patient with him. Ignacio and Stephen are going over to review the house where Carol Grover was murdered. For some reason Stephen feels he can solve the case by himself."

Geoffrey could be heard sipping water, "Oh, A.J. came by to see me on his gurney. He had the ambulance guys bring him down here to my room! He's a character all right and his son Marcus wanted you to call him. There is some information about the bomb found in Stephen's rental car."

Sophia interrupted him, "Geoffrey, do you know how sick I am of all of this? Do you? I feel as if the ceiling has fallen on us. It never lets up. We just have one catastrophe after another. My hair is turning gray. The girls have no way of getting to school tomorrow." She felt tears well up in her eyes.

"Hey, Sweetheart, hold on. I'm here, I know I'm way over here, but I am here on this planet. The bad thing is you can't get here and I can't get there. Damn, why didn't Stephen bring you guys with him when he came to the hospital?"

"I wouldn't have come. Geoffrey, the girls are hunkered down coloring, watching movies, having fun. The laundry is being done. The house is somewhat clean. Oh, the woman from the insurance company was here."

"What did she say about the van?"

She cleared the van's treasures off of the table. Some went into the waste basket, other's she took to the girl's rooms. She continued to tell him, "The van's frame is in good shape, which means the van is not totaled. She recommended we rescind our request to the insurance company, have the van sold off for parts, and buy a pre-owned van with what we can get for selling off the van's parts."

Geoffrey sighed, "Yep, she's right. If we do file a claim the cost of our insurance rises. Call her back and ask her to tear up our request." There was silence.

Sophia dumped Donna's clean clothes on her messy bed. "Geoffrey?"

"Yeah?"

"Is this house ours or is it Margaret's and Granger's?"

"Sophia, don't go there just yet. Let's not talk about the house. I'm working with Goldfarb on the counter suit against Margaret and Granger. He said he was going to call you this morning."

"He did, but I was still asleep. Stephen took the message. Did you know Granger has an ad in the Wall Street Journal to sell this place?"

"No, he doesn't. He said he doesn't have any ads out regarding our property. Goldfarb checked with the Journal. The ad was placed by persons unknown. There was no phone number, no address, and the ad was paid with a cashier's check. Granger was called on it by Goldfarb. Granger said he knew nothing about it."

Sophia sat on Donna's bed, "But Emily told me Granger spoke with her about it. She told me she was shocked he even considered selling our property."

"Someone is lying. Granger was emphatic in denying his involvement with this to Goldfarb. Goldfarb believed him."

"Geoffrey, Emily was here alone with the girls Friday night. Do you think she has something to do with this?" Sophia fell back on the bed.

"Emily? Do you believe Emily could plant a bomb?"

"Well, she knew about the dynamite. She may have had access to it at the Negara house. Oh, I don't know, what do you think?" Sophia moved the phone to her other ear.

"Sophia, she knew Carol well. Emily was over at your father's a lot of the time. She also knew Daisy. Daisy was Carol's constant companion. Daisy liked women and only barked at strange men. Emily is not dumb. She may have connections, but then she is such a prima donna. I can't see her rigging dynamite and hitting people over the head, can you?"

"No, I can't see Emily wielding weapons and carrying dynamite. She's a mother and a caretaker, but she is mad as hell about Granger and Katina. She may want revenge on Granger and be setting him up for this?"

"Sophia, she wouldn't hurt Carol. No, she wouldn't hurt people. Who else do we have on the list?"

Sophia groaned, "Oh, Stephen pushed me to put together a list of folks who might or might not be related to all of this. We went over it last night, but we couldn't come to any kind of solution. Stephen never gives up, does he?"

Geoffrey chuckled into the phone, "He loves you and the girls. Of course he won't give up until he finds the culprit. It's in his nature to seek and destroy. Please, be patient with him."

Tired of holding the phone, Sophia stood up to pace in Donna's bedroom, "You want us to be patient with him? What about us? We're in the middle of this. He keeps pushing and pushing and pushing and I'm so tired. What if the girls and I went to a hotel for the rest of the week?"

"Sophia, get a grip. We seriously don't have the kind of money needed to live in a hotel room. Where is the woman of steel I married? Once we have achieved the goal of catching this jerk, we can lead our lives just fine. There is no giving up or going back at this point. We must forge ahead with courage and gusto. Come on, work with Stephen. He will be gone soon and we need his help. I can't walk. We don't have a vehicle. Stephen can help you get a rental."

Pulling the phone away from her mouth, Sophia moaned, "Another vehicle? Are you crazy? All the vehicles around here get blown up or die! I don't want another vehicle. Can we get a horse and buggy?"

"Sophia, I have to go and walk with the nurse. Get your second wind, girlfriend. You need a car and the girls need to go to school. We don't have options here. I love you. Don't ever forget I love you. Say 'hello' to the girls and give them my love. Bye." He hung up on her.

The front door slammed shut. Sophia jerked when she heard her mother call out her name. Margaret was in her house. Margaret had taught the girls to slam doors. As Sophia moved down the hall, she heard Donna talking loudly to her grandmother, "Grandma Margaret, do not slam doors! There are bombs everywhere and if you slam the door it will be your last door!"

Margaret turned and stared down her nose at her six year old grand-daughter, "What are you talking about?"

Sophia quietly spoke as she met with them, "Mom, hi! Yes, we had another bomb found on the premises. Uncle Stephen told the girls to not slam doors or make loud noises. We don't know if there are more around."

Margaret paled as she turned and patted the door with her gloved hand of black leather. "Good door, it didn't blow up on me."

The six year old smiled, "There you go, Grandma. You better be careful around here." Donna ran back to the living room to be with her sister.

"Mom, come in the kitchen. I'll fix us a cup of tea. How is the storm outside?" Sophia pulled out a chair for her mother.

"The storm is fine. It's raining over by my house, but as I came through town the rain disappeared. I see you have a hard wind." Margaret placed a white bag on the table. "Here are your antibiotics. I went ahead and got them filled in town. Also, here are your papers. You shouldn't take a bath or soak your leg in water for at least ten days. If there is an infection you're to call the doctor right away. How is your leg feeling this morning?" Margaret took the mug of hot tea from Sophia's hand.

"My leg is fine. It throbs some, but otherwise it's fine." Sophia sat facing her mother with her mug of tea cupped in her hands. Margaret shoved the bag at her. "You should probably take some pills. Also, I got you some sterile bandages in case you have to change the bandage at some point."

Opening the white bag, Sophia noticed there were actually three bottles in the bag. "What are all of these for?"

"How should I know? Read the directions, you went to college." Margaret straightened all the brown plastic bottles, lining them up in front of Sophia.

Margaret lifted her tea mug, "Sophia, we had no idea all of this was going to happen to you and Geoffrey. You must believe me? I was shocked to find out Carol was attacked and killed. I had no idea about Geoffrey's truck."

Her serious face stared at Sophia, "You could have been killed. I love you, Sophia. I don't want anything to happen to you or my favorite girls!" She reached into her small purse to pull out a linen handkerchief. "Please, do not accuse your brother. He loves you and cares about you and his nieces with his whole heart. I don't know why you hate him so much? He really wants what's best for you."

Margaret stood to wiggle out of her full coat of gray herringbone. She gently folded it over the neighboring kitchen chair. "You have a way of always blaming your brother, Sophia. You know you do? If anything bad happens the first person you blame is your brother." She took a sip of her tea. "This won't do for you to blame him. The guilty party is out there doing these horrible things and you and Geoffrey are focused on Granger. This isn't right."

Sophia was busy reading the prescription directions. Margaret sighed, "You are always wearing old clothes. Don't you have any clothes that aren't from the Good Will?"

Noticing her mother's sweater of soft baby blue cashmere, Sophia answered hesitantly, "Mom, my appearance is not relevant to me right now. I put on my old jeans because I'm cleaning house. I have on my old work shirt because it gives me comfort. As for my boots, well, I was outside with the insurance adjuster crawling under the van. This is as good as it gets, sorry if you are offended."

Quickly Margaret responded, "Hey, don't get your knickers in a knot, I just asked!"

Ignoring her, Sophia tried to get one of the prescription bottle's lids off. Margaret took the brown bottle to open it for her. "They make these difficult so children can't get into them. Actually very few adults can get into them. Your father used to smash them with a hammer and of course then they were opened permanently!" She handed her the bottles she had opened. "Here, just push down and turn with the palm of your hand. These are to be taken with food, maybe you should wait for dinner." She shoved the bottles toward Sophia.

Sophia took a deep breath, "Mom, did you and Granger find dynamite at the house in Negara?"

Margaret nodded as she blew on the mug of hot tea, "Yes, we did. It was in the shed barn behind the well house. I asked Granger to remove it. Shirley is a little girl and she gets curious. If she found it, well, who knows what she would do with it?"

Sophia reached for the paper napkins behind her on the counter. "Mom, you need dynamite caps to set off dynamite."

"How was I to know? I don't dabble in dynamite on my days off, dear!" She took a paper napkin from Sophia, "Anyway, Granger put the dynamite in my used Toyota truck. It's outside. Do you want to see it?"

Sophia jumped almost knocking over her chair, "Mom, did you lock it? Did you lock all the doors?"

Her mother glared up at her, "Of course I did! Your brother had an alarm put in it. If anyone jiggles the door or hits the side of it—it sounds off a loud alarm. I just love it! Of course when I went to the bank yesterday, they had to come and get me to turn off the alarm. Some idiot bumped the truck and it was screaming in the parking lot. Hah, that will teach people to leave my truck alone!" She smiled with satisfaction.

Sophia leaned to look out of the kitchen window. The silver truck was parked beside the old van. "It's a nice truck, Mom. What made you buy a truck? Didn't you like the Mercedes you had?"

"The Mercedes was fine, but if you want to carry hay, or bring in dirt, you need a truck. I was tired of relying on other people for their trucks. The Perkal's helped us with their truck, but it's not good to always depend on others, don't' you think?"

Sitting back down opposite her mother, Sophia asked, "How's Katina doing with her problems?"

Margaret frowned as she primped her hair, "Katina's a funny one. Granger appears to love her and care about her, but she's strange. Katina disappears at night in her old car. Her faded blue car is scratched, dented, and the cloth in the interior hangs over your face when you sit in the passenger seat. You have to tuck it into the sun visor thingy. The car smells of dirty feet. She has these weird habits of only eating a head of lettuce or a bowl of dried cereal with no milk." Margaret shook her head, "I can't figure her out, Sophia. She says she has to go out at night and drive around or she won't sleep. How is she supposed to sleep if she's driving around all night?"

Sophia got up to pour more hot water in the mugs, "Do you know what she does or did for a living?"

Margaret nodded when her mug was filled, "You mean Katina?"

"Yes, what does she do for a living? Does she have a job or a supporter?"

Her mother's eyes glowed, "You know, I don't have any idea. I never thought to ask. She's not doing anything now, but being ill in the guest bathroom. Granger has her staying with me while he divorces Emily. Emily's belongings are still in the house. There really isn't any room for Katina at the moment."

"Mom, I know this is wrong, but could you look through Katina's things when she goes for one of her drives?" Sophia pointed her finger at her mother, "No, I don't mean to spy, just give a glance to see if there's something in the guestroom about where she worked last or if she had a job?"

Margaret studied her daughter's eyes, "You do want me to spy, don't you? I never thought I would hear such a request from you! You used to accuse me of opening your mail and now you want me to spy?"

Sophia clenched her teeth, "Yes, well not spy, just observe."

Chuckling to herself, Margaret twirled her empty tea mug in a circle. "I already checked her out, but not by going through her things. No, I am civilized. I had a private detective research her. After all she is marrying my son who has power of attorney over my estate. I'm not stupid. Please, don't give me that look! I was going to tell you, really. I was going to share this with you—before you were almost blown to pieces."

Studying the design on her tea mug, Sophia waited for her mother to continue. Margaret pushed back in her chair and crossed her legs. "Katina Combs was born in Los Angeles, California. She is the same age as Granger. Her birthday is three months before his, though, so she is an older woman. Granger and you were both born in October as you know too well. Her birthday is on a Wednesday in the month of August. You know about Wednesday's child, right?"

"Mom, you and you're superstitions!" Sophia grumbled.

"What? They are true these old English sayings. Remember this one from your childhood? Monday's child is fair of face—Tuesday's child is full of grace—Wednesday's child is full of woe—Thursday's child has far to go—Friday's child is loving and giving—Saturdays child works hard for a living—But the child who is born on Sabbath Day is bonnie and blithe and good and gay."

"Katina was born on Wednesday so she is filled with woe?"

Margaret took another small sip of her tea. "Yes, she has no siblings who like her or they would be here helping. Her mother is divorced and lives with a musician in Eunice, California. Her father was a railroad man who contracted cancer, probably from all those fumes, and is in a Hospice in San Francisco. Katina has three priors, as the detective put it. She was arrested for dealing drugs in the 70's and the 80's. She was arrested at a sit-in for Women's rights for abortion in San Francisco. Last month was her last arrest. She was put in the pokey for attempting to blow up the Santa Fe court house. She and a group of other people wanted gay marriages to be approved in New Mexico and since Santa Fe is the capital of New Mexico the gay groupies felt it apropos in order to make a statement."

Sophia's face blanched, "Is she gay? Does she have dynamite?"

Margaret lifted her tea mug, "If I am to be interrogated, I need more tea." Sophia got up and put the kettle back on the stove. "All right confession time, Mother, is she gay and does she know how to use dynamite?"

"How should I know if she has any dynamite? I believe the people she was with did the exploding. Her 'soul brother' is gay." Margaret put her fingers in quotes as she went on, "At least she told Granger he was her 'soul brother.' Any woman who has a 'soul brother' is suspicious to me." Her mother kept putting italics in the air as she spoke.

Margaret took her paper napkin and wiped her tea mug, "I told you, Katina just showed up at Granger's house for she had nowhere else to go. Her friends sprung her from jail. She was traveling with them and none of them have any money. It's a wonder they all didn't descend on Emily and Granger. They could have had a massive orgy."

The kettle whistled merrily. Sophia lifted it off the stove with a hot pad.

She placed the kettle on a tile square on the table. The bowl of tea bags was placed in front of Margaret next to the saucer holding the honey pot. "Here, Mom, you can help yourself."

"Sophia, I worry about your brother. Sex can be addictive, as you know only too well? Emily has been distant from your brother for years. Men need sex. We women are aware of this aren't we?" Margaret spooned honey into her mug. Sophia tried not to burst out laughing as she mumbled, "Mom, you know more about sex than I do."

"Oh, hush, that's not true. You lived with all those strange men during the seventies." Margaret rambled on, "Well, Granger is determined to marry this Katina. I'm not going to pay for a big wedding. As I told you yesterday, I'm embarrassed to be seen in public with her. Emily is beautiful. Emily has panache. Emily speaks my language. Katina is a rodent trying to forge her way into our family. Sophia, you have to help me get rid of her."

Sophia almost dropped the honey spoon, "What? What do you mean by 'get rid of her'?"

Margaret shook her head, "Well obviously we aren't going to hit her over the head, that's someone else's specialty. Granger needs to know she is a treasure hunter and my treasure isn't going to become hers, let me tell you. I will give you power of attorney over him if he marries Katina!"

Sybil ran into the kitchen, "Mom, listen! Do you hear the loud noise coming from outside?"

Margaret and Sophia almost knocked each other over running to the front door. The door was flung open before they could reach it. Stephen stood there with a red face, "Hey, I only peeked in the window. I didn't do anything. I just put my hands on the glass to peek in the window!"

Margaret smacked him on the back as she pulled her key ring from her pant pocket. She gave it a push and the screaming truck was quiet. She hit the button on the key ring again and it beeped twice. "There now it is reset. I don't want my vehicle going ka-boom!"

Stephen peered over Sophia's shoulder, "Where are the girls?"

She pointed, "They're in family room watching movies." She gave him a soft smile. "I'm sorry about earlier, Stephen. You deserved to be heard. I am sorry."

He gave her a quick kiss on the cheek, "The girls can help me unload the groceries. You were running low."

Stepping around Sophia, he was suddenly confronted by Margaret's angry glare, "Nice truck, sorry I set off your alarm." He disappeared into the family room.

Margaret took Sophia's hand and led her into the kitchen. "Let's get Katina to fall in love with Stephen. They're both rather dull, don't you think?" Margaret slid into her chair.

"Mother, no, Stephen is a rocket scientist compared to Katina." Sophia lifted her tea mug as she sat down, "Tell me is Katina an albino or does she have a serious medical condition?"

"Well, I asked Granger about her coloring. Evidently she is not an albino. Her mother burned her in a hot bathtub when she was around three years old. Her skin pigment never recovered its color. She's just white. Her eyebrows and her hair turned white as well. They couldn't do anything to help her. I suppose she could dye her hair, but it might look funny. She's a very strange duck."

The girls interrupted their conversation as they carried bags of food into the kitchen. The smell of moist air followed them. "Here, Grandma Margaret, you take this one, its heavy!" Marie shoved her bag at her grandmother.

Eight bags of groceries were unloaded before Sophia was able to ask her mother to take her to a rental agency. Margaret shook her head at her daughter, "You want to rent a vehicle? Darling daughter, are you sure? The vehicles at this house usually don't last long. This could be expensive."

Stephen leaned his long lanky frame against the counter, "Sophia, why don't I go with Margaret to the rental agency? I can get you a vehicle with a military discount. We can stop at the hardware store and get a car alarm. I might even get an alarm for my new rental van. Your mother's a smart woman having an alarm in her vehicle." Margaret gloated as she slid her arm through his.

Sophia thought for a minute, "You know you're right, Stephen. I'll let you two go and get the vehicle and the girls and I will make you a dinner fit for a king."

Margaret pouted as she pulled on her heavy coat, "Can I come back here for dinner? I don't think I could stomach another meal with Katina. I need her out of my house, out of my life, out of New Mexico."

Sophia helped her mother with her coat, "Mom, talk to Stephen about Katina. He knows about missiles and shooting items into space. Right, Stephen?"

Stephen handed Margaret her purse, "Well, I don't know about shooting a person into space without a missile."

"There you go. You two talk about it. Mom, we will expect you for dinner as well. I'll get the girls to help. Also, I better call Geoffrey and see if I can get a hold of Granger. He called earlier."

Margaret grabbed her daughter's arm, "No! Don't call Granger. He's in a meeting with Emily this afternoon. I think they were going to move some furniture to Negara. If they get involved with the bed, they might find love again. I pray they don't talk about the divorce. Oh, how I pray they forget Katina! Your brother's infatuation with having a son is driving all of us crazy! Children are children and he is going to lose the best woman he ever had because of dumb head Katina."

Stephen called to Margaret from the front room, "Hey, we better move it. The rental agency is waiting for us." She hurried to him. After several screams from the truck, they drove away into pelting rain and hard blowing dirt.

While Sophia inventoried the food for dinner, she called Marcus. He answered immediately. "Marcus, this is Sophia Vinder, you asked me to call you?"

His warm voice sounded pleased, "Yes, Mrs. Vinder. I just wanted you to know they did surgery on Dad's eye. He had to have a corneal transplant. The doc feels the surgery went well and Dad will have full use of his eye. Of course we have to wait until the bandage comes off, but knock on wood."

"Marcus, this is excellent news. How's his arm?"

"The doctor's are reviewing the x-rays on his arm tomorrow morning. The procedure on his eye had to be done promptly because the cornea came in this morning and they wanted to do the surgery right away. His arm has a spiral fracture and the nerves were cut somehow, so this may take months to heal. Oh, my Mom says 'hello.' We wanted you to know about Dad right away."

Sophia smiled, "Tell you mother 'hello' for me. Marcus, have you heard anymore about the bomber or Carol's killer?"

There was a pause, "Sorry, I wanted to move out of Dad's room. I'm in the hall now. The phone has a long cord on it. No, we just found out about Stephen's rental car having a bomb. Carl was by earlier and said he was at the house where Carol was attacked and did a full inventory. He said he was going to write up a report and share it with us and the State Police. Dad was still in surgery when he called." Marcus cleaned his throat, "Why don't we share tomorrow morning, probably after ten o'clock? There should be more news then."

Sophia pulled out some lean ground beef. Answering Marcus, she said, "Yes, tomorrow morning will be fine. Marcus, would you ask Carl to look into Katina Combs? Evidently, she was arrested in Santa Fe last month for attempting to blow up the county court house."

"Wow, this puts her in the hot seat, doesn't it?" Someone was speaking to Marcus, he quickly said to her, "I have to go, Dad is waking up now. Mom wants me with her." Dial tone echoed in Sophia's ear.

The spaghetti was boiling and the tomatoes were stewing in the lean hamburger when alarms were heard in the front drive. Sybil ran into the kitchen hurriedly. "Okay, Mom, I'm going to set the table. They're here in the front. I heard all the beeps telling us they have alarms in all the cars. Where is the fancy checkered table cloth?"

Sophia pointed to the cupboard, "On the bottom shelf, there. Where is your sister and what is she doing?"

Sybil yanked on the tablecloth, knocking paper towels to the floor. Sophia hurried over to help her put them back, "Where's your sister?"

"She's asleep on the floor with the movie running for the fifth time. She really loves that movie, Mom, I think because she was with Dad when he brought it home. She talks about Dad because she's really scared. I was scared, but not anymore. Uncle Stephen told us Dad's coming home and he won't leave until Dad is home." She opened the table cloth on the table. "No offense, Mom, but Dad is fun and you're all business."

"Really, you both think I'm all business? What about when we go to the zoo? What about when we go hiking or go to the movies? Am I boring?" Sophia put the table cloth over the table with Sybil.

"No, Mama, you're not boring. You just expect us to learn about stuff. Dad can be crazy and wild. That's all, gee!" Sybil took the silverware from the silverware drawer when Margaret entered the kitchen.

Her hair was wet, dripping onto her coat. She grabbed a dish towel. "It's really pouring. The weatherman said it will turn to snow later this evening." She rubbed her head with the towel. "Stephen is fixing his rental car with his alarm. He's going to be soaked. Sybil, take your Uncle an umbrella?"

Sybil pursed her lips at her grandmother, "No, I don't think I can. I'm setting the table."

Margaret threw the wet towel at Sybil, "Well, since I am already wet, I'll take him an umbrella. Sophia, your daughters have learned how to backtalk from you!" She disappeared out the door.

"Sybil, you could have taken the umbrella to Uncle Stephen." Sophia frowned at her daughter. Sybil shook her head, "No, I have to set the table. I can't do everything!" They both burst out laughing at Geoffrey's famous phrase.

"Mommy, my stomach hurts." Donna leaned against the kitchen door frame. "It really hurts like somebody stabbed me. It hurts right here." Donna pointed to her center abdomen.

"How much did you guys eat in there?" Sophia pointed to the family room. Donna shook her head, "I ate the rest of my Halloween candy. I found it under my bed yesterday. Sybil didn't want any she said it was too hard for her teeth. It was good. You just had to suck on it, that's all." Donna gave her sister a glaring stare.

Sophia reached into the kitchen medicine cupboard, "Donna, why don't you get into your nightgown and get into bed. I'll bring you some medicine. I'll be right behind you." The Cod Liver Oil was already in Sophia's hand along with a spoon. She smiled at Sybil, "Aren't you glad you didn't indulge in all the junk food?"

"See, Mommy, you're always teaching us stuff." Sybil tried to smile at her mother and the bottle she held in her hand. "I hate that stuff. Someday Donna will learn candy isn't worth it if you have to drink that yuck!"

"Sybil, you're in charge." Sophia turned the gas burner low under the spaghetti sauce. She put the lid on the boiling spaghetti and turned it to simmer. "Can you make the salad for me?"

"Sure, good luck with the liver oil." Sybil rolled her eyes as she opened the refrigerator. Sophia hurried to Donna's room. Donna was curled in a ball on her bed. She had on her pajamas and her pink socks. "Let's get you under the covers. You need to stay warm."

Donna kicked her legs straight out in front of her when she saw what her mother was holding, "No, I won't take that liver oil! Mama, I hate that stuff!" She started wailing.

Stephen raced into the room. "Whoa, what's going on in here? It sounds like someone is skinning a live cat!" He lifted Donna off the bed, "What's the matter with you? Are you trying to set off all the bombs in the county?"

Donna promptly shut her mouth. Tears fell from her large round eyes. She pointed to her mother's hand. Stephen leaned to read the bottle label. "Yuck, what are you doing with this stuff?"

Sophia glared at him, "Donna ate the last of her old Halloween candy by herself. She has a stomachache. There is only one way to relieve her stomachache. We're going to move the candy south and flush it away."

Stephen raised his eyebrows, "You don't fool around do you?"

"No, I do not! Not when it comes to the girls' health." Sophia shook the bottle to carefully remove the lid from the bottle. Donna squirmed in Stephen's arms as he held her in a tight hug.

"Donna," Stephen held her on his left leg as he pointed to the spoon, "You have to take a spoonful. You know it tastes like rocket fuel, but it will help you. Your mother knows what she's doing. You have to be brave for the rest of us."

She buried her head under his arm. She kicked, hitting Stephen in the thigh. He reached over and lifted her in his arms. "Sophia, here, hurry, she's like a wildcat." Donna jerked and kicked, trying to get away. Stephen had a firm grip on her. "Come on, Donna. Just swallow and it's over. Then you can have dessert with us. Margaret and I got a chocolate double cream cake and vanilla ice cream."

Donna froze, "Really vanilla ice cream?"

"Yeah, vanilla ice cream and cake is hard to pass up, right?"

She opened her mouth wide. Her mother poured the spoonful of Cod Liver oil into her mouth. "Yuck, it stinks! I'm gonna die, I'm gonna die!" Donna fell through her uncle's arms to lie on the floor. She rolled on her back to play dead.

Stephen tickled her. "Come on, it's not that bad. Now climb into bed and we'll call you when dessert's ready." He helped pull the covers over her, and gave her a kiss on her forehead.

Sophia walked next to him in the hall, "Really, Stephen, you are going to call her for dessert? You did get the part about her having a stomach ache, right?"

20

Rocoso, New Mexico
Sunday Night, January, 1988

Hot garlic bread was passed around the table. Sophia served each person, loading the plates with the spaghetti and homemade sauce. Sybil's salad of lettuce, spinach, sliced tomato, fresh avocados, and walnuts was the center piece. Stephen placed Geoffrey's chair next to Sybil. Margaret sat in Donna's chair and Sophia was at the foot of table in her usual place. Stephen had opened a bottle of Chablis, which was sitting to his left. He told them it needed to breathe before being poured. Sybil had a wine glass filled with ginger ale at her place.

Margaret twirled her spaghetti around her fork, using the spoon to hold it in place. "You know Granger is inebriated in his infatuation with the misaligned protoplasmic entity that is carrying his offspring to the point of disgust."

Sybil chortled, "Oh, boy, I get to translate!" She stared at her grandmother for a few minutes and then said, "You just said Granger is in love with a weird woman who is pregnant and you find her horrid. Am I right or what?"

Margaret gasped, "Sophia, your daughter is an enigma. How does she know such big words?"

Stephen lifted his hand, "Hey, I can answer this one. Sybil is a reader. She reads books from morning to night and her vocabulary is exemplarily, correct?"

Everyone laughed. Stephen started to pour some wine into Sophia's wine glass. Margaret quickly pulled the wine glass away. "No, no wine for you, young lady. You have antibiotics to take and the alcohol will defuse the antibiotic strength. You better have some ginger ale with Sybil here."

"Antibiotics?" Stephen put the bottle of wine on the table.

Sophia turned her wine glass upside down on the table. "Mom brought me my drugs from the hospital. Evidently we raced out of there without them.

She was nice enough to bring them here. She is a doctor's wife, remember, and she knows all about medications and alcohol, right, Mom?"

Margaret nodded, "Enough with this discussion. We were on the subject of my survival with the strange and bizarre Katina the rat. She is nesting in my house and making it foul with her nasty habits. What am I to do with her?"

"Mom, we discussed what to do with Katina. Margaret may be right about her being a treasure hunter. The one problem here is she pregnant with Granger's son?"

Stephen handed Margaret the basket of garlic bread, "Margaret, you are not completely honest. You want a grandson as badly as Granger wants a son. For some reason both of you put a lot of stock in birthing males, giving females the short end of the stick."

Smiling, he added, "No pun intended. The really big issue is if Katina is not pregnant. She may be on drugs. She was arrested for using heroine in the 70's and 80's. Heroine is not a drug people get off of easily. She could still be using and she may be driving around at night looking for a dealer. She may not have any money, aside from what Granger gives her. Who knows what she may be doing at night? She could be selling herself to get drugs? We don't know."

Margaret sipped the wine. She leaned back in the chair and sighed, "This is delicious, Stephen. You can pick my wine anytime." Putting her glass down, she asked, "It would be lovely to have a grandson, but not one deformed from drugs or born with brain damage. The thought of her giving Granger diseases, also, comes to mind." She gasped and put her fingers to her mouth, "What if she is leaving her diseases behind on my toilet seats? Oh, I really don't want that slut in my house! What do we do to find out where she goes at night?"

Stephen bit off a piece of garlic bread, "We follow and see where she takes us. You can't follow her because she knows you. She knows everyone at this table, but me."

Sybil interrupted him, "I've never met her and neither has Donna. We don't drive, but we could go with you as extra eyes."

Stephen leaned back to look at her, "Yes, and you do have fine green eyes. The only problem is you have to be in bed at nine. I am an old geezer who can follow odd ducks."

Pointing her nine year old finger at him, Sybil frowned, "True. You'll have to go it alone, Admiral."

Margaret held her fork over her plate, staring into her food, "Do you mean to say she may not be pregnant at all? But wouldn't Granger know about her pregnancy, he is a doctor after all."

Sophia pointed to the salad. Her mother handed her the wooden bowl filled with lettuce, avocados and tomatoes. Sophia said, "Mom, Granger is not a true doctor as you already know. He certainly hasn't examined her at least I can't see him doing any serious inspections. He may trust her. If they had sex and he let her know how seriously he wants a son, she may have told him what he wanted to hear."

Margaret coughed into her napkin, "Sophia, really, you have children here at the table that do not need to hear this kind of talk."

Stephen took the salad bowl from Sophia's hand, "Yes, I had a woman try to pull this trick on me when I was in boot camp. One female recruit was infatuated with me and my jeep. She told me all kinds of stories about being pregnant and being fragile. She wanted me to marry her before her father came to visit. I put her off believing her father would be the one to speak to about the situation. He sat down with me and cleared the air. She wasn't pregnant and she was already engaged to someone else back home. What a shock." He put the salad bowl on the table. "Sybil, don't you ever do that to a guy. You have to promise me you won't play stupid games with some poor sucker?"

Sybil put her hand over her mouth as she chewed, "Promise, Uncle Stephen. It seems stupid to me. Why would a girl want to tell someone she's pregnant when she's not?"

Margaret smirked, "She would lie to get his mother's money. Some of my money is supposed to go to you, Sybil. What do you think of that? Do you want Katina taking money from you to use for something illegal? I don't want her stealing the family blind with no intention of giving us a son."

Sophia put her hand on her mother's arm, "How do we know it's Granger's son? She may be pregnant by one of her friends in Santa Fe? We have no way of knowing if she is pregnant, who got her pregnant or if she is on drugs and pregnant. Whoa, this wouldn't be good at all. The baby could be deformed or drug dependent."

Everyone digested this thought as they ate dinner. Margaret explained,

"Katina has an odd habit of constantly rubbing her nose. She told me it was from the pregnancy, but I saw a program on the television about drug users and how their noses run. Granger has put this woman on a pedestal and his whole existence is rotating around her."

She handed Sybil her empty plate and pointed to the spaghetti, "Granger is talking now about leaving the H&G Clinic and starting his own. Sophia, you know he can't practice his trade unless he's working under a medically licensed doctor? His delusions are going to put him in the poor house with this creature Katina."

Stephen helped himself to another piece of garlic bread. "Will Henker and Enid be able to afford the clinic if Granger and Emily leave? It would seem to me if anyone was feeling threatened about Katina and the divorce between Granger and Emily it would be Enid and Henker. Has anyone spoken to them?"

"I have." Sophia handed her mother back her plate filled with sauce and spaghetti. "Enid called me several nights ago. She is very concerned for they all had to borrow money or take out loans to afford the property, the licensures, and the inventory they needed to keep the clinic going. Enid was worried about Emily leaving for Emily is the one who knows all the doctors and nurses who send them patients. Also, Emily knows the insurance companies and how they work. Enid is certain Emily's leaving is going to put everyone in a difficult position."

Stephen got up to get more ginger ale for Sybil, "You know it might be a good idea to drive down to the clinic and see Carl Henker. He might be the man who would know someone who wanted revenge on this family. Henker certainly wouldn't want Granger to leave or Emily for that matter." Stephen added wine to Margaret's wine glass. "What do you think?"

Margaret held her wine glass to her lips. After taking a delicate sip, she responded, "I never liked those people. They appear common to me. I mean they wear scrubs everywhere they go and have no sense of style. Enid is a remarkable woman who married beneath her. The German fellow Carl Henker is a slob. Granger said as much himself once. Henker never cleans or takes care to put the patient's files on the front desk. Emily is always running around trying to find the file in order to bill the patient or make an appointment. The Henker fellow is a poor relation of someone's. Also, the clinic is between Kelly's Liquors and an Auto Zone store on the main strip. Who would put a medical clinic between a liquor store and a car accessory store? They aren't our type of people, let me tell you." She took another sip of wine.

Sybil dropped her bread on the tablecloth only to shove it on her plate. "Grandma Margaret, you are a snob. You don't like anyone who isn't a Pino, not even my dad. Dr. Henker is a nice man who gives us lollipops when we visit him. He has a little boy who likes Donna. You should be nicer to people and they would be nicer to you."

Margaret glared at her granddaughter, "You have some lessons to learn, little missy, you should not speak to your elders in such a manner or you might find yourself with a sore behind from spanking."

Stephen lifted is hand, "Where is Carl Henker from? Isn't his name foreign?"

Before Sophia could answer, Margaret spoke, "Oh, yes, his family is German. He's very proud to tell you of his German family who served with the Third Reich. Henker has photos in his clinic of his great grandfather with Hitler standing outside a German Tank. He has a photo of his grandfather in full Nazi uniform with a troop of men around him ready to take on the French army."

Waving her fork, she continued, "Henker's whole family moved to the United States post world war two. His mother and father live in South Dakota, probably hiding from anyone who remembers the war. I can't imagine moving to the country of your enemy. They must have killed hundreds of Americans as well. What a sad group of people they are." She put her fork on her plate, "I find the man contemptuous and arrogant. I have not now nor will I ever let them into my house."

Sophia interrupted her mother, "Henker has had a hard life with his history. He went to medical school in Mexico City for he was attacked at several of the universities and colleges here in the U.S. He changed his name and moved to Mexico City for six years to receive his medical degree. His medicine is solid even if he prefers to use more Oriental Medicine than Western Medicine. Many people do like him and swear by his services."

Stephen passed the salad bowl around, "What about Enid? She doesn't sound as if she is from New Mexico."

Sighing, Margaret shook her head as she took some salad, "Enid is a spoiled trust fund child. Her parents are living in Connecticut. Her grandmother was a famous opera singer or something and her parents always had money. Enid marched against the Viet Nam war, she ran away and joined a commune, and finally she ended in New Mexico working for a clinic on the wrong side of the tracks. Enid said she enjoyed working with those who had less than she ever did and wanted to make their lives more bearable."

Lifting the empty salad bowl, Sophia took the salad from her mother and gave it to Sybil as she added, "Everyone loved your salad, Sybil. Look it is all gone now." She put it on the counter behind her. "Stephen, Enid is someone who felt displaced in her family. Her mother and father wanted her to go to one of those Ivy League colleges, marry above her class, and have a plethora of children. Enid wanted to explore, go on adventures and marry someone who would make a difference for those less fortunate. I think they are a great couple and have much in common."

Margaret made a growling grunt and gave her daughter a hateful stare. "You would say something like that, Sophia. You always stand beside those who I find despicable. If your brother were here he would tell Stephen how you only want to make your mother unhappy with your lies and your exaggerations."

Sybil placed her fork and knife on her empty dinner plate, "Mom, you are a great cook, of course, I did help, too."

"Yes," Sophia rubbed Sybil's back, "you are very helpful. Mom, what do you know about the wedge Carol placed in Papa's hospital bed? Do you know where it is?"

Margaret jumped as if she had been electrocuted, "Oh course, I know where it is. Why wouldn't I know where it is? The damn thing was stuck in the hospital bed making it look like some kind of medieval torture tool. I told Carol I didn't want it in the bed, I ordered her to remove it, but she refused. She was a pompous brat and she could learn to follow the requests of those who pay her." She threw her fork down onto her plate, "Stephen, certainly you are aware of the phrase 'never bite the hand that feeds you?'"

Stephen nodded as he grabbed more spaghetti. Not waiting for him to reply, Margaret explained, "The thought of the metal wedge, hammered into the back of the hospital bed as if it were a guillotine bed was appalling, grotesque, terrifying especially at night. I would lay awake at night and see it there in my bedroom."

Swallowing with some wine, Stephen probed her further, "Where is this wedge now?"

"Well," Margaret wiped her mouth delicately with the paper napkin, "I had Alfonso take it out and take it to the dump. He's my hired help, don't you know? He comes three times a week to help feed the horse, to muck out the barn, to get the hay in my fancy truck, and to help me around the house."

Sophia and Stephen stared at each other. Sybil piped up, "Did you tell the sheriff you took the thingy to the dump or did you just pretend you didn't know what he was talking about?"

"Sophia," Margaret spoke with contempt, "Your daughter is impertinent! How dare she address me in such a manner and in such a tone! Of course I didn't tell the sheriff. If I would have told him he would think I killed your grandfather and I did no such thing, young lady! It would behoove you to mind your own business, really!"

Suddenly, alarms started clamoring in the front yard. Stephen was outside in ten strides. Margaret leapt from her chair to grab Sophia's arm. They both leaned forward to look out the kitchen window. Sybil stood to hold her hands over her ears. Donna ran into the room, her face red and her pajamas wrinkled. "Mama, what's happening? What's all the noise?"

Sophia yelled at her mother over the noise, "Call the Sheriff, their number is on the wall. Call quickly while I see what Stephen's doing. Sybil, lock the door behind me. Don't let anyone in who you don't know. Uncle Stephen and I will call to you if we need to get in the house, all right?" She grabbed her jacket, pulling it over her shoulders while she flipped on the outside light.

A truck with a double cab was revving its engine as the driver frantically stripped the gears trying to put the truck in reverse. Stephen stood in the middle of the driveway holding a rifle, which was aimed directly at the truck. He fired at the front passenger tire of the brown truck. The tire blew with a 'pop.' Wasting no time, he shot out the back passenger tire of the truck. The driver was only a silhouette in the dark cab, but now had the driver's door open.

Sophia ducked behind a blue SUV that was parked in front of the house. The SUV's alarm was screaming a deafening scream.

Stephen stood with his legs apart, his hands firmly on the rifle held at his shoulder. He waited for the driver to move away from the cab. The driver's feet and legs were seen under the cab of the truck. Suddenly the truck began to roll forward. The driver crouched low in the driver's seat, turning the steering wheel. The truck was moving straight towards Geoffrey's ponderosa pine. The truck kept turning, moving slowly. The flat tires flapped on the ground as they moved. The truck missed the ponderosa tree by inches, as the driver sat up in the seat, gunned the engine and drove down the road with two radials on the pavement.

Stephen jumped into his vehicle and turned the lights on to bring the Army truck alive in the front yard. Stephen had the rifle in his right hand as he manipulated the Military vehicle to back out of the driveway and down the road. Sophia stood and stared, "Oh, my, Stephen didn't rent a car. He borrowed a military vehicle from the base. This is going to be war."

Running to the door, Sophia knocked frantically. "Sybil, its Mom. Open the door! Please open the door!" She heard the lock click and shoved the door open. "Margaret, Stephen shot two of the tires in the truck that was here. He's going after it in a military vehicle. Did you call the sheriff?"

Margaret gave her a crooked grin, "No, I didn't think you really needed me to, but I can if you want me to? Did you want me to call the police?"

Sophia laughed, "If you want something done it is best to do it yourself, right, mother dear?" She hurried around her to the phone. She called the sheriff's department and got Carl who was at work. She told him about the brown truck with a double cab. She thought it could be a Ford or a Chevy. He took notes as she continued to explain how Stephen shot out the two tires on the right side of the truck and was now in hot pursuit in a military vehicle.

"Stay where you are, Mrs. Vinder. Do not leave the premises. Keep the doors locked and I will call you when we catch the truck. The truck driver can't go fast and he can't go far with two flat tires. Stephen doesn't know these roads. Let's hope he doesn't lose the truck. Keep yourself and your family in the house, please."

Sophia put heavy jackets on the girls. They went outside to check on the vehicles. Margaret stayed by the phone in case someone called. Sybil held the flashlight. Donna held her father's baseball bat and Sophia held the keys to the rental SUV and alarm device attachment. She hit the black button and the alarm shut off. Margaret had already shut off her Toyota Truck's alarm. The SUV Stephen had rented for them was a deep tomato red with black interior. Beside the engine's hood on the ground was a crowbar.

The engine's hood was not dented nor was the paint scuffed. The alarm must have gone off immediately. The instigator must have backed into Margaret's truck because both of their alarms had sounded. Sophia couldn't remember if Stephen's military vehicle's alarm was sounding, but he was now long gone into the darkness.

Snowflakes fell around them as they cautiously slid open the back door of the SUV. The interior smelled of fresh peppermint. Stephen had placed Donna's car seat on the backseat. Nothing appeared to be out of place. "Mama, can we go for a drive?"

Sophia frowned at her daughters, "Not right now. We have to stay here. The truck driver may have messed with this vehicle. Carl told me to keep all of you safe near the house. We won't know until Stephen or Ignacio checks it. Maybe we should go in the house. The snow is seriously falling."

Donna took her mother's hand as they slid shut the SUV sliding passenger door. "Mom, can I have some dessert? I went to the bathroom and I think all the candy is flushed. Please, can I have some dessert?"

"Let's go inside. We may want to wait for Uncle Stephen after all he is the one who picked out the cake and the ice cream." Sophia hit the button at the top of the key chain. The SUV alarm went on. She pushed the girls back into the house.

Margaret was leaning against the counter, holding the phone in her right hand, "Yes, Sir, I understand sir. We shall wait here. No, we won't go anywhere in any vehicle until they have been examined. Yes, Sir. Good night."

Sophia pulled off her jacket and tossed it on a kitchen chair. "All right, who was that and what did they say?"

"Well," her mother grinned, "That was the State Police. Evidently, Carl called them regarding this hot pursuit business. The captain called us to let us know they have the driver and the brown truck in custody. Stephen was also arrested for reckless driving, driving while shooting a firearm, and for shoving an officer of the law."

Sophia burst out laughing, "Are we talking about Stephen Vinder? The Rear Admiral in the United States Navy is being held by the New Mexico State Police? Wow, this is serious."

Margaret pushed the kitchen chair up to the table, "Yes, and he wants you to go to the State Police place and bail him out. The captain would be grateful, too, if you would do so immediately."

"Then I better get my coat and get down there." Sophia grabbed her winter jacket off the kitchen chair.

"No." Margaret put out her hand to block her, "The captain ate his words. He doesn't want anyone of us to leave this place in a vehicle until all the vehicles have been checked and fully examined. He is stuck with Stephen. Stephen is stuck in jail. The truck driver is being interrogated. We are grounded here."

"When is the bomb squad coming over? Are they on their way now?" Sophia decided to put the kettle on to heat for tea.

Margaret sighed, "They won't be here until oh-six-hundred tomorrow morning."

"Six o'clock in the morning tomorrow? What are we supposed to do until then?" Sophia put her hands on her hips, "Mom, you will have to spend the night here. The girls are stuck here until the bomb squad is finished and who knows how long that will take?"

Donna gleefully smiled, "We can't go to school if we can't drive anywhere, right?"

Sophia turned to her daughter, "Yes, let's have dessert." She turned to her mother, "Do you want to call Granger and have him take you home?"

Margaret didn't wait to reply. She picked up the phone and called Granger. She held the phone watching the chocolate cake being cut and served onto the individual plates. Then she spoke into the phone, "Granger, I don't know where you are this late at night? It is almost nine o'clock, where are you? You are worse than your sister. She doesn't answer the phone either! Call me, I'm worried about you!"

She clicked the phone only to lift and redial. Sybil handed her a plate of cake and vanilla ice cream. "Hello, Emily? This is your mother-in-law Margaret. Do you know where my son Granger is at this time of night?" Spooning the dessert into her mouth she listened with an audience watching her. Finally she said, "All right, well then you aren't sure where he is either? Do you know of anyone who drives a brown truck with a double cab?"

More cake went into her mouth. She smiled and nodded. Then she said, "Thank you, Emily. Have a good night and give my best to Shirley." Putting the phone into its wall cradle, Margaret smirked, "Granger did help Emily move furniture today. They moved the bed to Negara. This is a good sign.

Granger left around four o'clock this afternoon and he was driving a friend's truck with a double cab. Emily didn't remember what model it was because she drove in front of it to the Negara house. She was sure Granger had to return the truck by six o'clock this evening to the owner."

Margaret put her plate on the kitchen table, "Now I need another slice of chocolate cake and a large spoonful of ice cream. Oh, the owner of the truck is one Henker, who we were speaking of moments ago as in Enid and Henker the business partners of Granger in H&G Clinic."

She happily smiled as she lifted a spoonful of chocolate cake, "Stephen has no idea what he's missing. We should eat it all just to let him know that chasing after bad guys in the night is not a wise decision."

Sybil shook her head, "No, it is not wise to leave a dessert this good with us to go running off chasing bad guys in the night."

Margaret pointed her spoonful of cake and ice cream at Sybil, "I stand corrected."

Sophia and Margaret tucked the girls into their beds. Margaret stood in the hall as she spoke to Sophia, "I cannot stay here with you and your daughters. This place is filthy and you don't have any of my necessaries. I have to go home and sleep in my own bed. Sophia, not to be unkind, but you really need to clean this place up and find a way to keep the girls' stuff in their bedrooms. You let them drop their things all over the house." She walked into the kitchen, "I will call Yellow Cab to take me home. They come from the airport, which will be a cost, but I need to get home. My main concern is in regard Katina. She will be alone in my house and who knows what she will do and what she will stick her nose into when I am not there. Sophia, I am going home and there is nothing you can do about it. I would rather pay for a cab than stay here. Thank you." She pulled out the telephone book to find the number. Sophia ignored her mother's nasty comments until the cab honked.

Margaret hurried out of the living room. "There it is, Sophia. Believe me when I say this, you need to get Stephen and Katina together. I mean it. They will go off and leave us all alone and in peace. You mark my words both of them would make a good pair. Now don't forget to call Geoffrey and get him to help you with this. I don't have time to push those two together. Granger has got to leave Katina alone. Sophia, what am I going to do if he really does marry her?" Margaret was out the door and gone before Sophia was able to reply.

It was too late to call Geoffrey. The hospital operator explained the phones were turned off to the rooms at nine o'clock. Putting the phone in the wall cradle, Sophia thought of Stephen in the State Police jail. She had to smile at the thought of him stuck behind bars. At least he had had a good dinner even if he did miss dessert. This made her believe he would find a way home before dawn. He wasn't a rear Admiral without connections. Somehow he took the military Hum-V off the base. Stephen must have connections and those connections would get him out of jail. She decided to make the couch bed for him just in case.

As Sophia remade the couch bed in the living room the front doorbell rang. She hurried to peer out of the kitchen window. There in the driveway was a sheriff's cruiser. Cautiously she asked at the door, "Who's there?"

A man's voice bellowed, "Deputy Sheriff Carl Owen is here, Mrs. Vinder, and I need to speak with you."

She let Carl into the front hall and decided it would be best to entertain in the kitchen rather than the living room with a bed. Carl followed her, unbuttoning his coat. She offered him a cup of tea, but he reclined. "Ma'am, I haven't seen much of you lately. Did hear officer Ignacio Cruz was working with your brother-in-law. I thought it might be a good idea for me to examine your vehicle tonight incase you need to take the girls to the school in the morning."

She returned the tea cup and closed the cupboard. "Are you planning on examining the vehicle right this minute?"

Carl patted his blonde hair, "Yes, Ma'am, I have had some bomb investigation classes and would have no problem finding a bomb or disarming a bomb if need be. I started my career in the bomb squad, but decided it was messy and wanted a job requiring less cleanup time. May I have your keys to the vehicle, please?"

Handing him the keys to the SUV of tomato red, she offered to hold the flashlight for him. The two of them forged into the falling snow. "We're going to need to get the snowplows moving by early tomorrow morning." Carl shut off the SUV alarm. He pulled the hood latch and turned on the headlights. "There, now we have light and we have the ability to examine."

Carl retrieved a pair of working gloves from his rear pant pocket. Slipping them on his hands, he took the flashlight from her. The flashlight was placed on the cloth he had centered on the frame of the engine compartment.

Lifting, he stood on the front bumper. He removed a hair net from his left jacket pocket and carefully placed it over his blonde hair. Carl inventoried the parts of the engine. Quietly, he hurried from the bumper to the open trunk of the cruiser and removed a black bag.

She decided to sit in the driver's seat of the van and watch. The falling snow was melting on the back of her neck. She watched Carl professionally trace each electrical line of the engine. Every now and then he would remove a mechanic's tool and fiddle with something. Finally, he put his tools into his black bag. Stepping on the ground, he moved to her. "There is nothing suspicious. No explosives and no bombs are in this engine."

He shoved the bag of tools under his arm. "Now, if you don't mind, I would like to look underneath the vehicle. Have you found anything you believe to be suspicious in the area?"

Sophia told him about the crowbar. Holding it in his gloved hands, he shone the flashlight over it. "This has printed on it, Property of the U.S. Military—Kirkland Air Force Base, Albuquerque, New Mexico. I'm going to take this with me back to the department. We may be able to get some prints off of this." He wrapped the crowbar in plastic and put it into the trunk of the cruiser. Taking a blanket from the trunk, he pushed it under the SUV and slid on top of it. Using the flashlight he examined the undercarriage of the vehicle. She could hear him knocking and hitting underneath her as she sat in the driver's seat.

"Mrs. Vinder, everything is clear. Don't think anyone had time to do any damage before the alarms went wild. Your vehicle is in good shape. Someone changed the oil recently and the oil cap was loose, I tightened it for you." He saluted her with the flashlight. She took it from his hand as he returned to his cruiser. Carl removed his hair net, his gloves, and waved to her as he backed out of her driveway and drove away. "What a calm man he is." She spoke to the falling snow.

Sophia sat in the vehicle staring at the white snow. The world was quiet and peaceful out in the freezing cold night. Everything appeared to be clean. She started the vehicle and listened. The engine was silent compared to her old van. She put the automatic gear into reverse. The SUV leaped backwards. She slammed on the brake before the vehicle hit the house. "Whoa, this thing has power." Parking the SUV closer to the old van, she pulled on the emergency brake. Relieved nothing had happened she dismounted the vehicle, locked the SUV, and hit the alarm button as she returned to the house.

Deciding to put her cares on hold, Sophia relaxed in a hot bubble bath. Her right leg stuck out of the bubbles with a plastic bag around her bandages. Six o'clock in the morning would be here all too soon.

21

Rocoso, New Mexico
Monday, January, 1988

The sound of water spraying from the shower woke Sophia. She rolled over in the bed to stare at the clock on the bedside table. It was five-forty in the morning. "Who is in my shower at this hour?" Quietly lifting back the quilt and blankets she kicked back the sheet. Pulling her soft blue nightgown to her ankles, she moved to the closed bathroom door. The door was locked, the handle didn't turn.

"Hah, the Rear Admiral has returned!" Sophia grabbed her robe from the chair in the corner of the bedroom. Pulling it over her shoulders, she went into the living room. Stephen's military coat was draped over the recliner. His clean underwear was neatly folded at the end of the couch next to his folded Navy pants of dark blue. His military watch was sitting on the toe of his polished black boots placed on the floor below his clothes. "Stephen is home, what do you know?"

Moving into kitchen, she fixed the coffeemaker to make twelve cups and put the tea kettle on the stove. As she returned to her bedroom, the shower had stopped and she could hear Stephen moving around. Quickly, she pulled clean underwear from her bureau drawer and hustled into the walk-in closet. She closed the door, pulled on her underwear and green corduroy pants. She pulled over her head the pink turtleneck and then her green cable sweater. Dancing on one foot and then the other, Sophia pulled on her jeans, socks and tied her hiking boots. Shoving open the closet door, she almost collided with Stephen who was wrapped in one of Geoffrey's big towels.

"Hey, beautiful, nice to see you so early in the a.m., hope I didn't wake you with the shower?" Stephen mockingly danced out of her way.

"No, well, it was time to get up anyway what with the bomb squad arriving any minute. How did you get here?" Sophia reached around him to make the bed.

"Your dutiful mother stopped by the police department on her way back to Calavera last night. She is a woman who is definitely male focused. She was worried about me being stuck in jail all night. Evidently, your late father had engrained in her brain that Navy officers should never be arrested." Stephen waved as he raced into the living room. His muscle bound body moved with impressive grace.

Hurrying into the bathroom, Sophia ran a comb through her hair, lined her eyes with her green eyeliner, put on her sunscreen lotion, and added some lip gloss to give her face a final touch. Pleased with the look, she flipped off the bathroom light, leaving the door open to let out the humidity. No sooner had she entered the kitchen to move the whistling tea kettle when the front doorbell rang. Stephen beat her to the door fully dressed and smelling of cologne. He smiled at her as he opened the door, "Hey, a team works in tandem. I am here to please." He opened the door to four men in olive green uniforms, holding helmets, and backpacks.

"Good morning, men! Welcome to the bomb center. Hope today is another day of no bombs, but one can never be too sure." Stephen stepped back to let them into the hall. Sophia led them into the kitchen where she grabbed mugs and put them on the kitchen table.

The men followed her hesitantly. "Ma'am, we are here to do a job. This is not a social call. Please, could we get right on it? Which vehicle is the vehicle in question?" A burley fellow with carrot red hair and reading glasses was the head of the pack. Stephen did an about face and chose to show them the vehicles. Sophia smiled to herself, she really should tell them about Carl's inspection, but then Stephen was seriously enjoying himself as head of the bomb unit. Those men could inspect away for all she cared, she just wanted her cup of tea and some peace. The smell of all those polished boots and starched uniforms was overwhelming at this time of day.

Leaning against the kitchen sink, sipping her tea, Sophia watched the men move from one vehicle to another. Stephen had all the keys and the alarm remotes in his hands. The bomb squad men first crawled under the vehicles. The doors were cautiously opened and then the hood of each vehicle was popped. Clicking devices were used all around the vehicles.

As the sun rose, the day warmed to reveal the ground wet from the night's melted snow. The pine trees glistened in the sun and the junipers were bent with moisture. Birds were flying low to the ground and a soft wind blew the tops of Geoffrey's cottonwood trees gently. Sophia stared at the horizon of black mesas. The brown expanse flowing to the edge of the earth's curve reflected the specificity of weather in New Mexico. There was no trace of snow on the other side of the canyon. It had only snowed on the east side. Closer to the house small cottontails and white-breasted quail were moving through the underbrush across from the men.

Finally, the front door opened to bring in the searching squad. They pulled out chairs in the kitchen to sit holding mugs of steaming coffee and confided in one another about the predicament. "There were signs of an attempted tampering on the silver truck. Although, the silver truck is pre-owned and after the snow last night, it is difficult to determine how fresh the marks are. The newly rented SUV had footprints around it, but no sign of attempted tampering."

Stephen stood leaning against the counter next to the sink, "Sophia, you moved the SUV last night, didn't you, even after you were explicitly told to leave it alone?"

"Ah, the cat's out of the bag." Sophia almost giggled as she wiped the counter down by the stove, "Carl Owen came last night and examined the SUV. He went through it thoroughly to tell me it was safe. He did find a crowbar in the yard on the ground." She smiled at Stephen with a sly look, "It had writing on it stating it belonged to Kirkland Air Force Base. You wouldn't happen to know anything about it, would you?"

"Damn, I felt something drop last night while I was fixing your alarm. I had to pry the side of the engine gently to run the wire of the alarm to the front. Guess, I forgot about it or it fell out of the bag." Stephen shook his head, "What did Carl Owen say he was going to do with it?"

"Check it for fingerprints and ownership." Sophia saluted him by lifting her tea mug. "Stephen, you haven't met Carl have you?"

"No, but Ignacio says he is a good guy. I'll call there later this morning and let him know it's my crowbar." Stephen took the coffee pot to fill empty mugs on the table. The men started sharing stories with Stephen. Sophia retreated to the Sybil's bedroom.

Sybil was up and dressed. Donna was grumbling in the girl's bathroom about how to fix her hair. They heard the men leave. When the girls came into the kitchen with their mother, they found Stephen washing out the coffee mugs. "Hey, here are the women of the house! How about I drive you guys to school? You can tell me how to get there?"

Donna growled at him, "I thought we weren't going to school today. I still have a stomachache, you know?"

Kneeling to be even with her six-year old face, Stephen spoke seriously, "No, I don't know. When I came home last night to have dessert, I found it had been eaten. Every bit of it was gone. No one thought to save me, the great Uncle Stephen a smidgeon of cake. A birdie told me, Donna, that you had helped yourself to my dessert without waiting for me. Is that true?"

Donna stuck out her lower lip, "I thought you were in jail. Why didn't you stay there?" She pushed around him to join her sister at the kitchen table for some cereal.

"Ouch, my feelings are hurt. I thought we were best buddies?" Stephen pulled out a chair to sit next to Sybil. "We are buddies, aren't we?" He put his arm around her.

"Sure we are. I like school. I'm glad we can go to school." Sybil smiled at Stephen. "We have to be out of here by eight o'clock. My school starts at eight-thirty and Marie's little kid school starts at eight-fifty. Besides it sure beats sitting around here waiting to get blown sky high."

Stephen smiled, "Pass me a bowl of cereal. A good breakfast is the only way to live."

Sophia wiped the clean mugs to hang them on the hooks by the kitchen window. Leaning, she put her mug of tea on the table next to Donna. "Stephen, you haven't told us who the culprits were and how they were captured? I am sure the girls would like to hear how all of that played out. Would you tell us before everyone disperses?"

Shoveling a spoonful of Shredded Wheat into his mouth, he nodded at her. Swallowing, he said, "The police were waiting at the bottom of the hill by Rincon with a road block. Carl is fast, I have to say that for him. He was on the phone to the State Police within seconds of hanging up with me. The truck with flat tires was trying to hightail it through the road block, but the truck was seriously leaning to the right. Steering it must have been damn near impossible." He put his hand up to Donna, "Sorry, I didn't mean to swear."

She smiled at him, "No problem. Mom said 'shit' yesterday. We're getting used to people swearing around us."

As if on cue the phone rang. Stephen swiveled in his chair and grabbed it off the wall cradle. "Yo, Stephen Vinder here, how can I assist you?"

Standing, Stephen burst out laughing. "Here, Sophia, it's for you. It appears your husband doesn't appreciate the way his younger brother the Admiral answers the phone." Stephen handed her the cordless phone. Sophia leaned over Donna to take if from his hand.

Sophia leaned back on the kitchen chair, "Hello, how are you feeling this morning? Are they going to send you home today?"

She could hear Geoffrey fumbling with the phone, "This thing has a short cord. I was trying to move it to the chair. Hell, I'll just sit here in the bed. What?"

Sophia repeated herself. Geoffrey replied, "Yes, they're letting me out of here around four o'clock this afternoon. I am free to roam with my crutches. The physical therapist from the Torment Camp has released me into your care with strict orders to do exercises. I have paperwork on how to change bandages. My next appointment with her is on Wednesday. Can you come and spring me from this place this afternoon?"

"You bet, handsome, I will be there with bells on and a crew of helpers who will be so pleased to have you home! Wait until you see the SUV Stephen rented for us. It's first class and has plenty of room for your foot. When do you want me to be there?" She smiled at her girls and gave them thumbs up for good measure.

"Can you be here around three-thirty and bring some clothes? All I have here are my favorite jeans that were cut off, the socks are shot. My white snap cowboy shirt stinks of smoke. Bring my work jeans and my blue and green flannel shirt with the snap buttons. Can you knock the mud off of my hiking boots by the back door and bring those?"

"Sure, I will even bring you some clean underwear, if you want?"

"Oh, yeah, my jockey shorts in the top drawer, but not the ones with the blue stripe, they have a hole in them." Geoffrey laughed.

"Why are they even in the drawer if they have a hole?" She reprimanded him.

"Oh, you know? There are days when a hole in the shorts is a good idea." Geoffrey became solemn. "I have to go. The doctor's here with some sort of torture instrument. See you after three?"

"I'll be there with the girls. They will be out of school by then and would love to escort you home. Love you, bye." Sophia listened to him moan and then the phone went to dial tone.

Stephen was standing in the hall holding Donna's backpack. "She's my friend again. I guess she thought I was brave to push the state cop out of the way of the moving vehicle. We are off. Do you want me to bring you back something from town?"

Sophia shook her head, "No, I'm going with you. We're going to drive in the new SUV. The girls and I want to experience driving in your choice of vehicles. Let me grab my purse. This time you are going to be the passenger. No more racing around in military vehicles."

Everyone was buckled in as Sophia shoved the key into the ignition. She leaned forward, "Girls, listen? There isn't any grinding or moaning from the engine. Isn't that amazing?"

Donna frowned, "What are we doing with the old van? I miss her. She woke us up with her sounds."

Sybil frowned at her sister, "When we pick up Dad he will be impressed with this new SUV. When we can we bring him home?"

Sophia explained how after school they would have to hightail it over to the hospital to get their dad. Stephen turned to her, "You know I just might take care of the old van this morning? Why don't you guys go ahead to the schools? I'll meet you back here. I can make some phone calls and Geoffrey won't have to deal with this on top of everything else." He jumped out of the red SUV before she could put the vehicle in gear.

Donna watched him as he stood to wave them off. "He can't wait to get back into his military vehicle, huh, Mom?"

"Probably, it is a spiffy looking vehicle. I wonder what they call it." She turned in the driver's seat to back out of the driveway.

Sybil smiled, "It's called an 'All Terrain Military Vehicle.' He told me they use it to cross deserts, rivers, and rocky terrain. He wanted to take us in it to go up the side of the mountain on the way to school." Sybil shook her head, "Mom, I 'm glad you're driving us."

Donna scrunched up her nose, "Smell? It has a new car type of smell or else someone sprayed it with perfume? Do you smell it?"

Sybil rubbed her nose, "Yeah, its kind of funky smell like peppermint sticks. Hey, these seats go back. Pull on that belt, see? The seats fall backwards."

Sophia laughed, 'This is an automatic, no more grinding gears to get going. What a fancy vehicle, we must thank Stephen for helping us rent this SUV. It is high class!"

The girls were deposited with a promise to get their father after school. Sophia decided she had time to go by the Sheriff's department and see Carl before Stephen could do anything with the old van.

The front desk had a new person sitting at the counter. Sophia nodded and asked to speak to Carl. The young man shook his head, 'Sorry, Ma'am, he's not in yet. He was busy last night investigating bombs. Can I take a message? He can call you when he comes in?" The fellow placed a clean pad of paper in front of her with a black ballpoint pen on the center of it. Sophia wrote down her name and phone number. Shoving the paper back to the young man, she asked, "Any news on Sheriff A.J. Martinez this morning?"

The young man tilted his head, "Ma'am, I'm sure any information regarding the Sheriff is confidential. Carl will be sure to have this message as soon as he arrives, good day."

Driving up the hill home, she noticed more heavy snow clouds hanging over the Puerco Mountains. The peaks had snow on them and the clouds fell over the peaks as if someone had poured whipped cream on top, letting it fall carelessly down to the valley below. Glancing in her rear view mirror, she saw a tow truck following her. It pulled into her driveway right behind her. Stephen was standing over the engine of the old van with his gloves in his pocket.

He waved at the tow truck as the driver came to a halt and starting backing up to the front of the van. Seeing Stephen waving at the tow truck gave Sophia a sick feeling in the pit of her stomach. She sat in the SUV and watched until the tow truck came to a complete stop. Hurrying to Stephen, she called out, "Hey, that was fast! What's going on?"

Stephen smiled at her over his shoulder, "Hey, this is Mr. Rover of R&R Engine Repair. He is going to buy the old van from you. He's got the best price and has serious designs on this van for a rebuild."

Mr. Rover walked to her with his hand extended, "Howdy, Mrs. Vinder.

We would be more than pleased to get this van out of your driveway. Heard about the explosion up here and your van is almost a collector's piece." He jerked his head to the other man who hopped out of the tow truck. This man was younger, more cautious, and had a scar running from the base of his nose to his right ear. The young man slowly put his hand to hers, "Howdy, I'm his son. I'll hook her to the truck."

Chains were fitted under the van and the tow truck began to haul her onto the back flatbed. Stephen was in serious conversation with the older Mr. Rover as Sophia stood and watched the younger man do the work. Finally, the van was firmly chained to the flatbed. The younger man mumbled to her, "Mrs. Vinder, I want to express my sorrow at hearing about what happened here on Friday. We knew the guys in the other tow truck. It was horrible for you, I'm sure. I have had a vehicle fall on top of me only once and after that I am extremely cautious about moving them around. To be honest I let my Dad drive because I wasn't real anxious about coming here."

She studied his face and then said, "I bet you'll need the keys to the van, huh?"

He appeared relieved at the change of subject, "We don't really need the keys, but if you want to give them to us it might help. We're going to be taking her apart and remaking her. She really needs a new paint job, huh?" He patted the back bumper of the old yellow van.

Sophia felt her eyes tear, "Yes, she is a love. We started out with her before we had children. The girls loved her and they are sad to have her move out of our lives. You will take good care of her?"

"Sure will, she's got a good body. The problem with these old vehicles is the engines get worn out and it's not much trouble to put in a new one. It takes time and some money. Of course, you have to know what you're doing." He bent over to feel the back rear tire. "These tires are shot. Good thing you didn't drive on them much longer or they would have blown and could have caused some serious damage."

Stephen called Sophia over to the older Mr. Rover. He was writing on a black notebook. "Mr. Rover, needs to know when you bought the vehicle and when and what you have done to it over the years."

Sophia stared at Stephen, "How should I know?" Then she smiled, "Yes, Geoffrey put all the work papers and oil change papers in the glove compartment. There is a small white paper in there where he recorded the cost and time of work. You can find it in..." She turned to go to the van's passenger door, but the vehicle was up in the air. The younger Mr. Rover grabbed the holding chain and pulled himself up onto the flat bed. He swung open the passenger door and slid his body onto the seat. Glass from the window fell to the ground. "Whoops, we can clean that up before we leave. No one needs a flat tire. We don't want a flat tire on the tow truck!"

The younger Mr. Rover retrieved the papers and Geoffrey's notes. He handed them to her and she handed them to the older man. He put them in the pocket of his notebook. "All right, we would like to make you an offer of nine hundred dollars for the van, is that acceptable to you, Mrs. Vinder?"

Before she could answer, Stephen interfered, "No, that's not acceptable. The main structure of the engine can be resold for four or five hundred dollars and the parts of the van are easily worth another five hundred. How about you offer her eleven hundred and we call it a deal?"

Mr. Rover scratched his head. He studied Stephen's face, "You're military right?"

Stephen stepped back, "Yes, so what?"

"Well, military folks have no clue about what goes on in the real world. That's what. Look at my son over there, he was in the army for six years and what good did it do him?"

Stephen looked at the son, "I wouldn't know, sir. I don't know your son."

"Damn right, you don't. You shouldn't be meddling in civilian matters 'cause you don't have any idea about the real world out here. Maybe you should go back to your platoon or whatever it is?" Mr. Rover was starting to sound hostile.

Sophia interjected, "Mr. Rover, please let's keep cool heads. This is an emotional decision for me. I love that old van and my brother-in-law here is trying to help us. We will have to buy another new van and the money you give us is vital in our doing this. The red SUV over there is a rental" She pointed to the vehicles as she took inventory, "All the vehicles here are rented or borrowed, aside from your tow truck and my mother's Toyota over there. My brother-in-law is just trying to help me and my poor girls afford a vehicle. My husband was badly hurt and his new truck was totaled. Please try to understand we want to be friends and work out a solid solution for everyone?"

Mr. Rover stared at her as if he had never heard anyone say so much at one time, "Mrs. Vinder, I have a family, too. My son over there lives with us and he's a mess." He pulled out a piece of paper and wrote a figure on it. He showed it to Sophia. She frowned at him. He crossed out the number and wrote another figure. She smiled and put out her hand. "All right, we have a deal."

A check was written. The R&R Engine Repair truck drove down the road with the yellow old van bouncing merrily along on the flat bed. Sophia stared down the road as they drove away. "So, how much did he give you?" Stephen put his hand on her arm. She smiled at him, "We do work well as a team, don't we? He wrote it for eleven hundred dollars and ten cents."

"Ten cents, huh, well, what do you know?" Stephen gloated, "Yes, we do work well together. I wonder what the problem is with his son. He appeared normal, aside from the scar on his face."

Frowning, Sophia answered him. "I think the problem with the son is the father." He shook his head as he followed her into the house.

She threw her purse on the rocking chair as she carried the check into the kitchen. "Now, I suppose we should get this check into the bank before he changes his mind. Stephen, I need to know what happened last night and who the people were who tried to blow up our vehicles. Can you tell me while I put the kettle on?"

"No, I can't." Stephen backed down the hall to open the front door. "Here comes your mother with Katina. They are probably here to get her truck. Maybe, you should put the kettle on somehow I have a feeling this may turn into a confrontation."

Sophia froze when she saw Katina. Her hair was a mess. Her blue eyes were puffy with red circles. She was wearing the same clothes she wore the last time she had come to their house, but now they were the hanging loosely all the worse for the wear. Margaret cautiously exited the passenger side of Katina's car. "Hey, we are here for my truck. You have no idea how difficult it was for me to get Katina to drive her pathetic car here. I had to wake her and explain how I could not drive two vehicles home at the same time."

Katina gave Margaret a drop dead look, "Did you know, Margaret, that other people have other priorities other than yours?" Katina shoved Sophia aside to enter the house. Sophia turned to follow her, but Katina hurried to the bathroom and slammed the door. Margaret's face went beet red as she pushed past Stephen and then Sophia. She raced down the hall to the bathroom door.

"You, little bitch, you don't know how grateful you should be! I have given you shelter when you had none. I have given you food when you were broke and I have allowed you to screw my son when he certainly doesn't need to be screwed by the likes of you!" She pounded on the bathroom door with her fists.

The door was flung open, "Me! I'm not ungrateful, you witch? I have told you how grateful I am every minute of every day and you, you conniving manipulating cow never cease to rag on me! You can take your damn truck and shove it up your ass for all I care and you can take your spoiled brat of an impotent son and shove him up there with it!"

Margaret gasped, clutching her chest, "Impotent! My son is not impotent! He got your sorry ass pregnant, didn't he? How dare you!" She slapped Katina in the face. There was a loud grunt and a scream. Katina fell back against the door frame. Shaking in anger, Katina returned the slap, hitting Margaret's right cheek with the back of her hand. Suddenly, Margaret lost her balance and fell to the floor. Katina jumped on top of her with fists flying. "You hit me, you nasty bitch! How dare you hit me! If I was pregnant I could have lost the baby, you really are a piece of work!"

Margaret started to give as good as she got. She screamed at her, "You are a rat! No, worse than a rat you are a leech and you lie. You lie about everything!"

Stephen hurried to the yelling arm flailing mess to reach down and lift Katina off of Margaret. He held Katina in the air as if she were a screaming, spitting puppet. "That's enough, Ladies! We won't have any fighting in this house. Sophia, help your mother!" Stephen turned to drop Katina on the floor in the living room. He put his hand on her arm and pushed her into the recliner. "Sit. Now what is going on with you two? Stay, sit, no moving, Katina, or I will hurt you." He put his hand in front of her face. She sighed and fell back into the recliner.

The kettle let out a loud whistle as Sophia helped her mother stand. "Mom, let's go into the kitchen and get some tea. We will let Stephen deal with Katina. Come, please, no more yelling or fighting. I know you're upset, but slapping people is not the solution."

"Sophia, shut up. You don't know what she does to me. The nasty she-devil has laced my toilet seats with disease and vomited for the last time in my house." Margaret sniffed as she let her daughter lead her into the kitchen. Plopping into a chair, Margaret fidgeted with her hair. "I can't take anymore from her. She called your brother impotent! Sophia, she insulted the whole family by saying such a nasty suggestive thing."

"Mom, chill. You two have a serious conflict of character going on and yelling isn't going to help. Please; tell me what happened this morning." Sophia put a hot mug of tea in front of her mother.

Margaret pushed the mug away from her. "Really, Sophia, every time anyone comes over here you shove tea in their face. I am sick of your tea. I need some chocolate and not just a little bit, I need a whole candy bar! Why do you keep shoving tea at people? It gets tiresome!" She rubbed her bright red cheek and then folded her arms on the table. "Chocolate, now, please!"

Frowning, Sophia reached into the cupboard over the refrigerator. She pulled out a fat Hershey chocolate bar and threw it at her mother. "Here, now talk."

Margaret ripped off the paper and shoved a large piece into her mouth. "Well, all I did this morning was to ask her to drive me over here to get my truck. I can't go anywhere without a vehicle, right? You would have thought I asked her to drink all the water in the Nile. I should have asked her to clean the toilets. She had a fit. She said she had been out all night and was not going to drive me anywhere. In that tone, Sophia, she spoke to me in that tone as if I was a prima donna and she was the queen." Margaret chewed more chocolate. "I think everyone hates me and I don't know why. I am thoughtful to those around me, help out my family, and only speak positive statements. Remember your grandmother always said, 'if you don't have something good to say then shut up.' Well, I only say nice about people, especially family because we only get our family once." She rubbed her lips with the back of her well manicured hand.

Sophia took the rest of the chocolate bar away from her mother. "Mom, you have enough. No more chocolate. Are you feeling calmer now?"

"No, give me my chocolate! What's the matter with you? You can't give people food and then take it away. What kind of a hostess are you anyway?" She reached over and grabbed the chocolate out of Sophia's hand. "Don't you think I've had enough grief for one day, damn it, what is the problem with that little bitch? She's now talking about not being pregnant! You heard her, right? She is a compulsive lying rat, that's what she is."

Sophia watched her mother shove the rest of the chocolate into her mouth. "You know, Mom, when you say only nice things about people you give it a spin that isn't exactly what grandma had in mind."

Margaret squinted at Sophia, "Oh, shut up, and you know about life? You are a miss goodie two shoes!"

Stephen brought Katina into the kitchen. She had pulled her hair back revealing the perfect hand print on her left cheek. Her blouse was still torn, but pulled appropriately over her shoulder. She sat across from Margaret to pick up the chocolate wrapper on the table. "You shouldn't eat chocolate. It'll make your face breakout."

Margaret held her breath and then let her face turn beet red, finally she spat at Katina, "This may surprise you, but I am no longer a teenager unlike some people I know who are living their lives as a permanent adolescent!"

Stephen slapped his hand on the kitchen counter. Everyone jumped as he said, "Enough, you two! Now it is time to work this out. What is the situation between Katina and Granger? We need to know if there is going to be relationship between the two of you or if you're playing with him." Stephen pulled out a chair to sit at the head of the table.

Katina pointed to the mug of tea, "Can I have that?"

Margaret shoved it at her, "Sure, choke on it. I hate tea and have drunk enough to sink a ship over here. My daughter pushes tea on every body!"

Katina tilted her head at Sophia and in a small voice asked, "Do you think I could have some organic honey?"

Stephen coughed into his hand, "Enough of this fooling around. Katina, you need to be straight with us. What's going on with you and Granger?"

She took the honey from Sophia. Pouring almost half the jar into her tea mug, she explained, "When everything we were trying to do in Santa Fe went bust, I decided to come down here and see Emily. Emily had written to me about their marital problems last year. I knew Granger was impotent and harmless."

Sipping her tea, she glared at Margaret who was as white as a sheet. "Well, Emily was very happy to see me as you can imagine? Her life was in misery with Granger. Granger didn't take any prodding at all to get into the sack. He couldn't do anything, but it was a good show." She poured more honey into her tea mug. Everyone in the room could hear Margaret grinding her teeth, but at least she listened.

Pulling her torn blouse to her shoulder, Katina went on, "Emily wanted a divorce. If Granger was with me and he believed I was pregnant he would divorce her and let her keep Shirley. I was helping my lifelong friend with her stupid husband." She sipped the tea.

Margaret pointed her red fingernail at Katina. "You said my son is impotent then how come he has a daughter? Huh? You tell us you were sleeping with my son and you are now pregnant. How did you get pregnant if my son is impotent? You, little twerp, you don't know anything!" She put her hand flat on the table.

Stephen put his hand on Margaret's arm, "Wait, let her finish."

Sophia sat next to her to hear the rest of this saga. Katina put her elbow on the table and her head on her hand, "Well, the pregnancy thing is a lie. I'm not pregnant and I did not have sex with your son. He is not someone I want to marry. The whole event was a charade and right now I'm sorry I came to New Mexico. All I wanted to do was help Ralph get married to his true love Sam. The whole trip was a bust." Katina's eyes welled up, "My lover Katie took off when she heard I had been arrested. She said she couldn't love someone who had conflict with the laws of man or woman." Katina wiped her nose with her hand and pushed her hand up to her forehead. "There is only one person I want to marry and that's Katie. We have been together for six years and we are meant to be together forever. But now I don't know where she went and for all I know she is desperately trying to find me." Sophia handed Katina a paper napkin that she used to blow her nose.

Margaret's face regained its composure as she stuck out her chest and slowly straightened to stand, "You mean to tell me you're not pregnant? But Granger is a doctor. He would know if you weren't pregnant. My God, what is this world coming to?" She walked out of the kitchen and could be heard going into the bathroom.

Sophia reached out to Katina, "Why were you so sick? You certainly aren't well, what is going on with you?"

Katina wiped her cheek as her tears fell, "I have cancer like my father. I was supposed to get chemo in San Francisco, but I wanted to live a little before going back to all of the sickness and the sadness my mother feels for me." She wrapped her arms around her waist as she leaned onto the table.

Stephen pushed his chair back and stretched out his legs, "This is certainly going to be a drama to watch unfold. Katina, do you know who set the bombs or who might have wanted to blow up Geoffrey and Granger?"

Katina lifted her head and pointed to the hall. "Her- the super witch believes Granger is going to steal all her money. She doesn't trust anyone. I wouldn't put it past her to blow everyone away. Somehow I know she killed her husband. It would have been so easy for her to do it."

Stephen leaned forward with his elbows on the table, "Katina, were you Carol's cleaning lady? What happened the night Carol was attacked, do you know?"

She sighed, "I knew this was going to come up again and again. I am not a murderer. I do not eat meat or kill bugs or try to steal food from orphans. Why can't people believe me when I say I had nothing to do with Carol's attack?" Tears rolled down her cheeks.

"Carol was my friend, or at least, I thought so at one time. She actually talked to me at the Vet's office. Most people don't even see me. It is as if I am invisible. Not, Carol, no she spoke with me and asked me what I wanted from life and she knew I needed I job."

Sophia watched Katina as she slurped her tea and then continued, "Carol asked me if I needed a job. She was thoughtful and kind. I told her I could do most anything. She asked if I would come to the house she was sitting and we could go over the place and I would give her an estimate as to how much I would charge to clean it up before the owner's came back. Carol said she wasn't really good at cleaning and found the whole process rather tiresome. When I went to the house, Carol met me at the door. She had the dog tied up or something in the backyard because I am allergic to dogs." Katina stared at one single point on the kitchen table.

"We walked through the house. She showed me the swimming pool. Wow, how glorious to live in a house with a pool, right?" Katina wiped her nose on the napkin. "She told me how she lived in the back guest room part because the main bedroom was just freaky weird with bad spiritual energy." Katina shook her head, "I went to the kitchen to get her doughnuts. She asked me to, you see, because we were going to sit on her bed in the back and talk about prices. She thought we should have a doughnut while we got down to it."

Katina took a deep breath and then sighed, "I walked through the trick door in the bathroom, down past the swimming pool, through the hall with the strange floor and into the kitchen. The doughnuts were right there on the counter." She puckered her lips, "Then just when I lifted the doughnuts there was this loud sound. A thump and then a drop from down the hall. Thinking that maybe she had let the dog inside made me fearful. When I get near a dog my face gets a rash and I can't breathe. So, I stayed put for a moment, listening, readying for a dog to attack me."

Stephen sat back, stretching out his legs under the kitchen table, "Did you see or hear anyone else at that time?"

Katina held her breath as she stared at him, "Everybody asked me that, but no. No. I didn't hear another voice. I didn't hear another car or anything." She took her paper napkin and wrapped it around her hand. "All I did was go to get the damn doughnuts. Evidently they were not a good buy for Carol. When nothing happened, I went back the way I had come and there...there... there on the tiles by the pool was Carol."

Katina hit the table with her hand, "She was bleeding, oh, it was awful. The smell of the blood on the tile, but she was breathing. I did what anyone would do, I called 911. There was no reason for me to hang there and wait. I had just gotten out of jail and was not anxious to go back to it. I left the front door open and got the hell out of there."

"So, you never actually cleaned the house for Carol?" Stephen leaned toward her.

"No, I never cleaned for her. She had three more weeks to be in the house and Carol only wanted me to clean after she had taken her stuff back to her own home. Granger tried to pry where Carol lived out of me, but I wouldn't go there. Granger is almost as ruthless as his witch mother." Jerking her chin toward the hall, she added, "I am more than ready to get out of here. It is time for me to go home to California. No love lost between Granger and me or her."

Sophia put her empty mug on the table, "Have you told Granger that you are not pregnant? This should come from you, not his mother or from me. You need to cut a clean break with my brother or you aren't much better than they are."

She shook her head, "No, I have no desire to speak to Granger again. I live to never hear his gravelly voice again. The sheriff's department won't be pleased with me leaving the state, but really, it is time for me to go and never look back." She pushed away from the table.

"What's the little liar talking about now?" Margaret returned with her hair primped, her face washed, and her self esteem returned. "I'm going home. Katina, I would appreciate it if you would follow me. Once we arrive at my home, you may remove all of your property and leave the premises. Leave my son and leave New Mexico. I will be glad to give you twenty dollars for your trip back to California. Twenty dollars should get you there with change."

Katina gasped, "Twenty dollars after the hell you have put me through?"

Sophia helped Katina up as they both stood, "Mom, twenty dollars won't even get Katina out of New Mexico. You need to give her about one hundred fifty in order for her to be completely out of your hair. Don't you agree, Stephen?"

Stephen winked at Sophia, "Absolutely, two hundred is a good round number. Katina, for two hundred dollars do you think you could make it home to California?"

"Yes, for a thousand I will stay away forever." She let Stephen escort her to her car.

Margaret scowled at her daughter, "She will get one hundred dollars and not a penny more." Margaret retrieved her lip gloss from her pant pocket and smeared it across her lips, "Sophia, I do enjoy your tea although you must spend a fortune on the stuff. After all you serve it to anyone who comes through your front door. I don't mean to be nasty, but Katina hates me, you know it. Call me later and let me know what you think we should do with Granger?" She hurried out the front door with her truck keys in hand.

Lifting the check from R&R Towing, Sophia folded it and put it into her jean pocket. The phone rang as she was cleaning the kitchen table. "Hello?"

"Sophia, Granger here. Where's Mom? She was supposed to meet me at the courthouse to get all of these legal papers filed. Do you know where she is?" Granger sounded subdued.

"Are these the papers taking our home away from us?" Sophia felt anger rise in her throat.

"These papers are of no concern to you. Where is Mom?" Granger was keeping his voice down. She could hear people moving around him in the back ground. "Sophia, just answer the question, where is Mom?"

"Um, right now I don't know. She was here earlier with Katina to retrieve her truck. At the moment I have no idea where she might be."

"Well, I'll wait ten minutes and call her at home, again. If I don't get her then we will forfeit our time with the judge. This isn't good. Why can't Mom ever get to an appointment on time?" The phone went to dial tone as he hung up on her.

Stephen called out Sophia's name as he came down the hall after closing the front door. She answered him, "Have the wild women left?"

Laughing, he met her in the hallway to the bedrooms, "I thought they were going to pull each other's hair out at one point. Good thing we were here or they could have seriously hurt one another. I bet your mother has a black eye by tonight."

She walked into Sybil's room to make the bed. "Stephen, Granger just called and was worried about Mom. Evidently, he is at the county courthouse waiting for her to file some legal papers. She won't make it in ten minutes, though, and he will be stuck." Suddenly, she hurried out of the bedroom to the phone. Studying Mr. Goldfarb's phone number, she called him.

Stephen sat in the chair and listened to the one sided conversation. When Sophia finished she gave him a warm smile. "He isn't worried and said he would meet us in Geoffrey's room this afternoon around three-thirty. Evidently, he put some kind of legal block on whatever it is they are doing and no matter who they try to get this house taken away from us, it ain't gonna happen."

Stephen told her he had some phone calls to make while she made the girls' beds and cleaned up their rooms. When she was finished with the rooms, the laundry, and the cleaning of the bathrooms, she decided to make Donna some gluten free cookies. Stephen helped her with the blender and by twelve noon the cookies were cooling on a plate and the kitchen was once again clean. "Making cookies with you was great fun. Donna will be pleasantly surprised as will Geoffrey. You know it was lovely being able to do something mundane without chaos. This was very special, thank you, Stephen."

Stephen pulled on his jacket, "Well, we got a lot accomplished this morning. Can I buy you lunch at the Range in town? Everyone tells me the food is excellent there."

She sat down to relax in her rocking chair. "Stephen, sit down for a minute, please." She nodded to Geoffrey's recliner chair. Stephen carefully removed his jacket. "What?"

"We have a minute. I need to know what happened last night. I haven't wanted to talk about last night because making cookies almost felt like the old life, the life without bombs and killings. Tell me who the state police took into custody and who was driving the truck?"

Stephen rubbed his large hands together. "Sophia, it isn't good. You won't like what I have to tell you."

"I don't care. Today appears to be the day everyone places their cards on the table. I have to know what is going on around here. Who is torturing my family?"

Stephen leaned forward to tighten the lace on his left boot. "You aren't the only one with sympathy pains for Geoffrey's foot." He wiggled his toes in his boot. "The strange thing about what happened last night is there was no proof when we caught the culprit."

He wiped the dust off of the toe of his boot, "The police tried to stop the truck with a road block, but the truck was basically incapacitated with the tires blown." He started to go on, but the door bell rang.

Sophia huffed, "Isn't there a moment's peace around here? We should have gone to the Range!" She jumped up to answer the door. Stephen was frantically pulling his jacket over his shoulders.

Patsy stood at the door with a covered paper plate. "Hi, are you all right? I heard yelling earlie . Thought it was time to bring some homemade cookies over to you. There certainly has been a parade of people coming and going this morning. Is someone here with you or do you want me to stay?" Patsy pushed her way into the house.

She froze when she saw Stephen. "You! You killer of trucks! You big oaf how dare you blow out my tires! I can't believe you shot at me! How dare you!" Patsy flung the covered plate of cookies at Sophia and raced out the front door. She slammed it with all of her might.

Sophia hugged the paper plate of cookies. Half of them were on the brick floor at her feet. She turned to stare at Stephen. "Patsy was the one in the truck?"

Carefully, she extricated the cookies from her sweater. Holding the plate steady she returned to the rocking chair, "Of course Patsy and Jim have a brown truck with a double cab. Geoffrey has borrowed it from them to move flagstone. Why would she want to blow up our vehicles? What do they have to do with bombs?"

Stephen leaned down to collect the broken cookies from the floor. He placed them gingerly in his large palm. "Evidently, she was coming over here with dessert for us. She saw your mother's truck and she saw me arrive in the military vehicle. She told the cops she was just delivering dessert when I started shooting at her. As she drove into the driveway all the alarms went off and it freaked her out. She was indecisive about what to do when I shot out her tires."

"But why would she drive down the road? Why didn't she drive home, just next door?" Sophia turned her head, "Then whoever was messing with the vehicles was on foot?"

Stephen chewed on a broken cookie, "I believe she thought we were attacking her and she was escaping with her life. The last thing she wanted was for us to come after her and shoot up her house or her husband."

He handed the broken cookies to her and she put them on the paper plate, "Yes, whoever was messing with the vehicles must have parked down a way or come on foot. Patsy swears she didn't have anything to do with the alarms going off and you know what? I believe her. She's not smart enough to know how to place a bomb or break into a vehicle. What about her husband, do you think he would have done it?"

Sophia frowned, "Jim, no. He's Geoffrey's friend. They work on the houses together. They are buddies. Jim worked for the National Transportation Company. He knows about roads and highways. I don't think he would have dynamite or bombs."

Helping himself to the broken cookie parts, Stephen sat on the floor. "Patsy makes good cookies. She also told us something last night that could be of help. Ignacio was up early this morning to check up on something in Santa Fe, but she mentioned something last night. You might want to think about." Stephen handed her a cookie.

Sophia shook her head 'no.' "What did she say last night?"

"She said there was a suspicious looking woman over here the night before Geoffrey's truck exploded. Patsy said she had never seen any woman with such white hair. It was put up, but the cap she had on her head kept sliding off revealing her white hair. Patsy asked Jim to come over and talk to her, because he had seen your van drive away. Nobody knew Geoffrey was here with the girls. She thought you had all gone off late at night."

"Did Jim come over here and talk to the woman with the white hair?" She finally took a cookie.

"No, the woman evidently cut through the arroyo and went down the other way. They thought she must have gone for a walk and lost her bearings late at night." Stephen pushed another cookie into his mouth.

She stopped chewing, "These are good. You don't think they're poisoned do you?"

Stephen muffled out, "No, they are good, but we should go get some lunch. It's after one o'clock. We have to get Geoffrey's stuff, pick up the girls, and get to the hospital. Let me treat you to a hot meal." He put the paper plate of cookies on the coffee table in the living room. "You know maybe Katina is the person setting the bombs? After all, Sophia, how many women do you know with white hair?"

"Two or three, there is Katina of course and Enid who has thicker longer hair and your mother who lives in Minnesota." She side stepped Stephen as he reached out to pinch her.

Sophia sat upright in the military vehicle. There were no springs in the seat and the ride was rough as Stephen headed straight down the hill into the arroyo behind the house. "We may be able to see footprints in the loose dirt or the snow if we drive through the arroyo. The person may have an all terrain vehicle and came in the back way, that's why we didn't see them out on the road."

"Stephen, you do realize it snowed last night and the heat from the day is causing everything to settle into a thick muck. How would be able to see footprints racing around in this vehicle?" Gasping, she held her breath as they went straight down into the arroyo.

"Give it a chance, Sophia. If nothing else you can enjoy the ride." Stephen gleefully wrenched the steering wheel to avoid a tree.

Grabbing the handle over the door, she said, "We weren't looking for anyone on the road or in the arroyo. We believed we were safe in our home." She was impressed at the agility of the vehicle. It didn't bog down in the muddy arroyo bottom. "Do you know how we are going to get out of this arroyo?" She spoke more to the deserted area in front of them than to him.

Stephen was completely in his element. His face glowed with excitement as he twisted the steering wheel to avoid boulders, rabbit brush, and cactus.

"No, we'll find a way or we can go back the way we came."

"Geoffrey won't be happy that you tore down the side of the hill behind the house. He has been trying to shore it up so the water won't cause a run-off. Let's find another way out. Remember you did offer me lunch in town. Town has paved roads."

Stephen laughed, "Yes, I remember. Hey, look there. There are some tire tracks. They look fresh. Those are from an all terrain vehicle with four wheels. It's a little one. Here, it went up the hill over here. Let's follow the tracks and see where they go."

She put her hand on his arm, "You sure you want to mess up the tire tracks? Maybe Ignacio would want to make a cast of them?"

"They are all over the place in the arroyo. He'll have plenty of tracks to cast. Hold on, we're going to climb the rise here." He gunned the engine as the vehicle climbed the steep hill. Only once did the tires feel as if they were slipping.

Stephen manipulated the steering wheel sharply and the tires dug into the wet earth. They topped the hill to find themselves bouncing onto the paved road. "Wow, this is where someone comes regularly to go wheeling. This could be the place the culprit used to get to your house or it could be just a way for kids to play in the arroyo."

"Enough, Stephen, let's go get lunch. This is fun, but we have serious issues we need to confront. Please, can we go and get some lunch?" Sophia glared at him.

"Sure, lunch. Here we go." Both were silent, taking in the magnificent views as they drove west. Sophia noticed the top of their house ahead. The stepped adobe bricks on the roof made the house appear to European. Stephen slowed down and pulled over behind a ragged juniper before he reached their driveway. Sophia turned to ask, "What are you doing?" When Stephen pointed to a beige Ford sedan parked in the driveway right by the fence. "Do you know who belongs to the car?"

She started to get out of the Military vehicle, but Stephen put his hand on her arm to hold her back, "Whoever owns the vehicle isn't in it. Why don't you walk to the house? I'll come around the back. If you know the person you can tell them you were out for a walk." Stephen watched Sophia walk into the driveway. He backed his vehicle into the open field behind a row of juniper trees. Jumping out of the vehicle, he quietly closed the door. He ran along the side of the junipers to circle the house and come along the outer wall by the arroyo.

Stretching her legs as she walked, Sophia moved easily to her front door. Standing under the porch, writing a note on the wall was Enid. "You're here at my front door. What a surprise!"

Enid almost dropped her pen. "Hey, where have you been? I've been calling and calling. Where have you been?"

Laughing at Enid's worry, she said, "I went for a walk. The day is gorgeous isn't it? Just look at the clouds rolling over the mountain into the valley." Sophia pulled out her keys to open the front door. She let Enid enter first. Twisting her shoulders around, she tried to see Stephen. He was nowhere to be found.

Enid stood in the hall waiting for Sophia. Enid appeared to be upset and in an emotional dilemma. "It's Granger and Henker, neither of them showed up at the clinic this morning! What an ordeal. I am beside myself with worry. Now, I know what you've been going through over here."

Sophia took her by the arm and led her into the kitchen. "Come in the kitchen its warmer. How about a cookie? We have gluten free or slightly mauled, which would you prefer?" She picked up the paper plate of cookies from in the living room. "Explain quickly for I have to get the girls soon and pick up Geoffrey from the hospital."

"Oh," Enid stuttered, "You, you, you are going to get Geoffrey this afternoon? Are the girls going with you?" Enid started pulling on her mittens which were attached with a string to her jacket sleeve.

Sophia tried to calm her, "Yes, finally the whole family will be together tonight. What is it that you need from me, Enid?"

Enid was now moving down the hall, she tried to explain, "When I get up in the morning with Alistair, usually Henker is already at the clinic. This morning was a usual morning. Alistair and I got up, we had our breakfast and I took the little fellow to preschool. But when I got to the clinic the doors were locked, the parking lot was filled with clients, and Granger wasn't there either."

Hardly taking a breath, Enid continued, "Both men had clients scheduled for the day. Granger won't answer his phone. I have no idea where my husband is and when I called your mother, she was aloof and distant. Evidently she and Katina drove to the clinic this morning and now Margaret says Katina has gone missing. Margaret wouldn't explain why they drove to the clinic or why Katina might disappear. Your mother is now being totally secretive, which is making me nuts!"

Enid gasped, "I had to cancel everyone's appointments. I am so humiliated after being yelled at all morning. When I called Emily she had no idea what was going on. She said she's glad to be out of the whole mess and loves the little house in Negara. Sophia, what's going on? Where is everyone? I'm all alone and feel completely abandoned! I feel a wreck and want to go home and climb in bed!" Enid cupped her hands over her eyes and started to sob.

Sophia watched Enid's face reddened, "Are you sure that my mother and Katina went to the clinic this morning?"

"Yes, of course! I was there and I know them, Sophia, why did the men not show up for work this morning? It was horrible being put on the spot like that!"

Sophia wrapped her arms around Enid. "Yes, I know the feeling well. Enid, go home. You might take a hot bubble bath and then get your son. I wish I could help you, but I have to go. Please be careful driving home and call me tonight, would you please?"

Enid hugged her back, "All right, I'll call tonight. Good luck with Geoffrey." Enid's angst appeared to leave her as she added, "Men are such babies, aren't they?" She tried to smile, but only managed a sad frown, "Thanks for listening." She went out the door.

Sophia ran into her bedroom. She pulled Geoffrey's small brown suitcase from the closet. Throwing in his jeans, she also grabbed his flannel shirt, and his underwear and socks, running to the back door she grabbed muddy boots. As she reached for the front door, it opened.

Stephen stood there with a grin. "Good for you, she's gone. Let's go and eat, I'm starving." Stephen placed the suitcase on the backseat of the military vehicle as he slammed the door to jump in the front seat. Sophia was already belted in and ready to roll.

Checking the time on the dashboard clock, she noticed it was one-thirty on the dot. "We have about one hour to eat and then get the girls, do you think we can do it?"

"Sure, no problem, the restaurant is probably emptying out about now. Here try these dark glasses." He handed her a pair of wrap around dark glasses. Sliding them on, she said, "These are incredibly dark. Where did you get these? Are they Navy?"

Stephen put the blinker on as he turned into the parking lot. "Yes, a friend of mine who is a Navy Seal gave them to me. He told me if I ever needed to play the role of a blind beggar they would come in handy. The Middle East can be blinding with the sunlight on the desert as well as in Saudi Arabia. He felt I could use them out here in New Mexico."

Sophia kept the dark glasses on as they crossed the street and entered the Range Café. Stephen smirked as he watched her stumble up the front ramp into the restaurant. "Here, put your hand on my elbow and I'll lead you. It's dark in here, my blind friend." She laughed, letting him play his game as they followed behind the hostess. The restaurant smelled of fresh pies and green chili.

The hostess apologized profusely at the inconvenience of being seated in the far back of the restaurant, but she explained, they were having a Moose Convention and the front and middle tables were taken. Sophia sat with her back to the main restaurant. Stephen sat facing her for he had made a point of always having his back to the wall. "Here, give me back my glasses."

Stephen put out his large hand to take them from her when two men walked past them and were seated at the table to the right of them. The reflective mirrored wall behind Stephen gave Sophia a full view of the restaurant and the men sitting behind Stephen.

Pushing the glasses back up her nose, she shook her head at Stephen. Whispering into the menu, she told him, "Don't look now, but to your right is Enid's husband. He went AWOL this morning. I wonder who he has with him. He has his back to us, but the fellow facing you appears to be military. Check it out?" Sophia lifted her menu to her face. Stephen laughed as he pulled the menu away from her, "Hey, you're blind. You can't read that menu. How about I order for you?"

She smacked him with her menu and threw it on the table. "Fine, but I already know what I want. I'll have the green-chili chicken chimichanga, thank you very much, and a glass of water with lemon."

The noise level in the restaurant was rising as they sat there. The Moose people were passing around a sign-in sheet for some sort of workshop. The representatives were going from table to table getting the folks to vote or sign a petition. Stephen leaned forward to Sophia, "The man with Enid's husband is in the army. He appears to be with Army and the small insignia on his right arm reflects he could work with the Black Op's. The other insignia on his jacket shows he's a sergeant. Don't know much about the Army, but Black Op's and Army personnel are folks who know about incendiaries and explosives."

Sophia purposely dropped her napkin on the floor, "Can you hear what they are saying?"

"He's talking about food. Enid's husband is disgruntled over something. He wants to know what happened and why it didn't happen." Stephen scooted his chair around to be closer to Sophia, thus putting him closer behind Henker's chair. The backs of the two chairs were almost touching. Stephen stretched out his legs under the table as the waitress arrived to take their order. He ordered for both of them.

Taking a ballpoint pen from his inside shirt pocket, Stephen wrote on the back of his paper napkin, "Enid's husband is Henker?"

Sophia took the pen from him to respond in writing, "His name is Carl Henker. Locals call him Dr. H." Sophia coughed and pointed to the mirrored wall in front of her. "Check out the two of them." She whispered. Henker was touching the Sergeant's face with the back of his hand. There was a lull in the noise for a few minutes, which allowed them to hear the neighboring conversation.

Henker spoke first, "Brad, you know I can't leave Enid now. This dope Granger is tearing the clinic to pieces. You were supposed to take care of him, what the hell happened?"

The man named Brad answered, "The guy with the truck screwed it when he came outside early to heat up his wife's old van. If he would have been ten minutes later I'd have finished with the wiring and everything would have worked. The timer was set, but the wiring was not completed. What a wreck. He went into the house and I couldn't risk going back under the hood, he could've come out at anytime. You saw it on the news."

"Did you find Granger last night?" Henker's voice had suddenly become quieter.

The Moose Club members appeared to be busy eating. The man facing

Henker shook his head, "How could I get to Granger when he was at his mother's? I followed him over there, but with the nosey neighbors and all the dogs there was no way I could get to his Mercedes."

Henker looked over his shoulder. Sophia put her hand up to hold the sunglasses and to hide her face from him. Henker put his hand on Brad's, "The only way we can save the family's money is to get the clinic free and clear. The only way we can own the clinic free and clear is to get rid of the Pino's." Henker raised his voice as a motivational speaker began giving advice to his club members. "Where is Granger now?"

The army man replied, "He took off early this morning in his green Mercedes. He has disappeared into the wind." He said something else, but the Moose conventioneers started singing a song about America.

Stephen's eyebrows went up as he smirked, "God Bless America, the land of the brave, who is this guy with Enid's husband?" The army man walked to the bathroom. Sophia nodded at Stephen, "Now might be a good time to find out. Don't you guys share while standing over the urinal?"

"We don't share urinals, Sophia! That's disgusting! It's when we wash our hands when we share, get real!" He quickly hurried down the hall to the bathroom.

The waitress came with their drinks. She placed Stephen's beside his knife and Sophia's she put in the center of her place setting. "Your water is dead center in front of you if you need it." The waitress swished away with her empty tray. Sophia lifted the cold glass of water and took a sip. She noticed Henker fidgeting in his chair. It appeared he didn't want to face the general public and made sure his back was to the room. The waitress arrived with Henker's drinks. On another tray she delivered Stephen's and Sophia's meal. She noticed Sophia had moved the glass to her right side. Not saying a word, the waitress plopped her plate down dead center in her place setting and left hurriedly.

Stephen returned before the army man. He slid into his seat, hitting the back of Henker's chair. Quickly, he spoke to Henker, "Hey, sorry, didn't mean to bump you."

Henker shook his head and without looking up at Stephen said, "No problem, we're packed in here like sardines." Henker scooted his chair closer to the table to let Stephen sit more easily.

Rotating his plate to have the steak in front of him, Stephen lifted his fork. Whispering he said, "His friend will have a bad headache when he wakes up. Let's eat and get out of here." Sophia didn't argue. After a few minutes, Henker rose from his chair and went down the hall to the bathrooms.

Suddenly, Sophia grabbed Stephen's arm, "What did you do? Is the other fellow all right? Tell me that you didn't resort to violence?"

Stephen chewed slowly, "This is absolutely delicious. No violence. The man didn't see the 'wet floor' sign and slid into the wall. He's going to have a headache, but he'll be just fine." Stephen cut another piece of steak, "Besides anyone who tries to hurt my brother or my family deserves a headache for his trouble, don't you think?"

She put her head down as Henker and the Sergeant came towards them. Henker was holding the man as they walked to the front of the restaurant. A tall man in a suit quickly met them. He pulled out a chair for the Army Sergeant. A waitress brought a glass of water for the man. Stephen scooted his chair back against the mirrored wall to watch the scene unfold. There was much talking, a lot of gesticulating, but no one pointed to him. Stephen inhaled his steak only to hurry to the front where the men were in discussion. Sophia held her breath as she watched the drama in the wall's mirrored reflection.

Stephen was kneeling beside the confused Army Sergeant. Henker was poking his finger into the suited man's chest and almost yelling. Stephen helped the Sergeant stand. He gave a smile and a handshake to the man in the suit. He helped the Sergeant to his feet, up the wooden ramp, and out the door. Sophia slowly chewed her green-chili chicken chimichanga as she looked out the window to see the men walk across the street to a large brown double cab Ford truck. Stephen helped the man into the passenger seat, speaking quickly to Henker he waved. Henker and his Army Sergeant drove down Main Street, allowing Stephen to run across the street to the entrance of the Range.

Striding up to Sophia's table, he slid into his chair. "Well, there you go. A kindness goes a long way around here." He took a drink of his water. She chewed while she waited for him to continue. "Evidently, Dr. Carl, as he introduced himself to me, has an office south of Albuquerque and will take Brad there for treatment. This Army sergeant is an explosive expert who is stationed at Kirkland Air Force Base in Albuquerque. They told me there's even a Navy crew at Kirkland, did you know that?"

She shook her head, 'no.'

Stephen said, "This Brad of Dr. Carl's is just back from his training at Fort Irwin, California. It's obvious they're close. They're not lovers, they're brothers. Brad is Dr. Carl Henker's youngest brother."

Sighing, Sophia felt the need to explain herself, "You know I don't have a problem with people being gay, but when they have spouses who are going to be destroyed from their choices, I just hate it."

She wiped her mouth with the napkin, "But this is even worse. Henker is using his brother to destroy my family and leave Enid. She is totally devoted to him and he treats her like this? They have a son who is a darling little boy, six years old and believes his father to be his hero."

"Carl was the one who should've had the nasty fall in the men's bathroom. Hey, we better get gone. It's time to pick up the girls." Stephen signaled the waitress for their bill.

As was usual, Sybil was waiting for them by the school's library. She had her nose in a book when they drove up to her. Oblivious to the world, she didn't notice the military vehicle. Stephen tapped the horn only to have her leap into the air, dropping her book and her backpack. She stared in disbelief at the driver, realizing she knew him. She set her jaw into a stubborn grimace. Sophia jumped out of the front passenger seat to help her gather her things. "Sorry, Sweetie, Stephen is in a hurry. He didn't know the horn was so loud. Come on, we have to get your sister."

Sybil pushed Donna's car seat over as she buckled her seat belt. "Uncle Stephen, I am going to get you! You just wait! When you least expect it, I'm going to get you big time!"

Stephen chortled, "Sybil, you know I love you. I didn't mean to frighten you, honestly. You're my beautiful niece, no harm was done. Besides you guys ate my entire dessert."

Sybil didn't respond. She stared straight ahead. They turned into the long drive to Donna's school. Her teacher was standing next to her as the military vehicle swung into the school's parking lot.

Sophia swallowed hard, "Oh, dear, this man really doesn't like me. Should I get out and speak with him or wait for him to come to us?" Stephen put the vehicle in park. He ran to Donna and her teacher, "Donna, how was school today? Who's this?"

Stephen put out his huge hand to her teacher, "Hi, I'm Donna's uncle. I specialize in missile launching with the Navy. You know this kid here is a pro on launching inanimate objects. Well, we better go. Have her mother in the vehicle, we're going to pick up Donna's father and then they're all going home. Hope you have a nice day!" Donna ran to the vehicle as Stephen took her backpack. Her teacher stood watching for a minute. Shaking his head, he disappeared down the long walkway back into a room.

Donna smiled as she was lifted into her car seat by Stephen, 'What did you mean that I'm good at launching? What does that mean?"

Stephen laughed, "It means shooting things in the air or up in space." He jumped into the driver's seat and they were off to the hospital. Sybil and Donna spoke in hushed tones in the back seat. Suddenly, Stephen pulled over onto the shoulder of the highway, "Sybil, leave my rifle under the seat. Don't mess with it, please."

Sophia whirled around to see Sybil holding Stephen's rifle by the stock. She took off her seatbelt and grabbed the rifle from her daughter. Pulling it into the front seat, she scolded Stephen, "What are we doing with this in the vehicle? Are you expecting another shoot out?"

"No, just put it down. I forgot it was in here. I thought it would be safer under the seat in the vehicle than in the house. Just put it under the dash." Stephen pointed to the area under Sophia's feet. He studied the girls in the rear view mirror. "Sybil, you should know to never ever mess with a gun until you know how they work, do you understand?"

"Yes, Uncle Stephen, but it was right under my foot. I just wanted to see what it was." She shook her head, "I didn't know what it was."

Stephen pointed to the rifle by Sophia's feet, "No worries, the safety is on. It can't fire unless the safety is off. Just leave it there for now. When we get to the hospital I'll put it in the back."

The four of them marched single file down the hall to Geoffrey's room. The first person they met was Dr. Baker. He stood at the foot of Geoffrey's bed with a plastic bottle of red orange liquid. He had on latex gloves and was rubbing the dye on his patient's foot. Geoffrey was wincing in pain, holding onto the side railing and trying to smile at Mr. Goldfarb. Mr. Goldfarb stood on the right side of Geoffrey, softly reading out loud from a legal paper. Standing to the left of Geoffrey was Granger who smiled when he saw them troop into the room.

Granger hurried to his sister's side and gave her a hug. "Sophia, how good to see you! I think we have everything figured out with the property. Mr. Goldfarb is trying to get the two of us to come to an understanding. Mom isn't too happy, but then when is she ever happy, right?"

Donna stared at Dr. Baker and the red dye. Sybil sat on the green cafeteria chair, hugging her backpack. Stephen pushed Sophia aside to reach for Granger's hand, "Hi, I'm Stephen Vinder, Geoffrey's brother, but you know that. We have met before only at the time you were trying to screw my family out of everything they own. What kind of property agreement is going on here?"

Samuel Goldfarb's attention was broken at the sound of Stephen's voice. "Another Vinder has arrived? Well, we can't have too many Vinder's in one room, can we?" He reached his hand to Stephen who pleasantly accepted it. Mr. Goldfarb removed his heavy reading glasses, "Here, maybe you would like to read this over while I say hello to Geoffrey's beautiful wife?"

Stephen took the papers. Mr. Goldfarb pointed to a row of figures and an outline at the bottom of the page. "This is the pertinent information related to Rocoso property owned by your brother and his wife and the ownership thereon." Mr. Goldfarb shuffled around Stephen to give Sophia a quick hug. He then knelt down to ask Donna how her day had been. While the two of them were in conversation, Sophia turned her attention to the doctor.

Dr. Baker pointed to Geoffrey's foot, "Here, young lady, let me show you what needs to be done when he gets home." Dr. Baker pulled a bottle of the red dye from his white medical long coat. "This is a beta dyne wash. To avoid infection, I recommend you use this wash on his foot at least twice a week once he is home. You don't want to overuse it for it will stop skin growth, but we do need to keep the new skin free from infection." He handed the bottle to her.

Reaching into his other pocket, he pulled out a rolled bandage of glittering material. It was sealed in sterile clear plastic. "I'll get you six of these before he leaves. Once the beta dyne wash is finished, wrap this filmy material around his foot. He's not to get his foot wet. Do not let him walk around with his foot uncovered. You might want to get a cardboard box for the bed to protect the sheets from touching his foot."

Dr. Baker lifted the sheet beside Geoffrey's good foot and showed her a welded metal square frame covered with blue sponge. It had an opening at one end. "We use these in the hospital, but you can use a box at home. Be sure his toes or the sides of his foot do not touch the sheets or blankets. Air must circulate around the foot."

Samuel Goldfarb, Stephen and Granger all watched as Dr. Baker explained. "His crutches are his mobility. He is not to walk on this foot until I see him again in three weeks. He doesn't need a wheelchair. The wheelchair has foot rests. His needs to keep the base of his foot free from weight bearing. The bottom of his foot received the most damage, as you can see here." Dr. Baker poked his finger at Geoffrey's heel. Geoffrey sucked in air, his face went white, and the guardrail jiggled with his grip.

"Keep his heel up off the sheet as well. I'll let you take this home with you. This little device is made from a sponge. Just shove it under his ankle. This rigid sponge will keep his heel from touching the mattress." Dr. Baker handed her a blue triangle of spongy material. "As for his meds—he has pain medicine, but I 'm only writing him a script for four pain pills. There is no reason for pain medicine if he's doing what he is supposed to do. I don't believe in giving pain medicine to patients who are going home."

He pulled out his prescription pad and wrote on it, ripping the paper off the top and handing it to Sophia. "Usually, the patient's family ends up taking the pain meds because the patient makes them crazy. We don't want that now do we?" Writing out another prescription, he added, "These are his antibiotics. He is to take these religiously for these will keep the skin from becoming infected, which would cause the loss of his foot. These are to be taken with food and he is to avoid all alcoholic beverages as the alcohol diminishes the strength of the antibiotic." He ripped off the white paper and handed it to her.

Sophia smiled as Dr. Baker continued, "Your husband has good stamina. He has been walking a quarter of a mile every morning and every afternoon. Make sure he continues. He informed me you live on a mountain. The uneven terrain may be difficult with the crutches, but you can take him to town and have him go up and down the street. The weather hasn't been too bad lately."

He turned to look out the hospital window. Sleet was falling. Dr. Baker chuckled and shook his head as he turned back to the foot, "The swinging motion in his foot helps with circulation. Good blood flow helps heal the wound." Pointing to the prescriptions in her hand, he added, "His discharge papers are at the nurses' station and he is free to leave anytime. Don't forget to ask for the extra bandages. They get used up quickly."

Turning, he put his hand on Geoffrey's arm, "See you in three weeks, my good friend. Take good care of that foot, remember no water. If you shower, put saran wrap around your foot with a towel or put it on a pillow placed on a stool beside the shower. No baths unless the foot is elevated out of the water. No skiing or roller blades until we meet again, all right?"

Geoffrey smiled at him, "Yes, doc, see you in three weeks for another appointment with pain."

Shaking his head, Dr. Baker spoke to Sophia, "He says that's my middle name, hah!" Dr. Baker left the room.

Geoffrey gave a sigh of relief. "Come here, Sophia, I need a hug and from the two of you as well." There was a pile up around the hospital bed as the family got a firm hug from Geoffrey. Sophia handed him his small suitcase and his boots. He held the boots out for all to see, "These still have mud on the bottom of them."

She shook her head, "Hey, we were running around today. Didn't have time to scrape off the mud, besides you can only wear one boot, right?"

Geoffrey with Stephen's help hobbled on his crutches into the bathroom. Sophia picked up the legal papers left on the bedside table. Geoffrey turned to her to say under his breath, "Read this. Take the deal. Granger will regret this, but then we will get the house."

The two brothers closed the door to the bathroom. Granger took Sybil's vacated chair, "Sophia, the property in Rocoso is really Mom's and mine. You need to accept that fact. We are trying to work out a deal with Mr. Goldfarb here, but Geoffrey has been extremely stubborn."

Mr. Goldfarb smiled at her, "Your father's will holds up in the courts. We have come to an agreement in which you and your husband agree to pay off the balance due of two thousand dollars to Margaret and Granger and the will to the Rocoso property is yours. The cost is final and they must pay for their own legal fees. Everyone can shake hands and walk away as friends."

Granger groaned, "I agree to this, but Mom will not want to sign the agreement. She is trying to gather up all the funds she can to maintain her farm."

Geoffrey yelled out from the bathroom, "Margaret has to keep the farm to feed the starving children of the world!"

Granger burst out laughing, "Yea, she never leaves her damn farm.

You'd think the world would end if she took a trip, went to visit her sister in Texas, or moved to a less expensive situation. The poor horse of hers is on his last legs and she won't give him up to God."

Holding the paper out to Mr. Goldfarb, Sophia asked her brother, "Do you want Geoffrey and me to have the property or are you just trying to get out of court proceedings, Granger?"

"Hell, to be honest, Sophia, I want the property. I'm in a divorce. My soon to be wife is running around and my mother hates me for even trying to be nice." Granger lifted his hands in the air and pushed back his curly hair. "What am I to do?"

Sybil walked over to Granger to stand in front of him, staring. In one quick movement, she slammed the toe of her foot into his shin. "You, big fat jerk, you can't take our home away from us!" Sybil raised her foot to kick him again.

Granger grabbed her by the shoulders, "You listen here, you little brat, you don't kick people. If you want to keep your home you need to learn some manners."

Donna who was standing beside Mr. Goldfarb, launched a full out attack. She raced full force into Granger. She landed on top of him in the chair. Donna was kicking, biting, and screaming at him, "You leave my sister alone! You're a slimy salamander and we HATE you! Go away, get out of our lives! We HATE you more than Grandma Margaret HATES you!"

He jumped, dropping Donna to the floor. She hit her head and began wailing at the top of her lungs. Sophia went to her aid, lifting her into her arms. "Granger, perhaps you had best go. Please, just go, leave us." She hugged Donna to her chest.

Granger brushed off his green corduroy trousers. "I'm the good guy here. I'm the one trying to help you keep your home! Why are you two little ones attacking me?" He lifted his left arm to examine it, "You, brat, you bit me. If it gets infected I'll sue."

Glaring as she lifted Donna, she snapped at him, "If it gets infected you can go see your buddy the doctor. Obviously you wouldn't know what to do with an infection. Granger, get out of here, now!"

Walking to the door, Granger suddenly grabbed his sister's left arm. "Hey, I want you and Geoffrey to have the house in Rocoso that's what we're working on for God's sake. What do you think I am a barbarian?" He let her go to walk down the hall.

Donna struggled for her freedom to attack again. Then she stopped, blood was pouring from her nose. "Mommy, help?"

Mr. Goldfarb yanked the top bed sheet off of the hospital bed. He knelt down beside them. He sat Donna on the floor. Pushing the sheet against her nose he leaned her forward with her head between her knees. "There, there, just keep your head forward and it will stop." He stroked Donna's hair as he gently spoke.

Glancing at Sophia who knelt on the other side of her daughter, he said, "You need to go to Granger. Apologize to him. He's trying to get this deal your mother set up with the lawyer in Santa Fe reversed. It's in your best interest to befriend him. Go to him, quickly, before he leaves and changes his mind." Mr. Goldfarb reached for Sybil. "I'll watch the girls, go!"

Sophia hurriedly kissed Donna on her the top of her head, "Will you be all right?"

Donna sniffed, "Yes, Mom, you better go. I'll stay here with the angel man." She pointed to Mr. Goldfarb.

Sophia hugged her leather purse to her chest as she ran down the hall. She righted her red wool cap to see Granger standing in front of the doors of the double elevator. "Granger, can we talk?" Granger turned slowly. "What? Are you asking if I am 'free??"

They both smiled at their Father's favorite line. "Yes, I guess I am. What happened in the room was most unfortunate and I apologize for the girls."

Granger abruptly sat on one of the chairs along the wall opposite the elevators. "Sophia, your property in Rocoso was paid for by the two of you. I checked into the loan Papa made with you two. He didn't give you any benefits. He charged you the same interest as the bank. The only difference was the money stayed in the family. It didn't go to the bank."

She nodded in agreement. Granger examined Donna's bite on his arm as he continued, "Mom is extremely unhappy with the way Papa spent her money. If you remember Papa bought a cabin at the Taos ski lodge for thousands of dollars and never used it. The cabin is still in his name. Mom has to pay taxes on it. Papa paid for the angel statue at the Negara cemetery and wanted to be buried beside it, but then he told me he didn't want to be left suffocating underground in the dirt for eternity."

Sophia nodded at him. Granger sat forward and took her hand, "We're going next week to spread his ashes over the Grand Canyon. This week turned into a nightmare and Mom postponed the ash dropping. Do you want to come with us?" His face was hopeful.

She shrugged her shoulders, "No, I don't think so. I have to stay and help out my family. Geoffrey can't drive and the girls still have school. My classes are going to resume in about five weeks and I need to prepare." She pulled her hand away from his. "Granger, I don't really want anything to do with dropping Papa's ashes. You and Mom decided on this, I haven't really had a say in anything around here."

Granger sighed and sat back, "I understand your feelings, but right now my life is one big mess. Our mother is mad at me for divorcing Emily and getting Katina pregnant. Do you know what she said to me last night over the phone? She called me on the phone to ask me if Katina was really pregnant and was I sure the child was mine! She asked me this over the phone, Sophia!"

Sophia shook her head, trying not to smile. "What did you say to Mom?"

"How the hell should I know if Katina's really pregnant? I have to believe what she tells me, right? She's in love with me. Why would she lie?"

Spittle flew from Granger's mouth, "Mom is really too much. If she isn't causing chaos, she finds chaos to throw at you." Granger crossed his legs. "Now, I can't find Katina. After Mom confronted me on the phone, the phone for God's sake! Yesterday, when I asked Katina about the pregnancy, you know what Katina said?"

Sophia put her hand on his, "I'm sure I don't know what she said?"

Granger studied his hand, "Katina told me she couldn't love me if I didn't trust her. Can you imagine?"

People waiting for the elevator moved closer to where they were sitting. Granger leaned forward with his elbows on his knees to put his hand on his forehead. His voice softened as he continued, "Katina said she didn't believe she could live with me if I didn't trust her! She says this out of the blue!" He shook his head, "She swore her love to me two days ago. We were planning a wedding for God's sake! She called me her soul mate! My soul mate for life is now in the trash!"

He stood and walked to the long rectangular window near the chairs. Touching the cold glass he turned to her, "She believes if there isn't the element of trust in a relationship there can be no relationship. If she wants trust, why didn't she tell me the truth? All I need to know is the truth. Is the truth so terrible?"

Sophia put her hand up to him, "Granger, did you believe her or do you think she was acting? Do you think Mom paid her to leave?"

He wiped his left cheek. "No, she took off. Last night in the dark, she jumped out of the Mercedes when I stopped at a stop sign! She took off! People behind me were honking their horns. I had to drive ahead. When I came back Katina was gone. She's vanished!"

Sophia opened her purse and handed Granger a tissue. "Here, do you know where she may have gone?"

He wadded the tissue in his hand, "No! I thought she would have gone to Santa Fe to see her friends. But I couldn't find them either. I did run into the deputy sheriff Carl at the court house. He was searching for Katina, too."

Granger wiped his nose with the tissue, "Sophia, when I finally found out Katina was doing drugs I was horrified. Drugs! She was with a group of people from California who were doing drugs."

Granger's voice became softer as people surged out of the elevator doors. He came back to sit in the chair, "My God, Sophia, the woman who is carrying my infant son is doing drugs. What else can possibly go wrong?"

He mumbled under his breath as he looked at her under his eyebrows. "Mother believes I am an idiot for getting involved with her. Right now I could use some advice from Emily, but she's divorcing me and you're my only family and you don't trust me either." Hanging his head, Granger wiped his nose again. "I did think Mom may have had something to do with this, but she didn't know anything about Katina leaving."

The elevators dinged and the doors opened. Their mother's shrill voice interrupted them, "Granger and Sophia, I have been searching for you every where!" Breathlessly Margaret hurried to stand in front of them. "What are you two doing out here? I called Geoffrey on the hospital phone. He told me you were here somewhere in the hospital. I had the operator paging you, don't you listen? Why don't you children answer your phones?"

Sophia chuckled, "Mom, it's probably because we're not near them. I've been out all day and Granger has been working with Mr. Goldfarb. We don't stay home and wait for the phone to ring, unlike some..."

"What's that supposed to mean? Are you going to insult me again? Really, Sophia, I do believe every morning you wake up thinking up insults against your loving mother." Margaret rested her hand on Granger's shoulder, "Listen, Katina came back this morning, late. She packed up all her things, screamed at me for twenty minutes and left in her junk heap of a car. She had a message for me to give you." Margaret winked at Sophia.

Granger's face paled, "What? What did she want you to tell me? Mom, tell me the truth not something you made up! I want to hear the truth."

Margaret put her gloved hand on her chest, 'The truth? I only tell the truth! What do you two take me for? I only tell the truth."

Sophia turned to watch people get on and off the elevator. Margaret continued, "Granger, Katina told me she isn't pregnant. She said her girlfriend left her in Santa Fe. Katina didn't have anywhere else to go. Thus she went to Emily's because she knew her in California. Katina told me you are a typical male and deserved to be lied to and you don't deserve a son."

Their mother held her chin high as she continued, "I told her to get off my property. She apparently didn't have any problem following my orders for she left. There is nothing of hers in the house. What little she did leave, I have had taken to the dump." She carefully pulled off her glove of black leather from her left hand as she sat down next to Granger. She placed the glove neatly in her lap as she worked on the right glove.

Granger hung his head, "Mom, she did love me. You paid her off, didn't you?"

Margaret snorted, "I most certainly gave her money. She told me you were a dirty animal. She even called you a sex starved orangutan."

Sophia shook her head at her mother, "Mom, no need to overdo things here."

Huffing, Margaret continued, "She had a locket around her neck with the photo of her 'significant other' placed in it. Granger, you were duped." Margaret folded her black leather gloves to put them into her coat pocket of long herringbone. "I still love you, my dear boy, but from now on if you wish to use your dipstick it might be best to talk to your sister or me first." She fluffed her brown hair with her hands, letting it fall into a perfect curl below her ears.

Now she turned her attention to her daughter. Leaning around Granger she asked, "Sophia, what are you doing here? Isn't Geoffrey home yet or have you decided to leave him here? He is rather accident prone, if you ask me." Margaret patted her coat over her knees.

"Mom, the girls are in their father's room. He's getting dressed. By the way, thank you for springing Stephen from jail the other night." She glanced at her mother.

"Stephen is a handsome young man. He doesn't wear those thick coke bottle lenses like your husband. Sophia, have you thought about taking him on for a husband?" She pulled a mint form her black leather purse. The mint's golden paper was unwrapped. The mint was popped into her mouth.

Lazily, Sophia put her arm around Granger's shoulders, "Mother, I love my husband. He's the father of my children and the man with whom I have chosen to spend the rest of my life. Get over yourself, please." Sophia showed her teeth to her mother. "Mom, you just dropped a bomb on Granger, don't you care?"

Margaret laughed, "The old ape teeth trick, huh? You're going to show me your choppers. It isn't going to work." She put her left hand on Granger's right, "You're all right, huh, Grange? This one is tougher than you think. He'll bounce right back and find a proper woman to have a proper son and take care of his mother as he should. Right, Granger? You'll be just fine because you have your Mama to take care of you, right?" She patted his hand.

Granger stood, "I think I have to go home now. All of this is too much to absorb. For some reason I'm exhausted and just want to sleep." He walked to the elevator door, which had just opened. He stepped inside and with a gentle wave disappeared behind the elevator's silver doors.

Margaret scooted over to sit next to Sophia, "Fat thanks he gave us, huh? Why don't you get your husband and go home. I will catch Granger and try to soothe his male ego. Call me this evening. Please call me this evening!" She hurried to the elevator doors as they opened once again.

Stephen was rushing down the hall, waving at Sophia. He came to her side, "We're ready to rock and roll. I spoke with Mr. Goldfarb. He's a fine lawyer by the way. He has a plan for you and Geoffrey. I believe it will work in the best interest of all concerned."

He spoke to her over his shoulder as they walked to the room, "We need to get home, though, and discuss what we learned at the restaurant. Come on, let's get the family and get out of here. Your husband is anxious to get out of here and get home. Donna's nose is no longer gushing red."

Sophia signed Geoffrey out at the nurses' station. She had the release papers with instructions, his prescriptions, but the nurse insisted on taking Geoffrey down the elevator in the wheelchair. He held his foot off the footrest as they rode down the elevator. Stephen had raced ahead of them to pull the military vehicle to the curb for easy loading. Geoffrey winced when he saw it, "Damn, Stephen, are you planning on a military invasion?"

They drove home full of conversation about hospital food, nurses and the development of car alarms in the driveway. Sophia sat in the backseat between Donna and Sybil. They laughed and sang songs until they pulled into the driveway.

Geoffrey screamed when he saw the truck was gone. "Where's my truck? Damn did you move my truck?"

Sophia tried to soothe his fears, "Geoffrey, the bomb squad had to take the truck. We didn't really get a choice." She patted his shoulder and shook her head.

Stephen tried to joke with him about how it was better off where it is now. Geoffrey made one curt remark, "Stephen, it was my truck, not yours."

They helped Geoffrey adjust his crutches as he exited the military vehicle. Donna ran to the outside wall, "Mom, look someone left us some stuff." She pulled open the top of the paper bag and peered inside. "It's not for me!" She ran into the house leaving the door open for the rest of her family.

Sybil and Donna disappeared into their rooms with no doors slamming. Their father hobbled on his crutches into the kitchen. He opened the refrigerator and took out a beer. "Ah, how I have missed the nectar of the gods."

Sophia quickly reached over and took the beer bottle from of his hand, "No beer for you. You can't take antibiotics and drink alcohol."

"If I have a choice, can I just have the beer?" His sad face glared at her. She put her arms around him, "No, you can have your beer when the antibiotics are all gone. This gives you something to work toward. I'm taking antibiotics, too. We'll have to be the sober ones around here. Now, Stephen and I have something to share with you." She helped Geoffrey sit in one of the kitchen chairs while she lifted his leg and placed it up on another chair. His foot dangled precariously in the air.

Sitting next to him, she went on, "Stephen and I were here this morning for the great conversion between Madame Margaret and the Illusive Katina. Katina is not pregnant and mom paid her to leave New Mexico. Aside from Katina's exodus from Granger and her involvement with the Gay Movement, she was at Carol's when Carol was attacked. Somehow I don't feel Katina killed Carol for she would have nothing to gain from it. She is a smart, educated, well travelled woman who was manipulating Granger. "

Geoffrey reached over to give Sophia a kiss on her lips, "You were just dying to tell me all of this weren't you? My goodness I have never heard you speak so quickly. So, what do we do now?" He watched Sophia put the bottle of beer back into the refrigerator. Stephen frowned, "I guess I better not have one then either, right?"

"Beer?" Geoffrey shot him a nasty look, "No, you better not touch my beer! I know where the shot gun is kept. Sybil told me."

Laughing, Sophia put her trusty kettle on for tea. After pouring out hot cups of water and handing out tea bags, she let them get comfortable. Stephen and Geoffrey listened as Sophia explained Margaret's behavior at the hospital. She held her tea mug in her right palm, "It was quite amazing to see Granger's face turn so white and Mom never flinched. She just kept on telling Granger how terrible Katina was without a thought. The poor guy must have been in shock. Wonder if Mom caught up with him in the parking lot?"

As if on cue the phone began to ring behind Geoffrey. He smiled as he pulled it out of its cradle and held it to his ear, "Geoffrey Vinder here, how can I help you?" His face sobered immediately. "Slow down, Granger, what do you mean she was dead?" He stared at his wife as he listened. Then he said, "Granger, I'll let Sophia know what happened and maybe she and Stephen can take a fast run up to Santa Fe, but I'm not able to drive." He nodded and then added, "Granger, I will tell her where you are and what happened. I do not control my wife and I would appreciate you not to tell me what to do. We can talk later, good bye."

He swung around in the kitchen chair to hang up the phone. "Well, we now have another development. Sophia, we have been home what, about two hours and in this amount of time your mother was on her way to see Emily.

The turn off to Negara is a dangerous turn and when your mother turned her steering wheel, the device came off in her hand and she flew onto the wrong side of the highway where her truck stalled out and she was immediately hit several times by vehicles coming down the hill from Santa Fe." He put out his hand to Sophia.

"The truck she was driving is completely totaled and the medics who arrived at the scene had proclaimed her dead, but while they were tending to some of the other injured parties, your mother started breathing on her own. She appears to be coming out of surgery. Granger is there and wishes you to come and help him deal with the legal as well as medical issues that have arisen from this accident. What do you think?"

Stephen quickly stood, grabbing the chair before it fell backwards to the kitchen floor. "Damn, you two can relay a lot of information in one long breath. So, Margaret the grand dame is alive and Granger is trying to pick up the pieces after his mother just dropped a bomb shell on him about the woman he was supposed to marry. Wow!"

When Stephen was finished, Sophia shook her head, "You know I have to go, right? This is my mother we are talking about and I do love her regardless." She took a sip of her tea, "Do you believe this was a true accident or do you think this was an accident waiting to happen?"

Geoffrey leaned back, lifting his foot to rest on the back of Stephen's chair beside him. "Who's to know? The insurance company will be the one to find out if this was purposely done or happened by accident." He stared at his wife, "Do you really want to go up there? I just got home and have hardly had a chance to be with you?" His face reddened when Stephen stared at him.

Sophia pushed her short bangs from her forehead, she said, "Honey, I have to go. We have a long life ahead of us, here or somewhere, but I better get up there." Glancing at the kitchen clock, she added, "If I leave right now I can be there before dark. Maybe I can help Granger with his emotional stability as well."

Lifting her arms over her head, she stretched, "Right now nothing feels real." She stood taking the tea cups from the table and placing them in the kitchen sink. "I can go by myself and Stephen can help you with the girls."

Stephen cleared his throat, "Sophia, I think I should go with you what with all the nasty things that have been going on around here. If there is someone with you who can witness whatever your brother chooses to do or whatever the doctors want to do with your mother, this would be a good thing. You have no idea how badly she may be broken."

Geoffrey stood, hopping on one foot he agreed, "Take Stephen with you. The girls can help around here. They aren't helpless little toddlers anymore. Go, go and have some support, but remember to call me every hour or I will be worried."

Sybil ran into the kitchen, "Dad, Mom, someone was in my room while we were in town getting Dad from the hospital." She held up her hand. There dangling from her fingers was a cloth bag with a ribbon handle. It was placed on the table with great care. "Why would someone put this right outside my window if they weren't inside my room?"

Sophia took two spoons and pulled apart the ribbons. There printed on the inside of the bag were Enid's name and Alistair's. "This is Enid's. She must have left it here when we found her out front writing me a note. Why would she have left this outside Sybil's window?"

Stephen put his arm around Sybil, "Good for you to find this. You will make a great detective someday. Now let's see what she has in this bag." Stephen took the spoons from Sophia to lift the bag by only the one ribbon. He let the linen bag drop on its side and then lifted the bottom of the bag, letting the entire inventory roll forward onto the kitchen table.

Stephen and Sophia pulled Sybil back as Geoffrey leapt away. Six sticks of dynamite fell out of the bag with two dynamite caps along with a small box of matches and some white wires attached to a small clock. The clock was not ticking. Geoffrey pushed the clock over to find the battery was missing. He lifted the bag again and the battery rolled out onto the table and was stopped by a roll of dynamite.

"A bomb has been found on the premises by the heroine of this tale." Stephen patted Sybil on the back. She stared at the battery. "Dad, my room would have blown sky high if the battery would have stayed in place, huh?"

Stephen walked to the wall phone in the kitchen. He lifted it and began to dial. Sophia gently shoved the dynamite away from the edge of the table with the teaspoon. Geoffrey asked his brother, "Who are you calling now?"

Without answering Geoffrey, Stephen spoke into the phone, "Carl, we have another development up here in Rocoso. The Vinder family found a bag of dynamite outside their daughter's window. It was loaded and ready to explode with a clock wire, but the battery had fallen out of the clock."

Sybil shoved her elbow into her uncle's ribs, "Uncle Stephen, I found the bag, not mom or dad!"

Stephen shook his head at her, "Yes, Mr. Vinder is here with the girls, but Sophia and I may have to go to Santa Fe. Sophia's mother was in a nasty accident and there are complications." He shook his finger at Geoffrey, "Yes, he can wait for you. I will tell him this is a direct order. Yes, Sir. I shall do this immediately." Stephen hung up the phone.

"Well, the verdict is there are probably more bombs. He doesn't anyone to go looking for them and he will be here within the hour to assist with searching for more explosives, but he recommended everyone who was planning to spend the night here leave and spend the night at a hotel. He is going to stay the night here in case there is another attempt on anyone here in the house."

Sophia's face blanched, "My God, Stephen, you were right. Enid was here for an alternative reason. She has white hair, she was parked conspicuously in the bushes, and she was caught so she decided to run to the front door and pretend to write a note." She stared at Stephen, "But then why was she crying? Why did she make up that crazy story about her husband not being at work and Granger disappearing? Why? I thought she was our friend?"

Moving the battery from the clock on the table, Geoffrey moved the dynamite to the side, "Right now we have no idea who our friends are and who aren't. The weird thing is that she was here, that she has kept in touch with us regardless of what Granger has done to her and her husband."

He stopped and looked at her, "Maybe she is trying to destroy Granger's family. Carl has put all of his money into the clinic and so has her family. If Granger takes a walk and removes his financial obligations along with Emily's, this would leave Enid and Carl in a very dark hole financially. Sophia, if they are desperate to save the clinic, they will stop at nothing."

Moving Sybil to the side, Stephen picked up a stick of dynamite, "A mother will do anything to protect her young. You know this? If Granger is planning to sue them for his investment in the clinic, wow, this would destroy the Henker's lives."

Stephen lifted the dynamite cap from the stick of dynamite, "This may be why he called in his brother from the Army. If Carl and Enid lose all their money they will have no one to help them. Sophia, you even said that even Enid's parents helped out with the buying of the inventory, right?"

She nodded 'yes.' Sybil watched Stephen pull the dynamite cap off of the other stick, "What are you going to do with those?"

Stephen stuck the undetonated dynamite back into the linen bag, "We need to keep this in a safe place for evidence."

Sybil glared, "Mom, what if those would have gone off? Donna and me would have been blown up to the sky!"

"What could have happened?" Donna walked into the room carrying her Social Science textbook. "What could have happened to us, Sybil?"

Geoffrey stared at Sybil, "Oh, dear, you don't think she had a backup plan do you? Stephen, we better go through everything in the girls' rooms and, Sophia, why don't you get ready to go to Santa Fe. Do you think we should just pack and go to a hotel?"

Sophia raced down the hall ahead of the men to her youngest daughter, "Donna, where did you put that brown bag you found by the wall when we got home? Where did you put it?"

Donna scrunched up her face and started to cry, "Why? What did I do wrong now?" Sophia knelt down to hug her. "Just tell me where you put the brown bag you found outside."

Donna shook her head, "I didn't. I left it there because it was too heavy for me to lift. It's still outside by the wall." She pointed her chubby finger down the hall, "I didn't like what was in it. The stuff was used, it wasn't pretty or new, I don't like old stuff."

Stephen ran outside to the wall. The brown bag was where it had been when Donna had first noticed it as they were getting Geoffrey into the house. Stephen hurried to the military vehicle. Opening the back, he pulled out a hand held fire extinguisher. Pulling the pin from the side, he aimed and sprayed it across the yard at the brown bag. The bag now soaked sank into itself. Bending down, Stephen grabbed a stick and poked at the bag. A loud ticking started and then there was a beep.

Sophia, Geoffrey, and the two girls were watching him from the open door. Geoffrey yelled out, "Stab it with the stick. Stab it and pull the bag to pieces, we can't take any risks." Just then the phone in the kitchen began to ring. Geoffrey nodded to Sophia, who ran into the kitchen to get it. As she lifted the phone to her ear, she heard a loud 'bang.' Dropping the phone, she ran back to the front door to find Geoffrey sitting on the ground with the two girls in his lap.

"What happened?" Sophia knelt down beside her husband.

The men started laughing and the girls joined in with him. Finally, he took a breath and explained, "The bag was soaked as well as the wires yet when Stephen jabbed at it with a stick it imploded. Look?" He pointed to the far side of the wall. Stephen was on his knees covered in a white whipped creamy substance. "The fire extinguisher foam certainly shot into the air! The stuff covered me!"

The girls laughed and pointed at Stephen, "You look like a marshmallow man who is starting to melt."

"Thanks a lot. You really do give good advice, little brother!" Wiping the foam from his forehead, he shook it off his hand onto the ground. "Stab it with a stick, my ass, the stick caused the stuff to explode."

Sophia carefully moved to the bag that was splayed on the ground only inches from Stephen. She took the dropped stick and continued to pull the bag apart. A small stick of dynamite rolled out with wires trailing behind it followed by a small clock similar to the one on the kitchen table. The clock was attached by wires, but the clock was soaked through with the fire extinguisher foam. She tore the wires free, using the stick and then kicked the small clock away from the bag.

"Well, someone was certainly interested in blowing up our environment." Sophia suddenly remembered the phone and ran back into the kitchen. She picked up the ear piece which she had left lying on the counter. "Hello?"

"Hey, what in the world did you do? You pick up the phone, drop it on the counter, making me wait for you to come back and pick it up again, what is going on?" Granger's voice was terse and sharp.

She took a deep breath, "Granger, we just found two bombs planted around our home here in Rocoso. Stephen was detonating one of them when you called. Sorry, but I needed to be sure my family was safe before even thinking of this phone. What do you want now?"

"What do I want now? Hell, I could use some peace and quiet and a lack of hysterical women, that's for sure. I thought you were on your way here to help me out with Mom, but if you are too busy, well, then I will try to deal with this crazy accident by myself." His voice started to crack.

"Granger, listen, I am sorry, I'm on my way now. I do believe we have found all the bombs there are and you are important to me and I can help you. Let me pack a bag in case I spend the night in Mom's hospital room with her and you can figure out what to do with the insurance company." Sophia leaned forward to peer out of the kitchen window. "Granger, do you believe this accident of mom's was an accident or do you think someone tinkered with her truck?"

"I don't know, Sophia, and the insurance people are sweating it big time. It appears Mom was at fault. You know Margaret? She never seriously learned to drive a stick shift. When she had the Mercedes or the BMW they were automatics and she didn't have a problem, but with this truck it was a stick shift and sometimes she couldn't get it out of second gear." He paused, "If this is her fault, oh, God, she will be sued by at least four different groups of people who are here in the hospital as well. One of the children in one of the vehicles that hit her is in critical condition. This is truly a nightmare. Also, I have been trying to find Katina for she could help. Supposedly she is in Santa Fe."

"Oh, Granger, don't go there. Just take care of Mom and then we can think about Katina. From what Mom said Katina is not pregnant and she is a lesbian who needs to find her soul mate and that soul mate is no longer you. Don't hurt yourself anymore, stay clear of all of that and just deal with the insurance folks and if you can, talk to the other family members. Mom didn't hurt them on purpose; she had a problem with her truck." Sophia watched Stephen carry Donna into the house. Geoffrey hobbled on his crutches as Sybil followed him. "Granger, I'm on my way. Stay at the hospital and I will be there within the hour."

"Sophia, be careful. Bring Stephen with you if you can. Something is seriously going wrong with all of us and I don't think whoever is doing this is going to stop. See you later, oh, and bring food. The cafeteria here just has microwave food and you know I can't eat that stuff. Bring some apples or something healthy, please?"

Reaching to open the refrigerator, Sophia replied, "Sure, I have some cheese, rye crackers, and two oranges and some strawberries, how's that?"

"Great, now get up here before something else happens and thanks, little sister, thanks for your understanding." He hung up the phone.

Stephen had put Donna down on her bed while Geoffrey and Sybil were searching the house for more bags. Sophia put the food in a cloth bag she had hanging by the back door. She grabbed some napkins and a butter knife and dropped it in with the food. Stephen met her in the hall, "Ready to go? Geoffrey and the girls have packed backpacks. We are going to drop them off at the small hotel at the bottom of the hill. Your husband can't drive and we are their only transportation right now. Carl is speaking with Geoffrey in front of the house. I have my overnight bag and toothbrush. Do you need to grab anything?"

Sophia gave him a thankful smile, "Wow, you military types are like James Bond. You guys can pack in thirty seconds and still have a smile. I better get some of my things, just in case we stay near Mom tonight or the house..." She ran into her bedroom and pulled out a bag pack from the closet. She could hear Geoffrey talking to Carl in the hall.

After she had her toiletries in the back pack and her nightgown on top of everything, she met up with her family right outside the front door. The smell of pinion smoke from people's fireplaces hovered over the area.

"Mom, do they have food at this hotel? We haven't had any dinner yet." Sybil pouted her lips at her mother.

"Yes, and there is a Breakfast Café open all hours of the day and night right beside the hotel. Be sure to take your Dad with you though if you go over there, right?" Sophia brushed her daughter's hair with her fingers.

Noticing Sophia's maternal instincts, Stephen added, "...and guys don't forget to feed your dad. There are plenty of places near the hotel that have food. Donna, you need to be in bed by nine o'clock for tomorrow you may need to come up to Santa Fe to help me. Sybil, watch your father and make sure he takes his pills and no alcohol of any kind, got that?"

Sybil hugged her father's good leg, "I will be the nurse as long as he is a proper patient. Oh, and I can put the butterfly wing wrapping on his foot, too. I watched the doctor do that in the hospital." She hurried around Stephen's vehicle to sit behind her father. "Don't worry, Mom, we got Dad all taken care of and we will keep our eyes open for anymore 'spicious bags."

Donna frowned as she pulled herself up into the large back seat, "Mom, we could all sleep in this thing. It is big enough."

Stephen threw everyone's bags into the vehicle's back area. "We will call you at regular intervals to make sure everyone is safe."

In the hotel parking lot, Geoffrey reached for Sophia's hand and pulled her into his embrace. He held her face in his hands close to his, "Remember, don't trust anyone not even Stephen. I love you and want you to come home to us. Please, if you can come home tonight. My life is horrible unless you are here by my side and for the last week I have felt like an orphan without you." He kissed her lips.

His glasses magnified his sparkling blue eyes, "Let Stephen drive and you rest. Don't listen to Granger, but follow your gut. Call me when you get there. Stephen has our room numbers and the phone numbers. Remember I love you with my whole soul!"

"Me, too!" Sybil threw her arms around her mother's neck as Stephen lifted her off the back seat. "Mom, please, please, please, you be careful. We just got Daddy back and we need you two together 'cause I can't deal with Donna by myself. Promise we won't slam any doors."

Sophia kissed her girls on the top of their heads and gave Geoffrey another kiss on his cheek. She grabbed her heavy coat to sit up in the passenger seat of the large vehicle. As they backed away, she waved at her little family standing outside the open hotel doorway.

The sun fell slowly, as the clouds in the sky changed from a yellow pink to a dark azure blue and then a dull black. The traffic north was light considering it was after rush hour. Mostly there were large trucks and some delivery vans moving in synchronization up La Bajada Hill and to the flatlands. Stephen was quiet as he drove. Sophia held her hands in her lap, trying to think of why Enid, who had been her friend for at least three years, would want to blow up their family, their house, or destroy their lives.

The turn off to the hospital came abruptly after the exit signs into Santa Fe. Stephen asked her for directions and they were soon in the hospital parking lot. White emergency vehicles were lined up under the yellow street light and the visitors were to park behind them on the far side of the building. Sophia looked up at all the lit windows. Many of the rooms had windows where the blinds had not been put down yet. Maybe the patients wanted to see the sunset or were unable to pull the blinds down and give them privacy.

"Come on," Stephen jumped out of the vehicle and was running around to her door. "Let's just leave the baggage here and if we need it I can come out and get it. Let's go find your favorite brother, yes?"

Sophia didn't move from the passenger seat, she stared at him. "Stephen, for some reason right now I am extremely tired. I feel like curling up in the back seat and going to sleep, pretending nothing happened. You have to admit, it has been one thing after another and for all we know there are more bombs around the house or Enid may come back tonight and blow our home to kingdom come."

He put his hand out for her to take, "Give it up, you're letting your mind get the best of you. One thing at a time, Geoffrey and I searched everywhere and we found nothing more that resembled a bomb at the homestead. We even looked in the other cars." He slammed the door behind her as she started to walk into the Emergency Room. "Your husband will take care of the girls and Enid is probably freaked out by the whole attempt. I think that's why she was crying. She was terrified she would really hurt someone. Now, let's deal with this accident and think about Enid later."

The automatic glass doors of the hospital slid quietly open as they walked in side by side. There were three nurses at the front station and they all looked up as they walked to the counter. Stephen took control, "Hello, we are here to find Margaret Pino, who is a patient and also we need to speak to her son Granger Pino who may be with her."

The plump nurse shook her head, "Oh, yes, we know the Pino's. Mr. Granger Pino told us he was a medical doctor and wanted to remove his mother from the hospital and take her home with him. She was on oxygen, vital signs were failing, and she seriously needed emergency surgery for a collapsed lung and shattered femur. Oh, yes, we know Mr. Granger Pino who is indeed not a doctor at all." She sat down and typed on her computer key board.

Then she stated under her breath to Stephen, "Mrs. Margaret Pino is in the recovery room on the fourth floor. Where Mr. Granger Pino is, I have no idea, but he better not be messing around with any of our patients!"

The other nurses chortled as she laughed. "The elevators are over there to your right. Go to the fourth floor and there is a waiting room to your left as you get off of them. Good luck!"

Sophia was about to make a snide remark when Stephen took her arm and pulled her down the hall. "No need to make enemies. If Granger has pulled his act here, then we have to watch ourselves. The question is why would he even consider taking Margaret out of here when she was in such sorry shape? What in the world was he thinking? She would die on the drive home if he tried to do that. Sophia, something smells pretty damn rotten around here."

The elevator rose slowly with several other people around them. Sophia kept closing her eyes, hoping this would all disappear and she would be at home safe and sound. As the elevator doors opened, there standing in front of them was Granger. He was holding several pieces of paper. Beside him was an older woman with reading glasses on the end of her nose and she was holding his elbow. The woman had her salt and pepper hair pulled back in a tight bun with straggles of hair falling close to her mouth. Her lipstick had faded. She glanced up at Stephen and Sophia as they departed the elevator. Her eyes appeared to be tired and her demeanor was of someone who had worked too long with too little pay.

"Granger, what is going on?" Stephen pushed Granger back and away from the older woman. "Why in the world would you want to take your mother home? Your mother is in need of serious immediate attention of which you are incapable of giving?" Sophia stood behind Stephen to watch her brother's face turn beet red.

Flustered Granger stuttered as he greeted them, "Stephen, oh, hi, this is Mrs. Ortiz of Alpine Insurance Company. She is representing mom or Margaret Pino in this accident. Evidently, her inspectors found a lose engine part in her truck, which caused her to lose control and thus caused this accident." Granger stepped aside allowing Mrs. Ortiz to greet them.

Stephen stared at the woman. Sophia moved around him to take her hand. "Hello, I am Sophia Vinder. I am the daughter of Mrs. Margaret Pino and the sister of this fellow Granger. This is my brother-in-law Stephen Vinder and we are here to help in any way we can." Mrs. Ortiz took her hand and stared at Stephen over her reading glasses. Under her breath she mumbled, "You have no idea how glad I am to see you both. Mr. Pino here has been arguing with me for over an hour."

Mrs. Ortiz opened a red folder she had in her free hand to pull out several pieces of paper, "You need to read through these and sign the bottoms. It appears the victims of the accident are all suing your mother for several million dollars. We will of course represent her in court and provide her with an attorney, but she will need to be healed and fully cognitive in order to stand trial or the law suit will be dropped. At this point it is too soon to know if she will be able to regain her memory or even if she will be able to function at all." Mrs. Ortiz nodded to Stephen and then walked around them to get into the elevator.

Granger waved his papers at them, "I have the same papers and believe me they make no sense, no sense at all. I tried to explain this to Mrs. Ortiz, but she said they are standard forms and not to worry. She told me to just sign them." Granger's face got redder and redder as he thrust the papers at them, "Why should I sign a paper agreeing that my mother was to blame for the accident? I don't know this! I haven't inspected the truck, how can I sign something that says I submit when indeed I most vehemently do not submit at all!"

Other families were trying to walk around them to get on the elevator. Granger continued to ignore them, "Sophia, you should read these. It makes Mom out to be an outlaw, a mass murder, a horrible person who vindictively tried to kill all these people." He shoved the papers under his left arm as he ran his fingers through his wavy hair, "Sophia, my god, what are we going to do now? She was at fault. She was parked in the middle of a damn freeway for goodness sake and these people were streaming at her at high speed only to crash and smash themselves and mom to pieces!"

People coming out of the elevator were bumping into them. "Come on, you two. Let's find a place to talk." Stephen took Sophia's hand and led her away from the busy hall. They moved to a quiet room where a woman dressed in a pink jacket was sitting next to a table with a black phone. Granger nodded to the woman, "She will call us when we can go in and see Mom. Mom though is completely messed up and a wreck." He plopped down on one of the plastic chairs. "Her face is cut from the broken windshield. Her lung was punctured by her rib and her legs are shattered. She looks like a broken bloody doll."

Stephen sat on the other side of him, "Granger, answer me this. Why did you want to move her in your vehicle to your house when they had her here before her surgery?"

Sophia stood with her hands behind her back. Granger looked up at her, "I just wanted to take her home and fix her by myself. She has had so much sadness, so much grief, and I guess I was in shock."

Sophia lifted her foot and stepped down hard on his foot. "Granger, you were never a good liar. You wanted her to die, didn't you?"

Granger stared at her foot on his. Stephen studied Sophia's face, "What do you mean he wanted her to die?"

She moved her foot and sat down with her knee touching her brother's, "He killed my father with my mother's help. Didn't you?"

The ringing phone broke their concentration. The woman at the table called to them, "Anyone here a member of the Pino family?"

Sophia raised her hand, "I am and this poor flunky. This fellow over here is the military escort."

The woman smiled not knowing what else to do, "Your mother is out of recovery and she is being moved to a room in the intensive care unit. If you go to the end of the hall and turn right you can follow the blue stripe on the floor to the intensive care unit. The nurse there will tell you if you can visit with your mother or not."

Sophia and Stephen walked down the hall with solemn faces. Granger didn't move. He sat in the plastic chair with his head in his hands. Stephen whispered to her, "What was that all about? What do you mean Granger and Margaret killed your father?"

She shook her head as she searched for the blue stripe on the floor, "They did it. They killed him and right now I wouldn't be surprised if he tried to kill Carol and my mother got someone to go to the house and make sure Carol was dead by hitting her over the head. Stephen, things are falling into place."

Stephen grabbed her shoulders and spun her around, "Are you accusing your brother and your mother of murder?"

She pulled his hands from her shoulders, "You bet I am and right now I would like to go and see my mother and give her a scolding or a slap or something. But she is a mess. She has always been a mess. Oh, my, Carol knew." Sophia wiped tears from her face, "Stephen, I bet you Carol knew all the time and she was trying to tell me carefully and they, oh, dear, they killed her." She dropped her arms and leaned against the wall in the hospital hall. "They are killing machines and they are doing all of this for money. Granger wanted to get my mother out of here, let her die, and then there would be no one to sue for the accident and there would be no one to confess to killing my father with his help."

Moving out of the way of a gurney coming down the hall, Stephen leaned against the wall beside her. "Sophia, these are serious accusations you are making. Killing your dad who was already on the verge of death was one thing but what good would come from killing Carol?"

He rolled onto his shoulder as he leaned against the wall to look at her, "And then there is Geoffrey's truck and A.J. and all of the troubles there. What is the purpose of all of the blood lost and all of the terror if all they wanted was money?"

Tears welled up in her eyes, "Money, money is all they think about for they never can have enough. They want our home to sell and thus they will have more money. Granger was divorcing his beautiful Emily to marry Katina the lesbian to have a son who would carry on the family name. Stephen, you live in a world of military dynamic where there is a good reason to shoot folks or blow them up, but in my family all you need is a couple of dollars to turn into a murdering culprit."

"Damn," Stephen pointed to the notice on the hall wall, "There is the intensive care unit down that way. Sophia, I wouldn't recommend you getting into your mother's face at this point for she is probably unconscious."

They walked slowly to the double doors and rang the bell. A nurse pulled open the door to greet them. "Yes, can I help you?"

Hugging her purse, Sophia smiled, "Yes, I am Margaret Pino's daughter and I was hoping I could see her?"

"Just a moment, please." The nurse disappeared back through the double doors.

Stephen shook his head, "Granger was really stupid to tell everyone he was a medical doctor and he was going to take his mother home with him. Probably everyone in this hospital has heard his story. It's a wonder the nurses downstairs didn't call the cops and have him arrested."

The door opened again and the nurse reappeared. "I am sorry, but your mother is not able to have visitors at this time. Her condition is critical. She has a breathing tube and is in a medical coma to keep her from moving. If you come back in the morning there might be a better chance of seeing her. I know she would be pleased to know that you are here." The nurse turned and was gone once again through the double doors.

Sophia turned to walk back to the waiting room, "Well, there you go.

She is knocking on death's door, but will the door open as easily as the one for my father?"

Stephen took her hand, "Come on, we need to sit down somewhere and read these papers and find your brother."

She smiled at him, "First, let's find a phone and I can call Geoffrey to make sure everyone is all right."

"Yes," he put his arm in hers, "and we might just find a bathroom and some food, not necessarily in that order."

The sharp odor of disinfectant was strong on the first floor. Granger was sitting with his legs crossed in an easy chair opposite the front doors of the hospital. Sophia found him quickly and Stephen left her to talk to him as he located the men's bathroom.

"Hey, mom's out of surgery, but she can't have any visitors probably until morning." she pulled a plastic chair toward Granger.

"Well, there you go. She's going to be talking in her delusional speak and who's to know what will come of it?" Granger fanned his face with the papers. "At least we have plenty of reading material. Evidently the five year old girl who was in the front seat of one of the vehicles that hit mom has died. Her mother and father are inconsolable and they believe all of this is my fault."

Sighing, Sophia studied the papers she had been given. "Basically these papers state mom was in the wrong, right?"

"Right, she was parked in the center of a fast moving freeway. Her truck was sideways not allowing for anyone to zoom around her, every single one of those four vehicles had to hit her or go through her, or fly over her, or take the impact. The first woman who hit her was alone and her legs were pushed past her into the back seat. She has severe spinal damage and may be paralyzed for life. Another vehicle which was a small sports car had a middle aged couple in it. They are both still in surgery. The third vehicle was an old Chevy truck and the old man who was driving it, swerved to hit the back of her truck. He has some serious damages to his left arm and left leg, but he will probably be all right. The fourth vehicle had the family in it. The father was driving with his little girl in the front seat. The mother and sons were in the back seat. The mother broke her neck and one of the young sons may lose his leg. The son in the middle had hardly any scrapes or bruises. He is unfortunately the only one sitting in the waiting room, waiting for his grandparents to arrive. The father is in surgery and it doesn't look good for him." Granger shook his head, "Damn, why not me in the truck? I would have taken the beating, but not mom."

Stephen returned to sit in the chair next to Sophia, "It would have been better if it was you. You're younger and more flexible than your dear old mom."

Sophia jabbed Stephen in the ribs with her elbow, "Well, right now we need to find out how mom is doing and if she needs any more medical care. Also, we need to see the families of the accident and let them know how sorry we are for their pain."

"No, no can do!" Granger lifted his hand to them, "Mrs. Ortiz stated clearly that we were not to have contact with any of the other folks. She said it was a legal matter and the lawyers talk to one another and we are to leave them alone in their suffering." His face reddened, "There weren't supposed to be any other people involved with any part of our problems and now the whole world has been invited into inspect us under a microscope."

Unzipping his jacket, Stephen piped up, "What do you mean 'there weren't supposed to be any other people involved?' What does that mean, Granger?"

"Oh, damn, I suppose by now, Sophia, you have figured out all about Dad's death and what Mom was doing to me? You got it right?" Granger studied her face for a reaction.

"Oh come on, tell me that you figured this whole business out? You know my life is a living hell with Mom now pushing my buttons after what happened with Dad. Carol figured it out faster than anyone and she was ready to pounce on me. I didn't have a choice! I had to react quickly or everything would have been lost? Sophia, come on, say something?"

She shook her head," Granger, it was fairly obvious what happened. Even Dad's doc knew what had happened, but it was over. Dad was a vegetable waiting to die. There wouldn't have been any point in bringing the law into the messy situation. Yet, you and Mom kept acting as if this was the biggest coo since Little Big Horn."

Stephen put his hand on her shoulder, "What we need to need know is how you plan to deal with Enid and Carl Henker?"

"What?" Granger stared at Stephen, "What the hell do they have to do with anything? They are running the clinic and I am not part of their establishment anymore. What do they have to do with what is going on here, now?"

Turning to watch the elevator doors, Sophia interrupted them both, "Granger, what did you do to Mom? Were you the one who fiddled with the steering wheel pin and caused the accident?" Before Granger could speak, she went on, "You have to tell us the truth now. We are a family and we need to work as a team. No more lies. No more making stuff up just to look like an angel. There are lots of other people involved here and some are dying, others will be in pain for the rest of their lives. Granger, no more false hopes and misinformation, please tell us the truth!"

Granger suddenly leaned back letting the back of his head rest on the hospital wall. His face went gray to ashen. "Oh, hell, why not, yes, yes and yes! I fiddled with her truck steering wheel, but only because she kept going up and down to see Emily and Shirley. Why couldn't she put her energy into her son, the namesake of the family? Why did she insist on going to see them and financially help them when I have found myself in a horrible situation?" Granger looked around him, "I'm not feeling very well. I have been up all night with this and now the terror!"

Stephen smiled at Granger, "Granger, your conscious must be eating itself up what with the weight of the world on your shoulders?" Stephen nodded to him, "There are no other people around us, there is no one else is around."

Granger moved slowly as if all his joints were hurting. He turned his body to face them in the white plastic chair and said with a sigh. "Stephen, do you think you could get me some coffee? Before I unload my story it would be nice to have some hot coffee."

Sophia jerked her head to the side, "Sure, get some coffee for the vegetarian homeopathic doctor. There should be some by the nurses' station." Stephen followed her pointing finger to the hall crossing where the nurses' station was situated.

"All right, Granger, now cough it up, what the hell happened?" Sophia let her unzipped jacket fall into her lap. She pushed back her bangs and studied Granger's face.

"What was I to do? Katina led me to believe she was pregnant. Somehow I still believe she is pregnant. She has to be! Then Emily went ape nuts and wanted a divorce. I was perfectly willing to take care of both of them. Emily and I go way back, too, and Shirley is my daughter. How could I just cut them off from my life?" Studying his hands, he squeezed his right hand into a fist.

"Then there was mom, the Madame Margaret Pino of the world who must control all and everything around her. She insisted that the manly thing to do would be to divorce Emily and marry Katina for to have a male heir is a priority in this family. What a two faced lie!" He hit the side of the plastic chair with his fist. "Damn, why did I believe any of them?"

Sophia sat forward and pulled her jacket off to fold it and place it in the chair beside her. "Granger, there is an old saying, "One can only blame oneself for their own wrong choices.' Remember Dad taught that saying to us?"

"Look what happened to him? He married a leech who killed him in the end and what has he got to show for it? A bunch of kids who wanted him to support them, guide them, and help them get their feet on the ground. Oh, Sophia, my life has been one huge hoax all put together by my mother." He pushed his hair back from his forehead. "Look what he left behind! I am so tired, Sophia, tired of all of this fighting to survive business. When does it get easy? When can I just get up, go to work, make money, come home to a loving family, and not have my mother sticking her nose up my ass?"

Stephen pulled one of the plastic chairs around Sophia's to give Granger a paper cup of steaming coffee. "Here you go your last wish." He winked at Sophia. She gave him a funny frown and turned her attention back to her brother. Stephen leaned into Granger as if he was about to hug him. Sophia glared at Stephen, but he ignored her

Sophia spoke cautiously, "What happened with Katina? Did you purposely sleep with her or did Mom push you into a relationship with her?" She put her hand on Granger's knee.

"No, no, no Katina didn't even know Mom. Katina came to the house because she was in trouble with the law. She got me stoned on some strong pot she had and we ended up making love. Emily walked in while we were lying naked together on the floor smoking another reefer of pot. Emily went ballistic. She took Shirley and they left. I believe they went to Mom's. That was the Margaret Pino no-no. No smoking pot, no having sex with someone other than the person she had picked out for me. Mom then decided to pick up her wicked spoon and start the mix."

Sophia shook her head, "Granger, it takes your participation if you are going to be manipulated. What did mom expect of you?"

"Mom wanted this and that and then more demands on me! She wanted me to earn my money and to get you and Geoffrey out of the house in Rocoso so Katina and I could live there with our male heir. She wanted Emily to leave the county so no one would know about the ugly adultery, as if anyone couldn't guess." He took a sip of the coffee and made a wincing sound. "This is hot stuff, Stephen."

Sophia watched Granger puckered his lips. She poked his arm, "All right, you got pulled into a situation that put you and several other people at risk. Why did you try to kill Geoffrey or for that matter why did you try to kill me and the girls?"

Sighing, Granger put the hot cup of coffee on the floor. "I didn't try to kill anyone. For God's sake, Sophia, I'm a total wuss when it comes to hurting people. Sure, I helped mom with Dad, but she was the one with the plan. I don't plan these things." He shook his head, "These things aren't in my head. They're not on my page for life! Mom is the one who manipulates and plans, pushes, and threatens, blackmails, until finally she gets what she wants without ever getting her fingers dirty. Haven't you noticed this, Sophia?"

"Why would I notice? I am not around her unless I feel guilty. She makes me feel guilty and when the guilt becomes larger than my laundry pile, I go and see her. No more, no less and we talk about incidentals and nothing personal. This is vital to my existence. She has no business in my business and she knows this." Sophia shook her head, "But, Granger, you told us you would tell us the truth now. What happened with this accident? What did you do?"

Stephen took off his jacket, patted his shirt, and folded his jacket on his lap. His voice softened as he asked, "There are some issues here, Granger, that aren't adding up at all? Geoffrey was almost blown up and two other people were hurt and one was killed by the truck explosion. Several times your sister has been shot at and had her vehicle blown up almost in front of her." Stephen studied Granger's face, "There are inconsistencies in what you are telling us right now and we need clarity."

"All right, all right, clarity, my God, Stephen don't' push so hard. I just might change my mind." Granger reached down and lifted the coffee cup to his lips. "I didn't get involved with the bomb incident. That was Mom and she was in touch with Carl Henker and they were the ones who plotted that whole scenario. Carl was going to sue me while I sued him for the money I put into the clinic. I made an agreement with Mom, only with Mom, that if I got the house in Rocoso then Carl and his family could have the clinic free and clear. That was all I did. I didn't hire anyone to kill anyone. I just made a verbal agreement, which Mom then later had written up by one of her lawyers. That was all I did. That was it." He bent over to put the coffee cup back down on the floor.

Sophia glared at him, "Then what about Carol? What did you do to Carol?"

"Oh, for the love of God, why are you dragging up all this ancient history? Carol was going to sue me! She was going to take me to court and destroy my life, Emily's life, Shirley's life, everyone's life because she had some stupid photographs. I mean, come on, photos of drugs in a closet are not going to sink the Titanic!"

Granger was becoming more and more addled as he spoke. His eyes were darting around everywhere, but he did not make eye contact with Sophia or Stephen. "I didn't want to hurt Carol, but she was being a pest. I followed her to her rental home after you had lunch with her one day at the Range. She had a stupid dog that ran out and wanted me to pet him. While she was in the back of the place, I switched out her insulin. No big deal. It would've been enough to make her have a slight stroke or something, but I didn't kill her. Oh, no, I'm a medical doctor! I don't go around hurting people!" He rubbed his hands together.

Stephen shrugged and asked, "What did you do with your mother, here?"

"Here, I didn't do a damn thing. She was stupid enough to try and drive back up here to see Emily. I told her clearly and emphatically that I didn't want her involved in Emily's life. Why is this so hard to understand? Emily is not blood kin and why my mother wanted to treat as if she is—is beyond me! I couldn't take it anymore. I just couldn't take it." His voice got softer and he stopped talking.

Sophia turned to Stephen, "Did the insurance papers say anything about the accident's cause?"

"Oh, yes, it is on page three." Stephen stood up and pulled the bulk of papers from his back pant pocket. He sat back down and pointed to the sentence, "Here, it states clearly that the steering wheel pin had been manually removed at some point with metal pliers for the impression is still noticeable even after the accident. Evidently, the belief stands that when Margaret was aware that the steering wheel was loose and in her hands, she let out the clutch and the truck stalled out right in the middle of the highway."

"Sophia," Granger shook his head as tears fell down his cheeks, "I am guilty of killing that child and of hurting all those people. I did it. It was easy to remove the pin and somehow I believed the only problem would be the steering wheel would come off in her hands and she wouldn't be able to drive. No one would get hurt. No one would know but me. Mom would be stuck at home and not able to see Emily." He wiped his cheek with his left hand. "None of this was supposed to happen, none of it. I swear to all that is holy, no one was supposed to get hurt."

Stephen nodded at Sophia as he stood to walk down the hall. As he moved toward the nurses' station he unbuttoned his shirt and pulled out a box that was small and black with wires attached to his collar. Mrs. Ortiz walked around the counter to greet him. Both Sophia and Granger watched in disbelief.

The elevator doors dinged and opened. Both of them turned to study the elevator doors. Carl Henker and his wife Enid walked directly to them. Suddenly everything started to happen at once. Stephen handed the black box to Mrs. Ortiz and as swiftly as a cat he hurriedly trotted over to stand behind Carl. Carl had his hands in his jacket pocket. Enid was wiping tears from her cheeks and her face was flushed. Granger stood to greet them. Sophia nodded, but she moved away from the trio.

Stephen quietly stood behind Carl. Enid was facing Granger with what looked like a sheet of paper. Carl moved his right hand out of his pocket. He was holding a pistol. "Granger, you have done enough damage to too many people. This has to end. You have my wife running around the countryside trying to destroy people that she loves. You are threatening my family with bankruptcy and now you have gone too far with the killing of people including your mother."

Carl lifted the pistol. In a blink of an eye, Stephen had Carl on the floor of the hospital. Carl's was face down with Stephen's knee in the center of his back. Stephen held Carl's hand with the pistol down toward Carl's chest. Stephen pushed down hard with his knee and Carl called out in pain as he dropped the pistol. Enid started screaming and shaking. She fell to her knees beside Carl.

Sophia took Granger's arm and pulled him into her embrace. The nurses had called security and by the time the whole event had happened there were four guards in black uniforms pulling Carl from the floor. He was handcuffed and in raging anger. Enid remained kneeling, crying, and shaking.

Sophia stared at her. She was not going to help her. She couldn't. Not when Enid had made the attempt to kill her family. Enid pushed her white hair back from her face and crying put her hands up and out to Sophia. Sophia shook her head 'no.' Enid fell over on the floor, shaking. Stephen knelt down next to her and pulled her into his embrace. She grabbed his shoulder and shivered as she cried.

Stephen pulled her to stand. "You need to go with your husband and help him with the security and the police. Come on, pull yourself together. You have a small son who is counting on you to do the right thing. Let's go and see where they are going to take your husband."

He practically pulled her into the elevator. Granger's face was ashen gray. "Oh, Sophia, he was going to try and kill me! He was going to kill me!"

There was one guard standing by the nurses' station talking with Mrs. Ortiz. The two of them walked over to Granger and Sophia. Mrs. Ortiz put her hand on Granger's shoulder. "I am sorry, Mr. Pino, but you are under arrest for the attempted murder of the freeway incident. You attempted to kill your mother and right now you are responsible for the death of the ten year old girl. Please come with us."

Granger glared at her, "What are you talking about? How could you possibly know what happened? How could anyone possible know what happened? It was a flipping accident, nothing more nothing less. Leave me alone!" He pulled his arm free from the guard. The guard quickly pulled Granger's arms behind his back and put handcuffs on him.

"What the hell is going on here? I am not guilty of anything! Unhand me or I shall call the cops!" Granger pulled and fidgeted, but the guard had him firmly in his control.

Mrs. Ortiz nodded to Sophia, "I recommend that you stand back and let us do our job. We shall notify the authorities in Rocoso of this development and I believe they will be relieved to know that you helped with this arrest."

Granger pushed away from the guard, "Sophia, what is she talking about? What the hell is she talking about?" Sophia shook her head. The three of them went into the elevator and disappeared behind the automatic closing doors. Sophia sat down, holding her shaking hands in her lap she tried to calm herself.

Stephen reappeared after twenty minutes. He wiped his face where someone had raked their fingernails over his cheek. "Well, life can't be too simple. They gave a full confession to setting bombs, which were gotten by Carl's military brother. They did hit Carol over the head with the ceramic figure, which they hid somewhere on the road. They did attempt to blow up half of Rocoso to get to Geoffrey. They did try to get you and the girls out of the house. Evidently, Enid has a copy of the written agreement Margaret made with them. The agreement was that if they could remove you from the property by whatever means, then Granger would not file for financial repayment by the Henker's."

Sophia put her hand on his arm, "Take a breath. What happened to Enid and Carl?"

Stephen shook his head, "It won't be good. They both confessed to all the atrocities they committed. It looks as if their son Alistair will be going to a Foster Home for both of them are guilty of attempted murder."

She put her head down. "Damn, what a day of it." She stood and gathered her jacket into her arms. "I'm going to call Geoffrey. Then I recommend we go home. I have no interest in what or how my mother is doing at this point. I just want to go home and be with my real family who doesn't blackmail or attempt to kill anyone."

Stephen turned to follow her to the elevators, and under his breath he added, "At least as far as we know?"

Readers Guide

1. How do the descriptions of Margaret influence the setting of the story: like her relationship with her son, her husband, and her daughter?

2. Do you feel that Granger and his mother Margaret have a common bond of more than just one goal? Explain how their personalities are alike and dissimilar.

3. What differences can you find between Sophia and her personal family versus the relationship she has with her mother and her brother? Do you feel she handles conflict well?

4. How does your first impression of Sophia change as the plot develops?

5. When Sophia's life is described in the book, regarding her dropping the girls off at school and her relationship to her own work, is this a realistic depiction of someone's life? How do the day-to-day events enlighten the reader?

6. Do you feel that Sophia's questioning by the doctor in the barn shows Sophia's stubbornness to accept what has happened or is she in denial?

7. In Sophia's house, where is the main place of communication and realization? Does this add flavor to the development of the story? How so?

8. Is Geoffrey and Sophia's relationship solid, strong enough to handle the emotional chaos that comes into their lives? Is Geoffrey showing weakness by leaving his wife?

9. How does Carol attempt to sway Sophia into taking legal action against her brother? Does she turn Sophia's view of her brother or does she bring new angst into Sophia's life?

10 The sheriff's department plays an important role in finding the truth regarding Carol's finality. Do you feel they were efficient in their attempts to find facts? How so?

11. Geoffrey's accident places him out of the main frame, but is his point of view forgotten? How does Sophia keep the girls from being upset about their father?

12. Geoffrey's brother Stephen has a specific background, which may or may not help Sophia. How does Stephen use his training to help in her cause or does he bring confusion to the plot?

13. The dynamite plays an active role in this story. How does it help to find the true perpetrator?

14. Has Margaret chosen sides, or does she radiate in regards to special interest? Use examples to explain.

15. A.J. is not only the sheriff for the county, but he ends up saving Sophia, how?

16. Sophia attempts to prove Granger's innocence falls flat at the end. Who finally brings to light the cause and the effect of Granger's choices?

17. Who was the main mastermind behind the murders? Why did so many people do what was wanted with no remorse?

CPSIA information can be obtained at www.ICGtesting.com
Printed in the USA
LVOW13s0138270514

387203LV00003B/163/P